# OVERPOWERED

# OVERPOWERED

## MARK H. KRUGER

SIMON & SCHUSTER BFYR

New York   London   Toronto   Sydney   New Delhi

An imprint of Simon & Schuster Children's Publishing Division

1230 Avenue of the Americas, New York, New York 10020

For information about special discounts for bulk purchases, please contact Simon & Schuster Special Sales at 1-866-506-1949 or business@simonandschuster.com.

The Simon & Schuster Speakers Bureau can bring authors to your live event. For more information or to book an event, contact the Simon & Schuster Speakers Bureau at 1-866-248-3049 or visit our website at www.simonspeakers.com.

Book design by Hilary Zarycky

Jacket illustration copyright © 2013 by Kareem Iliya

The text for this book is set in Janson Text.

Manufactured in the United States of America

2  4  6  8  10  9  7  5  3  1

Library of Congress Cataloging-in-Publication Data

Kruger, Mark H.

Overpowered / Mark H. Kruger. —1st edition.

p. cm

Summary: Sixteen-year-old Nica Ashley moves to sleepy Barrington, Colorado, to live with her father and discovers a mysterious pulse of energy has given her and her friends superhero–like powers.

ISBN 978-1-4424-3128-7 (hardcover)

ISBN 978-1-4424-3130-0 (eBook)

[1. Science fiction. 2. Conspiracies—Fiction.]  I. Title.

PZ7.K9414Ov 2013

[Fic]—dc23

2012043190

FIRST

EDITION

*For Emily, Annie, & Maddie . . .and Nica's everywhere.*

# 1. HOME, SWEET HOME

It all started with a stupid sandwich. Chicken curry and spinach stuffed inside a homemade pita pocket. I found it in my backpack one Friday morning when I was getting ready for school. Neatly wrapped inside a neon-green plastic bag, one of those flimsy sacks used by the local Bangkok markets, along with a handwritten note, which tumbled out:

> *Nica:*
> *Remember to recycle!*
> *Love, Mom.*

"What's this?" I stood in the doorway of my mother's bedroom, dangling the suspect package in front of her face like it was radioactive plutonium.

"Your lunch. I made it last night." Dressed in a colorful peasant skirt and ivory silk blouse, she grabbed her over-sized shoulder bag and swooped by me, out of the room.

"What possessed you to do *that*?" I followed her into the kitchen.

"You don't like chicken curry?" She was rummaging through a stack of magazines and guidebooks on the kitchen table. "By the way, have you seen my notebook? I know it must be here somewhere. . . ."

"No, I love chicken curry, Mom," I said while handing her the book, which was lying on top of the fridge, right where she'd left it the night before. She was always misplacing things. "That's not the point."

"Well, the point is, Nica, you're sixteen and you need to take better care of yourself. A bag of prawn crackers is not lunch. Not to mention you need some nutrition with kickboxing practice this afternoon." My mother dropped the spiral notebook into her bag and then rushed out the front door of our large 1930s colonial Bangkok apartment with me close behind.

I would not let the conversation end. "Which I've had every Friday for like the last six months. All of a sudden you're auditioning for Mother of the Year?" If I sounded a wee bit suspicious, it was with good reason. My mother never made lunch for me. *Ever.*

Let me rewind: I'm not saying that Lydia (aka my mom) had never once made my lunch since I was born. But she certainly had not since we'd moved overseas ten years ago. I'm not complaining or trying to be all Judge-Judyish about her less-than-stellar parenting skills. Honestly. I'm not even suggesting that she was a bad mom or the least bit neglectful (though the word "maternal" doesn't immediately pop to mind when describing her attributes). All I'm saying is that my mother was always preoccupied. Enthusiastically self-obsessed, with her own life and the fate of the world, for starters. Concern for my food intake and emotional well-being ranked way lower than, say, worrying about the vanishing polar bear population or where she could find a good Ashtanga yoga workshop.

Not quite buying Lydia's newfound concern, I chased her down the stairs out to the busy street in Soi Tonson, determined to get to the bottom of things. If there was one thing I knew for sure in my young life, it was when my mom was trying to butter me up, getting ready to lower the boom about something or other I wasn't going to like. And that day she was most definitely avoiding me big time.

"We'll discuss it all later, honey. Hurry, or you'll miss your bus." She kissed me, pointing to the approaching bus, anxious to leave. She was going to check out the quaint Thonburi canals along the Chao Phraya River for an article she was writing for some travel magazine.

"The next one's in eight minutes." I stood there at the corner, not getting on, refusing to budge. Not till she came clean about what was really on her mind. "Tell me what's going on. What's the big secret?"

My mother knew she couldn't dodge me any longer. She took a deep breath, sighed, and said, "Antarctica."

"As in the continent at the South Pole? What about it?" World geography was most definitely something I was up on.

"They want me to go. *National Geographic* magazine. To do a cover story."

"Mom, that's awesome. When do we leave?"

I was all ready to find my passport and hop on the next plane south. Not that I didn't love Bangkok. I did. It was insanely beautiful, with golden palaces and ancient Buddhist temples. It was also insanely crowded, with twelve million people, but incredibly welcoming, with the most delicious seafood I'd ever tasted. The weather was hot and humid and always felt like summer. Shopping heaven with everything from inexpensive clothing and jewelry markets to fancy bazaars. All in all, a fantastic and totally amazing 24/7 metropolis that never slept. But we'd already been in Thailand more than nine months. Our longest stretch ever, anywhere. It now was time for us to move on.

Traveling had always been my mother's passion, bordering on mania. She was an ecotravel writer (her description, not mine)—a globe flitterer who loved immersing herself in far-flung, exotic locales for months at a time. Living among "the people" and not in fancy five-star hotels, soaking up their culture and respecting their way of life, hopefully without inflicting too much damage, while she wrote about all the exciting adventures awaiting the daring tourist. As a result, we'd moved around the world as often as some people changed Facebook status. Nineteen times over the last ten years (with as many schools), from Zanzibar to Patagonia, with stops in Morocco, Kazakhstan, Tasmania, Botswana, India, and Thailand, among many others.

In fact, I'd lived on every continent except Antarctica. And now I'd be able to cross that off my list of things to do before I died. It was going to be epic.

I knew I was kind of a freak. Not a two-headed circus type or bearded-lady variety. But more like the "Really, you lived where? You did what?" type of freak, which I totally didn't mind at all.

Believe it or not, I was happy. I loved seeing the world. Not having a permanent home or school seemed kind of liberating. Really. No emotional complications or bad break-ups with boyfriends (not that I had ever really had a serious one yet). No big expectations or letdowns from friends. No realizing you were hanging with the wrong crew. And most important: no obligations. I would move on to the next place and dazzle the kids at my new school with my sparkling personality before life got messy and confusing.

My mother apparently had other ideas.

"You're dumping me?" I felt sucker punched, like the wind had been knocked out of me. "You're going to Antarctica alone? Without me?"

"Honey, they want me to live at McMurdo Station for nine months. There isn't a school at the South Pole."

"Who needs a classroom? You can homeschool me." I admit I was grasping at straws. McMurdo Station, Antarctica, was the most remote outpost on earth, according to Lydia. A science station and research center, it had about one thousand residents in the summer but fewer than two hundred in the winter.

She hastened to add, "We're talking months with no sunlight. Not to mention being confined indoors twenty-four/seven." My mother had a point. Antarctica was hardly the place for a teenager who loved exploring new cities and cherished her independence.

And yet I wasn't prepared to give in without at least putting up a fight.

"I'll adapt," I insisted brightly. "You know how great I am at fitting in to new places."

"Yes, but you're a teenager," my mother was quick to remind me. "You should be hanging with kids your own age. Not holed up in some climate-controlled research station in the middle of nowhere with a bunch of overeducated scientists."

"Sounds like a perfect learning opportunity. Think of how much I'll get out of the experience," I retorted brightly, desperately trying to put the best spin on my argument. "Besides, you always said I was precocious."

"Believe me, I'd do anything to take you along," my mother admitted.

"Then do it. Take me, Mom," I pleaded, playing on her heartstrings, feeling her resolve weakening. "We'll have so much fun together. We always do."

"I know," she replied with a remorseful sigh. "It's just . . ."

*"Just what?"* I asked with trepidation.

Still, I wasn't quite prepared for the biggest shock yet to come.

"Honey, it's just not possible. Besides, I've been thinking . . . about your future and all." Always a bad sign when my mother uttered those three words: "I've been thinking . . ."

"What about my future?" I held my breath, anxiously waiting for the other shoe to drop. And boy, did it ever.

That is how I ended up jetting solo from Bangkok to Denver on a fifteen-hour red-eye flight less than two weeks later. My mom shipped me off to live with my dad in some Podunk hick town in southern Colorado.

For the next two years, until I graduate. (Please, just shoot me now.)

My free-spirited mother suddenly thought a traditional high school education with all the homespun trimmings in small-town America was the best thing for her worldly daughter. It made no sense to me. She had lived there with my father briefly after they got married nearly twenty years ago. I thought she never had any intention of going back, since my dear old mom got the hell out of there with me when I was two and never looked back, though she never exactly explained why. After four years living with my mom's parents outside Philadelphia we then moved overseas. And now she was shipping me off like some FedEx package—with overnight delivery guaranteed.

The night after she told me my life was about to change, we had a huge fight. The biggest fight we'd ever had.

"Why are you doing this? Can't you see you're ruining my life?" I'm usually not a drama queen, but desperate times called for desperate measures.

"Nica, it'll be great. You'll see. It'll be exciting. Finally putting down roots."

"I'm not a tree. I don't need roots."

"What about having good friends? And dating. Going to the mall. And to football games. And the senior prom. Not to mention more quality time with your dad. Believe me: You'll thank me for this later."

"I wouldn't hold my breath if I were you." My mother was really doing the hard sell, and I wasn't buying. "Besides, if Barrington was *so great*, why did you leave with me the first chance you got?"

"Nica . . . you *know* why I left," my mother argued back, suddenly looking away from me and avoiding all eye contact as she pretended to be sifting through some mail. "Your dad and I divorced. He wanted to stay. *And I had to get away from there . . .* you know, to see the world."

I could tell by Lydia's uncomfortable reaction that the past was still a sensitive subject with her. Especially where my dad was concerned. She rarely brought it up on her own. And even then her memories were limited to stories about what I was like as a child and my penchant for doing weird things like peeling back wallpaper. ("When I asked the pediatrician if I should be concerned, she said it was because you were so curious and inquisitive.")

"Anyway," my mother continued, adeptly evading my question and turning the argument back on me, "didn't you say you were tired of all this moving around? Living out of suitcases? You'll have stability and consistency. You'll finally have a permanent house and really feel like you belong." Perhaps that's what made Lydia such a good journalist. She was relentless in her pursuit of a story or an interview. Not to mention getting her way.

"You don't have a clue who I am or where I belong." Okay, neither did I, but I wasn't ever going to admit that to her. So I stomped off to my room and slammed the door shut.

Yes, maybe I did complain a tiny bit sometimes to my mother that I was tired of changing schools and all this moving around. And maybe I had said once or twice that it might be kind of nice to spend more time with my dad. But why did my mother decide this time to listen to me?

Well, the joke was on me.

Early the next morning I awoke to the sound of my mother arguing in a hushed tone with someone over the phone. This was unusual. Lydia rarely got angry. She prided herself on her easygoing nature—very little fazed her. So the fact that she was arguing with my father, of all people, made me more than a tiny bit curious. Though her bedroom door was closed, I could still overhear her side of the conversation, demanding to know "how safe" everything was in Barrington, Colorado, where my dad lived. Her sudden concern infuriated me. As if I were this little child who needed constant supervision. I felt the urge to barge in there and tell my mother off. Instead, I swallowed my anger and snuck back to bed, secretly praying that Mom would have a change of heart about sending me away.

Twelve days later my mother escorted me through the sleek, ultra-modern Suvarnabhumi Airport terminal. I wore my favorite peacock paisley flip-flops, vintage Levi's jeans, and hot-pink camisole (courtesy of the Bangkok flea markets). My mom looked quasi-stylish in her jade Thai silk blouse and ivory linen slacks. I thought about all the amazing places we'd lived the last ten years and decided that sultry Thailand was probably my favorite. Not just because of the yummy pad thai and massaman curry, the vibrant people, and the gorgeous white sand beaches, but because of its very Zen attitude about life—an enlightened attitude that I still lacked.

I mean, how could I ever meditate and look inward at myself for life's answers and spiritual wisdom when I didn't even know what most of the questions were?

"Nica?" My mother finally broke our awkward silence amid the din of arrival and departure announcements in five different languages. Her voice had a slight inflection, like she was posing a question: "Keep an open mind?"

"About boys?" I snapped back, quite pissed to see Niagara Falls suddenly threatening to gush from her normally lucid hazel eyes. No way. I was not about to have my dignified farewell dissolve into some hideously hormonal blubberfest to be witnessed by thousands of gawking travelers in the middle of the Bangkok airport.

Luckily, my snarkiness had the desired effect. Dialing back her tears and pangs of maternal guilt (as I knew she would), she shot me one of those classic Lydia looks of exasperation tweaked with wry amusement—head tilted slightly, the right corner of her mouth upturned just a bit.

"About *life*," she replied with a smirk, indicating she understood this would be an emotion-free zone. Then, suddenly darkening, she looked me right in the eye and said, "And listen to your dad. *No matter what.*"

I promised. As if there were any mischief to be had in Barrington, Colorado.

Still, I'd never seen my mother look so serious—almost worried. I immediately brushed aside all thoughts that anything was off. I just assumed she didn't want me to give my dad a hard time.

Yet there was something lingering in her eyes when we hugged.

I pulled back first. My mother almost didn't let go. Fortunately, my plane was already boarding, so she had no choice but to release me. That was when she had handed me a bag loaded with food she purchased at the local market. I was so surprised that I actually forgot to thank her.

Mom's parting words were "I'm going to miss you." Mine were "Take care, Mom. Don't forget to charge your phone." She had an annoying habit of letting her battery die in the most inconvenient places (like the time we got lost in Mae Hong Son, accidentally crossed over the Thai border into Myanmar, and almost became captives of the Burmese army).

Mom grinned and promised to remember, then watched me stroll down the ramp to my plane, at which point I heard her burst into tears.

I didn't look back.

My flight landed in Denver, Colorado at four forty-five p.m. Exactly on schedule. Weather in the Mile High City was amazingly perfect for late October: midsixties, afternoon sunshine, a cloudless blue sky, shimmering office towers with the magnificent Rocky Mountains in the distance.

There were so many flights landing around the same time that day it took forever for my two beat-up suitcases to finally come tumbling down the chute onto the baggage-carousel. I scanned the baggage claim area for my father, but there was no sign of him anywhere. I figured that he probably didn't want to park and was waiting outside for me in his car. However, when I rolled my two bags to the passenger pickup area, I didn't see him either. I tried calling and texting him but kept getting his voice mail. I thought of all sorts of reasons why my father wasn't there. Maybe he got stuck in traffic? Or maybe he was held up at the hospital with a patient? I wasn't concerned. I was so used to traveling and navigating my way through strange airports that Denver was no big deal. After waiting almost an hour for my dad to show, I trotted over to the taxi stand and grabbed the first car I could.

The taxi ride from the airport to my father's house in Barrington took nearly ninety minutes, during which my driver, Sami, a chatty guy in his twenties originally from Peru and now residing in Denver, regaled me with a whole history lesson about the all the towns in the foothills of the Rockies. Sami prided himself on knowing more about Colorado than any other taxi driver in Denver. He had taken a slew of adult-education classes and was like Wikipedia come to life.

"Barrington was settled during the nineteenth century as a trading outpost along the infamous Santa Fe Trail. Back then Barrington had a reputation as a Wild West town complete with gunfights, Indian raids, and bloody battles during the Mexican-American War. Today it's known for a low crime rate, excellent schools, steady property values."

"Sounds thrilling." Especially if you like quiet and boring. Which I definitely did not.

"The town also *claims* to be one of the safest in the state." I detected an awkward hesitation in his voice—in the way he said it.

"What do you mean, 'claims'? They're not?"

"No. Sorry." He fumbled around. "It's just . . . my English. I get a little messed up with words sometimes."

Still, Sami's English sounded fine to me. After that he went radio silent. The rest of the ride he didn't speak another word.

By the time the taxi arrived at 33 Whisper Glen Road (I didn't hear any whispering, much less see a glen, whatever that is, but that's suburbia for you) it was just after eight p.m. and dark. I was exhausted and ravenous (I'd long since eaten my mother's bag of food somewhere over the Pacific Ocean) that I actually fantasized about devouring a rich, creamy dish of panaeng goong over noodles followed by a huge bowl of Thai coconut ice cream with palm sugar. In my semidelirious, famished state I actually believed that my father would read my mind and have a big spread waiting for me when I walked in through the door. Surprise! That was the reason he didn't come pick me up at the airport. Instead of doing rounds at the hospital, he was preparing a traditional Thai meal for me.

Sami took my two suitcases out of the trunk and walked them to the front door while I snapped several photos of the house (soon to be number twenty on the hit parade of places I'd lived) with my phone for the record. I thanked Sami, paid him, and waved as he drove off. Then I practically skipped up to that bright cherry-red front door and rang the bell, expecting an idyllic father-daughter reunion. I told you I was delirious. I hadn't seen my dad since he'd visited Bangkok a few months earlier.

I hadn't been back since I was two. I had never even been to this house, a cute three-story Victorian in a well-manicured neighborhood of similar homes. Well, at least not that I could remember. My father always preferred visiting me two or three times a year wherever I happened to be living at the moment. He thought it was easier on me and more fun. Made sense to me.

Those days were gone. Now I was standing right outside the house that would be *my home* for the next few years, at least until I went off to college, and I felt like a complete stranger. Totally discombobulated. What a weird concept—my home. Doubly weird that I'd be sharing it with my dad, who—let's face it—was basically my vacation buddy. Weirdest of all, though, was that Dad didn't answer the door. No one did. I waited a minute, then rang the bell a second time.

Again, no answer.

I stood there staring at the house, assessing the situation. I realized there weren't any lights on. Nor was there a car parked in the driveway. Dear old Dad was most definitely not at home. And he wasn't answering his cell phone either. Now unless my father had been kidnapped or brutally murdered or suffered some equally heinous fate that left him incapacitated, it became crystal clear to me that he'd forgotten I was arriving. Some welcome.

Instead of getting all weepy-eyed and feeling sorry for myself or pissed off at being forgotten by my own father, I took matters into my own capable hands. I fished around in my oversized suitcase and pulled out my trusty Swiss Army knife, which was handier than a horny prom date. (You'd be amazed how often in my travels I'd found I needed scissors, or pliers or even a screwdriver.) Then I circled around the house to the backyard for some privacy away from any prying neighbors' eyes.

Now, mind you, I wasn't a professional burglar or anything, but a locked window never presented much of an obstacle to me. Moving around a lot had made me extremely resourceful, especially since my mother had an annoying habit of losing her keys about every other week. Anyway, I wasn't about to sit on the curb all night waiting for Dad to have a sudden epiphany and remember that his one and only child was arriving and return home. For all I knew, he was hanging with some girlfriend—not that he'd ever mentioned one, but how was I supposed to know what went on between weekly Skype calls and his semiannual visits?

I scanned the property and immediately found my point of entry—a first-floor bathroom window tucked away on the side of the house. After a quick look up and down the block to make sure no one could see me, I popped out the window screen (easy, really, with the aid of a nail file). Then I wedged my Swiss Army knife blade between the upper and lower portions of the double-hung window and tried to trip the inside lock. Not to brag or anything, but I was doing a good job of working the blade without breaking any glass or splitting the wood frame. Unfortunately, opening the lock was another matter entirely. It refused to cooperate. I couldn't get it to budge even one millimeter, which was truly annoying. I'd never encountered this secure a latch on any window before.

Then I felt a hand grab my shoulder. I whipped around in full self-defense mode (courtesy of my Muay Thai kickboxing training), fists tightly clenched, knuckles ready, and power punched my assailant in the arm. Imagine my complete and utter shock when I found myself standing face-to-face with my own father! All six foot two inches of him.

"God, Dad! Trying to get yourself killed?" I yelled, realizing I had actually punched him. My heart practically exploded out of my chest it was pumping so fast.

"No more than you're trying to get yourself arrested," he quipped back, rubbing his arm. "You got quite a right jab." It was clear he was equally surprised to find me standing there. He quickly added, "By the way, what are you doing here?" He gave me an awkward hug. "Not that I'm not thrilled to see you."

What was I doing there? The words hung in the air, as I thought about how I had just flown halfway around the world to move to stupid Barrington, Colorado, of all places. "Uh, last I heard, moving in with you, Dad." I stared at him in disbelief and plenty annoyed. Clearly somebody had gotten some major wires crossed.

"Tomorrow, Nica. You were supposed to arrive tomorrow morning." He scrolled through his BlackBerry, rechecking my flight information.

"My original flight got canceled, so they put me on the one arriving this afternoon. Mom said she called you. Didn't she?" I brushed past him on my way back to the front door, hoping he wouldn't see the hurt in my eyes. Even if my mom had forgotten to call (which was totally possible), my dad could have shown a little more excitement at seeing his only daughter.

"Oh, she probably left a message on the home phone. I've been on call since last night." Don't think for a minute I believed that one. Mom had spaced, and Dad was now covering for her. Despite their divorce almost fourteen years ago, Dr. Marcus Ashley still defended his ex-wife every chance he got. In fact, I've never heard him utter even a mild criticism of my mother. Sometimes I suspected that he still (inexplicably) loved her. Perhaps that was why he never remarried. My father always claimed it was because of his demanding job. But I couldn't help but wonder if he just used his job as an excuse. Another one of life's elusive mysteries I won't ever get.

My dad turned and followed me across the front lawn, obviously concerned. "Honey, I'm really sorry about the mix-up." I could tell by the tone of his voice and the expression on his face he felt pretty awful about such a major screwup.

"That's okay. It's not your fault." I'd already decided I was willing to give him a pass for the less than ecstatic greeting. I was never one to hold a grudge, at least not against my father. He always went out of his way to be Mr. Responsible (unlike my mother), and I was so hungry and tired that I didn't have the energy to make him feel any guiltier than he already did.

"Well, glad to see you made it. Safe and sound." My dad always used these quaint catchphrases when he was trying to act all parental with me. I think it was due to his ultratraditional upbringing in Youngstown, Ohio, with my grandparents, who were teachers at the state university (Grandma taught literature and Grandpa economics) and only bought American products. In any case, I so didn't get why, much less understand what, my dad was trying to say. "It's just a colloquialism," my mom would respond when I complained. But to me it was like he was speaking Urdu or something.

I just looked at him and shrugged: "Yeah, I made it all right." If life with Lydia had taught me anything, it was that I wouldn't be too disappointed if I just relied on myself. I started to feel cold and asked if we could go inside.

My father took out his house keys, which dangled from this silly lanyard key ring I had given him for Father's Day five years ago when I lived in Botswana. I had actually woven the braided rope out of red, green, and black leather strips I'd bought in a Gaborone flea market for about two dollars.

He stood at the doorstep, keys in hand, for what seemed like an eternity, deep in thought. I looked over at my dad, waiting for him to unlock the door. He glanced back at me, and I thought I detected a flash of anxiety in his expression, which was quickly covered over with a forced smile.

"C'mon, let's go inside. *Through* the door," he said as he unlocked the front door for me and grabbed my big suitcase. I picked up the smaller suitcase and crossed the door-step into my new abode.

Home sweet home it was most definitely not. I surveyed the marginal furnishings in the large living room—worn black-leather sofa, streaked glass coffee table, and a battered nineteen-inch television set that was most definitely older than me. The walls were white and bare, except for a lonely Escher poster titled *Relativity*; one of those freaky black-and-white mind benders where faceless people walked up and down a series of never-ending staircases. At the bottom was a quote: *I walk around in mysteries.* Imagine waking up to that every morning.

The dining room was even more pitiful. It only had a collapsible card table (the prefab faux wood type) and four folding chairs, probably courtesy of Staples or OfficeMax. I mean, I'd lived all around the world and moved so many times—from a stone house in northern Morocco to a vast sheep farm in Patagonia—but my mom hung up photos and a few personal knickknacks and always tried to make our temporary digs feel like home. My dad, on the other hand, had lived in his house for twelve years, and it still looked like he'd moved in only last week.

It was like a bachelor pad without any of the cool stuff. I knew he was a dedicated cardiologist, not to mention an extreme workaholic, but the decor was beyond tragic.

"You've certainly put your personal stamp on the place, Dad."

"Yeah, I've been hearing motel minimalism is ripe for a comeback," he said glibly, getting me to smile. No surprise where my sense of humor came from.

It was then I noticed that all the doors and windows, and I mean all of them, had a series of major locks on them exactly like the one on that bathroom window I'd tried to open. And not just the usual dead-bolt or window-latch variety. These were like super-duper industrial-strength megalocks. The kind I'd seen used in bank vaults and jewelry stores.

"With just the right accent of high security," I muttered flippantly as I wondered exactly what valuables my father needed to protect. It certainly wasn't the furniture.

"Would you like to see your room? It's upstairs." He was just about to take the first step when I interrupted the royal tour.

"Actually I'm dying to see the kitchen first. I'm starving." I desperately needed to get some food in my empty stomach before facing what I imagined would undoubtedly be another sad white cell (aka my new bedroom).

Dad directed me to the airy, traditional kitchen that ran along the back of the house. It was a pleasant room with big windows and a set of French doors, which opened onto what looked like a brick patio with a built-in barbecue. I couldn't imagine Dad throwing any parties out there, but maybe he had a whole other secret life that I didn't know about? That thought was wiped away once I opened the fridge and saw what was inside.

"Sorry, honey," Dad said. "There's not much food."

"That's an understatement." The upper shelves held four eggs, a jar of mustard, two bottles of white wine, some Tupperware containers with unidentifiable food groups, plus a ziplock bag with the remnants of a half-decent-looking chopped salad.

The bottom shelves of the refrigerator were less appetizing, if that's possible. They were crammed with all sorts of vials, IV fluids, and medicine bottles. It looked like a hospital infirmary or something.

"Thankfully, you've got plenty of penicillin, should I get a sudden attack of strep throat." I shut the refrigerator door. "Can we order sushi? Do you have any decent sushi in this town? Or is it strictly burger country?"

"Actually, we've got everything. Even sushi."

Relieved, I picked up the phone and was about to ask Dad for the number of the nearest Japanese restaurant when he added, somewhat hesitantly, "Unfortunately, everything closes at nine p.m."

"Ha, ha. Nice try." I shot my dad a dubious no-way-I'm-gonna-fall-for-that look, totally convinced he was playing one of his practical jokes on me. He was known to do that. And I always fell for them. Like the time he convinced me that you could make popcorn without a microwave by just surrounding the bag with four simultaneously ringing cell phones. My dad assured me that cell-phone radiation could really pop those kernels. I even enlisted seven friends to help me prove it was true. I felt like such a moron when we all stood there for several minutes waiting for the kernels to pop, and nothing happened, except that my mother yelled at me to turn off the phones while she was trying to work. Anyway, I was now sixteen and not about to be so easily snowed. Except that one look at Dad's face told me he wasn't kidding.

"Nothing in this town is open past nine p.m.? How's that possible? I mean, this is America. Land of perpetual consumption, twenty-four-hour supermarkets and fast-food joints giving you whatever you want whenever you want it. I know I've been away for a while, but something's *always* open for business." I couldn't quite wrap my head around this concept.

Not in Barrington, apparently. "Barrington prides itself on being a sleepy, family community," Dad curtly explained.

"Sleepy? More like comatose."

"People like having a curfew, Nica. Makes everyone feel safe." He nonchalantly slipped that in, almost as an afterthought. Talk about burying the headline.

"*Curfew?* This stupid town actually has a curfew? I mean, even Amish and Mormon communities allow teenagers out until midnight." I was horrified. "Is it a legally mandated thing?"

My dad tried to put a positive spin on this bombshell. "What Barrington lacks in nightlife it more than makes up for in livability. Great schools, low unemployment, and almost no crime." He sounded like one of those lame marketing ads states use to drum up tourism. ("Virginia is for lovers!") But my bullshit meter was bouncing off the charts. I wasn't buying what he was trying to sell.

"House arrest will definitely keep criminals off the streets," I said, "and everyone else for that matter."

Dad laughed. I guess I was trying to make light of the depressing situation I found myself in, because I didn't want him to feel bad. I didn't know what else to do. The fact was, this wasn't some boring little town I could drive through and forget the next day. I was stuck here. This was going to be my life—one with a tragically limited social existence and a way-too-early curfew. I mean I'd seen sleepy towns and all, but this, doors locked, all inside at nine p.m. was ridiculous. It wasn't like Barrington was in the middle of a war zone or even had a gang problem. Even Sami the cabbie had said it was the safest town in Colorado.

"What do you do if someone has a heart attack at ten p.m.? Text your diagnosis?" I was unable to hide my irritation at this point. I think I also used the words "stupid" and "insane."

25

Fortunately, my dad swatted away my comments; he always was way more even-keeled than my mother. "I'm allowed out if someone needs a doctor."

"What a huge relief," I said, not hiding my sarcasm. "Though what happens if, like, your car gets a flat or you can't get home in time? Not that I'm planning that or anything."

"I hope not. I'd hate to have to bail you out of jail your first week here," Dad replied jokingly, but with a definite undercurrent of seriousness and caution. Then his expression darkened as he stared me right in the eye. "Just promise me you'll respect the law. That you won't do *anything* stupid."

"Of course." I nodded, taken aback by the harshness in his voice.

My father quickly steered the conversation back to the crisis at hand—my growling stomach. He apologized for being so woefully unprepared for my arrival and cheerfully said we'd have to "wing it." He pulled out the bag of leftover chopped salad, which he said he'd prepared the night before, and he also took out a couple of frozen enchiladas to nuke them in the microwave. The next day, he said, he'd do major shopping. And then he handed me a pen and a pad and said I should just make a list and write everything I wanted on it.

"Sushi, most definitely," I muttered, as I started to fill up the page.

· · ·

After I devoured the enchiladas and salad, I felt ready. "Okay, let's see my bedroom," I said, heading up the stairs. Dad quickly got ahead.

As he led me through the upstairs hallway past his bedroom—which was pretty basic with a large bed, two nightstands, a chest of drawers, and a comfy reading chair—a sky-blue tiled bathroom, and a linen closet, he was trying to give me a pep talk.

"Honey, I know you never envisioned living in such a small town like this. But you're here, and we might as well make the best of the situation. And the thing about Barrington is, as long as you abide by the rules, you'll find it's a great place to live."

"I'm sure it is." I tried to be upbeat, but that word "rules" sounded so rigid and constrained. It was such an alien concept for me. I had lived in many different communities and countries with lots of diverse people—from the Masai in Tanzania to the Mapuche in Chile—and never once had anyone ever said that word to me much less tried to limit my freedom.

Then Dad stood in front of the closed door to my room. "Here we are. It's not much, but it's all yours." When he opened it, I saw a surprisingly cool and kind of perfect bedroom. In fact it was far and away the nicest room in the house. Painted a pretty shade of pale yellow, it had a large picture window with a built-in seat, which overlooked the tree-lined neighborhood. The furnishings—a big bed with an upholstered brown suede headboard, plus a sleek white dresser and desk set—were funky and modern with a sixties retro vibe. On the dresser was a framed photograph of my dad and me trekking through northern Thailand back in February. We'd celebrated my sixteenth birthday in the provincial capital of Chiang Mai, riding elephants and getting soaked during the water-splashing festival of Songkran, honoring Buddha. It was one of the best times I'd ever spent with my dad.

"I really like the color." Lame, I know. But that was the first thing I could think of to say at that moment.

"It's called honeycomb," he said with a bemused shrug. "I had no idea there were so many different shades of yellow."

"Neither did I." I looked at his face and saw that worried expression he got when he thought I really hated something. "It's great, Dad. Thanks."

My dad had obviously put a lot of care and thought into getting the room ready for me, and it showed. I wanted him to know I loved it. I kissed him on the cheek.

He smiled, visibly relieved. Finally, something his hard-to-please (okay, bratty) teen daughter approved of.

"Get some sleep, honey. You've got a big day ahead of you tomorrow."

As if I could sleep. He shut the door as he exited the room. I sat on the bed and sighed. Despite not having to live

out of a suitcase anymore and my somewhat cool new bedroom, this was not going to be an easy adjustment for me.

Two hours later I was staring out the window, my mind
racing, totally wired, despite having been up for more than
thirty hours straight. My cell phone said it was 11:46 p.m. I
had unpacked all my clothes plus laid out the few personal
mementos I'd brought along, including a cheesy digital
picture frame that flashed dozens of photos of my mother
and me. All my beloved books and knickknacks were supposedly en route from Bangkok. I'd had them shipped last
week in six boxes, and they were due to arrive (hopefully)
within a few days. That was if they didn't get lost or held up
by the US Customs department, which undoubtedly would
inspect them for drugs, illegal contraband, and terrorist
connections, all in an effort to keep America safe. Funny,
but in all the years I had lived abroad—and Mom and I had
decamped in some pretty rugged and remote areas, including a Sivananda ashram in rural India—I had never once
worried about *not* being safe. Now that I'd been back in the
US for barely eight hours, safety seemed to be my father's
and this town's priority. Their number one concern.

Sitting at the window seat (it was already becoming my
favorite spot), I looked out at all the well-kept houses that
lined Whisper Glen Road. Every one of them was dark,
unlit. Completely and totally pitch-black. Weren't there any

night owls in town besides me? Only the bluish glow of the ecofriendly streetlights gave any sense that people actually lived in the neighborhood.

It was really weird, but I suddenly felt this sadness, a vague yearning for what I used to have. I was homesick, which was a novel and somewhat strange feeling for me. I'd never gotten homesick before. Weirder still, I was now in my actual home and didn't really have an old home to miss. I assumed what I was missing was a way of life, a carefree, footloose existence I led, as opposed to a particular place. I pulled out my cell phone and immediately started calling my mother, who was visiting an old boyfriend in Buenos Aires before making her way to Antarctica the following week. Halfway through punching in her number I realized there was no phone service. No dial tone. Absolutely nothing.

Great. Here was another wonderful selling point of life in Barrington—miserable, nonexistent cell-phone coverage. Frustrated, I tossed the useless phone over to the bed.

That's when I saw a classic black Mustang GT cruise slowly down the street with its lights turned off. Quiet. Stealth. Like a Japanese ninja creeping along undetected. It occurred to me that I hadn't seen another car, let alone another person, since my dad had caught me trying to break in more than three hours ago. And yet here was this rogue vehicle, flagrantly violating curfew and patrolling the streets on some kind of covert mission.

Who was this mystery driver? A rebel or kindred spirit, perhaps? Or maybe a burglar on the prowl for a big score. Whoever he or she was, I was dying to know. I squinted and pushed my face up the window, trying to get a good look at the driver of this admittedly killer car, but it was way too dark to see much more than a shadow in the front seat. The figure looked like a guy, but it was hard to be totally sure. I wondered if the driver even lived in Barrington, or was just some random person passing through, in which case I might never know his identity. The thought occurred to me that I should run down the stairs and out the front door to flag him down. I could beg him to drive me to the nearest cur-few-free town and then pig out on junk food and do regular teenage things, like maybe go bowling or hang out at some mall. That was what kids did, right?

But as I fantasized about what to do, the car rounded the corner and then zoomed out of sight, disappearing like some kind of ghost or phantom in the night.

## 2. DANA FOX

"Nica, two-minute warning!" my dad shouted at me from the kitchen downstairs. It was 7:28 a.m. and I was already running late for school.

"Okay! Be right down!" I yelled back, trying not to completely lose it as I rifled through every stitch of clothing I owned.

I had slept through my hateful cell-phone alarm, which chirped and tweeted like some nightmarish invasion of parakeets tweaked on Red Bull. A few months earlier I had chosen it because it was usually way too effective in waking everyone within shouting distance—the dead and me included. But not today. By the time my dad realized I had overslept and dragged my sleepy ass out of bed, it was seven fifteen a.m. I had barely fifteen minutes to wash my hair and pick out the perfect outfit. Normally that would have been plenty of time.

But today was most definitely *not* any normal day.

It was my first day back at an American school after ten years abroad. My first day at Barrington High, filled with six hundred twenty (hideously judgmental) teenagers who would undoubtedly enjoy watching the freaky new junior humiliate herself publicly. What better entertainment for a bunch of hicks who were locked up every night.

You would have thought I'd be used to the whole "first day" thing by now. That it wouldn't bother me. I was an experienced world traveler, after all. I'd survived nineteen such first days in the last ten years. How bad could number twenty be, right? But I was intimidated. I knew just how wretched that first day could be. Like the time at Hobart Middle School in Tasmania, when some boy thought it would be hilarious to superglue my locker shut so I couldn't get my books out. Or the time in Kyoto, Japan, when I was so naive I walked straight into the boys' locker room, thinking it was the library, because I couldn't read the signs.

Still, as awful as all those first days were in other schools around the world, I knew an American high school in white-bread suburbia would be that much worse. All because of the clothes.

I quietly panicked. I hated everything. And was completely clueless about what to wear for my first day at Barrington High. I'd never had to contend with such a major decision while I lived abroad. Students in Thailand (and every other country where I'd attended school) wore uniforms. They were mandatory from kindergarten up through college. Boys wore navy or khaki pants with a white open-collar short-sleeved shirt, white socks, and black sneakers. Girls wore knee-length navy blue or black skirts with an open-necked pale-blue blouse, white socks, and dark blue or black sandals. It made life easier and uncomplicated. No one stood out (even coming into school four weeks into the first semester). You never had to worry about not being cool enough or having the right shoes or jeans or designer purse. All my tropical colored tank tops and perky denim shorts and cute skirts that I wore after school and on weekends in Thailand suddenly looked way too slutty and crass in milquetoast suburbia. Nothing seemed right.

I didn't need that kind of pressure. And neither did my totally uncooperative mop of mousy brown hair, which had its usual waviness sucked out by the excessively dry mountain air. No amount of mousse or whip or volumizing foam altered the fact that I looked like a freeze-dried sewer rat.

Totally desperate and ill-equipped to handle the pressure so early in the morning, I threw on an old pair of faded jeans, a vintage Patti Smith T-shirt I'd stolen from my mother, and a pair of laceless knock-off Converse sneakers I'd bought from some random street vendor in Bangkok. Hardly the back-to-school look one normally saw featured in *Seventeen*, but with no other options I hoped it would do.

The car ride to school felt like it lasted an eternity, even though it took less than ten minutes. It was all I could do to restrain myself from jumping out of my dad's silver Prius and fleeing for the hills. He must've realized how freaked I was, because he was a little too cheerfully pointing out all the town highlights, which amounted to a bunch of restored old buildings from the 1800s along Main Street.

"And there's our library, which used to be the jail. And that's the old hotel, which is now medical offices . . ."

"What's that?" I pointed up the hill to a sprawling campus of impressive postmodern buildings. They were the newest structures in town.

"Bar Tech Industries," my dad announced.

"Bar Tech has an office here?" I asked, somewhat incredulous.

"You've heard of them?" My dad acted surprised that I knew who they were.

"Who hasn't?" I retorted. "They're one of those huge international companies, always in the press. Into all sorts of high-tech stuff like green energy and communications."

"And health care, too," my dad added. "Anyway, that's their headquarters. Speaking of green, did you know we've got the highest recycling rate of any community in the West?" My dad proudly rambled on about how Barrington was such a "green community," while I zoned out.

His valiant efforts to distract me and put me at ease didn't work. Instead of listening I kept hearing a terrified voice inside my head warning me of impending doom. *They're all going laugh at you. You're wearing that?* The voice in my head scared the hell out of me, and yet there was nothing I could do to stop it. I sat there mindlessly picking my cuticles while staring out the car window like a zombie, hardly registering the flurry of homemade MISSING—HAVE YOU SEEN posters of a pretty Asian-American girl named Dana Fox that were stapled to every telephone pole.

By the time we pulled into the busy parking lot at Barrington High School, I felt nauseous and on the verge of losing my quasi-breakfast of yogurt and berries. Which would have been a great way to introduce myself to my new classmates. *(Hey, check out the new girl barfing in the parking lot!)* And that would not have been pretty. Luckily, Dad offered me a stick of winter-mint gum. My obsessively chewing helped settle my stomach and keep things down. Barely.

The Prius finally made its way up to the entrance drop-off behind a parade of other fuel-efficient hybrids.

"Good luck," my dad said with a great big smile as I grabbed my bag and opened the door, ready to jump out.

"Thanks," I mumbled, and quickly exited the car, praying I could survive first period without any major disasters. Maybe I'd just blend in and no one would even notice me.

Just as I slammed the passenger door shut, my dad opened the window and called out to me. "If you want, I could go in with you. Help you get oriented."

Oh my God. I bit down my lip, desperate to fend off an all-out panic attack. Having my daddy walk me into high school like I was six years old was the last thing I needed. That would be one humiliation I'd never be able to live down. I didn't care if his feelings would be hurt; I had to nip that idea in the bud, and quick.

I shook my head. "Thanks, Dad, but I got the whole first-day thing pretty well covered." I waved him off, sounding just the tiniest bit confident—enough, at least, to reassure my dad. I breathed a sigh of (temporary) relief as he shifted into gear and drove away, allowing me to suffer in silence.

I looked around the school grounds and tried to get oriented. Three ivy-covered brick buildings were built in a U shape around a lushly landscaped quadrangle, where friendly students congregated in various cliques. The campus looked more like a small elite college than any school I'd ever seen. And the surprisingly clean-cut student body—boys in argyle sweaters and cardigans, girls in plaid skirts and colorful tailored blouses—only added to the idyllic impression. They looked like they had jumped out of the pages of a J.Crew or American Eagle catalog. Everyone, that is, except for me, of course. I was the square peg among all these perfect round holes.

Still, as I stood in the middle of the quad, no one was giving me dirty looks. Which was disconcerting by itself. In fact random kids passed by and gave me big hellos and friendly smiles as if they were my friends. I mean, the high school years, no matter where you lived, were supposed to be the meanest and most insecure time of our lives. Surely there were one or two Queen Bees in this Disneyland who would shoot withering looks my way and take great pleasure in reducing me to tears. I was prepared for such nastiness. I could handle being royally snubbed by the cool kids. What I wasn't prepared for was being showered with warmth and friendliness. *That* was freaky and a little unnerving.

I was immobilized for a moment in kind of a daze when I remembered I had to pick up my class schedule. I scanned the quad, searching for a sign or map that would direct me to the main office.

That was when I first saw *it*. Or heard it.

A low, dull rumble came from somewhere behind me. I turned around. A shiny black Mustang roared into the student parking lot. There was no mistaking: It was the identical car I'd seen cruising by my father's house at nearly midnight the night before, out way past the town curfew. I suddenly got excited and wanted to tell someone about it. Until I quickly remembered that I didn't actually know anyone and therefore had no friends to confide in. Clusters of students were clutching books and chattering away, not paying the slightest bit of attention to the fine Mustang as it glided into a primo parking space right in front of the entrance.

Just when I started to think that maybe the mysterious driver was some loser creep that everyone loathed, the door swung open and out stepped this gorgeous boy. Even from where I stood I could see that he was tall and athletic. Not to mention insanely sexy in his tight, faded jeans, cowboy boots, and black hoodie. He had this retro rebel aura about him—a wildness and defiant swagger, almost—like he'd leaped out of an old-fashioned movie Western. He was the kind of dangerous boy mothers usually warned their daughters to steer clear of.

Luckily for me, my mom skipped over that lesson.

As Rebel Boy brushed by me, he flipped that mane of jet-black hair off his chiseled face with the toss of a hand. My heart practically burst out of my chest it was beating so fast. Though he seemed not to notice me standing right there, I couldn't help but stare. Absorbing every little detail about his beautiful face. Especially those shockingly bright blue-green eyes, which seemed haunted by a rage that nearly took my breath away. So much so that I actually felt woozy and had to steady myself against a nearby tree.

A moment later the school bell rang and snapped me back to reality. But by then Rebel Boy had disappeared among the crush of students filing inside through the main entrance. I pulled myself together, remembering it was my first day, and quickly joined the stream of kids.

• • •

I discovered that Barrington High School was as beautiful inside as it was on the outside. It may sound surprising, but beautiful this school was. And so spotless you could practically eat off the polished tile floors, not that I planned on ever doing so. A far cry from the Morogoro Primary School I'd attended for two months in Tanzania, which used an old farmhouse with dirt floors for its classrooms and open cubbyholes for lockers. Here rows of shiny navy-blue and burgundy lockers (school colors, of course) perfectly complemented pastel-colored walls unmarred by grime or graffiti. Everywhere I looked, I saw evidence of nauseating levels of school spirit. Professionally made banners and posters touted sporting events, club meetings, and countless charity drives, all sponsored by Bar Tech Industries. To top it all off the hallways even smelled good—kind of sweet, like a candy shop.

Somehow I found my way to the main office amid all this cheerfulness. A pair of very helpful middle-aged women immediately greeted me with warm smiles and a welcome package that included a T-shirt, baseball cap, and several notebooks emblazoned with the school mascot.

*Go, Cougars!*

Clearly they had expected me, although a day later. They all knew my dad ("such a wonderful doctor") and treated me like I was some sort of VIP. Even going so far as to quiz me about all my travels and what it was like to live in Thailand and India. Just as they were printing out my class schedule and reassuring me about how quickly I would fit in with everyone, a girl burst into the office, breathless and just a hair shy of frantic.

Taller than me and naturally pretty, she had wavy black hair and green eyes, and she wore a dark-blue embroidered baby-doll dress. She looked like the kind of fresh-faced beauty who never needed any makeup and probably washed her zit-free olive complexion with generic bar soap and water and yet still looked amazingly perfect when she bounced out of bed every morning.

"Sorry I'm so late, but I thought you were arriving tomorrow."

I realized she was talking to me. "Parental miscommunication. Happens when neither one is in the same time zone." I shrugged, suddenly feeling surprisingly relaxed.

"Well, we're glad you made it. I'm Maya Bartoli, FYI. Principal Hellinger asked me to show you around. Help you get acquainted. And see why Barrington is the absolute greatest high school in Colorado, if not the entire country." She said it like some slick politician at a campaign rally.

"Sounds like you've got your work cut out for you," I replied, totally straight-faced.

She barked out a nervous, giggly laugh. "Not at all. I mean, I really do *love* our school. Which reminds me, do you prefer Nikaela or Nica? Just so I can let everyone know."

"Nica's cool. Actually, I prefer it." Standing next to me, I could see her type *Nica* into her cell phone with a big, approving smile as if she was preparing to text the info to the entire student body. It was all a little too much energy and perkiness for barely eight in the morning, but I decided to roll with it. Then she took my arm, waved good-bye to the kindly office ladies, and whisked me off to start the grand tour.

Maya's enthusiasm continued full throttle. "Every new student is assigned a buddy so that they have an instant friend from their first day."

"And you're mine." I looked at her and couldn't believe how tightly wound she was.

"Yes, lucky for you. You could have been stuck with some real geeks . . . not that I'm judgmental or anything." Maya blathered on about the "super teachers" as she proudly pointed out the state-of-the-art auditorium with digital projection, the enormous gymnasium with bleacher seating for one thousand, and the Olympic-size indoor pool. I nodded and tried to seem interested in what she was saying, but my mind wandered.

Suddenly I imagined I was back in Tanzania, studying the chimps with Jane Goodall, and Maya was the leader of the group. Perhaps I could learn a thing or two from her about surviving in this strange new world I'd been dumped into. On the other hand, she was exactly the kind of girl I was naturally suspicious of: pretty, perky, and way too happy with herself.

· · ·

The last stop on my tour was the school cafeteria, a large, airy dining hall with skylights and huge picture windows overlooking the quad. It was as cool as any trendy café I had ever seen.

"They serve salads, pastas, sandwiches. Nothing freeze-dried or prepackaged," she said, adding with a smug look of satisfaction. "And best of all, it's totally free of charge."

*Free? As in it won't even cost me a dime?* How could the school afford to provide free lunches to more than six hundred students every single day?

I didn't say any of that, but I'm sure Maya caught the look of complete skepticism on my face.

"I know. Pretty amazing. All compliments of Bar Tech Industries, of course," she said. "They're like our school's biggest sponsor."

Maya then launched into a Hamlet-like soliloquy praising their corporate generosity. The company had donated millions, not only for books, sporting equipment, science labs, and computers. They had also built this school and paid for the entire renovation of downtown. On top of everything they were also the town's biggest employer.

"Bar Tech is just awesome. They've made this place," Maya said. "This town."

A benevolent corporation—that *was* impressive, not to mention highly unusual.

Maya then rattled off a list of clubs she thought I should join: Yearbook, Student Council, and Future Leaders of America, to name a few. "Colleges look at that sort of thing. So better not wait till senior year to take your future seriously."

That had never been my problem—*not* taking life too seriously. If anything, everyone was always telling me to lighten up and chill. As if there were a special pill you could take for that. Well, actually, I guess there was one (or several), but it wasn't like I was depressed or suicidal. Just terminally bummed at being shuttled off to live in the town that time forgot. Still, I was determined to make the best of it, so I actually listened and asked a couple of questions about the clubs.

All of which culminated in Maya urging me to try out for the cheerleading squad.

"We're desperate for a sixth since we lost our last flyer." She said it as if she were giving me the opportunity of a lifetime—a personal invitation to join the "in crowd."

I shot her a horrified look and blurted out, "Are you on crack?" Maya's eyes nearly popped out of her head, and I apologized for making such an obviously lame joke. I quickly added, "Of course, I know you never, ever would do drugs."

Maya breathed a sigh of relief. "Great. So then we can count on you?"

"Thanks for your tempting offer, but cheerleading and me are *so* not happening." Finding me on a cheerleading squad would be as likely as finding a Prada outlet in North Korea. I'd try my best to fit into this school, but even I had my limits. "I'm really not much for group activities," I added.

But Maya persevered. "Oh come on, Nica. We have way too much fun, not to mention it totally fulfills your PE requirement. Health is paramount, you know. I'm sure your dad tells you that all the time."

"Never, actually." True, my dad did live a healthy life-style, but he never preached or tried imposing his values on anyone else—least of all me. In fact he was the least judg-mental person I knew. Two years ago when I'd impulsively dyed my hair deep red and sported this unfortunate emo shag, he'd told me how pretty I was despite the fact that I looked like some preadolescent skater boy.

With the school tour nearly concluded, I tried to politely slip off to first-period World History, but Maya insisted on escorting me to the classroom. I couldn't exactly decline, since (miracle of miracles) she was in the class too. Maya had thought it would be nice for me to have her friendly face in my first class, so she'd helped arrange my schedule. So much for my desire to be anonymous and go unnoticed.

To make matters worse, my World History teacher, a jovial, middle-aged man with a slight paunch, named Mr. Ghiradelli, introduced me to the class like I was some exotic species they had never seen before.

"Everyone say hello to Nica Ashley. She came here all the way from *Bangkok*. In Thailand." His saucer eyes nearly bugged out of his head he was so excited.

The students greeted me politely. I stood there and said, "Hi."

And, as if that weren't completely humiliating enough, Mr. Ghiradelli turned to me and said, "Maybe you could enlighten the class about the differences between Theravada and Hinayana Buddhism."

I looked at him, waiting for him to say he was just kidding. But he wasn't. He stood there, waiting expectantly, his thick sausage fingers clasped together as if he were praying. I swallowed and looked at all the kids just staring at me. The truth was, since I had lived in Thailand and other parts of Asia I could actually answer the question. But being put on the spot like that was mortifying.

"Mom and I are atheists. Don't know," I lied, then quickly grabbed a seat at the back of the room, much to his and the other students' bewilderment. All in all, an extremely desperate and totally unsuccessful attempt on my part to fade into the woodwork, as the rest of the class kept turning around and staring at this rare bird that had landed in their classroom.

The rest of my morning classes (English, gym, Spanish) were pretty much a blur of unfamiliar but friendly faces.

Enthusiastic teachers ("Welcome to Barrington, Nica!") who were eager to inspire their students to reach new intellectual heights and cheerful students who seemed all too willing to soak it up—all before noon. They were all so relentlessly upbeat I started to wonder whether everyone was on Paxil or some other serotonin inhibitors. Maybe it had been slipped into the water supply?

Forget Disney World: Barrington seemed like the happiest place on earth. To me, however, it was quickly becoming the world's most annoying.

Lunchtime was a welcome relief. I breezed through the school cafeteria line, impressed by its array of nutritious offerings, and grabbed a garden salad with Tofurky along with a zucchini nut muffin. Maya was right about the food. All the salads were made fresh daily with only the finest organic ingredients, as were the free-range turkey and veggie burgers, whole-wheat pasta salads, and Margherita pizzas with basil. And all the plates, cups, and utensils were made from biodegradable corn products, which would naturally decompose in only a few months as opposed to the usually indestructible plastic crap festering in toxic garbage dumps. My ecoconscious mother would have approved of all this "green" living. I was just relieved to get some food in my system before my blood sugar crashed and I turned into a total raving psycho.

I passed by the neatly spaced rows of empty tables and wandered outside to the quad, where most students were sitting at picnic tables, eating their well-balanced meals under the bright noonday sun.

I spotted Maya perched atop a table, practically holding court with her perky crew of Neutrogena-fresh cheerleaders. She waved and called me over. I pretended not to hear and headed in the opposite direction. All I wanted was to be able to stuff my face in peace without the extra added pressure of having to make small talk or, worse, justify my not wanting to complete their precious pyramid squad at the next football game.

I had no sooner avoided jumping into the proverbial frying pan then I found myself heading straight for one major fire.

Rebel Boy sat underneath a giant oak tree at the far end of the quad. Alone. He was busily typing on his laptop, as oblivious to everyone else as they were to him. It seemed as though the other kids deliberately went out of their way to avoid him, and he them. I had a thought. Maybe underneath that tough-as-nails exterior lurked a fellow outsider like me. I figured he might have a really interesting story, because anyone *that* gorgeous and athletic was usually leader of the pack, not ostracized by it. So I headed straight toward him, not thinking about what I would say or do if he actually acknowledged my presence.

As if he detected an alien intruder about to invade his sacred space, he looked up and glared directly at me with those intense blue-green eyes. My throat went dry. *Just look away*, I told myself. And yet I couldn't help but meet his gaze dead on and stare right back at him. He projected a rage that was so blistering and naked that I actually thought I might spontaneously combust right then and there. Barrington High's very own Salem witch.

Yet I continued walking toward him.

A sensible girl would have found somewhere else to eat lunch and tried to forget all about him. A normal person would have turned away.

Not me. I wasn't wired like that. "Normal" wasn't part of my genetic code (not that I was ever deliberately reckless or actively stupid). When I was attracted to something, or someone, I couldn't pretend otherwise. There was something about Rebel Boy that was pulling me toward him.

I never stopped or broke stride even for a nanosecond. Though slightly terrified I was determined to at least introduce myself. Our eyes locked. I became completely oblivious to everyone and everything around me.

Until a trio of jock asses slammed into me as they played catch with a leaky chocolate milk container over the head of a cute but feisty Harry Potter type balancing a lunch tray. While the tormented kid, dressed in jeans and faded plaid shirt, didn't look like your typical geek, he was most definitely the runt of his litter. I realized that as friendly as kids appeared to be in this welcoming school, the age-old social pecking order most definitely applied, with jocks presiding on top and geeks relegated to the bottommost rung. So the happiest place on earth maybe wasn't so happy after all.

My bottle of dragon-fruit Vitaminwater went flying like a Scud missile, narrowly missing the feathered coif of Señora Gibbons, my new Spanish teacher, who was on her cell phone chastising her husband *(en inglés)* for buying regular yogurt instead of nonfat. Luckily, I was able to prevent my salad from turning her tangerine-orange pantsuit (she looked like a giant Popsicle) into a Jackson Pollock splatter mess.

I, on the other hand, was not nearly so fortunate. Nonfat vinaigrette dressing sprayed my Patti Smith T-shirt. Meanwhile the clueless Three Stooges continued abusing the runt without even tossing off a "my bad" or "sorry" in my direction.

"Yo, the O-man's hoping to jump-start a growth spurt," said a fireplug wrestler sporting a severe buzz cut as he caught the pint of chocolate milk from one of his equally buff teammates.

I yanked the idiot's arm and flipped him to the ground before he knew who or what had hit him. Then I poured the rest of the milk over his head without missing a beat.

"Oops," I said with a sweet smile, pissed as hell that I was going to reek of garlic and onions for the rest of the day. No amount of winter-mint gum could neutralize that.

Fireplug stared up at me, his mouth hanging open, totally flabbergasted. His jock-ass buddies were equally stunned, as were the other kids who had witnessed my swift moves. All I was conscious of was how Rebel Boy had turned back to his laptop, not giving me another glance, as if I had never existed.

At the same time, the Three Stooges, humiliated at getting their butts kicked by the new girl (all five feet six inches of her), bolted off before they became the laughingstock of the entire student body.

"Impressive moves," said the cute runt, who chased after me while blotting chocolate milk off his curly mop of auburn hair. He was easily half a head shorter than me.

"Living in Bangkok for almost a year had two benefits. I learned kickboxing from a master. And I developed a fierce addiction to prik king."

"Which I hear is highly curable."

"As is the need for being a human piñata." I handed him some extra napkins.

"What? And deprive the steroid six-packers of their reason for being? That would be way too cruel." He flashed a playful smile, which I returned. I liked his refreshing I'm-no-victim attitude. Not to mention his very deft ability to throw back the witty banter.

"Live to annoy. That's my motto." He held out his hand. "I'm Oliver Monsalves, by the way. You must be the new girl."

"So I've been told. Nica to my friends." Hearing that phrase "new girl" made the tiny hairs on the back of my neck go stiff. "Speaking of cruel and annoying, was my photo and résumé texted to everyone before school this morning?" Was there anyone in this school who *didn't* know my life story?

He shrugged apologetically. "No need. There aren't many secrets in this town."

Over what remained of our respective lunches Oliver proceeded to recount the highlights of my young but event-filled life with alarming accuracy, right down to my mother's fanatical quest to discover the most unspoiled Eden on earth. Here I was an open book and I hadn't even made it through my first day of school. How weird and depressing was that?

Still, I was more than happy to find a kindred spirit and make my first real friend.

The bell rang, signaling the end of lunch. Five minutes until afternoon classes began.

Oliver and I headed for the main entrance. He must've seen me glancing back at Rebel Boy, who was stealing off to the parking lot toward his Mustang instead of to sixth period along with the rest of us.

"Oh, FYI. Steer clear of *that*."

I felt myself blush, embarrassed that I'd been caught staring at Rebel Boy. Still, I decided to play dumb. "Of what?"

"Jackson Winters." He shot me a mocking look and shook his head disapprovingly, clearly not buying my naive schoolgirl act one bit. "I may be vertically challenged, but I wasn't born yesterday."

I was so busted that I chewed on my lower lip in an effort not to smile. So that was Rebel Boy's name. "He looks harmless enough." I watched Jackson Winters slide into his car and then speed away.

"So do most serial killers. Anyway, you're about six months too late." Oliver held the door open for me.

"For what?" I looked at him questioningly, pausing a moment before entering the school building. Was Oliver really comparing Jackson to a psychopathic murderer? Was he really suggesting that the guy was on track to be the next serial killer? I have to admit that he most definitely had my attention.

Oliver sighed in frustration as he nudged me through the doorway into the corridor, where we joined the sea of students trudging off to their respective classes. It was becoming quite clear that my new bud was hoping to squelch my unhealthy interest in Jackson.

He tried a different approach, pulling out the big guns. "How can I best put this? Jackson is on what we sociologists call a downward spiral to Outcastville. Mind you, his wounds are mostly self-inflicted."

"Those are the most interesting kind." Now I was most definitely intrigued. God knows I felt like an outcast myself most of the time.

Oliver shook his head. Once again this was *not* the reaction he was hoping for. I could tell I was starting to exasperate him. I've been known to do that sometimes, become fixated with things that I should let go for my own good. The summer I was thirteen, when we were living in Bali, I developed an unnatural obsession with Facebook, at least according to my mother. By the end of my first month I had eight hundred forty-two friends (remember, I moved around a lot). Pretty soon it got to the point where if I didn't check my page at least four or five times an hour I'd have these severe panic attacks, like I was missing something important. I'm talking full-on heart palpitations and difficulty breathing. Finally my mother held an intervention and canceled my account. Forcing me to go cold turkey. Withdrawal was utter torture. I literally felt physically ill for a week like I had the worst case of food poisoning imaginable. But it broke my addiction. And I never logged on again. Oliver's valiant effort to keep me on a straight-and-narrow path with regard to Jackson gave me all the early signs of a similar compulsion developing, which I chose to ignore.

Meanwhile I was rocked by a surprising jolt of emotion.

A feeling that could only be described as sadness. I imagined that Jackson Winters must be a tortured soul. Maybe even a masochist. And despite the fact that I had never even said one word to the guy, for some bizarre reason I felt drawn to him. Even a little sorry for him, though I wasn't sure why.

"Well don't leave me hanging. Tell me everything about Rebel Boy. From the beginning." Oliver's sensible words of warning aside, I was eager to know the whole story, every last detail about Jackson Winters's tragic and no doubt misunderstood life.

As we wound our way through the crowded hallways, Oliver recounted Jackson's shockingly rapid descent from school star to pariah in less than six months. I was riveted.

"Seriously, Nica, you don't know the half. Dude was the zenith of cool ever since kindergarten. Had it all. Straight As. Natural athlete. Champion snowboarder. Coolest friends. Respect. Plus super-hot girlfriend Dana Fox."

*Dana Fox?*

My ears immediately perked up. I shot Oliver a puzzled look. For some reason that name rang a distinct bell, though I couldn't exactly recall why. I thought she might be one of the many kids I'd met that day.

"Her name sounds familiar," I said, racking my brain trying to remember which super-cheerful girl I had met was Dana.

"No wonder. There must be hundreds of posters with her face plastered all over town."

Of course, now I remembered why I knew her name. "She's that missing girl. The one I saw on the way to school this morning. What happened to her?"

Oliver shrugged. "Nobody knows for sure. Other than Jackson's one true love up and split one night without so much as leaving a 'Dear John' text or e-mail. Hence all those posters that Jackson keeps displaying, hoping someone will report *something*."

"How awful. Do you think she ran away?" Needless to say, I was highly intrigued.

"Conventional wisdom says she did," Oliver responded with a shrug.

"What do her parents say?" I asked.

"Very little other than she left town to get away from Jackson and is living with relatives," Oliver admitted. "They're pretty vague on the details. They've urged him to stop with the posters and all, but he refuses. In any case, heartbroken JW did a one-eighty James Dean bad-boy flip-out. Let everything go to hell. His grades plummeted. Friendships dissolved. He got in trouble with the cops and local security. Even blew off the Olympic snowboarding team trials. Now he's practically a ghost that people barely notice anymore. Other than occasionally working in his family's sporting goods store, he barely interacts with anyone unless it has to do with finding Dana."

"That's so tragic." Forget about Heathcliff and *Wuthering Heights*: Emily Brontë would've had a field day with Jackson

Winters and his tale of woe. I wanted to know more. "So what was this Dana Fox like?"

"She was awesome. Never had to work hard at anything," Oliver said, without any hint of irony or judgment.

"Sounds a lot like Maya," I remarked pointedly.

"On the contrary. She and Maya were polar opposites," Oliver proclaimed. "Whereas Maya's super competitive and works harder than anyone to be Queen Bee—with all her clubs and cheerleading and volunteering—Dana was always totally chill. Never sweated anything. And yet Dana always managed to excel at *everything* she did. Academically, athletically, socially."

"Let me guess. Maya *hated* being number two." I have to confess I thoroughly enjoyed hearing about the Dana-Maya rivalry. Perhaps Maya wasn't so perfect after all.

"Not only that," Oliver continued. "Maya made sure she and Dana were besties, from preschool on."

"Keep your friends close and enemies closer," I retorted.

"You'd think a girl like Dana, who had the golden touch, would be a stuck-up bitch. But truthfully, Dana was really sweet. Even to me." Oliver shrugged and shook his head, completely mystified, as though he were the world's biggest loser.

"And now with Dana out of the picture, I guess Maya finally gets her wish to be numero uno." I declared. "Triumph out of tragedy."

The class bell rang loudly. The remaining stragglers

scattered off to their classes. Oliver and I lingered, now officially late.

"What'll really be a tragedy is if I miss all the fun in bio lab. It's frog-dissection day. How awesome is that." Oliver held his right hand up to his head, cocked it like a gun, and pretended to fire two rounds into his temple.

I smirked in amusement. "It's awesomeness squared. Just remember to pith Kermit between the atlas and axis of the vertebral column." I pointed to the base of my neck, just to tweak him a bit.

He cringed at the thought. "Thanks. I'm sure Kermie will appreciate it." And then he flipped me off with a grin as he shuffled reluctantly into the last classroom at the end of the corridor.

I stood alone in the quiet hallway and took a deep breath before entering my Algebra 2 class, where they were learning about sines and cosines and triangle identities.

Given that I enjoyed math as much as a trip to the dentist, I silently slid into an empty seat in the back of the room and tried not to call too much attention to myself. Fortunately, Mr. Ramirez was a wiry, no-nonsense math nerd in pressed jeans and a bow tie, who happily kept new student introductions to a minimum rather than lose one minute of precious time discussing the exciting law of tangents. As he droned on in a monotone bass voice, my mind drifted back to Jackson Winters and his missing girlfriend, Dana Fox.

## 3. LIGHTS OUT

The last bell rang precisely at two forty-five p.m. Classes were thankfully over for the day. After a few wrong turns, I finally found my way back to my locker. I sorted through the stack of deadly boring textbooks, figuring out which ones I really needed to lug home.

My heart fluttered for a few brief seconds. It did that sometimes when I felt anxious. Kind of like having butterflies in the stomach, only it lasted longer. I steadied myself, stood up straight, and took a long, deep breath. I had survived yet another first day in a new school in a new place. If only they gave out prize money for that kind of thing.

I felt exhausted (still fighting off brutal jet lag) and slightly overwhelmed by the amount of busywork (aka homework) that was assigned in each subject. I was probably looking at four hours of work, and it was only my first day. Not that I'd never had homework before—believe me, I had. It was just that I was used to a less rigid and more creative approach to education, especially the time spent outside the classroom.

Which is what had led me to Master Kru at the Fighting Spirit Gym in Bangkok, where I'd learned Muay Thai kickboxing, also known as the Art of Eight Limbs.

It's not that I had a burning desire to kick some serious butt or become this awesome fighter—a female Tony Jaa. Not in the least. The truth was, I had already run through the usual "girl" pursuits of music lessons (piano, guitar, and viola) and dance lessons (ballet, jazz, and modern), followed by five years of soccer (it was the one sport that was played in every town we lived in). Anyway, I was bored and itching to try something different. Something new and challenging, very out of the box. Not to mention I *was* living in Thailand, and kickboxing was considered the national sport. So, as the saying goes, "When in Rome . . ." Or Bangkok, in my case . . .

Not that I wasn't a tiny bit nervous. Believe me, I was. Totally terrified and intimidated. Which made me all the more determined (or stupid, depending on your point of view) to go for it. Plus my good friend Lai, who was a serious gymnast in trampoline and tumbling, came along for moral support. She was petite and adorable with a bubbly personality and always pushed me to try everything Thai. The first afternoon I entered the Fighting Spirit Gym, a sprawling warehouse devoted entirely to kickboxing, I heard Master Kru instructing two ripped young guys in neon-blue silk boxing shorts who were sparring in a padded boxing ring.

The boys, both shirtless and barefoot (and yes, totally cute), jabbed and kicked each other with lightning speed and efficiency while Master Kru watched with his laser-beam eyes.

He seemed to sense my fear and waved me over. A compact, soft-spoken man in his forties, Master Kru was no taller than me. And yet he commanded such authority and respect from everyone in the gym without ever demanding it that I felt compelled to obey. He was one of the greatest kickboxers in Asia, I later learned.

I stood there, fidgeting, expecting to be taught some basic moves. After a minute of silence, which felt like an eternity, he finally spoke, uttering one word: "Breathe."

*Breathe?* That was it? My first big lesson? I almost laughed, but one look at his calm and fixed expression told me he was dead serious. I was familiar with meditation, so I tried a yoga inhalation that I'd learned from my mom. After a few breaths, Master Kru held up his right hand, stopping me. Wasn't I breathing properly? Apparently not. I felt like a total dork.

Master Kru inhaled, taking in a long, deep breath. He held it for a moment, then slowly exhaled. I watched in amazement how his entire body seemed to inflate and almost grow taller before my eyes. I swallowed, and then I breathed in again, this time more aware of the air rushing into my lungs. I felt the muscles in my abdomen tighten while I held the breath for a moment longer than usual before slowly exhaling. My body was suddenly overcome by the strangest sensation. I became aware of my heart beating and the blood pulsing through my veins, sensations I'd never noticed before.

*My entire body felt alive.*

I shot Master Kru an astonished look. He acknowledged me with a quick nod and then explained that breathing is "the source of life." With proper breathing, he said, we can control our bodies and everything we do.

"When the breath wanders, the mind is unsteady. When the breath is still, so is the mind."

That may sound simple and New Agey, but I found it deceptively difficult to pull off.

I stood in the middle of the Barrington High School hallway, shut my eyes, and breathed: slowly and deeply, exactly the way Master Kru had taught me. I tuned out every sound and every thought from my head. I felt my heart rate slow down. My breathing became steady. Within seconds I felt calmer and more relaxed. After a minute I opened my eyes and sighed. Momentary relief.

But just because I might be able to face hours of homework tonight didn't mean that I was happy about my predicament. One day here at Barrington High and I knew the school sucked and the kids were freaks. Maybe that sounds melodramatic, but I had fit in better at my last school in Bangkok because, since I was an American, no one had expected me to fit in. Here I was supposed to fit in, and there was no way I could or wanted to.

I shut my locker, then zipped up my shoulder bag, which was weighed down with almost twenty pounds of textbooks and class handouts, and headed to the exit.

As I hurried down the stairs to the first-floor administrative offices (I remembered I had to hand in my signed class schedule to my new guidance counselor, which would confirm that I hadn't ditched any classes), I heard deep voices arguing in the hallway—male voices. At first I thought it was two students and barely paid much attention. But then, as I turned the corner, I caught a glimpse of my object of desire, Jackson Winters. He was getting reamed by what I assumed was a very pissed-off teacher near one of the exits. When Jackson tried walking away, the well-dressed African-American man grabbed his arm to stop him. It was then I realized he probably wasn't a teacher. *A teacher wouldn't do that*, I thought. The man angrily ordered Jackson to "stop looking for her." Jackson yanked his arm free and shouted back, accusing him of lying about Dana and something else, which I couldn't catch.

Part of me wanted to hang around and eavesdrop, of course. But the other part (the occasionally sane and cautious half) knew better than to butt into someone else's business and turn a tense situation into an ugly one. So I decided to sneak off in the opposite direction to the administrative offices.

At the very last second, though, Jackson looked away from the man and over at me. I was mortified. All I could think about was getting the hell away. So I rushed off, praying he didn't know who I was.

Five minutes later my heart was still pounding as I stood quietly in the office of Mrs. Julie Henderson, listening to her thank me effusively for turning in my schedule so promptly. She was cute and a lot younger than I expected a guidance counselor to be. Thirty-nine years old, I was guessing, courtesy of her Northwestern University diploma, class of '96, which was prominently displayed on the wall alongside photographs of her riding an elephant somewhere in Africa, posing in front of the Parthenon in Athens, and at her wedding. With a pixie haircut and cool sense of style and dress—most probably Betsey Johnson—Mrs. Henderson seemed like a welcome change from most of the other staid, vanilla-bland teachers I had met. After she politely inquired about my first day, she suggested scheduling a meeting for the following week to discuss my goals and future.

"Before you know it, all your time will slip away if you don't plan ahead," she chirped with a bright, eager-to-please smile as she scrolled through her calendar on her computer, searching for an available time slot. "No matter how prepared you think you are in life, there are always *unexpected adjustments*."

Goals and future plans, as in college and career and the great beyond known as adulthood? Was she for real? Here I had barely finished my first day in this new school in this new town, and she was already pressing to know what I wanted to be when I graduated in two years?

My disbelief and horror must have been pretty apparent, because she immediately got this apologetic look and quickly dialed everything back to zero.

"You know, on second thought . . . there'll be plenty of time to discuss all that stuff later."

She closed her calendar file and put her computer to sleep. Then she stared at me. I squirmed about in my chair, feeling scrutinized.

"Listen, I hope I didn't freak you out too much," Mrs. Henderson remarked, pushing her computer to the side and smiling self-critically. "I have a tendency to get a little carried away with all the planning. As my husband so often reminds me."

And I had a tendency to run for the hills when facing down a control freak, but instead I kept my cool, muttered something noncommittal like "no problem," and then took off before she had time to think of any other helpful suggestions.

• • •

The parking lot had thinned out considerably, as most kids had already left for the day. I spotted my father standing by his Prius in the drop-off zone. He was chatting with a tall, sandy-haired boy I didn't recognize.

My dad smiled as he saw me approach. "Here's my girl. How did your first day go?"

"It went," I replied, in no mood to go into details about my exhausting day with some blond dude I didn't know standing right there.

My father smiled indulgently at my flippant response but knew better than to pry or prod me for further details, especially in front of a stranger. "By the way, you guys know each other?"

"Don't think so." I stared right at the guy. "I'm Nica."

Blondie stared right back, supremely confident and not the least bit intimidated by my prickliness. "Chase Cochran. Pleasure to meet you, Nica. I heard a lot about you today."

"Interesting. I didn't hear a word about you." Snarky, I know, but I hated feeling like all the kids were dishing me before I even knew them. I couldn't hide my grumpy mood even with a smile.

Chase chuckled, easily amused. "Lucky for me."

Okay, so the boy was quick-witted, with a sense of humor. Points for that. He also had the brightest megawatt smile I'd ever seen. Which no doubt he whitened twice a month for maintenance. And he apparently had already won over my dad, who was beaming brightly at the sight of his daughter getting acquainted with this boy. It was a little unnerving how smooth a player Chase was, not to mention how good-looking.

Though to call Chase Cochran good-looking was an understatement. Excessively handsome was more like it. The kind of handsome that almost hurts your eyes—like one of those unnaturally ripped Abercrombie models who look like they've been genetically engineered. Yes, those boys are gorgeous hunks, but they're not quite *real*. Chase had a strong, chiseled profile and such a sharp jawline it probably could slice steel. And judging from his school jacket, which he wore proudly with its numerous varsity letters, Chase was undoubtedly an awesome athlete. Odds were he was also incredibly popular. Guys that good-looking invariably are, no matter which school they attend. The guy every boy wanted to be—and every girl wanted to know. And adults admired. A star.

And he was staring at me. Checking me out.

"Mind if we go, Dad? I'm really fried." And, I admit, I was more than a little self-conscious with Chase scrutinizing me that way. I was so obviously *not* his type. And neither was he mine.

"Ready when you are. Can we drop you somewhere, Chase?" My dad would have to be Mr. Polite and offer blond Adonis a ride.

"Thanks, Dr. A. I got my own wheels," he responded with a grin.

*Dodged a bullet on that one,* I thought. The prospect of being trapped in a car with Chase and my dad literally made me nauseous. Just like I didn't do group activities, I didn't do charming very well.

"Catch you later, Nica." Chase grinned and gave me a lingering and, if I was not mistaken, lascivious look before heading off. But still, I wasn't sure if he was flirting with me or merely acting attentive in front of my dad.

"Yeah. Later." Very much relieved, I hopped into the passenger seat and watched Chase stride confidently over to a posse of guys who were goofing around on the lawn. There was a flurry of fist bumping as they opened their arms and made room for Chase, like he was their prodigal king returned from battle.

"He acts like he owns the place," I muttered, half under my breath.

"Actually, his dad does." Dad pressed the ignition button, then drove the Prius out of the school parking lot onto the main road.

There was an edge to my father's voice, which made me sit up and press further. "Who's his dad?" This was the second time my dad had slipped something into conversation (the first being curfew), and I was curious why.

"Richard Cochran. He's president of Bar Tech Industries.

And chairman of the hospital board, among other things."

That explained a lot about Chase's egotistical attitude. His dad's company was literally everywhere in Barrington. I stared out the window at the Bar Tech logo, which was emblazoned over the school sign.

Fortunately, Chase Cochran's name was never mentioned again during the ride home.

My dad dropped me off at the house before heading back to the hospital for the rest of the afternoon. He had patients to see and promised to be home no later than seven with a delicious sushi dinner. Meanwhile I was more than happy to have a few hours of much-needed alone time.

I immediately logged on to my laptop to check e-mails. There were several from Lai in Bangkok, who filled me in on her latest boyfriend woes (she finally had a date with Pak, a senior on the gymnastics team), and one from my mother down in Buenos Aires. My mom hoped I was settling in okay with the new school and making friends. She also said that although she missed me terribly, she was busily preparing for her long trek down to the South Pole. That meant shopping for just the right kind of water-repellent, fleece-lined Canada Goose parka and rubber boots and snow goggles and turtleneck sweaters and whatever else one needs in the coldest place on earth. All in all the e-mail was vintage Lydia— short and sweet with just a splash of sentimentality. Rather than wait to send my reply I shot back a brief e-mail telling her that school was great and that the kids were awesome and that I was doing fine.

In other words, I lied.

It was best for everyone: less drama all around. The last thing I needed was having my mother feeling all guilty about shipping me off to live with my dad. The last thing I needed was her calling him and them conspiring to turn me into a happy camper. No, it was much better for everyone—especially me—if they were kept totally in the dark about my current emotional state.

Someone once said, "Ignorance is bliss." Well, if not total bliss, then way less misery.

And misery is exactly what I felt after wasting more than two and a half hours on mind-numbing tedium—aka my homework. I desperately needed a break. So I plugged in my iPod and chilled as it shuffled through *Rolling Stone*'s top five hundred rock-and-roll songs, one of the truly cool gifts my dad had gotten me last year. By the time Blondie's "Call Me" came on, my mind had drifted to thoughts of Jackson Winters.

Next thing I knew I was online reading all about his many snowboarding medals in halfpipe and parallel giant slalom at the US Juniors the year before. Oliver was right. Jackson had had a bright future. Not only was he nationally ranked, but he was also on the brink of breaking into the top ten. He'd had a real shot at making the US Olympic team. That is until Dana Fox left Barrington and he threw it all away.

I couldn't help but wonder: Who was this girl who broke Jackson's heart? Was she really as special and as awesome as Oliver claimed?

A Google search on Dana Fox turned up little information—surprisingly little. Other than Jackson's website, *Dana Fox Is Missing*," which had a dozen pictures of her and claimed she'd been kidnapped, scant media attention had been given to her disappearance six months earlier. Odd.

Usually if a popular and very pretty young woman, let alone a high school cheerleader, goes missing, reporters trip all over themselves to interview the anguished family and friends and write about the tragic story. And yet in this case there was just one story written about Dana's disappearance. It was a short, vaguely written article in the local Barrington paper in which her parents claimed Dana was "alive and well" and living safely "somewhere back east with relatives." End of story. Reading between the lines, it sounded as if her parents and the police were suggesting that Dana Fox had left Barrington to get away from Jackson, "the intensely attached boyfriend." As if he were this crazy nut job or stalker with severe emotional problems. I knew that was what Oliver, and perhaps the other kids at school, believed. I was sure of one thing: Jackson Winters was obsessed with Dana Fox.

I studied the pictures of Dana—her bright, smiling face—and her equally attractive family. She really was gorgeous, with striking, exotic features: shiny black hair, green eyes, and beautiful full lips. Her beautiful mother was fifth-generation Chinese American, whose family had apparently helped build the transcontinental railroad way back in the 1860s. Her distinguished father was an African-American science nerd who'd moved from Washington, DC, to Barrington in the late 1980s. I recognized his picture. He was the man who'd argued with Jackson at school. By all accounts the Fox family was successful and happy. Dana seemed to have it all. Then she was gone. And poor Jackson was left out in the cold.

The battery on my laptop started flashing a warning that it was running out of juice. That was okay. I looked at the time and saw that it was already after six. I logged off, plugged in the power cord, and called my dad. I was hungry and wanted to find out how much longer until he came home with dinner.

My father returned home at seven p.m., with enough sushi to feed a small army. He'd had trouble deciding what to order, so he'd gotten an assortment: unagi, hamachi, toro, ebi, and tako among others. And all skepticism aside, I must admit he was right—the fish was pretty tasty.

We chatted about unimportant things: the weather (unseasonably warm), college football (Ohio State's rivalry with USC), and my new teachers, along with several other (mostly boring) topics I forgot by the time we retreated to our rooms to finish our work. Dad disappeared into his study to work on some research paper about heart valves or something like that. I had at least a couple more hours ahead of me of homework.

By the time I'd finished, it was after eleven p.m. Still, I wasn't the least bit tired. I grabbed my laptop and snuggled in the window seat, looking forward to chatting on Skype with Lai in Bangkok to give her the full report on my first day. Given the fifteen-hour time difference, she would most likely be arriving home from school by now.

But when I tried logging on to Skype, I kept getting error messages. After a half dozen futile attempts, I discovered that Internet service was down. I walked down to my dad's room and saw his light was out, so I couldn't ask him what was wrong. I then tiptoed around the house and finally found the cable modem underneath the large oak desk in my dad's study. The connections were fine. Maybe my room had become a dead spot? I sat on the floor and hooked up my laptop to the modem. Still no Internet connection. Then I opened my cell phone. That wasn't working either. It was as if the entire network had been deliberately shut down, just like this town after curfew. How annoying was that. I closed my laptop and cell phone in frustration, pissed as hell.

"Nica, what are you doing in here?"

Startled, I looked up to find my dad standing in the doorway in a T-shirt and sweatpants. He sounded really irritated and looked perturbed, as if I had done something horrible.

"Oh, sorry," I said, rising up from the floor. "The Internet was down and I tried hooking up my laptop to your modem to see if it would work."

"Well, it won't," he announced, swooping over to his desk and checking to see if I had disturbed any wires or medical files on his desk or any of the locked cabinets lining the wall.

"Yeah, I kind of discovered that. Should we contact someone to report it?" I asked quite innocently.

"*No*," he snapped back at me. I must've reacted to his sudden harshness with surprise, because he quickly softened. "The network goes down a lot. Erratic service. They're probably just doing maintenance."

"Okay, whatever," I replied, not quite sure why he was having such a strong reaction to me being there. I hadn't looked at any of his files, nor had I touched anything on his desk. I turned to leave, but stopped when I heard my dad speak again.

"And Nica?"

"Yeah?" I turned around, feeling embarrassed at being scolded like a six-year-old.

"In the future, please stay out of here and don't touch anything. Ever." I'd never seen my father act this testy before.

74

"Sorry, Dad."

I left my dad's study and hurried back to my bedroom, trying to shake off the unsettled feeling that I'd violated some unspoken rule and done something horribly wrong.

Licking my wounds, I sat in my window seat in the dark, feeling sorry for myself and very much alone. The lights were already out in all the other houses in the neighborhood. People in this town obviously went to bed earlier than I did. It was creepy to be looking out into a completely black landscape. Even in rural Thailand, when my mother and I visited small villages at the edge of the jungle, we would see lights from nearby houses. I felt a wave of homesickness again overtake me, and I wished I were in any of the other places I had lived with Mom, anywhere but here in Barrington.

Then I saw Jackson's car cruise by my house with its lights off. It was just like the night before. Was Jackson really just searching for Dana Fox, even when all evidence pointed to her leaving town? Or was this nightly ritual, a deliberate violation of town law, a statement of some kind?

## 4. BORN TO BE WILD

I finally fell asleep sometime after midnight and woke up on time at six thirty a.m., my alarm having done its job quite efficiently. Taking advantage of the extra time I even managed to throw an outfit together (moss-colored long-sleeved V-neck T-shirt over black skinny stretch jeans) that I didn't totally detest. After finishing his 10K morning run, my dad made me a hearty, well-balanced breakfast. And he insisted I eat it.

"The most important meal of the day," he declared, quite serious.

I was taken aback. He always seemed so relaxed about what I ate—especially in the morning. Now suddenly he was micromanaging my breakfast? I chalked it up to our new (permanent) living arrangement.

After I dutifully ate a bowl of fresh fruit mixed with plain Greek yogurt, he fed me one hard-boiled egg (hardly my favorite food at seven a.m.) and a slice of dry wheat toast, hold the jam and butter. Heart healthy, as they say. I obeyed because it seemed to make him so happy to see me eat it all. You've got to throw the parents some crumbs once in a while.

"Sorry I flew off the handle like that last night," my dad said contritely as we straightened up the kitchen before leaving the house.

"That's okay." I shrugged, not wanting to make a big deal of it. "I shouldn't have gone into your study without asking in the first place." It was always best to accept an apology from Dad and move on without rehashing matters too much.

"It's just I've got medical files and other sensitive documents in there that need to remain private."

"Of course. It'll never happen again," I vowed as we walked out the front door.

On the drive through town, Dad ran into a local java house for his double dose of coffee with nonfat milk and two Splendas (his one vice, as far as I could tell). I snapped a few photographs of the oh-so-quaint shops along Main Street, which I intended to send to Lai, just in case she doubted that I was living in the land of the Brady Bunch and apple pie. There was Will Wright's, an old-fashioned ice cream parlor where they still made their own flavors daily. Then there was the original movie theater from 1926, the Odeon, which showed only classic films made before 1980. There was also a mom-and-pop grocery and a retro bookstore specializing in mysteries and thrillers, along with other assorted home-grown businesses. At least Barrington was not the land of ugly strip malls. It was a friendly, hospitable town that looked like it came out of a Norman Rockwell painting.

As I looked around, I noticed that every single store had identical red-and-white BTS decals prominently displayed in their front windows. Curious, I asked my dad what the deal was with all those BTS stickers. Did they represent some kind of community organization like the Elks or the Barrington Better Business Bureau? All he said was that they were for Bar Tech Security, a private patrol company, and then he flipped on the radio to listen to the morning news.

I got the hint he didn't want to discuss the topic any further. I was wondering why and how it was that a sleepy, ultrasafe town like Barrington needed a private security force, especially one run by a corporation, anyway. Not to mention a silly curfew. I was thinking so much about these questions that I never got around to asking Dad because I knew it would just annoy him.

My father dropped me off at school with twelve minutes to spare before first period. Rather than immediately head to my locker, I hung around the quad, secretly hoping to run into Jackson again. Maybe this time we might actually have a conversation. Maybe he'd even tell me about his late-night rides. I knew that was unlikely, but even just being introduced to the guy would be a start.

So I hung around and waited. Minutes ticked by. I tried not looking like a total douche just standing there all alone, so I greeted every familiar face that passed by me with a friendly hello. I felt like one of those smiley flight attendants standing by the cabin door, cheerfully welcoming passengers as they boarded the plane. And Jackson never showed up.

When the first bell rang, I was forced to make a mad dash off to my locker, where I ran into Chase Cochran and his clean-cut band of brothers. The four of them had all just finished morning football practice and were strutting along like they owned the hallways. With Chase clearly the top dog—always the alpha. Given the high school pecking order, I guess that made them all something like royalty.

"Well, if it isn't the doctor's daughter." Chase smiled, super friendly, casually brushing his sandy blond locks out of his big brown eyes. "Finding your way around school okay?"

"Yeah. No problem," I responded with a forced, awkward smile.

"You know my boys?" he asked, gesturing to the trio like they were his trusty lapdogs. "Kyle, Vox, and Alex."

Kyle, the big one, was an utterly faux beach boy, with a deep, even tan (courtesy of the local tanning salon, no doubt) and a couple of beaded bracelets on his right wrist. No way had he ever been within a thousand miles of Malibu. Vox, the skinny one, stood ramrod tall and sported a severe military buzz cut. Alex, a strapping lad with curly black locks, had a nervous and very annoying habit of laughing at everything anyone said.

"Hey, guys," I replied with a little wave, feeling incredibly gawky as I nearly dropped all my books.

"Dudes, this is Nica," Chase announced. "She's cool."

They all grunted politely.

"So you going to the game after school?" Chase asked.

That was the first I'd heard about any game, and I did a lot of hemming and hawing, trying to think of an excuse. The last place on earth I wanted to be was at a football game, cheering Chase. "Sorry, I can't plan that far ahead." As I heard those lame words come out of my mouth, I cringed. How utterly lame.

"Yeah. Hate to tie you down, Miss World Traveler. With your busy schedule and all, given you've been living here what, forty-eight hours?" Chase teased with a mix of bravado and conceited charm, which I found oddly appealing. His buddies riffed off him and razzed me about being some kind of "alien foreigner." A phrase they all found rather amusing.

*Alien foreigner?*

I held my tongue and let the nonsensical redundancy slip by without comment. For some reason I was reminded of an old Confucian proverb Master Kru liked to quote: *Ignorance is the night of the mind, but a night without moon and star.*

Anyway, I just smiled and walked off, with Chase following and the boneheads following him.

For a split second I actually had the thought that Chase might have been waiting around for me to arrive. But I realized that was totally ridiculous when a moment later Maya appeared from around the corner and kissed Chase right on the lips. Not a gentle peck you give a friend or relative, either. It was the kind of long, lingering full-on lip-lock that cute cheerleaders give to hunky quarterback boyfriends.

News alert: Maya and Chase were a couple.

Of course, that didn't surprise me. In fact it made perfect sense, as if it were biologically predestined. They were a textbook example of evolution: survival of the fittest. Charles Darwin would most definitely approve of such a pairing.

As we headed toward class together, Maya jabbered on about how I should totally hang with them after the game. Chase and his crew chimed in.

"It's going to be awesome," bragged Kyle, the team's star wide receiver. "Watch me score a few TDs."

The Cougars were going to annihilate their archrivals from Fairview High. I was about to beg off with a feeble excuse about needing to unpack and having too much homework, but then I had one of Oprah Winfrey's famous "aha" moments. (Yes, we got that show even in Thailand. And, amazingly, pretty much wherever we were. My mother was a fan, so I watched it a couple times, under duress, believe me.) Anyway, my epiphany was simple: Why fight it? They were being friendly and including me, so what was the harm in me being sociable in return? My mother always preached "stepping out of your comfort zone." She said it would help me grow. I thought, *Why not try to fit in for a change?*

I took a deep breath, swallowed all my cynicism and foolish pride, and chirped out, "Go, Cougars." *Rah, rah, rah.*

Well you would've thought I'd told Maya she'd won some lame-ass reality show competition. She literally jumped up and down and made a noise that sounded like "whoop." Then she promised to introduce me to all her cheerleading pals at lunch, and vowed to get me into a cheerleading uniform if it was the last thing she did.

"Don't hold your breath," I told her. I mean, fitting in was one thing, demeaning myself quite another. I did have my limits. Cheerleading ranked high on the list.

True to her word, Maya caught up with me on the cafeteria lunch line and introduced the entire cheerleading squad to me: Emily, Annie, Maddie, and Jaden—an enthusiastic clique of tanned limbs, well-blended natural highlights, and winning smiles. Even though they looked like they'd burst out of the pages of a Neutrogena ad, they seemed extremely down to earth and couldn't have been nicer. Within seconds of our meeting I was invited to go to the mall with them and to the movies over the weekend. I graciously accepted. This was the new Nica, throwing caution to the wind.

"Wow. Talk about a meteoric rise. Maya will have you running the school dance committee before you know it," Oliver teased me as we snagged a shady spot in the quad to eat our grilled chicken Caesar wraps five minutes later.

"Hardly. I'm just going to a stupid football game."

"That's what they all say. It's just *one* game. But it's the gateway sport. Next thing you know . . ."

I let out a small, involuntary laugh. I was just getting to know him and wasn't sure he was actually joking. "Wait, you're actually comparing watching football to getting addicted to drugs?"

For dramatic effect, he shook his head like a parent scolding a naughty child. "Don't you get it, Nica? This is how they hook you. After football, it's basketball games. Then baseball and hockey. And then maybe even cheerleading. Who knows where all this school spirit will lead?"

He looked at me with a most serious expression. I stared back. Okay, maybe he was serious. But then he burst out laughing.

"You had me going there for a minute! You're seriously warped, Oliver. You know that?" *And I thought I was weird.*

"Highly imaginative, according to my mom and all standardized exams."

Even though I didn't know his mother, I thought she was right. I was learning that Oliver had a wicked sense of humor, and he could make me laugh hard. Which counted for a lot.

"And your dad? What does he think?"

"Not much. What I mean is I don't know, since he died before I was born."

"That's awful. What happened?"

"An accident or something. I'm not really sure."

His tone was matter-of-fact and casual, but when I asked him why he wasn't sure, I immediately saw that he was putting on an act.

He shook his head and shrugged. "My mother doesn't like talking about it. Too many painful memories, I suppose. Anyway, no dad."

"Sorry. I really am." I felt terrible about raising the subject and pressing him on it. Sometimes I was as clueless as my mom. Like the way she could grill me about sensitive topics, like boys or sex, as if I were the subject of some article she was writing.

Oliver shrugged it off. "You can't miss what you never had." But then he kept talking. "I guess. I mean, I don't remember my parents ever being together. You know, married. And yet I've always felt like something's missing. Like there's a big void I keep trying to fill."

It was as if he was confiding in his dearest friend, but we'd only met a day ago. I realized I had never admitted such deep dark feelings to anyone before. But even though we barely knew each other, Oliver trusted me, and I him. Still, I wasn't sure why.

"Curse of the only child," said Oliver. "We've got no older siblings to fill in the blanks. The things we missed." Oliver's face suddenly crinkled. Sadness mixed with regret.

I nodded, thankful to have found a friend who understood what it was like to feel alone in one's own family. Even though I loved my parents, I didn't think they knew me or understood me. Not what I was really feeling, otherwise they never would've shipped me here to live. It was like we were these three planets orbiting the universe, occasionally coming into contact with one another. I took a big gulp of Vitaminwater, suddenly uncomfortable with the awkward silence that hung between us.

Quickly changing the mood, Oliver smiled brightly and said, "By the way, how excellent are these wraps?"

"They're genius," I replied, as I finished mine off with an approving smile. But I was still wondering why Oliver's mother would be so mysterious about how his father died.

After school I persuaded Oliver (begged, bribed, then bullied, actually) into tagging along with me to the football game. As cool as I pretended to be about the whole event,

I knew I wasn't quite brave enough to stomach sitting near Maya and her friends for the entire game by myself. And forget about hanging out afterward. I needed Oliver's moral support. All this togetherness, perpetual grinning, and rah-rah school-spirit stuff was still alien to me (in Thailand team sports like basketball and soccer were popular, but after-school games weren't big deals. Neither were they in most of the other places I'd lived either). Plus being a social butterfly didn't come easily to a natural loner like myself.

Turnout was surprisingly huge. The thousand-seat bleachers were filled to capacity. It seemed like at least half the school was in attendance, along with parents and friends. Oliver said it was always that way, though he'd only gone once before. Going to the game was a major social event. Especially for Maya and her girls, who did an impressive job stoking the enthusiastic crowd with lots of cheers, high-flying moves, and fancy routines. I was exhausted just watching them.

The game started promptly at four p.m. That seemed a bit on the early side to me but no surprise given the town curfew was ridiculously early too. The game was a real nail-biter as high school games go, or so I was told. Fairview High was a pretty tough opponent. The score was tied 7-7 until late in the fourth quarter, when our star quarterback, Chase Cochran, threw an epic pass to his buddy Kyle that helped the Cougars score the winning touchdown. Game over.

The bleachers erupted with a chorus of cheering, bringing everyone to their feet. Even me. I had to (begrudgingly) admit it was all sort of *fun*. Not that I was intending to make a habit of attending football games, but even Oliver got into the spirit. By the final seconds we were both on our feet, shouting at the top of our lungs along with everyone else.

I looked around at all the kids in the stands, respectfully cheering and incredibly well behaved. There was no raucous shouting or name-calling like I had witnessed at soccer games overseas. "So what's the deal with this town anyway?"

"What do you mean? It's just a town." Oliver looked truly puzzled, like I had just asked him a question in Swahili.

"One where all the teenagers are relentlessly cheerful, well dressed, and polite. It's sort of bizarre, like we're in some sort of time warp, from fifty years ago."

Oliver scoffed. "Only fifty?"

"What about this curfew? It's ridiculous," I snapped back. I couldn't believe he was actually debating this point.

"Keeps the riffraff off the streets," he replied flippantly.

"Hasn't stopped Rebel Boy from cruising about at all hours." I looked over at Jackson, who much to my delight and surprise was watching the game alone from way across the field.

"Some dudes are just asking for trouble." Oliver sighed and shook his head as we climbed down the stands toward the field along with everyone else.

. . .

We met up with Chase and Maya, and I congratulated them on their stellar performances. It was nearly six fifteen p.m. They asked me to join the team and cheerleaders for their ritual postgame pizzas, but I had already promised Oliver we'd do something after, so I declined.

"You've got to come," Chase insisted. When he saw me steal a glance at Oliver, he added, "And Oliver can come too."

Oliver shrugged and replied, "Whatever."

And so the matter was settled. It was a quick half-mile stroll to the center of town from school. We took over Violetta's, a traditional pizzeria with red-and-white-checkered tablecloths, empty wine bottles recycled as lamps, and walls lined with black-and-white photos of old-time singers like Frank Sinatra and Tony Bennett. I felt like I was watching an old American movie, except I was in it. Chase and Maya sat at the center of a long table like a king and queen. Everyone was joking and laughing, while scarfing down seven delicious pepperoni-and-extra-cheese pies in record time. I had three slices. Who knew that merely watching a football game could make you so hungry?

When it came time to pay the bill, Chase threw down two crisp one-hundred-dollar bills, picking up the hundred-forty-nine-dollar tab for everyone without discussion.

"You rock, Chase," a couple of the kids said. It was ridiculously generous. But I felt a little weird about him paying for me along with sixteen others. Back in Thailand and most of the other places I'd lived, people would invite each other over for lavish home-cooked meals, but none of the kids I knew walked around with more than just a few dollars in their pockets. I slipped an extra five dollars into the tip jar as we all left and went our separate ways home.

"Does Chase always do that?" I asked Oliver as we hiked through some dense woods at the edge of town. It was 7:05 p.m. and I was conscious of the hour. This town did have that annoying curfew. Oliver conveniently lived just a few blocks away from my dad's house, so he was showing me this shortcut as we walked home together.

"Do what?"

"Pick up the check like it's no big deal?"

"It isn't a big deal to him. He's rich. As in *rich* rich. His dad owns most of Bar Tech Industries. And Chase likes to spread the wealth among friends."

"Which explains his extreme popularity." Not that I was envious or anything. In fact I was always pretty careful when it came to spending money. Super frugal, according to my mother. Some kids might be impressed with Chase's ostentatious display of wealth, but not me. Living in third-world countries like India, Tanzania, and Morocco, I saw real poverty and suffering, and I never took anything I had for granted.

"That and the fact Chase is also a total hottie," Oliver quipped with a shrug of his shoulders. "According to most girls."

"If you like that sort of thing. Muscles and all," I joked, even though I had to begrudgingly admit that Oliver was right. Chase was hot.

I was surprised to find my dad at home when I walked up the driveway a few minutes later. It was not even 7:25 p.m. He was in the backyard busily grilling some kind of white fish for dinner—halibut I think.

"You're home late," my dad commented as he expertly flipped the fish on the grill. I had texted him not to pick me up after school.

"My friend Oliver showed me the scenic route," I admitted as I opened the door to go inside the house. "That's allowed, isn't it? *Walking home from school?*" I couldn't help but make a pointed remark about curfew and all the rules in Barrington.

"Of course it's allowed," he replied with an unusual trace of paternal concern. "I just like to know where my daughter is."

I nodded, though I was a bit surprised by my father's unexpected overprotectiveness. He then said he had to get back to the hospital later and didn't want to miss having dinner with me. Which was kind of sweet but also very much my dad.

I didn't have the heart to tell him I was so stuffed on pizza that I might not eat for a week. Instead I sat with him at the kitchen table and forced myself to eat fish and salad while telling him about my eventful day, football game and all.

"Sounds like you're really settling in." He acted pleased and maybe even a bit relieved by my apparent social evolution from outsider to (almost) Miss Popularity in a matter of days. I wasn't quite sure how I felt about the whole situation, so I just nodded back, which seemed to reassure him that his only child was happy.

My father left the house to go back to the hospital. He had patients to look in on or something medical to attend to; he wasn't very specific. Later that night I was feeling pretty antsy and took a break from homework. I went online and checked e-mails. There were two from my mother, both asking if everything was okay. She was traveling to Tierra del Fuego at the tip of Argentina, so she said it would probably be several days before I'd hear from her again, but if there was an emergency I could contact the magazine and they would track her down. I told her that I was fine and not to worry. Lai texted me to say she'd had a great second date with Pak and she'd give me the details later. Just as I was replying to Lai, my dad called and said he'd be home late and not to wait up. No other explanation. I was still jet-lagged, so I told him not to worry.

I sat on my bed and sighed, just staring at the four walls, assessing my somewhat limited amusement options. It wasn't even eight thirty. My dad had an ancient TV set with only basic cable and marginal picture quality. I was hardly in the mood to watch the super-thrilling *CSI* marathon or equally exciting *MTV VJ Hunt: Exposed*. Nor was I the least bit tired.

I slipped out the kitchen door into the backyard. It was nearly pitch-dark except for a tiny sliver of a crescent moon hanging high in the blue-black sky. I stood there and gazed up at it. A sea of stars surrounded the moon, twinkling and sparkling, way too many to count. It was a beautiful, warm night. I really had no intention of doing anything other than just lazing on a chaise, when I noticed that the garage door was open. I realized my father must've forgotten to close it when he left for the hospital.

The two-car garage was a separate, freestanding structure at the back of the property. I hadn't bothered to pay too much attention to it before that night. It was only a garage, after all. I walked over, intending to hit the electric button to shut the door, when something inside caught my eye.

It wasn't my father's impressive set of power tools, which were neatly displayed on the left wall. My dad prided himself on being pretty handy around the house. He always hated calling a plumber or electrician, convinced he could fix any problem big or small. Judging by the leaky faucet in the downstairs bathroom and the two unhinged cabinet doors in the kitchen, the jury was still out on whether he could.

What drew my attention was the black tarp that was covering up something in the middle of the garage. I lifted it up, ever curious. Underneath I was stunned to discover a beautifully restored Indian motorcycle—a relic from my father's more adventurous youth, no doubt. I recalled my dad once telling me that Indian was the first American motorcycle company, even before there ever was a Harley-Davidson. This bike in particular—a gorgeous, copper-colored, completely restored 1948 Indian Chief Roadmaster—was all shiny steel and curvy fenders.

I hopped aboard the molded black leather seat. It felt amazingly cushy and comfortable, as did those sleek handlebars, which elbowed out and down at a forty-five-degree angle. When I glanced down at the speedometer and fuel gauge, I saw a key dangling from the ignition.

*The key.*

I couldn't help but touch it. My fingers couldn't resist temptation. I bit my lip, debating whether I should jump off the bike, pull the tarp back over it, and just close the garage and forget I ever saw it . . . or turn that little key. . . .

Under the dim glow of the streetlights, I wheeled the bike down the driveway to the deserted street. It wasn't even nine o'clock yet, and there wasn't a person in sight. I turned the key in the ignition and heard a click. Then a purring like a tiger waking up—a low, guttural sound.

My dad had taught me how to drive smaller bikes before—mopeds and 125cc motorcycles, mostly in Chile and Thailand—so I wasn't too worried about being able to handle my dad's bike. I only intended to take her for a quick spin around the neighborhood. A few short blocks—ten minutes max and then back into the garage. I'd be home before curfew. No one would need to know, least of all my dad. But once I was on her and we got going, I lost track of what time it was. I felt totally revved up. Forget about being jet-lagged and getting a decent night's sleep.

I turned the corner and just kept going . . . feeling free, wind in my hair. Born to be wild, as the song says. I realized it was something I hadn't felt since arriving in Barrington.

I had been riding on the old service road for what felt like just a few minutes when suddenly bright red and white flashing lights whirled behind me.

At first I thought it must be the Barrington police. Great. Just what I needed: to get arrested for riding a motorcycle. My dad would be furious. I could already imagine his massive disappointment: his good girl gone bad. For a split second I thought about racing off. But even I knew better than to try and outrun the cops—even on a fast bike—so I quickly pulled over, prepared to face the grim consequences. Like being grounded for a whole year without my cell phone or the Internet, or something equally horrific.

But when I glanced in the rearview mirror, I saw that these guys weren't the police at all. Their large white van was inscribed with the red BTS logo. They were Bar Tech Security—Barrington's private security patrol. I remembered what my dad had said about them. I wondered if they were more like mall cops or if they had any real authority.

Two security guards in navy-blue uniforms got out of the van and walked toward me, shining flashlights in my face. The first was a big beefy dude with a goatee and huge hands who looked to be maybe thirty. He wore a school class ring, a big badge with his name on it, and a very stern expression. He was a lot more threatening than I'd expected.

"You have any idea what time it is?" Officer Lorentz glared right at me.

"Sorry, Officer. I left my watch at home." Which was totally true, I never wear one, but Officer Lorentz wasn't buying my lame excuse.

"Which is where you should be. That your bike?"

I shook my head rather guiltily. "It's my dad's."

"Does he know you're breaking curfew?"

"Of course. He thinks curfew is for losers." That's what I *wanted* to say, but no words would come out of my mouth. The truth was, I was terrified. I had lost track of time and had had no idea that it was already after nine p.m. I just shook my head.

The other guard, a young brunette in her late twenties, shone her flashlight right in my face, probably to see if I was drunk, or high, or just plain nuts. She introduced herself as Officer Korey, and she looked even tougher and meaner than her partner, despite a beautiful French manicure.

"Can I see your license?" She held out her hand, demanding it.

I fished through my pockets and pulled out a ratty slip of paper, which I handed to her. She scrutinized it, then gave me a cold look. I started to imagine what the punishment could be for curfew infractions—a huge fine and maybe being locked up in jail for a week—when I heard her speak again.

"This is only a learner's permit. From *Thailand*." She exchanged a harsh glance with her partner. They didn't say a word, but I could almost read their thoughts. They were going to teach me a lesson.

Feeling desperate, I started rambling, pleading for mercy. "Officers, I'm really, really sorry. I got lost. You see, I just moved here from Thailand—only a few days ago, in fact . . . and, um . . . well, I didn't realize how late it was, not to mention I am totally planning on taking the driving test here as soon as I can. Weather permitting."

Just when I thought all was lost and they'd be snapping on the handcuffs and sending me to a gulag somewhere, Officer Korey surprised me. "Nica Ashley. You're Dr. Ashley's daughter?"

"Yes. I am."

I wasn't sure exactly what happened, but suddenly their body language changed. Officer Lorentz nodded to his partner, and for once I was thankful that everyone knew everyone else's business in Barrington.

Officer Korey's tone softened considerably. "Tell you what, Nica. Given that you're new and we like your father, we're going to cut you some slack. But if we ever catch you out again after curfew, you're going to have a problem. Now go straight home."

I swallowed, greatly relieved, but could tell they were serious. "Thank you." She then gave me back my learner's permit.

I turned the key and started up the bike. I waved appreciatively. What a close call. The security guards watched as I rode off; then they drove off in the opposite direction.

I was doing thirty on the service road, totally intending to return home, when I passed a small clearing. Something among the trees glinted off the bike's headlight. I slowed down and moved in closer and spotted a black Mustang GT parked there beneath the aspens. It was Jackson Winter's car. I'd know it anywhere.

I immediately circled around the spot, pondering my options. I could hurry back home and definitely avoid arrest like the good girl I should be. Or I could linger just a bit longer (I mean, I had already broken curfew, what was five more minutes?) and maybe finally find out exactly what Rebel Boy was up to every night.

It was one of the easiest decisions of my life.

I got off the bike and followed a winding footpath to a hilly area overlooking the town. There was an awesome view. I scanned around but saw no sign of Rebel Boy anywhere. Why had he come here? And where had he gone?

Disappointed, I stood at the edge of the bluff and stared down upon sleepy Barrington. It was idyllic and peaceful—and so, so boring. I began to contemplate my next thousand-plus days living here, when I heard a sharp sound—like a twig snapping. I spun around and nearly jumped out of my skin.

Someone was standing right behind me.

"Doctor's kid is out a little late." Jackson Winters slowly emerged from the shadows.

"Or everyone else is in way too early," I heard myself answer. I was excited to see him and could not believe I was actually able to utter a coherent sentence. I was also thrilled that he knew who I was.

"Maybe for good reason." He stared back at me with those intense blue-green eyes. Was he interested in me or irritated by me? I wasn't sure, but I was just glad he was deigning to talk to me.

"Yeah. I'm bummed about missing that Kim Kardashian

marathon." For some reason his imposing presence and startling good looks were not intimidating me. Exactly the opposite: I was feeling emboldened, and weirdly self-confident.

"What are you doing out here?" I heard the anger rise up in his voice and then watched it flash across his face. He took a step toward me, almost threatening.

"Me? What about you? Cruising the streets at all hours. The pope gave you a special dispensation?" I stared back at him and didn't back away. I just stood my ground, intently curious about this mysterious guy who lurked in shadows, avoided the happy crew, and was out after curfew every night. Was his strange behavior all just a reaction to being dumped by Dana Fox?

Suddenly his face relaxed, and I saw a slight smile take shape at the corners of his mouth. "This town is going to have its hands full with you."

"From what I hear, you're doing an epic job yourself." Cool. We were now flirting, or at least I thought we were. I actually tossed my hair back, like I was inviting him to open up and confide in me.

"It's easier for them to believe I'm the bad seed than . . ." His voice trailed off.

"Easier than what?" I desperately wanted to know every-thing he was thinking. All his intimate secrets.

"Easier than dealing with the truth." He glared at me, as

if his eyes had X-ray vision and could see right through me.

I burst out laughing. Did he really think I'd fall for such a lame-ass line like that? "Shouldn't we be having this conversation in some creepy cemetery during a full moon with a pack of howling wolves?"

Jackson didn't crack a smile. In fact he got this mean, wounded look on his face as if I had struck a nerve. I immediately regretted opening my big fat mouth.

All of a sudden a huge swath of bright light, an unearthly green light, flashed across the inky sky. It was a fluorescent green. And glowing so much I had to look away for fear I would be blinded.

Seconds later, I felt a soft *WHUMP*, which pulsed right through me. Heat ran up my body, surging from my toes up through my legs and torso to my hair follicles. Every cell in my body was vibrating. All my synapses and billions of nerve endings blasting at full throttle.

When it stopped, the entire valley—all of Barrington—had lost electrical power. The town was plunged into complete darkness. Then, just as quickly, the electricity returned.

"Get out of here. *Now!*" Jackson yelled, shoving me down the path toward my bike.

Before I could protest, or ask what the hell had just happened, he had jumped into his car and turned on the engine. "Get home!" he shouted, before driving off at warp speed.

For a minute, I must admit, I stood there in shock. I

didn't know what had happened or why. It was something otherworldly, and had scared even the toughest dude in the high school. Frightened and trying very hard not to dissolve into tears, I gunned the bike and flew down the road toward home. I hoped I'd make it into my bed, under the covers, safe and sound.

## 5. SHOCK AND AWE

The birds were dead.

I'm saying that *every* single bird in town had died, like in some cheesy horror movie. What had happened in Barrington looked random at first. A few small bodies here, several more there . . . enough that I noticed them, lying on the ground. Lifeless. Their glassy black eyes just staring up at nothingness. It was an unsettling sight, to say the least. But I blocked it out of my mind, not wanting to think about what might have killed them. The truth was, my mind was so overwhelmed with figuring out what had gone down with Jackson the night before that I couldn't process much else of the outside world.

And then I went to school.

My dad had planned to drive me as usual, but I told him that I preferred to walk. He kept pressing to know why. I hemmed and hawed a lot and avoided telling him the truth. I was afraid that if I rode with him, I might blurt out something incriminating about being out past curfew and breaking his one cardinal rule. This would lead to all sorts of unpleasant questions about the bike that would land me in hot water. It was much safer for me to walk to school and avoid Dad altogether.

"You sure you're all right? It's nearly two miles." Dad stared at me, his eyes narrowing skeptically, refusing to let the matter die. He placed his palm on my forehead to feel if I had a fever, no doubt convinced that I was pulling his leg.

"I walked all the time in Bangkok." I brushed his hand away, not wanting to make it into any big deal. My paranoia kicked in. Why was he prying and being so insistent? Was he testing me? Did he know what I'd done last night? "Besides, it's a nice day." I zipped up my bag and casually tossed it over my shoulder, ready to fly out the front door, anxious not to field any more questions. Fortunately, Dad accepted my explanation, gave me a peck on the cheek, and allowed me to go on my way.

The fact was, I wasn't lying. It really was a lovely morning: bright sunshine, clear blue sky, with a slight autumn chill in the air. The flaming reds, bright oranges, and golden yellow leaves falling from the trees only added to the illusion that Barrington was still a normal town. Not the end of the world, black-sky Armageddon I'd half expected to see when I looked out my bedroom window at the crack of dawn that morning.

For all I knew, that fluorescent green pulse I'd seen (and

most definitely felt, and was still feeling) was nothing more serious than a freak mountain lightning flash or benign electrical discharge from a nearby power plant. Or perhaps it had been one of those meteor showers? Nothing worth flipping out about in the light of day, that's for sure.

But I couldn't explain why it felt like my body was *still vibrating*. Or was it all just in my mind?

That morning I replayed the events of my encounter with Jackson in my mind. I felt confused and unsure about exactly what I had witnessed. Maybe Jackson had just been messing with the new girl's head, ordering me to run home as if the world were about to end. Oliver had warned me to steer clear of him—that Rebel Boy was bad news. And now I had firsthand proof.

I shook my head and chuckled at how gullible I had been the night before, racing home on my dad's bike, then staying up half the night freaking out that a nuclear bomb had exploded or that we were being attacked by space aliens. I had finally calmed down around two a.m. when I heard my dad roll in from the hospital. He tiptoed up the stairs and down the hall to my bedroom. I shut my eyes and pretended to be fast asleep, half expecting him to wake me to tell me something truly awful had occurred. *Honey, pack a bag. They're here.* Instead he lingered in my doorway like any dad before padding off to his own bedroom, where he went to sleep.

By five thirty a.m. I was actively trolling the Internet, seeking out information on what exactly had happened the night before. I searched dozens of media sites, from CNN and the Rocky Mountain News to the Huffington Post and the Durango Herald. I even broke down and checked my old nemesis Facebook for the first time in two years to see if any kids were talking about it. To my surprise I didn't find one story or discussion. Not a single mention of any bizarre light flashes or strange astronomical occurrences in Barrington, or the rest of southern Colorado, for that matter, either. Another hopeful sign that last night wasn't anything to freak out about.

So I showered and dressed, then tried my best to put on a happy face. Apparently the earth was still spinning. I was relieved. I kissed dad good-bye and trudged off to school at seven fifteen in the morning as if nothing were wrong, despite mounting evidence to the contrary.

But I had barely turned the corner of my block when I spotted my first dead bird. A sparrow, small and brown, lay lifeless on the front lawn. From afar it looked peaceful. I stopped and cringed to see it just lying there, with its black eyes fixed wide open. For a second I contemplated scooping up the poor thing and giving it a proper burial. But then I thought about all the gross diseases birds carry, like avian pox and salmonellosis, and decided it was far wiser to let a medical professional (aka my dad) dispose of the body.

So I texted dear old Dad as I hurried down the block: *Dead bird on lawn. Gross.* I'd no sooner hit send than I came upon my second dead bird at the corner. This one—a crow—was bigger and looked considerably nastier than the first victim. Its head had been ripped off. Super gross. Still, I felt compelled to snap a photo of the disturbing remains before I sprinted across the street, not wanting to be late for my first class. Along the way to school I encountered several dozen avian fatalities scattered around—even on Main Street—and now Jackson no longer seemed like an alarmist or a nut job messing with my head.

By the time I arrived at school, I knew things were slightly *off*. Well, actually way more than slightly. They were off by a whole lot.

Normally, in the morning the quad reverberated with soft, respectful voices mixed with muted laughter. Super polite. Nothing raucous nor that jarring. Instead, this particular morning I heard people shouting. Angrily. Loudly.

I immediately spotted Chase and his football posse at their customary table, arguing heatedly with one another. Red-faced and antagonistic, they gesticulated wildly, jabbing fingers in one another's chests. Kyle and Vox were really going at it. The spectacle of jocks turning on their own, like a group of crazed alpha-male baboons, was highly amusing—though not nearly as entertaining as what was happening a few tables over. The members of the normally sedate geek squad, instead of solving differential equations, were aggressively pushing and shoving one another around as if they were inner-city gang bangers. A couple of mathletes in neatly pressed jeans and white collared shirts actually began punching each other, egged on by a crew of prepster girly-girls in casual cardigans and pleated skirts.

"Go for it!" one girl screeched as a circle of fervent onlookers gathered around.

I was so engrossed by the surreal vision of awkwardly flailing bony limbs that I collided head-on with Maya. Her usually coiffed black hair was inexplicably wild and unstyled.

"Maya. I didn't see you."

"What are you, like suddenly blind or something?" she snapped back with all the sweetness of a piranha tasting blood. Before jostling past me in an angry huff.

Completely thrown by Maya's sudden psycho turn from America's Sweetheart to the Bitch Who Ate Barrington, I felt the urge to grab her by the hair and throw her to the ground, but I quickly restrained myself. Then I slowly looked around the quad at all the various cliques. It became clear to me that Maya, Chase, and the geeks weren't the only ones who were seriously bugging—it was *everyone*.

"Tell me: Is the entire school PMSing, or just inhabited by body-snatching aliens?" I shouted this as I jogged up to

Oliver, who valiantly tried keeping pace with everyone else running laps around the track during third-period phys ed.

"Is this going to be another of Nica's 'Barrington sucks' rants? Because frankly, it's way too early," he barked back as he blotted the beads of sweat dripping off his forehead with the bottom of his red-and-black anime tribute T-shirt.

I glanced around to make sure nobody else was within earshot before spilling my guts. "Okay, so don't think I'm crazy. But I kind of went out last night after curfew and had a close encounter of the strangest kind with Jackson Winters."

Oliver's big brown eyes practically popped out of their sockets. "Holy crap, Nica. Do you realize how much trouble you could get into?" He was so shocked by my confession he came to a complete stop on the track. I grabbed Oliver's arm and yanked him along, not wanting gung-ho Coach Lurrell and his ubiquitous stopwatch to penalize us for goofing off.

"Listen, before you start going ballistic on me, can you at least let me explain?" He could see by my tense expression that this wasn't some bad-girl escapade I was about to regale him with but something much more serious.

He nodded and listened silently while I quickly downloaded the details of last night's motorcycle adventure.

"That's all? Just a slap on the wrist from security for breaking curfew and driving without a license?" Oliver shook his head in disbelief, amazed I hadn't been locked away for life.

"Only *after* security realized who my dad was."

"Just goes to show you: In Barrington it's who you know. So how does Jackson figure in your Hell's Angels drama?"

"I was kind of on my way home when I spotted his car parked up on the bluff."

"And you couldn't resist. You and him together under the moonlight . . . it's like some trashy romance novel gone super 3-D," he scoffed, considerably amused with himself.

"Thanks, Oliver. I love being reduced to a sappy cliché. Anyway, we were in the middle of this truly cryptic conversation—about me, and the town, and him. Then out of nowhere this freaky green flash lights up the entire sky for about five seconds."

"Like a meteor or fireball or falling star?" Oliver sniped, wanting specifics, which I didn't have. "Or a UFO?"

"I'm not sure what it was, Mr. Science, other than blindingly bright. And it produced this intense blast of energy," I confessed, recalling how I'd felt when it happened.

"You felt a blast of *energy*?" Skepticism oozed from Oliver's every pore.

"I literally felt the power pulse through my entire body. From head to toe."

"Maybe it was the power of love? Or just bad sushi?" he joked.

"Ha, ha. Look, whatever *it* was really spooked Jackson." *And freaked me out*, I almost shouted, but Oliver already heard the anxiety in my voice without me adding any more fuel to this fire.

"Listen, there must be a logical explanation. We're always getting heat-lightning storms here in the foothills this time of year. And October is supposed to be an active month for astronomic activity." Though a bit troubled by my report, Oliver still wasn't ready to accept that it was anything to get alarmed about.

"I thought that at first too, but haven't you noticed everyone's bizarro moods today? I mean, Little Miss Sunshine practically sliced and diced me for breakfast this morning." I gestured across the field, where Maya argued with Jaden while the rest of the fighting chick squad ran cheerleading routines. "I swear that girl's a little bit cheerleader, a whole lot bipolar."

Oliver shrugged, trying to blow off my concerns. "Maybe she forgot her Lexapro?"

"Joke all you want, Oliver. I'm beginning to think Jackson's onto something."

"Onto what? Everyone knows the dude's crazy." Oliver shot me a dismissive look as he chewed his lower lip, his brow knit questioningly.

"That underneath this town's pleasant facade, something's not right." I stared back at Oliver, challenging him.

As if on cue, barrel-chested Coach Lurrell launched into a full-throttle hissy fit with the girls about them practicing their cheers too loudly. Spittle flew out of his mouth while he berated the cheerleaders. Instead of apologizing to the coach—a teacher—the girls actually argued back, taunting him mercilessly. They were all so angry the altercation almost turned into a brawl, until one of the other gym teachers ran out and broke them up.

Oliver turned and watched the other students jogging around the field. They were grumpy and tense. No one was smiling. In total contrast to how contented and sociable people normally seemed.

"So you think last night's *flash* . . . ?" Oliver looked back at me, groping for understanding.

"*Pulse*. It was more like a *pulse*." I immediately recalled how it felt the exact moment when it hit me. The way my body vibrated. The experience forever scorched into my brain.

Coach Lurrell blew his whistle loudly and angrily waved the students back into the gym. Oliver and I obediently left the track and headed toward the entrance.

"You really think this pulse did a shake-and-bake with people's minds?" Oliver was starting to take me seriously.

"That's not all." My eyes drifted down to the ground. Oliver followed my gaze. A small brown-and-gold finch was lying on the grass in front of us. Dead. Just like those other birds I'd come across on the way to school. "I saw dozens of dead ones on my way to school."

We stepped around the dead finch and continued inside to the gym, neither of us saying another word. I could tell Oliver knew that something was definitely off too. Unfortunately, neither of us had the slightest clue about what that might be.

The rest of the morning was a big blur. While my physical body dutifully showed up for Spanish, my mind was somewhere else, endlessly replaying what had gone down the night before with Jackson and that freaky light show. The more I tried to make sense of it, the more questions I had that needed answering. Jackson was the key. I was convinced he knew a whole lot more than he had let on. I had to talk to him. But first I had to find him.

During lunch I searched the entire school for Jackson. I started with the quad. He wasn't hanging in his usual place under the old oak tree. Next I scoped out the cafeteria and the hallways. No Jackson. I even checked out the gym and library—not that I really thought he'd be hanging in either—and no Jackson. Nor was his car parked in the student parking lot. He really was like some kind of elusive ghost—nowhere to be found. No one seemed to know his whereabouts or much less care about him. I couldn't help worrying that maybe something had happened to him after we'd parted ways the night before.

• • •

It was during seventh-period biology that Principal Hell-inger made an announcement over the school PA system. Mr. Bluni, a lumbering teacher with an annoying habit of pacing up and down the aisles, was lecturing about the various ways genetic mutations occurred in the animal kingdom, when he was so rudely interrupted. Principal Hellinger rattled off a long list of students to report to the nurse's office, when I thought I heard my name called out. I didn't spring out of my chair like everyone else. I hadn't been paying complete attention (my mind preoccupied with tracking down Jackson), so I wasn't quite sure if I hadn't just imagined hearing my name.

"Are we waiting for an engraved invitation, Ms. Ashley?" Mr. Bluni snidely quipped. He peered at me over his tor-toiseshell bifocals, arms crossed, impatient. He also had an equally pompous habit of using the royal "we."

"Sorry." I quickly gathered my books and hustled out of the classroom, humiliated and irritated at his condescend-ing attitude. Also a little mystified. What could the school nurse want with me, not to mention the thirty other kids whose names were called? I had turned in all my medical forms the first day of school. I hadn't been at Barrington High long enough to get into any trouble, much less pick up any communicable diseases.

"We're getting physicals? No way." I was unhappily wait-ing outside the nurse's office with Maya, Emily, and many other students I didn't know, totally outraged by the news. I mean, pop quizzes were one thing. Pop physicals were downright creepy.

"Maybe you have no regard for your health, Nica, but thankfully the administration does." I could practically see Maya breathing fire the way she was bristling and so on edge.

"Don't they need parental approval or something? We do have rights, after all," I challenged her. Suddenly all the kids started to argue and disagree, until everyone was yelling at one another like a bunch of raving lunatics.

Before I could launch into a full-blown inquiry concerning Maya's and everyone else's erratic behavior that morning, the nurse's door swung open. To my absolute astonishment and horror, my father suddenly stepped out of the office, looking all doctory in his white lab coat. Followed by Chase Cochran, of all people. They were laughing about something.

"Catch you later, Dr. A." He then bumped fists with my dad. What a kiss-ass. And my dad actually fell for it. I was so grossed out that I practically ran screaming from the office. The entire visual was almost too much to stomach.

"Dad?" I prayed my eyes were playing tricks on me. No such luck.

"Nica, come in." I took a deep breath and breezed past Chase, who winked at me as I approached the office.

"Won't hurt a bit," Chase whispered as he swaggered over to Maya and kissed her on the lips, immediately brightening her mood. It made her so happy she lit up like an overdecorated Christmas tree.

Once I was safely inside the nurse's antiseptic office, my dad shut the door for privacy.

"So what's this I hear about you giving physicals?" I tried acting cool about the whole thing despite the fact that I was (not so quietly) freaking out on the inside. My heart was racing. I'd always thought that doctors were not allowed to treat their family.

"Just some routine blood tests for a research study I'm conducting."

"You mean the kind with *needles*?" I nervously sank into one of the Lucite chairs. I hated getting shots, and I really hated giving blood. It made me nauseous. "Which arm do you want?" I felt my stomach tighten into a knot.

"Neither." My dad leaned against the examination table, his arms crossed. I normally would've felt relief at not having to give blood, but his face took on this serious demeanor with his dark brown eyes laser-focused right on me. The way I imagined he delivered bad news to his cardiac patients. "That's not the reason I called you down here."

"It's not?" I played coy and innocent, all the while choking back this uneasy feeling of impending doom that was creeping up my throat.

"Did you really think I wouldn't find out about your little joyride last night? What the hell were you thinking, *Nica*?" He glared at me, clearly upset. I heard the anger and disappointment in his voice, the way he said my name.

I knew I wasn't going to be able to charm my way out of this mess the way I sometimes did with my mother. Like last spring when she found out that Lai and I had gone clubbing in Bangkok instead of studying for exams. I'd convinced her that blowing off steam dancing had actually helped me ace them all. Unfortunately, no amount of As would appease Dad. Total honesty was the only way to go with him. Throw myself on the mercy of the court.

"I'm sorry, Dad. I really am. I was just going stir-crazy home alone. The whole curfew thing seems so unnecessary." I couldn't help but put in my two cents about the lame curfew.

"I don't care how it seems. *It's there for your own protection.*" Maybe I was delusional, but my dad actually seemed more worried than angry.

"Protection from what?" I probed, wondering if he knew anything about that freaky green pulse. "I thought Barrington had the lowest crime rate in the state."

"How long did you stay out?" He quickly turned the interrogation back on me, not answering my questions.

"I don't remember." I shrugged. It was mostly true, since I'd been more absorbed with my encounter with Jackson.

"Not long. I wasn't exactly paying attention to the time. I just drove around."

"*Where?*" he pressed, demanding to know. "Where exactly did you go?"

"How am I supposed to know? Everything looks the same to me in the dark." I leaned back from him, feeling very defensive. "Winding roads and lots of trees. Does it make a difference where I went?"

"Yes. Because you don't know your way around here. These roads can be treacherous," he shot back, upset, before quickly recovering. "I just don't want you to get hurt. So then nothing happened to you?"

"No," I lied. "Nothing."

"Just promise me you won't do it again. *Ever.*" It might have sounded like a request, but the harsh look he gave me demanded total compliance. It wasn't in my dad's nature to yell or curse or even threaten. He just stated what he wanted, in no uncertain terms. And you were expected to follow.

I nodded my agreement, silenced by his reprimand. No way was I going to challenge him or risk saying another word right now. I was lucky he wasn't grounding me forever—or at least until I graduated high school. Which was a total possibility.

Dad stood and walked over to the door. He was about to open it but hesitated, exhaling audibly. He then turned back to face me.

"Nica, I know how difficult this transition must be for you. We're both bound to make some mistakes along the way. Anyway, I hoped maybe this weekend we could spend some time together. Go hiking. The trails around here are really beautiful."

"Fine. So long as the tofu jerky stays behind." I desperately wanted to lighten the mood.

"Hey, that stuff's highly nutritious, not to mention quite tasty." He pretended to be insulted, but I saw the hint of a smile break through his scowl.

"Precisely the problem: I'm still tasting it from the last time we went hiking in the Andes." My face cringed from the awful memory of chewing that heinously salty cardboard the summer before last.

"Deal." Dad grinned. "Now get back to class. And head straight home after school." He opened the door for me to leave. Our father-daughter chat was mercifully over.

"Thanks, Dad." I left the office, not having to give blood and well aware that I had dodged a major bullet.

"Wow. I wish my mom were that lenient," Oliver said to me over the phone about an hour later. I had my Bluetooth in and was walking along Fox Hollow Road, a relatively new development of modern homes. "Do you know she actually took away my PlayStation and Wii for an entire week after I got a C on a math test? Claimed God of War and Guitar

Hero were sapping my potential. As if anything could sap my potential more than school does. Speaking of parents, turns out our moms knew each other way back when."

"Seriously?" I responded, taken aback by the news. Though the truth was, where my mother was concerned, nothing really surprised me.

"According to Mom. I mean, not that they were good friends or anything," Oliver added, "but she said they knew each other. Which means it's *fate* that you and I should be friends."

"Absolutely. It's our manifest destiny," I joked.

"By the way, where are you?" Oliver asked.

"Outside Jackson's house." I had just turned the corner onto Field Point Circle and was staring up at the multilevel, green-designed contemporary with solar panels on the roof. Made of cedar, natural stone, and glass the residence resembled a mountain lodge.

"Girl, you're seriously wack-a-doodle. I thought you promised your dad to go home after school." Oliver's reprimand was no big surprise given his earlier reaction to my previous night's misadventure.

"I will go home. *After* I talk to Jackson." I approached the house, which sat at the end of the woodsy cul-de-sac, surrounded by other well-tended homes.

"*Stalk* him is more like it. Haven't you heard of texting? Or phoning?"

"Calls and texts can be ignored. Besides, I don't have his number. Bye." I hung up, proving my point. Then I proceeded up the flagstone path to the frosted-glass front door, took a deep breath, and rang the bell, which played some awful mellow-jazz riff. Then I waited patiently for Jackson to answer.

Unfortunately, no one came to the door. Was he hiding? I actually put my head to the door but didn't hear any sounds coming from inside. I peered through a window into the two-car garage. Both spots were empty. No one was home. Where might Jackson be at three thirty-five in the middle of the afternoon?

I bit my thumb cuticle as I quickly ran through—and discounted—the other possibilities: He was hanging around with friends? Unlikely, since his old buddies seemed to have contempt for him. He went snowboarding? Doubtful, as it hadn't snowed yet. Hospitalized? Unlikely, as word of some horrible accident would've certainly reached school.

I then had an idea about where I just might find Jackson.

Winters Sporting Goods was located in a huge warehouse on the edge of the Barrington business district. Oliver had mentioned that Jackson worked here a few days a week after school. The enterprise reminded me of one of those big-box megaplexes with extra-wide aisles, hideously bright lighting, and colorful, eye-popping displays. Except this family-owned store was cleverly laid out in four distinct quadrants—each representing a different season.

I went directly to the winter section of Winters, pretending to check out the slick ski boots and snowboards, expecting (and *hoping*) to run into one-time Olympic contender Jackson. (*I didn't know you worked here! What a surprise.*) But unfortunately, Rebel Boy was nowhere to be found in winter.

I methodically cycled my way through the other seasons without any luck spotting Jackson either. Though I did manage to find an awfully cute retro bikini in black-and-white polka dots, which was on sale and which I didn't buy since I wasn't there to shop.

An attractive middle-aged woman, an outdoorsy type with wavy black hair pulled back in a no-nonsense ponytail, strolled the aisles. I first noticed her while I was lost in the baseball section of spring. Who knew there were so many different-size cups and jockstraps for guys?

Anyway, I thought the attractive woman might just be another random mom shopping for her kid, but then I never saw her with any child. Finally I realized she was actually following *me* around the store when I spotted her again in summer and autumn. Was she the store undercover detective? Did she think I was there to shoplift? It started to creep me out a bit.

Having had no luck finding Jackson, I thought it was

time to leave. But as I was heading toward the door, the woman intercepted me.

"Excuse me. May I help you?" she asked, suddenly appearing out of nowhere, her bright blue eyes staring me down.

"Oh, no. I was just . . ." Flustered was what I was at that moment and supremely tongue-tied. "Browsing."

"Anything you're looking for in particular?" she pressed with a beautiful smile. I wondered if she was going to search me. "Winters prides itself on having everything for every sport. It's our motto." She pointed to the big sign emblazoned over the main entrance.

"Actually, I was looking for *someone*, but he doesn't seem to be working here today," I muttered, feeling terribly embarrassed and guilty, like I was being a *stalker*.

"Are you looking for Jackson?" she asked knowingly.

"Oh. Yeah," I responded, surprised that she knew the reason why I had been roaming the aisles. "I'll catch him at school tomorrow. It's nothing important." I tried to act nonchalant, when in fact I felt myself perspiring.

"Important enough that you made a special trip to see my son," she declared quite pointedly before continuing. "Unfortunately, Jackson doesn't keep regular hours here anymore. Or anywhere, for that matter."

Oh my God. I realized I was talking to Jackson's mother. I felt even more humiliated and exposed. I wanted to split, and pronto.

"Mrs. Winters, it's no big deal. *Really*. I just didn't see Jackson at school today, and I had to ask him something . . ." I was digging a deeper hole, and I felt like Jackson's mom knew it.

"Hopefully, I'll see my son at home this evening and let him know you were looking for him. Though with Jackson I never know," Jackson's mother admitted with a hint of sadness. "By the way, I didn't catch your name."

"Nica. Ashley," I timidly confessed.

A flicker of recognition registered on her face. "You're Dr. Ashley's daughter," Mrs. Winters remarked, flashing her intense stare my way.

"Yes. The one and only," I retorted with a nervous smile. Everyone really did know my dad. I felt like I was living in Tiny Town.

"You remind me of your mother," Mrs. Winters said, almost knocking me off my feet.

"You knew her too?" I asked incredulously. "I mean, you knew my mom?" First it was Oliver's mom, now Jackson's mother. I had gotten quite used to people knowing my dad, since he still lived in town. My mother was another matter, since she hadn't set foot in Barrington in fourteen years. It would take some getting used to for it to not feel a bit strange to me.

"Back in our younger days," Mrs. Winters replied, somewhat vaguely. "We worked together very briefly. Haven't seen her since she left Barrington. How is Lydia?"

"Fine. Great. She's a journalist," I answered, impressed that she remembered Lydia and even referred to her by name. "Actually, on her way to Antarctica for a long time. Which is how I ended up here." I was doing my best to sound upbeat.

"Lydia never really was one for settling down. Had a major case of wanderlust. She always said she'd see the world," Mrs. Winters admitted forlornly.

"And she did. Is still seeing it. I was too, until she sent me here," I lamented sadly. "You know, my mother barely mentions the past or this town. Where did you guys work together?" I was hoping to get some good dirt on my parents' past, since they never would tell me much.

"*Barrington's not for everyone,*" Mrs. Winters curtly answered, her expression visibly darkening. For some unknown reason she had shut down and was deliberately avoiding my question about where they'd worked together. "Well, I'll tell Jackson you stopped by."

And Mrs. Winters turned and abruptly walked off—leaving me confused about what had just happened.

"I just had the weirdest encounter with Jackson's mother," I reported to Oliver as I bolted out the door of Winters Sporting Goods, tapping my Bluetooth headset pressed tightly against my right ear.

"Did she catch you trying to break into the house?"

Oliver asked, eager to hear the details of my latest escapade.

"No. I was actually looking for Jackson at Winters. I thought he might be working today." I hurried down the block at a quick clip, feeling a rush of adrenaline pulsing through my body.

"I take it he wasn't," Oliver said, stating the obvious. "So what happened with Mrs. W.?

"Turns out not only did she know my mother," I declared, "but they also *worked together*."

"*And?*" Oliver replied, seemingly unimpressed, waiting for something more exciting.

"And nothing. She blew me off when I tried to get the specifics. Anyway, I still don't know where Jackson is. Neither did she," I confessed, having hit a major dead end in my search.

"Maybe Rebel Boy finally ran off to find Dana?" Although Oliver said it quite flippantly, a lightbulb went on in my brain.

I stopped in my tracks. "Oliver, that's totally genius." I then did a complete one-eighty and strode across the street from Winters Sporting Goods heading in the opposite direction.

"It is?" He sounded pretty stoked by the compliment, until he thought about it. "Why?" His confusion and surprise were audible.

"Dana Fox. She lives over on Stony Wylde, doesn't she?"

I'd found out her address when I'd Googled her the other night. I heard Oliver suck in an apprehensive breath as I turned back onto Fox Hollow Road.

"Don't."

I arrived at the Fox family's imposing gray-and-white McMansion after less than ten minutes, most of which I spent listening to Oliver vainly try and talk me out of going. It was an exercise in futility for him. I'd spent the entire day trying to hunt down Jackson. I had to see if he was there. I thanked Oliver for his genuine concern, then hung up because my phone battery was nearly out of juice.

Unlike most homes in Barrington, which seemed to have the standard security system of reinforced door and window locks and a burglar alarm, Dana's house was fortified like San Quentin prison. I'm talking maximum security. With a huge iron gate and a six-foot-high wall surrounding the sprawling property. There were even video cameras strategically placed along the perimeter to discourage trespassers. My mind immediately wondered whether all this high-tech security was really necessary to keep intruders out, or just Jackson Winters.

I followed the property wall around to a quiet country road that ran behind the three-story imitation French château and its lushly landscaped grounds. (It never ceased to amaze me how unnecessarily big houses were built in the US;

did a family of four really need two formal living rooms that they would never use?) That was where I discovered Jackson's Mustang tucked under some willow trees. There was no sign of Jackson inside the car, but I knew he must be close by.

I scanned the area and immediately understood why Jackson had parked here. The road was deserted. And there were no video cameras or other houses within sight. Equally important: The Mustang was parked beside the wall, which was under one of the willow trees. For a moment I thought about just hanging by the car and waiting for Jackson to return. But with the sun setting behind the mountains, it would be dark in less than thirty minutes. If I wasn't home before my dad got back at six p.m., I might as well kiss the rest of my teenage years good-bye. I had to find Jackson now. Time was of the essence.

Next thing I knew, I was standing on the roof of Jackson's car, hoisting myself up onto the thick branch. I balanced myself upright. Then I carefully inched my way across the limb until I hovered over the other side of the wall. I looked down at the ground below. It was at least a ten-foot drop. Worst case I might sprain an ankle, which would make walking home rather difficult. If I landed on both feet just right, I'd probably be okay. I steadied myself, making sure my weight was evenly distributed. Then, channeling Master Kru, I breathed slowly and deeply. On the count of three I jumped.

My landing on the grass was less than Olympic graceful but good enough that I wasn't injured. I got up and brushed the leaves off my butt. Then I crept through the overgrown bushes and shrubbery toward the big house, which resembled a wedding cake on steroids, to find Jackson.

I began to wonder exactly why Jackson was here. Did he come every day, searching for clues about Dana's disappearance? Or did he believe she was really locked inside the house, held prisoner against her will by her controlling parents? Or was he merely an obsessed psycho, who was unable to face the truth that his girlfriend had dumped him?

Speaking of being obsessed, what about me? Why was I here, really? I was not only trespassing, but I was spying on this potential nut job. Stalking, according to Oliver. I felt out of control, more than I ever had. And I didn't know why. Something was compelling me. Hormonal lust? Maybe. Whatever it was, it was a strong, almost primal instinct that I felt helpless to resist even though I knew it could put me in danger.

I snuck closer to the house. A pair of French doors opened onto a large patio. Had Jackson actually broken into the house? Just as I got nearer, I heard howling. Deep, doglike howls coming from inside. Followed by a loud, thunderous thud. As if an enormous piece of furniture had toppled over. And then: ominous silence. The kind of eerie quiet that made me wished I'd never climbed over that wall.

I immediately turned to leave and ran straight into Jackson Winters, who was standing right behind me. Flustered, I opened my mouth to scream, when he clamped his hand over it and dragged me behind a hedge of willow bushes.

"Let me go." I wrestled free from his powerful grip, even though I didn't think he was actually going to hurt me.

"You're lucky it's only me," he whispered through a clenched jaw, his anger apparent. Our faces were less than a foot apart, as we crouched down, hidden among the thicket.

"I'll count my blessings after you tell me what the hell's going on," I whispered back, all the while staying close beside him. The tiny hairs on my arms stood up as my body barely touched his. I couldn't help but notice his well-toned arms and the pulsing vein running down the side of his taut neck.

Jackson looked at me, about to say something. I felt his heart thumping as rapidly as mine. Before he could utter another syllable, we heard glass shattering from within the house. He instinctively held me back as a large black mastiff came barreling out of the house through the open French doors. The dog was so huge it almost looked like a pony.

"What the hell is that?" The voice came from nearby. Jackson and I both jumped as we discovered Oliver crouching behind us. Unfortunately, big, bad devil dog heard him too. The monster charged across the lawn, barking and snarling.

And he was hurtling straight for the three of us.

Jackson pulled Oliver and me to our feet: "Run!"

We took off in the direction of the wall. But that dog was so fast he was nearly upon us in seconds, snapping at our heels. I was terrified and so was Oliver. We just ran as fast as we could, our legs pumping like pistons.

Without warning Jackson whirled around and thrust out his arm like one of those attack-dog trainers, motioning to the dog to stop. Except he wasn't a trainer offering a treat; he was a teenager with an exposed, meaty arm that was about to be bitten off.

Oliver and I both turned and looked at Jackson like he was suicidal. I think Oliver shouted, "You're crazy!" Even the dog thought so, because instantly he lunged up several feet in the air to take a chunk out of Jackson's flesh. Cujo bared back his slobbering mouth and exposed those huge canine fangs. I screamed.

Except instead of getting a hefty taste of Jackson's forearm, what Cujo got and what I saw were *silvery bolts of electricity* blasting from Jackson's outstretched fingertips like lightning discharges.

*Full-on, sizzling, white-hot currents of power exploding out of his body.*

Zapping the dog, which literally sent it flying thirty feet across the lawn like a soccer ball. It landed on the grass with a giant thud. And just lay there. Eyes wide open. For a second I thought it was dead—just like all those birds. Except with one major difference. This dog was still alive, but immobilized. I could see its heart thumping in its chest. Stunned by the powerful electrical discharge that had shot out from Jackson's hands.

Oliver and I looked at each other, mouths hanging open, too shocked to speak.

*This can't be happening. We must be imagining this. Did we really see what we just thought we saw?* We turned to Jackson, who shrugged. And then, for the first time, I saw his dark scowl turn into a wolfish grin.

# 6. JUMP

"Is he alive?" Oliver stood over the big dog lying on the ground, nervously watching for any signs of sudden movement.

"Resting like a baby," replied Jackson, quite matter-of-factly.

"Yeah, one who just sucked on some live wires." I was about to nudge the dog's hind leg with my foot when Jackson grabbed my arm.

"Don't. Cujo's still *hot.*"

"And you're not, Mr. Generator?" I squirmed out of Jackson's grip and took a half step back, admittedly wary of what he could do to me.

"Harmless as a kitten. Unless of course I choose not to be." Jackson sounded sincere, but I was still less than completely reassured. He acted as if what Oliver and I had just witnessed was the most natural of activities—like jogging or swimming—instead of a mind-blowing, what-the-hell-was-that-shooting-out-of-your-hands astounding occurrence.

"How can you be so laid-back about the whole thing?" I asked Jackson, incredulous, still trying to fathom the phenomenon I had just witnessed.

"Believe me, I'm not," Jackson snapped back, his intense eyes fixed on mine. "I didn't ask for this. *For any of it.* It first happened six months ago. Thanks to the pulse."

"And again last night," I reminded him.

"And one other time in between," Jackson added, revealing just the slightest hint of unease.

Oliver's eyes, on the other hand, lit up like a Las Vegas marquee. "A real-live power source. Think of the possibilities." Totally stoked, he beamed as though he'd just discovered a cure for cancer or at the very least an awesome new video game.

"Limited," Jackson interjected. "Far as I can tell, this only happens to me *after* the pulse. Twenty-four hours later I seem to go back to normal."

"There we go with that *pulse* thing again," Oliver replied sarcastically, rolling his eyes for my benefit.

"Told you I wasn't hallucinating." My eyebrows raised, I shot a look of absolute vindication back at Oliver.

"I wouldn't broadcast it around town, if I were you." Jackson stared right at me. He wasn't smiling, and he definitely wasn't joking. His warning was severe and unambiguous.

"Why not?" I folded my arms and bristled at being told what to do—even by someone as sexy as Jackson. I was not about to roll over and just accept his edict without an explanation. Neither was Oliver, for that matter. Not after what we'd witnessed. I was relieved when Oliver moved next to me, silently declaring solidarity.

Jackson sighed in exasperation. This was obviously a moment he had dreaded. A moment of absolute truth. He could either risk trusting someone else with his secrets or just walk away and continue being the lone cowboy. I hoped he'd choose to come clean. I hoped he'd choose me.

I didn't know exactly what was running through Jackson's mind. He seemed to pull back and withdraw into himself. Was he thinking about *her*? About the elusive Dana? Finally Jackson spoke. "Six months ago I was like every other deluded fool in this town. Believing that Barrington was the best place to live—a kind of suburban Eden. Until some freaky green flash lit up the sky and changed everything."

"Was that the first pulse?" I casually asked, trying my best to cover my excitement at being taken into his confidence.

Jackson shrugged and shook his head, uncertain. "I'm not sure. But all of a sudden my body was vibrating at warp speed."

"These pulses have always happened at night?" Oliver questioned Jackson as if he were part of a research experiment.

*"Always."* Jackson emphasized. "After curfew."

"Is that why you're sneaking out every night?" I probed

him even harder. "You're waiting for the next pulse to occur?"

Jackson coolly nodded. "I'm hoping to find what it is and where it's from."

I listened intently as my mind processed the information. Things were starting to make sense to me. Jackson's mysterious personality change six months ago and his sudden fall from the social pecking order all dated back to that first pulse.

"There's no way of predicting when it'll occur again?" I asked, pressing for more information.

Jackson shook his head. "I still don't even know what's causing it. The only hint that anything unusual has happened is how moody everyone gets afterward." He took a beat, pensive, before adding: "The dead birds are new. Maybe it's gotten more powerful."

Oliver and I exchanged looks of comprehension. "That might explain why Maya and everybody else seemed so unhinged today," I said. Still, I had significant questions that remained unanswered. "So why hasn't the media been all over this? There's not a single link on Google. I've searched everywhere."

"I'm not sure how many people know," Jackson said. "But those that do are maybe keeping their mouths shut. When I asked my parents and Coach Lurrell about it, they got angry and insisted it was just a nightmare I had."

"You make it sound like it's part of some giant conspiracy." That seemed a bit extreme—even paranoid—to me.

"Is that so hard to believe?" Jackson stared right at me, definite, unwavering. "I have my theories."

"Well I, for one, have never seen it." Oliver's voice revealed a healthy dose of skepticism mixed with irritation at being left out of the conversation.

"But you did see all those dead birds today," I reminded Oliver quite pointedly.

"True." Oliver nodded, a bit begrudgingly. "But then again it could've just been a weird coincidence. The scientific record is filled with them."

"I doubt it's a coincidence," Jackson interjected forcefully. "I bet it's some kind of an escalation—a cumulative effect of the three pulses. There's no telling who will be affected or what might happen after the next one hits."

"Does the pulse have anything to do with why Dana Fox left town?" I couldn't stop myself from blurting it out. Someone had to ask Jackson the tough question. Oliver's eyes opened wide as saucers and his mouth was agape; he was surprised but also impressed that I was being so direct with Jackson.

"Dana didn't leave," Jackson barked back. "She *disappeared*. The day after that first pulse hit. We were supposed to meet in the quad at school. She never showed. *Coincidence?* I don't know." His blue-green eyes cast a resolute glare my way, erasing any doubt that Dana Fox was still an extremely painful topic for him to discuss after six months.

Just as I was about to press him further on what he thought had happened to Dana, we heard loud voices coming from the house. I turned around to see who was there. Through the trees I caught sight of a pair of very distinctive navy-blue-and-white BTS uniforms—and they were heading in our direction. The sophisticated security system had obviously done its job and alerted BTS.

"Time to go, kiddies," insisted Jackson as he waved us in the opposite direction. "And remember: Promise me you'll keep your mouths shut. No matter what."

Oliver and I nodded and quickly followed as Jackson broke into an all-out run toward the back wall, which was well over a hundred feet away. I kicked into a healthy sprint. The last thing I needed was to get caught by the friendly folks at Bar Tech Security. Not only would Dad be furious with me for disobeying him a second time (not to mention trespassing!), but he would never trust me again.

Unfortunately, Oliver was lagging behind. I heard him panting as he tried keeping up with me. I looked over my shoulder and yelled, "Hurry!" I could see the bushes moving in the distance and suspected that the security guards were not far behind.

"I'm trying!" Oliver's scrawny legs pumped harder and harder, but he was in less than optimal condition.

"Maybe if you cut back on the video games and science journals, you'd be in better shape." I slowed my pace. He glared at me, huffing and puffing and pushing as hard as he could to catch up.

Jackson, meanwhile, had already reached the wall and was urgently waving us over. I knew by his tense expression and the way his jaw was rigidly set that the security guards weren't too far behind us.

I grabbed Oliver's arm and yanked him along. I couldn't leave him behind to take the fall for Jackson and me. The only reason Oliver was there in the first place was because he'd been worried about me.

"Go ahead without me," Oliver shouted.

"Come on! You can do it," I called back, trying to will him to go faster.

Just as it seemed like we might not make it to the wall in time, Oliver's feet miraculously kicked into hyperdrive. Suddenly his legs began pumping like a couple of racing pistons. *He was moving so fast that he was dragging me along.* I glanced over at him, stunned by his newfound speed and power, as was Oliver. He didn't know what the hell was happening either, but he was now moving at the speed of an Olympic runner.

And then something really strange happened. Oliver's legs pumped so fast that he literally *left the ground and took flight*, like a cheetah chasing its prey in the wild. I hung on to Oliver's arm for dear life as he leaped over the wall with me in tow.

We soared at least forty feet in the air before landing safely on the other side, without getting even a scratch.

"What the hell was that?" I muttered, dazed.

Oliver just shook his head, breathless and in a state of shock, totally staggered by what he had just done too.

"Get in!" Jackson, having already scaled the wall, hopped into his Mustang and threw open the passenger door, revving the engine.

Oliver leaped into the backseat. I took shotgun and slammed the door. Jackson shot me a look, equally amazed by Oliver's unexpected athletic prowess, then threw the car into gear. In seconds we were speeding down the road before the guards had even made it over the wall.

"Have you been holding out on me?" I shouted, spinning around in the front seat of the Mustang and glaring back at Oliver as Jackson sped through the back roads.

"No. *I don't know* . . . ," Oliver sputtered, doing his best to not completely lose it. "I mean, one second I'm barely keeping up with you and the next my legs become these turbo-charged booster rockets."

"*How long, Oliver?*" Jackson demanded to know, glancing at him in the rearview mirror. "How long have you had this?"

"Honestly, Jackson, I don't know. I swear I don't know what the hell's going on with me," Oliver babbled, obviously confused and overwhelmed. "Other than I've felt *really different* for a while now."

"Different how?" I couldn't stop myself from pushing Oliver hard.

"Weird sensations in my legs," Oliver confessed. "Like intense heat mixed with nonstop tingling. I just assumed they were intense growing pains. How was I supposed to know?"

"And you never once ran like that?" Jackson asked, suspicious.

"Uh. Hello?" Oliver snapped back sarcastically. "You forget who you're talking to? Oliver Monsalves, boy most likely to flunk phys ed when he's not cutting it. My idea of a good workout is playing video games for six hours straight."

My mind raced as I tried to comprehend the implications. This pulse seemed to affect everyone in town, causing all those cranky moods today. But what that didn't explain is why a select few—Oliver and Jackson, of all people—were suddenly endowed with superhuman abilities.

I looked over at Jackson and demanded answers: "Are there any others? Like you and Oliver?"

"Possibly. I don't know. I didn't know about him. I thought I was the only one!" Jackson admitted, trying to keep cool despite fraying slightly around the edges. He wouldn't look at me. He kept staring straight ahead as he turned back onto one of the main roads, which cut right through town. But I could tell by Jackson's clenched jaw that he was unnerved by the fact that the pulse had affected Oliver too.

Just as we were passing the main library, I heard Oliver nervously clear his throat.

"Heads up. We've got company." A visibly anxious Oliver pointed out two BTS cars that were suddenly following us from a few blocks behind.

"What should we do?" I turned around and saw the cars gaining on us. My nerves were already pretty rattled, and this wasn't helping.

"Nothing," ordered Jackson.

I looked at him in disbelief. He didn't panic or lose his cool. He just continued driving at the posted speed limit as if he'd done nothing wrong. While Oliver and I sat quietly, holding our breath.

Jackson watched the security cars from his rearview mirror. They were picking up speed, pulling up closer to the Mustang. I glanced at Jackson and could see that prominent vein in his neck pulsing away like crazy. He may have been acting all cool with Oliver and me, but I could tell he was worried too. The body doesn't lie.

Just as we approached the last major intersection in town, Jackson flipped on his turn signal and made a hard right into a church parking lot. I was prepared for the security guys to pull in and surround us, guns drawn like in some bad action movie. Instead both security cars just drove right past the church. Never even slowing down to look at us.

Surprised and more than a little relieved, we sat there in the parking lot until they'd disappeared from view. Once they were gone, Jackson silently shifted back into gear and headed off in the opposite direction.

We were safe for now. Though none of us were celebrating.

Ten minutes later Jackson, Oliver, and I stood in my kitchen, chugging back Vitaminwaters, not quite knowing what to do next. Luckily, my dad wasn't home yet. Jackson finally broke the uneasy silence: "The effects should be wearing off pretty soon. I've never seen them last longer than a day."

I know he was trying to be reassuring, but it didn't comfort me one bit. Something unnatural had transformed both Jackson and Oliver from relatively normal teenagers into superboys. Oliver, on the other hand, cracked a smile, apparently pleased by Jackson's news that he had a few more hours left to indulge his newfound abilities.

"Well, in that case . . ." He set his water bottle down on the counter, opened the French doors, and exited to my backyard. I looked at Jackson and shrugged, before following Oliver outside.

Jackson joined me on the deck and we watched Oliver

walk to the edge of the property. He saluted us like a good soldier and then broke into an all-out run. Within seconds Oliver was soaring high into the air again, sailing nearly fifty feet across the yard with a loud, Tarzan-like yell. He landed on the ground with a tumble and roll, laughing loudly. A moment later he was racing back in the opposite direction, again flying through the air, this time landing squarely on his feet, his arms raised in victory like a triumphant Olympic gold medalist. Oliver was reveling in his new strength.

Jackson called after him with a cautionary warning: "Hey, O-man: Use, don't abuse."

Oliver made a hand motion indicating he thought Jackson was overreacting. Then he launched into a series of running leaps, crossing back and forth with amazing speed and ease. Each time, he jumped just a little bit farther and higher than the previous time.

"Can't blame the boy, can you?" I remarked, understanding Oliver's impulse to play with his newest toy—his amazing ability.

"Guess not." Jackson nodded, amused. Then he leaned closer to me and confided, "I did a bit of my own . . . *playing*."

I was quite intrigued. "Mind giving me a little demonstration? I mean, as long as no other dogs are involved."

Jackson smirked. He walked over to an outdoor light and grabbed hold of the base. Tightly. All of a sudden the bulb lit up. Bright as a Christmas tree. He grabbed hold of another light fixture and it lit up too.

"Wow," I muttered, impressed by his awesome display.

"Yeah, well, don't try this at home, folks," Jackson joked in a rare moment of levity as he let go of the lights. Off they went.

"What do you do for an encore?" I asked while Oliver continued having the time of his life sprinting across my backyard.

"I can power up your computer," Jackson replied as he came back over and sat beside me at the picnic table.

"My own personal energy source," I said teasingly with a smile.

He looked right at me. "You should smile more often."

I laughed nervously. "Oh . . . okay. Thanks. I'll remember that," I blathered back, as my face must've turned ten shades of red from self-consciousness. I had to change the topic fast before I really embarrassed myself. "So . . . what's your theory?"

"About what?" Jackson shot me a quizzical look.

"About who or what's behind the pulse and your giant conspiracy. You said you had a theory. So . . . *theorize*." I gestured for him to enlighten me.

"I'm formulating it," Jackson responded, ever so cryptically. His right hand rested on the table, nearly touching my left shoulder.

*"Formulating?"* I challenged him with a dubious look. "So

then the truth is you really don't know what the hell's causing it—whether alien or otherwise."

He turned and looked at me. I gave him the slightest hint of a grin. He didn't smile back, just shook his head and exhaled. I smelled a trace of spearmint on his hot breath. It was sweet and almost intoxicating.

"Anyone ever tell you you're trouble?" Jackson remarked, glancing at me, then at Oliver running loop-de-loops around my yard like a hyperactive Jack Russell puppy dog.

"You mean other than my mother and you last night?" I shrugged coyly. "I have been known to ruffle a few feathers."

"Guess we have that in common," Jackson replied thoughtfully before adding, "You need to think long and hard before you get *involved*."

Was he talking about the pulse or something else? Either way I wasn't going to run for the hills. "I think that ship has already sailed." I leaned in close to him, not letting him off the hook. "So are you going to share your theory with me, or not?"

We locked eyes. Jackson didn't reply.

"What? You really think aliens have landed? That they're causing the pulse?" Exasperated, I started to get up, when he grabbed my hand. I looked at him. He leaned in close to me. My heart nearly skipped a beat.

"Can I trust you, Nica?" He stared at me. "Really trust you?"

"Of course you can." I nodded, feeling the tiny hairs on my arm stand up from his touch. I so desperately wanted to be taken into his confidence.

"This probably sounds crazy, but I think Bar Tech Industries may be involved." He delivered this explosive allegation without fanfare or elaboration. Just stated it softly, barely above a whisper.

Before my brain could process what he had just said and before I could press Jackson for specifics as to why he believed it, I heard a car pull into the driveway. I was immediately yanked back to the here and now.

Oliver was about to launch into another run when I called out to him. "My dad's home," I announced loudly, clearly anxious that he not find out what had occurred that afternoon.

Oliver stopped himself, not the least bit exhausted. In fact he seemed incredibly exhilarated. "I could've done that for hours."

"C'mon, O., I'll drop you," Jackson said. He then turned to me and reminded me of our oath: "Promise you won't say a word about this. *To anyone.*"

"I promise." I stared into Jackson's eyes, hoping he knew that he could trust me. Then he turned and slipped out through the side gate with Oliver, heading back down the street to where the Mustang was parked.

• • •

Once they were safely gone, I hurried back inside the house and greeted my dad, who was at the kitchen table sorting through the mail.

"How was school today?" he asked probingly. "Other than being surprised by your dad and all."

"The same. Boring," I replied with a casual shrug, pretending that I'd just suffered through another dull day at school.

He looked at me and nodded, though I wasn't quite sure whether he believed me or not. I couldn't tell him the truth—that picture-perfect Barrington was driving people crazy—even though part of me was dying to tell him everything. Maybe he could explain how a scrawny geek like Oliver had suddenly soared through the air or how Jackson could fire electrical bolts out of his hands? Because it was really scaring the hell out of me. I instead opted for a less explosive topic.

"By the way, I met Mrs. Winters at the sporting goods store on my way home."

"What were you doing there?" my father asked inquisitively.

"Browsing," I lied. "Anyway, it turns out she knew Mom from a long time ago. Said they even worked together."

"Yeah, I think they did. Writing press releases or something," my father replied somewhat vaguely. Then, suddenly seeming a bit guarded, he turned his attention away from the mail to searching through the pantry.

"Turns out a lot of people still remember Mom," I added nonchalantly, but pointedly.

"By the way, how do you feel about pasta for dinner?" He held out a package of spinach pasta, deftly changing the subject.

"Whatever. Pasta's cool," I responded, grabbing my things to head upstairs. "Just no heavy sauce or anything."

I was nearly through the kitchen door into the hallway when my father asked, "So did Mrs. Winters say anything else about your mom?"

"Nope. Not a thing," I answered as I left the kitchen and went up to my room. But I wondered why my dad had been so squirrelly about talking about my mom.

That night I power-ate my way through pasta primavera in eight minutes flat. We dined in silence. I wasn't sure if it was because my dad suspected something . . . or was he just happy not to have to talk either? My dad watched me the whole time, sensing something was up. "What's your hurry?"

"Sorry. I just have a ton of homework." I stood up from the table, grabbing my plate and silverware.

"Guess they're keeping you pretty busy." He got up too, picking up the salad bowl and the rest of the dishes. I was relieved he accepted my explanation, which wasn't entirely false.

"They won't be happy until everyone gets into Harvard,"

I joked as I loaded the dishwasher. Dad laughed but didn't say anything else. I wasn't about to break my vow to Jackson, especially when I thought that he might be right. Jackson's secrecy made sense to me until we knew more, even if it meant keeping things from my dad.

I started to leave the kitchen but then stopped in the doorway, a million questions buzzing around my brain. "Dad?"

"Yes, honey?" He turned around and looked at me.

"So what did you think about all those dead birds today? They were everywhere." I couldn't ask him about the pulse, so this seemed like a safe alternative.

My dad barely reacted to my question, as if people asked him about dead animals every day, but he did offer up an explanation. "A severe weather system moved in from the Rockies last night. It caused the birds to be disoriented."

Sounded plausible to me at first. But then when I thought about it for a minute, I realized it was really ludicrous. "They died because they were *confused*?" I couldn't help but mock what he'd said. I imagined all these mixed-up birds flapping around in circles as if they were drunk.

Hearing the disbelief in my voice, he quickly added, "Blackbirds and starlings don't have particularly good night vision. They probably flew into some power lines, causing a traumatic stress event."

"A traumatic what?" He was talking in supergeek-speak

that I didn't quite understand and avoiding all eye contact with me. Was he deliberately trying to be vague? Was he hiding something? Or was he just so wrapped up in the science of it all that he was having a hard time explaining it to me?

He looked at me impatiently. "Like a panic chain reaction. One bird freaks out, causing the others to go crazy . . ."

"Sounds like they could've benefited from some strong antidepressants," I joked.

My dad barely reacted at my rather lame attempt at humor. It wasn't that I thought the image of the birds flying into things was funny—it was just that his "scientific theory" that the birds had died from a massive panic attack sounded ridiculous to me. By the way he suddenly shut down, I knew I wouldn't get much more out of him, so I nodded thoughtfully, then said, "Well, I better hit the books."

And then we both trotted upstairs to our respective rooms—me to my bedroom and him to his study. I heard my dad lurking around in there, pacing back and forth. Was he practicing some sort of exercise regimen? I snuck out of my room and crept down the dark hallway to see what was going on there. Through the half-open door I caught him locking his desk drawers, then walking back and forth between the two windows in his study, just staring out into the darkness. It was a little eerie.

Not wanting to get caught spying on my own dad, I quickly retreated back to my bedroom and shut the door.

I opened my algebra book but couldn't concentrate. It all got me thinking. Was my dad telling the truth about what had happened to the birds or was he just putting me off for some reason? I searched every bit of relevant weather data I could find online—from temperature readings to humidity tables—hoping for answers. But I didn't find a single website that corroborated my dad's theory. In fact not one weather bureau reported any severe weather events anywhere in Colorado last night at all. Just higher than normal winds.

I was about to end my search when I found several graphs from the University of Colorado (*Report on Solar and Geophysical Activity*) that I hadn't noticed earlier. Each graph had a multitude of wavy lines with irregular peaks and valleys, measuring the electromagnetic radiation index. They were accompanied by lots of scientific formulas and mathematical calculations, none of which I understood. The one thing I did understand, however, was the big spike on the graph at the time of the pulse. I had no idea if it might be a coincidence, but I thought it might be something. So I downloaded the charts as PDFs to show Oliver and Jackson the next day at school.

Feeling very much alone, I tried calling and texting my mother, without success. She was "out of area," as the cell network kept telling me. It would probably be days before she got back to me, if not longer. Not that I really expected her to know anything or even be able to help. I mean, how could she, being nine thousand miles away at the bottom of the world? And what would I even tell her that didn't sound crazy? *Hey, Mom. There was this bright green spark in the sky and now my friends have these awesome superpowers.* Truth was, Lydia hated messy situations. She'd probably think I was just making it all up so I could come stay with her. It was all so confusing and unsettling.

Oliver and I texted each other back and forth before the Internet and cell phone service went radio silent for the night, thanks to Barrington's mysteriously "erratic" service. We were trying to make sense of our surreal situation. He said his mother reacted strangely when he questioned her about the reason for the town curfew. She'd gotten defensive and insisted it was for his own good. Not accepting her explanation he'd pressed her a little harder, and she'd shut him down, ordering him to focus on his schoolwork rather than try to stir up trouble. Something about the way his mother flew off the handle made him realize he had to keep his promise not to say anything about the pulse or his extraordinary ability to leap through the air.

There must be some way to find out the truth about the pulse. Then again, Jackson had devoted the last six months to trying to figure things out and had come up totally cold. Other than a vague, unsubstantiated theory that implicated Bar Tech Industries. About the only thing that did seem crystal clear was that Jackson, Oliver, and I were completely on our own.

# 7. NOW YOU SEE ME

Jackson was right about the effects of the pulse wearing off after about twenty-four hours. By early the next morning both he and Oliver—and everyone else at school—had returned to "normal." Whatever normal was. It felt like that bad dream you quickly forget as soon as you wake up and get out of bed. Except the three of us were wide awake and knew exactly what had gone down and couldn't forget it.

Oliver, Jackson, and I met up in the quad during lunch for a bit of a reality check. All around us kids were chatting, laughing, listening to music. Acting totally cheerful. As if yesterday's harsh moods had suddenly evaporated or been wiped clean from their brains.

"I'm not sure if this means anything, but check it out." I took out my laptop and showed them the *Report on Solar and Geophysical Activity* with all the graphs I'd downloaded as PDFs.

"They're measuring electromagnetic radiation," Oliver said, eyes lighting up in excitement.

"Of course *you'd* know what they were," I teased Oliver as his eyes eagerly devoured the scientific data like they were puffs of cotton candy.

Oliver continued, his technogeekness unharnessed. "Solar activity was very low. A few low-class B flares observed here." He pointed to a couple of small spikes in one of the graphs. "But check out those spikes there. The geomagnetic field is majorly unsettled."

Jackson grabbed my laptop, intrigued. "Where did you find this, Nica?" He scrutinized it more closely.

"I'm not really sure," I admitted, shrugging sheepishly. "It was from the university in Boulder. I was looking at so many sites last night I kind of lost track."

"Check out the spike right there," Jackson interrupted, pointing to one of the graphs. "Ten eighteen p.m. Exactly when the pulse hit."

"Yeah, I noticed that too," I acknowledged.

"So, the big question is . . . ," said Oliver, expounding like he was Albert Einstein or Stephen Hawking, "did the pulse cause the huge spike in electromagnetic radiation? Or did the EMR spike cause the pulse?"

Science was not my passion. I was more like my mother: Studying human behavior and people's interactions fascinated me. While Oliver attempted to unpuzzle the graphs, I couldn't help but notice Maya and her cheerleading clique giggling and flirting with Chase and his crew. They seemed happy and carefree, with no trace of tension or animosity. "So we're just supposed to act like everything's okay," I blurted out. "Like nothing happened?" This keeping my mouth shut was easier said than done.

"Yeah. That's *exactly* what we're doing." Jackson shut my laptop and handed it back to me, leveling his intense gaze my way. "At least until we know what we're dealing with. And who to trust."

"And how do you propose we figure all that out, Jason Bourne?" In the cold light of day Oliver seemed considerably less excited by his short-lived burst of extraordinary abilities.

"By working together." Jackson looked at Oliver and me, dead serious.

"A team? As in the three of us?" I asked, staring back at him, secretly hoping that was precisely what he meant.

Jackson nodded. "People already think I'm wacko. That I've gone over the edge. Which means *they're* always watching *me*."

"You're talking about Bar Tech," I muttered skeptically.

Jackson pressed a finger to his lips, shushing me. The guy really was paranoid.

"What?" Oliver flashed a look of complete incredulity. "You think *they* . . . ?"

"Maybe. I don't know," Jackson admitted, eyes nervously darting around the quad. "Point is, until I've found proof, it's best not to take any chances. Meanwhile you guys—"

"Can blend in. The perfect cover," I interjected, finishing his thought. "Act as if nothing's happened while keeping our eyes and ears open."

"Like Desmond in Assassin's Creed. Awesome." Oliver smiled, hopping to his feet, totally stoked for the team to get to work. "Where do we start?"

"At the beginning," Jackson replied as he stood up. "Oliver, why don't you focus on the science of it all? See where that leads you."

"Aye, aye, Captain Winters. I'm on it," Oliver replied, giving him a *Star Trek* salute as he grabbed his things and scurried off, intent on his covert mission.

"What about me, Captain? What should I focus on?" I kidded, eager to hear what assignment Jackson had in mind for me.

"You can still walk away, you know. Steer clear of all this shit," Jackson whispered as we stood next to each other under the oak tree. I noticed Maya checking us out across the courtyard. One could almost think we were a couple chatting about what movie to see over the weekend instead of two kids conspiring to unravel the biggest mystery of their lives.

"Are you serious? After everything I've seen?" I looked at him, perplexed, wondering if he wanted me to back off because of what had happened to Dana. "For all any of us know, aliens really have landed in Barrington."

"I just want you to know what you're getting into," Jackson answered. I could tell by the pained look in his eyes that he was trying to protect me.

"I appreciate your concern, but I can handle things," I countered, not wanting him to think I was some scared little girl that had to be coddled. Walking away wasn't an option. Working closely with Jackson and confiding in each other sounded so enticing. A dream come true. Except for all that paranoia stuff.

For the next two weeks the three of us alternated night-watch shifts, staying up late and looking out for any unusual activity in the sky. At the end of my nightly three-hour stint, I'd text either Oliver or Jackson depending who was up next to make sure he was awake and let him know if anything looked suspicious before his shift began. And vice versa. Despite us being hypervigilant, our neighborhood watches didn't produce any useful clues or stop Jackson from continuing his nightly rides through town. In fact, life went on as usual at home and at school.

Fifteen days after the pulse Maya cornered me in the bathroom before sixth period. "What's the deal between you and Jackson?" She was definitely not one to beat around the bush.

"Nothing. What are you talking about?" I was more than

a little bit defensive. Partly because I'd promised Jackson I wouldn't tell anybody about what we were doing. But mostly because of how much I wished her insinuation were actually true.

"*Lunch.* Every day in the quad." Her voice had an annoying singsongy quality. "You guys looked awfully cozy." She grinned knowingly as she stared in the mirror and expertly applied pink-sparkler lip gloss to her mouth.

"It's hardly romantic. Are you forgetting Oliver eats with us too?" I hastily added with a casual laugh, hoping to convince Maya she was wildly off base.

"The Three Musketeers," she said with an eye roll. "I can't imagine what you all have to talk about. But that's just me." She capped her lip gloss and tossed it into her bag, obviously skeptical. "Listen, Nica. Can I give you some advice?"

"Sure." I took a deep breath and braced myself for her words of wisdom.

"You're still new here, and you don't know that Jackson is crazy. And you certainly don't want people to think that *you're* crazy. It's bad enough you're hanging with that nerd Oliver. Anyway, I just want to help you out because we're friends."

Though I wanted to reply, *You're a bit crazy yourself,* I bit my tongue and politely replied, "Thanks."

"Well, don't linger. I hear Ramirez is giving a pop quiz

in math." Maya then swept out of the bathroom just as the class bell rang.

I sighed in exasperation and quickly followed, realizing I was as unprepared for a surprise algebra quiz as I was for Jackson's covert operation. *But that's just me.*

On the sixteenth day after the pulse Jackson stopped hanging with Oliver and me at lunch. In fact he pulled another of his I'm-not-coming-to-school disappearing acts. I texted him, but he never replied. Even Oliver became concerned by Jackson's longer-than-usual absence, which extended to four days. He stopped by Winters Sporting Goods and spoke to Jackson's parents, who claimed that their son was home sick. It made me suspicious. Had Jackson vanished like Dana did, never to be seen again? Or was he off on his own looking for Dana or pursuing clues about Bar Tech and the pulse? Or was he just avoiding me for some reason?

I went to Jackson's house after school, but no one answered the door. If Jackson was sick, wouldn't he be home in bed? I went around to the backyard and boldly knocked on the living room sliding glass doors.

"Jackson? You home?" I kept knocking on the glass, but the house seemed totally still, empty. If he wasn't at home, then where could he be?

In a last-ditch effort to find out what had happened to Jackson, I stopped by his family's store and tracked down

Mrs. Winters. She was assisting a customer with a merchandise exchange in the autumn section. Hiking boots. I hovered around a display case, trying on various leather gloves, until she finished.

"Looking for a different size, Nica?" Mrs. Winters asked, gesturing to the pair of mocha open-back leather driving gloves I was holding in my hand, as she walked over.

"No. These are awesome. It's just . . ." I hesitated, not wanting to come off as too clingy or stalkery. "I haven't seen Jackson around school for several days. Is he *okay?*"

Mrs. Winters's face grew visibly strained as she formulated her answer.

"My son is . . ." Before she could say another word, I heard a familiar voice interrupt.

*"Right here, Mom."*

I turned around as Jackson suddenly stepped out from the turtleneck rack.

"Jackson, I wasn't expecting you," his mother remarked, clearly on edge. She was as surprised to see Jackson as I was.

"I promised to help Nica check out snowboards," Jackson snapped back without missing a beat. "Right, Nica?"

"Yeah . . . absolutely. Might as well, now that I'm stuck in the land of mountains and snow." I went with Jackson's story, not wanting to get in the middle of anything.

"Well, maybe you can get Jackson back on a board again," Mrs. Winters commented sadly, giving Jackson a guarded look before walking off toward the front of the store.

"Was that a note of tension I detected?" I remarked as Jackson navigated me toward the snowboard section. Mrs. Winters was definitely keeping her eyes on us.

"More like a symphony of major disappointment ever since I gave up competitive racing. She had this fantasy that I'd actually compete in the Olympics," he replied dismissively, changing the subject while picking up a totally tricked-out board. "So, do you need a freestyle, Alpine, or all-mountain board?"

"I haven't a clue." I shrugged. "One that goes downhill, hopefully." They all looked vaguely similar to me. Just decorated in wild colors and exotic designs. "So why did you give it up? Boarding."

Jackson exhaled before responding, his expression darkening with pain. "After Dana disappeared . . . everything seemed so . . . *ridiculous*."

"Football, too?" I wanted to understand Jackson. I wanted to hug him, to make him feel better.

"Yeah, football. And good grades and honor society and class president and every other frickin' lame-ass activity I'd been dutifully performing for the past seventeen years." Jackson looked at me and laughed as he shook his head at the pointlessness of it all.

"I know. I mean, not to get all existentialist about life, but sometimes it all seems so absurd. High school. Being stuck

**161**

in one place for so many years." I empathized with what he was going through. The world suddenly seemed incredibly ridiculous to me, too. "Maybe my mother has it right after all? Always staying on the move so she avoids complications and never gets bogged down. I kind of miss that life . . . that freedom."

We stood there staring at each other, connected, if only for a moment. It felt as if we were two kindred souls trapped in this insane universe called Barrington.

"So," Jackson said, shifting tack, shaking off all emotion. "Beginners generally look for shorter boards to enable them to maneuver easier." Jackson stood a bright red one adorned with black Japanese characters alongside my body to demonstrate. "Between the collarbone and chin is a perfect height."

I felt a shudder of excitement as his fingers grazed the middle of my neck. Jackson looked at me and held my gaze. I worried that my face was turning red from embarrassment. Could he tell how I was feeling?

"By the way," Jackson added, "all of these boards have been evaluated by our expert testers."

"Testers?" I laughed, shooting him a skeptical look. "You actually have testers?"

"All right, *tester*. As in yours truly," Jackson whispered with a sheepish grin. "When it comes to boards, I know my shit."

"So I see," I said, checking out the many photos of Jackson boarding that were plastered up and down the nearby wall. "What about *other things*?"

"I'm working on it," Jackson responded solemnly, circling around me with the board, alluding to the pulse.

"Anything specific?" I gently probed, hoping for some new insight or information.

"The less you know the better. Get on the board," he instructed me, laying the board on the floor, fully aware his mother was still watching us.

I obeyed, cautiously putting my left foot forward on the wobbly board. Jackson grabbed hold of my arms, steadying me. I exhaled and steadied my breathing as he adjusted my body position with his hands, gently shifting my right leg to the back of the board. I tried to focus on my feet instead of how close Jackson's body was to me.

"Don't come back in here again," he ordered, whispering in my ear as his body suddenly tensed up. "It's too risky."

I followed Jackson's gaze and spotted a couple of Bar Tech Security guards chatting with his mother.

"I'll be in touch once I know something more." Jackson nodded, stepping away and disappearing toward the rear of the store.

And that was the last time I saw Jackson for the next week.

• • •

While I waited in limbo for Jackson to contact me, I spent every night aimlessly trolling the Internet at night for any more unusual phenomena—weather or otherwise. It wasn't like I could follow a trail of bread crumbs out of the woods to an answer—I was flying blind. Hoping for that one-in-a-million hit that would unlock the mystery of the pulse.

I pursued all possibilities, no matter how irrelevant they seemed, from strange bird behavior and unusual encounters to random UFO sightings around the country. Oliver, meanwhile, investigated every mysterious incident from NASA rocket launches to missing planes in the Bermuda Triangle. He even scoured the most outrageous alien-conspiracy-theory blogs. All of which he dismissed as bogus and none of which had anything to do with explaining the pulse.

"The effects of EMR upon biological systems . . . ," Oliver began, trying to explain exactly what he was tracking, while we huddled at the back of the school library during lunch.

"On biological what?" I immediately interjected, needing a translation.

"On *humans* . . . ," Oliver clarified in a hushed whisper. "Our bodies are powered by bioelectric impulses to the brain. The effects of EMR on humans depend both upon the radiation's power and frequency."

"So in theory, the more often the pulse happens . . . ," I replied, keeping my voice down in case anyone was trying to eavesdrop, "the greater the effects on you and Jackson."

"Exactly," Oliver answered, happy that I was following his train of thought. "Though I'm seeing nothing out of the ordinary since that night."

Which meant another dead end for our investigation.

I felt a bit directionless without Jackson. Not that he was our official leader or anything like that, but Jackson did seem to have a gut instinct about what might be going on beneath the surface in Barrington. That got me wondering: Did he know more than he was letting on? Was he possibly withholding information from Oliver and me? About Dana or Bar Tech?

Unfortunately, since Bar Tech was a privately owned conglomerate, there wasn't much publicly available information beyond the standard corporate PR bullshit about their awesomeness. What little I could find out was that they were one of those ultrasecretive companies that manufactured an array of high-tech equipment—everything from medical supplies to solar and green technology. Not to mention they also gave very generously to a host of charitable causes. Other than their private security patrol in Barrington, there wasn't much else suspicious I could find online that made me believe they were causing the pulse.

Nevertheless I found myself constantly glancing over my shoulder wherever I went. Whether walking down a hallway at school or along Main Street through town, I checked out every person and vehicle I passed. Perhaps some of Jackson's paranoia had rubbed off on me, but I was also hyperaware of every word that came out of my mouth, no matter how trivial. Every seemingly innocent conversation I had with fellow students or teachers or even my dad, I filtered through a lens of wariness and suspicion. I was afraid of making a misstep by inadvertently revealing a clue about what had happened to Oliver and Jackson.

Oliver tried to step into the void and take on a leadership role, but it wasn't the same. While he did know a lot about science and math, he didn't have the knowledge that Jackson possessed. We needed Jackson's insight to help unravel what was going on. I needed him. More to the point, I missed being around him.

When nothing had happened twenty-two days after the pulse, I started second-guessing myself. Wondering if what I'd seen that night with Jackson hadn't just been a fluke—a random event. After all, I only had Jackson's word to go on that he had actually experienced the pulse twice before that night. Still, despite Maya's warnings, Jackson didn't strike me as a crazy person who made things up for attention. If anything—other than the whole Dana-Fox-is-missing mystery—he went out of his way to be left alone. That and the fact that I had witnessed him shoot electricity out of his fingertips, not to mention seen Oliver leap fifty feet across my yard, convinced me we weren't suffering from the same delusion. And yet there was no guarantee any of this would ever occur again.

I shared my doubts with Oliver one afternoon after school while grabbing a couple of slices of pizza at Violetta's. "You think we're on a wild goose chase here? That the pulse I saw was just a meteor shower or some other cosmological event?"

Oliver shrugged and shook his head. "I'm beginning to wonder. But then I can't totally explain what happened to Jackson or me that day either. There have been studies about the physiological effects of electrical energy in humans causing temporary abilities."

"So you suddenly becoming the bionic man and Jackson this high-powered generator was just a happy coincidence?" I shot Oliver a dubious look, not quite buying that theory either.

"Maybe that's all the pulse was—concentrated electrical energy, similar to a bolt of lightning?" Oliver theorized. "And for whatever reason we don't yet know, it just affected Jackson and me."

It sounded rational. Up to a point.

"That doesn't explain why my dad and your mom pretended nothing was odd about all those dead birds, let alone that anything unnatural had ever occurred," I said. "Or why they shut us down any time we questioned them about the town curfew, or the need for excessive security. And what about Dana Fox's disappearance the morning after the first pulse? Did she leave town simply to get away from Jackson? Or was she really abducted, like Jackson said?"

Oliver looked at me, shook his head, and exhaled audibly, totally stumped. "I wish I knew."

*"Knew what?"* my science teacher, Mr. Bluni, asked as he suddenly appeared at our table and spotted the printouts on bioelectrical energy and electromagnetic radiation that Oliver and I were reading.

"Nothing, Mr. Bluni," I answered, panicking as I quickly gathered up the documents and stuffed them into my bag. "Oliver and I were just . . ."

"Doing some extra reading on the brain-nerve cell connection in vertebrates," Oliver interjected, doing his best to cover our tracks.

"We're not covering that until next semester." Mr. Bluni eyeballed us skeptically.

"Just trying to get a jump on things," I announced like I was the world's biggest ass kisser.

"Really," said Mr. Bluni, not quite buying what we were shoveling. He then proceeded over to his table, where he sat with several other teachers from school. He said something to them and they all turned and stared at Oliver and me. It was very unsettling.

"I'm not a hundred percent sure," Oliver muttered to me, "but I think they're talking about us." He stood up from the table, wanting to leave.

"I think you may be right." I grabbed my things and hastily followed Oliver toward the exit.

"You're sure we weren't followed?" I asked Oliver as we hurried down Main Street away from Violetta's.

"Yes. No. I mean, I don't know for sure," he replied, as paranoid as I was about our strange encounter. "Just like I don't know for sure if maybe Jackson isn't onto something."

"Well the one thing I do know for sure," I asserted, my mind reassessing our previous conversation, "is that the whole Dana story doesn't quite add up."

"In what way?" Oliver asked, eager to hear my reasoning in light of what just happened.

"By all accounts Jackson was Mr. Perfect his whole life *up until Dana disappeared.* It's only *afterward* he melts down and becomes rebel-without-a-cause-meets-town-crazy. Right?"

"Right," Oliver affirmed, suddenly following my train of thought. "*Right.* So then if that's true, why did Dana feel the need to run off in the first place?"

"One of two reasons," I answered. "Number one: Jackson was secretly crazy and Dana was the only one who knew it."

Oliver shook his head, not buying it. "Highly unlikely. What's the second reason?"

"Dana's parents lied about what really happened to their daughter," I responded. "The question is . . . *why?*"

• • •

Twenty-seven days after the pulse I woke up early and dressed without even thinking about what I was going to wear. As opposed to my usual habit of trying to at least wear something that didn't make me stand out. After kissing Dad good-bye, I walked to school with Oliver, which had become our morning ritual. Attended all my classes and completed all my assignments like a good little girl. By all outward appearances I was fitting in and making friends. And I did nothing to ruin this impression. But inside I still felt like an outsider who would never really belong.

Oliver had to take a makeup history exam, so I ate lunch with Maya, Chase, and their friends. It wasn't awful. For a few brief moments I actually forgot about everything and found myself laughing over some silly conversation we were having about whether the ultra-uptight school nurse was getting it on with the super-hairy football coach. I must've gotten distracted, because next thing I knew I was scanning the quad, hoping to spot Jackson. I didn't think anyone noticed my momentary attention lapse.

That is until Chase suddenly startled me: "He skipped again."

"Who did?" I quickly recovered and looked over at Chase, acting like I had no idea what he was talking about.

"Jackson. Dude's gone AWOL. Hasn't been around in almost a week." Chase gave me a sympathetic look, like he cared about me, which was totally out of character for him.

I figured Maya had shared her suspicions about my feelings for Jackson with him.

"Actually, I was looking to see if Oliver finished his exam early," I replied in total denial that Chase might be right. Luckily, the bell rang. I grabbed my bag, anxious to go.

Chase leaned in close, whispering in my ear, making sure no one else could hear him. But his lips touched my ear. "Word is, they may expel him."

"Too bad." I pulled away from Chase. "Why are you telling me?" I shot Chase a look, pretending I couldn't care less about Jackson. While deep down I worried about whether it was true and how he knew this information.

"Because the asshole used to be my best friend. And whether you believe me or not, I just want to help the guy with whatever shit he's going through. Anyway, I'd just hate to see you get hurt," Chase added before walking away, slipping his arm around Maya, and heading off with her to class.

"You think we should go to Jackson's house to make sure he's really okay? Let him know what's happening?" I asked Oliver as we exited the school later that afternoon on our way home. I normally wasn't one to repeat gossip, but this seemed out of the ordinary.

"Jackson can take care of himself," Oliver declared, trying to keep me from worrying any more than I was. "Besides, I think Chase was playing you. Hoping you'd admit how you felt about Jackson so he could report back to Maya." Oliver shot me a wary look and I nodded back, even though I wasn't sure he was right about this.

"I just hope Jackson knows what he's doing." I couldn't mask my anxiety any longer.

Neither could Oliver.

He chimed back, "Me too."

A few hours later I was sitting at my bedroom window, staring out at the pitch-black darkness. My many texts to Jackson over the last few days had gone unanswered. If Jackson really was all right, as Oliver believed, why wouldn't he just let me know he was okay? My initial concern about Jackson's well-being had given way to frustration and anger. Why was he icing me out like this? Had I done something wrong? Weren't we supposed to be working together?

I sighed and looked back out the window, dutifully continuing my watch.

*Bzzzz . . . Bzzzz . . .* I heard the annoying sound even before I opened my eyes. *Bzzzz . . . Bzzzz . . .* I woke up in bed, still dressed in my clothes. As I looked around my room, trying to figure out the source of that buzzing, I realized I was clutching my cell phone in my right hand.

It was vibrating. I looked at the screen. Jackson had sent me a text with just one word: *PULSE.*

I threw down the phone and rushed over to the window, all my anger at him dissolving into relief that he was okay, as I glimpsed the telltale flash of shimmering neon-green light lighting up the night sky. Instantly followed by that powerful *WHUMP!* shooting such a forceful wave of energy right through my body that it literally blasted me back from the window, slamming me into the wall with a resounding thud.

The pulse was happening again, much stronger than the last time. I saw it. I felt it.

My fingers frantically texted Jackson: *Saw it! What do we do???* A moment later my phone vibrated with another incoming text. This one was from Oliver: *OMG!!!* He had seen it too.

I stood in the middle of my bedroom, worrying about what to do next. *Do I tell my dad? Do I go outside?* I started to dial Oliver's number when I received another text. It was a warning from Jackson: *Don't go out. Keep quiet.*

It didn't make me feel any better. I texted Jackson: *U OK? Where r u??*

Jackson replied: *Home. C U tomorrow.*

Morning came none too quickly for me. Despite feeling woozy from being slammed against the bedroom wall, I hadn't slept a wink since Jackson's ominous text had woken me up almost four hours before. I spent all my time checking out those University of Colorado weather sites again, poring over graphs and charts. Sure enough, I found a huge spike in electromagnetic radiation at 11:13 p.m., the moment the pulse hit. It matched the previous spike, which had occurred during the last pulse. I e-mailed the information to both Jackson and Oliver with a note: *U think it's a coincidence??* Oliver replied: *Hard to know.* Although we didn't exactly have a smoking gun about what caused the pulse, it was a start.

I heard my dad fixing breakfast down in the kitchen. He called up to me, "Nica, do you want a ride?" He still asked me every morning, even though I had been walking to school with Oliver. He was leaving for work earlier than usual. I was thrilled. That meant I could get to school a half hour earlier, so I hitched a ride. I said I wanted to get to school early because I had to study for a quiz, when in fact I wanted to see how everyone at school was reacting. I texted Oliver to see if he wanted a ride too, but he was just getting up and said he'd meet me in the quad. I didn't even have time to change my clothes before heading out the door.

The car ride to school was uncomfortable. My dad seemed distant and even more preoccupied than usual. He'd glance over at me periodically. I was concerned that his silence had something to do with me.

"Everything okay, Nica?" he finally asked, looking over at me with a long stare.

"Yeah," I lied, forcing an uncomfortable smile, when

what I really wanted to do was shout: *Do you have a freaking clue what the hell's happening in this town?* "How about you?"

"I was just wondering," he responded. "You and Oliver seem pretty tight."

"Yeah," I shrugged guardedly. "I guess we are."

"Who else are you hanging with these days?" he asked probingly.

"I don't know," I answered with a shrug. "Lots of kids." My suspicions were definitely raised along with my blood pressure. *"Why?"*

"No reason," he replied before he turned his attention back to the road.

Was his questioning purely innocent, or was he fishing around for something specific? I hadn't a clue, and I wasn't about to ask.

I was relieved when my father finally dropped me off at school. It was more than a replay of the day after the last pulse four weeks earlier. Kids and teachers alike seemed bad-tempered and very much on edge—even more so than the last time. I caught Mrs. Henderson slamming the car door shut on her belligerent husband as he gruffly dropped her off near the front entrance in his silver Mercedes sedan. Then I overheard a very angry Maya berating Chase over some math assignment he hadn't finished the night before. People were pushing and shoving and wound up all around me, as if they'd been given massive doses of testosterone. Even I felt these scary waves of pulsing rage, like I had this burning urge to kick some major ass for no reason.

I started walking toward the quad, anxious to find Oliver and Jackson and avoid an altercation, when suddenly Maya confronted me.

"Have you ever felt so angry that you wanted to rip some asshole's head off for no reason?" Maya demanded to know, blocking my path, her eyes wild. "Or worse, your own?"

"Only like every other day," I wisecracked, hoping to defuse her anger. I was leery of her volatility—and I also had no interest in getting dragged into a fight with her.

"Well that's not me," she barked back. "*Happy is me.* Perky is me. School spirit is *f-ing* me. I sound totally insane, don't I?"

"No more than the rest of us." I was trying to make light of the situation, but suddenly I felt concerned and a bit afraid of her, as well as afraid of my own unpredictable feelings. I might not have been Maya's biggest fan, but she seemed genuinely unhinged—and weirdly aggressive. About tenfold more than she was after the last pulse.

"Are you going to be okay?" I tentatively asked. I'd never heard Maya curse before.

"Once I ditch this heinous cheerleading outfit after practice," she growled, pulling at the zipper. "I'd torch this piece of shit if it weren't a hundred percent fire resistant." And then she charged off in a major huff, knocking kids aside like bowling pins.

Meanwhile my head was left spinning from the encounter as I staggered my way into the quad. I paced back and forth, looking everywhere for Oliver. I needed to hash out what I was seeing. And we needed to come up with a strategy about what to do next with our investigation. He'd promised to be at school in time to talk. It was already seven fifty a.m. First class would start in fifteen minutes. The minutes ticked by. He was nowhere to be found. Was he now blowing me off like Jackson? A girl could develop a complex. Instead, I got annoyed—really angry. It wasn't like the boy had major wardrobe issues to deal with in the morning.

After anxiously waiting outside the front entrance twenty minutes I finally saw him sprinting down the street toward the school. Even though his feet barely touched the pavement, I could tell Oliver was putting the brakes on how fast he was running. He was deliberately concealing his extraordinary abilities so that no one would know the truth.

As I stood on my tiptoes and waved my hand so that he'd find me among all the students congregating near the entrance, I felt this momentary rush of heat throughout my body. I didn't pay much attention to it, because I was more focused on getting Oliver's attention as he darted across the street and jogged through the center of the quad. I gestured for him to hurry over, as the morning bell was going to ring in less than five minutes. There was a lot I wanted to discuss with him before school started.

He walked up to me and then breezed right by as if I weren't even there.

"Really mature," I called out. I was in no mood, today of all days. But he kept on walking. Ignoring me. I thought Oliver was playing games, pretending he didn't see me, and I was in no mood for it. "Hey, *Oliver!*" I found myself yelling.

He stopped dead in his tracks, hearing me, and promptly spun around. A couple of students froze and stared right past me. Oliver scanned the crowd with this bewildered look on his face. As if he was looking for me but not seeing me, which was totally ridiculous, because I was standing not more than twenty feet away, staring back at him with one hand on my hip, quite exasperated. But he stared back as if he was looking right through me. Then after a few more seconds he just shrugged, turned away, and continued toward the school entrance.

Now I was really fuming. So I shouted again, this time even louder: "That's so not funny."

Oliver stopped and spun around, looking a bit angry himself. And then I noticed something: He wasn't the only one ignoring me. Everyone else was striding past me too. Acting like they didn't see me at all. I was getting paranoid. Was this some kind of class joke? I'd kind of expected this on my first day, not my twentieth. Or was my wardrobe so pathetic that everyone was ignoring me? I looked down at what I was wearing just to make sure I hadn't committed a serious fashion crime, and suddenly I let out a long wail. A horrified, Oh-my-God-this-can't-be-happening-to-me kind of scream. Which was when I realized the horrifying truth:

*I couldn't see myself! I was totally invisible!*

I started hyperventilating and began to panic. No wonder Oliver was acting like I wasn't there. He couldn't see me! Even my clothes had disappeared. How was that possible? What was going on? What the hell was happening to me?

"OHHHH! MY! GODDDDD!" I screamed. It was the loudest, longest scream I'd ever unleashed—louder than the time I found a snake crawling in my bedroom in Tanzania . . . louder than the time I dived off the Maui cliffs into the Pacific Ocean. This time I screamed the loudest scream I'd ever screamed in my life—even louder than the time I rode the three-hundred-eighty-foot-tall Tower of Terror roller coaster in Australia.

Suddenly kids were scrambling in all directions, covering their ears and spinning around to see which tool had just screamed her bloody head off at 7:55 a.m. in the middle of the school quad. Luckily, they couldn't see me, or how humiliated I must've looked. Maya angrily accused Jaden of doing it. Jaden blamed Annie. Chase and his crew were scanning the crowd for who the lame-ass girl was. Most just shrugged my scream off as some sort of prank, continuing on their way inside as the school bell rang.

Except for Oliver, who stood there, just staring straight ahead. Did he sense I must be close by? I walked toward him, trying to figure out the sanest way to break the obviously insane news that his new friend had suddenly become invisible. I was standing right in front of him, nose to nose, when all of a sudden I watched his jaw practically drop to the ground and his eyes grow wide with absolute astonishment. As if he'd just seen a ghost.

Well, not exactly a ghost. Just me. For when I looked down, I was amazed that I could actually see my feet and my legs and all the rest of me. Somehow I had rematerialized. I was back in the flesh. Looking exactly the way I had when I'd arrived at school just minutes before. And then I realized that everyone else could see me again too. Oliver stood frozen like a marble statue, staring at me, totally speechless. Completely freaked myself, I swooped over and grabbed Oliver's arm.

"Don't say anything now," I urgently whispered through my clenched jaw, as I whisked him into school, wondering what other fabulous surprises the day had in store for us.

## 8. DUCK AND COVER

Oliver, recovered from the shock, looked me in the eye. "I'm dreaming, right?" He poked my arm as I hurried him through the crowded hallways. "Because there's no other explanation for what I just witnessed out there in the quad."

"If only," I replied, trying to rein in the considerable panic I was feeling. "It's the pulse. It has to be." My eyes locked with his. "How else could I just vanish into thin air along with my clothes?"

"The pulse must've altered your refractive index or something," Oliver hypothesized excitedly.

"My refractive *what*?" My brain was already reeling from shock. I certainly couldn't process a bunch of technojargon on top of that.

"How your body reflects and absorbs light," Oliver explained in a whisper. "There's so much electrical energy in your body that the electrons are repelling light. A negative refractive index causes light to bend away from you.

Think of it as built-in camouflage. You're really there, but it doesn't look like you are to anyone else."

"I think my head's about to explode," I groaned.

"We better find Jackson." Oliver knew I was right.

"Yeah, pronto." I then quickly texted Jackson, hoping he'd be able to help, though I wasn't exactly sure how. He was more invisible than I was.

"In the meantime, let's just go to class and pretend everything's normal."

"Awesome idea," I said sarcastically. "And we do that how? I mean, given my current . . . *situation*?"

"You think I know?" Oliver shrugged, as flabbergasted as I was.

"Well, I don't have a clue what I'm supposed to do. Other than try not to vanish during class." I was also desperately trying not to lose it in the middle of a crowded school hallway, but it wasn't like I was in control of my body. All I could do was hide behind my frozen smile and wave hello to kids I knew as I passed them by.

"Listen. Just hold it together till third-period phys ed," Oliver implored. "We'll figure something out then." Oliver squeezed my arm, hoping it would reassure me, and then rushed off to his first class.

World History was pretty much a blur to me. I sat in my assigned seat near the back of the room and pretended to pay attention, barely noticing that Maya was absent. She had skipped class—probably a first for her. I was too caught up in my own drama to wonder what had happened to her. Mr. Ghiradelli rambled on about the concept that became popular in the eighteenth century during the European Enlightenment: free will. Something I was painfully aware I lacked at the moment, considering I was trapped there. Needless to say I wasn't happy about my situation.

All of a sudden I felt a powerful surge of emotion washing over me. Anger like I'd never experienced before. A tidal wave of rage rose up from the pit of my stomach and coursed through my veins until my entire body pulsated with energy. I felt like the Incredible Hulk bursting at the seams, about to trash the room. I glanced down at my hands and watched in shock as my fingers literally began to disappear before my eyes. Quietly panicking, I yanked my sweater sleeves down over my hands so that no one could see what was happening. That only seemed to speed things up. It was as if all the molecules in my body were separating from each other and disintegrating into thin air.

Terrified that I might totally disappear if I didn't do something quick (try explaining *that* to your dad!), I did the only thing I could think of not to flip out. I recalled Master Kru's simple wisdom and started to *breathe*. Slow steady breaths. Focusing my mind and body. A few kids gave me strange looks. I rolled my eyes, acting like I was bored to distract them. Until, quite amazingly, my hands started to become visible again. Incredibly relieved, I summoned all my powers of concentration to keep breathing like that until the bell rang, at which time I bolted out of the room before the other kids had even gotten out of their seats.

During second-period English, I was slightly better able to handle my panic—until we started discussing Mary Shelley's *Frankenstein*. The discussion turned to Victor Frankenstein's hubris and transgression against God and nature in creating a human out of spare body parts. Most everyone viewed Dr. Frankenstein as somewhat of a villain in the novel. Chase, on the other hand, argued vehemently that Victor was heroic for pushing the limits of science.

"That's what Watson and Crick did when they discovered DNA and won the Nobel Prize," he said with authority, like he knew what he was talking about and he wasn't some dumb jock. But this time he was making a forceful argument, one I might have followed with more interest had I not been watching the clock, eager to reconnect with Oliver.

Then it occurred to me: I was relating to Frankenstein's monster—I was extremely confused and not quite sure what had been done to me, or how to handle it. And I certainly wasn't up for having an in-depth conversation with Chase when he cornered me after class.

"Hey. What's up with you?" he asked, checking me out more than usual.

"What do you mean? Nothing. Why?" It was difficult for me not to sound incredibly defensive.

"You're just acting . . . *weird*," Chase replied with his usual bluntness.

"Yeah, well. That's me." And I bolted toward the door before I started to disappear in front of Chase's eyes.

"Or maybe you're hanging with Jackson too much," Chase shouted as I fled into the crowded hallway.

I hurried down the stairs to the gym, nearly tripping over my feet. Oliver was in my phys ed class. I avoided talking to anyone along the way—I was afraid I wouldn't be able to control what was happening to my body. Fortunately, I made it safely to the girls' locker room and was changing into my sweats and sneakers when all of a sudden Maya's quartet of high-strung BFFs ambushed me.

"Oh my God, here you are! We've been looking for you!" Annie cooed.

"You have to hear—" Jaden squealed.

"Let me tell her!" Maddie interrupted.

Aggressively jabbering over one another like Alvin and the Chipmunks, Annie, Emily, Maddie, and Jaden were saying something about planning a surprise birthday seventeenth birthday bash for Maya at Chase's house in a few weeks. They hoped I'd be on the organizing committee.

"A committee for a birthday?" I muttered incredulously. That was a new one.

"It's a theme party—Katy Perry," Jaden confided, quite excited, as if that clarified the matter.

"No, it's not!" Annie angrily retorted, her face twisted in a dismissive grimace. "No one ever mentioned *theme*." She was so pissed I thought her head might explode.

"I thought we wanted it to be fun?" Jaden replied, hurt and indignant.

"*Fun*, yeah. Katy Perry is so middle school." Annie rolled her eyes, condescendingly.

"Whatever, bitches," Emily interjected, having no patience. "It'll be wicked no matter what."

I didn't dare say a word. The hostility among these girls was spinning out of control.

"As long as we have a *fabulous* menu. Like sushi or tapas. That's where we really need you, Nica!" Maddie glared at me, the world traveler, hoping I'd help calm the choppy waters they were swimming in. But I couldn't get used to how they celebrated birthdays here. Back in Thailand and most other places I'd lived there were no parties, or birthday cakes, or presents. The most lavish gift I ever gave a friend was a book.

They were all dressed identically, in navy-and-white sporty workout ensembles with painfully cute pink, green, and white clipettes in their hair. I knew the only way I could get out of there quickly was to simply smile and say, "Count me in." I added, "Absolutely. Sounds genius." I figured I'd bail on them later, telling them I had to go out of town for the weekend to visit my grandparents in Ohio.

They perked up, extremely happy to have recruited me for their committee. Mission accomplished. And then they continued to argue about the menu, party color palette, and a million and one other mind-numbing details. They were so engrossed in their bickering I was able to slip away and hightail it out of the locker room before something really weird happened. Like my legs or head began disappearing.

By the time I found Oliver out on the field running soccer drills with the rest of the class, I was almost a complete basket case. I didn't know how I'd make it through the rest of school, without suffering a mental breakdown.

"Glad to see you're still in one piece," joked Oliver, checking me up and down with amusement.

*"Don't even,"* I warned him, in no mood to banter.

"Sorry," Oliver replied as he kicked the ball, pretending to be into dribbling. "Has it been awful?"

"You mean other than almost disappearing in the middle of history?" I nervously tugged my sweatshirt sleeves down over my hands, worried about a repeat performance. "Boring it's not."

"Well, I've got just the thing to cheer you up," he said cryptically as Coach Lurrell blew his whistle and ordered the class to run laps around the track.

"Follow my lead." Oliver started to jog very slowly, drifting to the back of the pack, with me obediently trailing behind him. I couldn't help but notice two Bar Tech Security officers striding across the field.

As we circled around the first bend in the track, I saw Officer Korey and Officer Lorentz chatting with Coach. I had this momentary fit of paranoia. Were they looking for me? Before I could find out why they were there, Oliver grabbed my hand and whisked me off the track. We were underneath the bleachers in two seconds flat. Out of view from the rest of the class.

I opened my mouth to chew Oliver out for pulling such a risky stunt when I saw Jackson standing there. Wearing faded jeans and a black-and-white flannel shirt he was also sporting a three-day growth of beard, looking as scruffy and unbearably handsome as always. My heart practically skipped a beat. I hadn't seen him in days and I felt this urge to run up to him, jump into his arms, and kiss him.

"Hey." Jackson acted like he could care less that he hadn't seen me in a while.

"Nice of you to make an appearance," I responded with attitude.

Jackson gave me a small smile. "Oliver filled me in on what's happening. How you holding up?"

Even though I wanted to remain annoyed at him for ignoring my texts and dropping out of sight the way he had,

I could feel my anger melting. "Excellent. Can you explain it to me? Because I'm about to lose it—literally." I held up my hands, hoping he had an answer. (And maybe a long kiss—you can't blame a girl for fantasizing.)

"It'll be okay. Just roll with it. The first time is really scary, I know. And you'll probably have a headache the day after. But you'll be fine, really." Jackson was doing his best to reassure me, but it wasn't good enough. I needed some tangible proof that I wasn't going to spend the whole day disappearing again.

"Can I quote you? Because I'm not exactly feeling it." However, I was starting to feel something else: a vibrating sensation radiating out from my spine. It was all too familiar a sensation to me that day. Kind of like when you hit your funny bone, except with the tingling feeling magnified a thousand times.

"Oh no." I held out my hands and watched as they started to disappear. "Here we go again."

I didn't fight it. I didn't try and stop it from happening. Not this time. Not with Oliver and Jackson watching. I wanted to appear tough. I disappeared within a matter of seconds, vanishing without a trace right before their eyes. And yet I was still standing next to Oliver and Jackson. They just couldn't see me. It was both unsettling and thrilling at the same time—for me. For Jackson and Oliver it was also awesome, but in different ways. Oliver thought it was kind of cool, while Jackson took a more clinical, dispassionate approach.

"Freaky," Oliver said.

"Can you control it?" Jackson asked, as he slowly circled the spot where he had seen me standing a moment earlier.

"If I concentrate hard enough. With my breathing."

Jackson turned around toward the sound of my voice. I was now standing right behind him, though he couldn't see me. I pondered the possibilities and realized that being invisible had its advantages. What would happen if I wrapped my arms around Jackson? Yes, the thought did cross my mind, even while I sounded quite rational—a lot less emotional than I actually felt inside.

"Pretty crazy stuff, huh?" Oliver said to Jackson. "Now you see her, now you don't. Must be some kind of negative refraction going on. It's as if Nica's been shielded from electromagnetic radiation. The light is actually going around her body and clothing rather than being reflected by it. Sort of like infrared waves or microwaves."

"So theoretically," said Jackson as he pondered the possibilities, "*anything* inanimate Nica touched would be hidden or invisible as well."

"Yeah." Oliver shrugged. "I suppose it would."

Jackson nodded, running his right hand through his hair, deep in thought. I noticed he did that whenever he was feeling troubled or uneasy, one of a million sexy habits he had.

And today he couldn't help being spooked by my newfound ability. But there was something else going on, something that was bothering him even more than my sudden disappearance.

"It can't be a coincidence," blurted Jackson. "*The three of us.*"

"I highly doubt it's contagious," Oliver declared. "Maybe we're part of some giant alien experiment?" Jackson's paranoia seemed to be rubbing off on Oliver.

I knew Jackson was right, and by the ashen look on Oliver's face he did too. However, before either one of us could say anything else, a large figure suddenly appeared by the edge of the bleacher stands. It was Coach Lurrell in all his blustery glory.

"What the heck's going on here? Last I looked, gym class is going on out there," Coach Lurrell growled, reminding me of a cartoon bull angrily stomping its hooves, steam billowing out of its flared nostrils.

I held my breath and didn't move a muscle, not wanting to suddenly reappear. How awkward would that be?

"Hey, Coach," replied Jackson as he stepped in front of Oliver. "Just had to give my man O. the good news." He sported a friendly demeanor, trying to defuse the situation.

"What news?" Coach eyeballed him suspiciously, waiting for an explanation. I was hoping Jackson would be able to come up with one. "Well, nice of you to finally make an appearance, Jackson."

"Sorry, Coach," Oliver bravely interrupted, not wanting to let Jackson take all the heat. "Those rad Vans I ordered two weeks ago from Winters Sporting Goods finally came in, and Jackson knew I'd want to know ASAP." Everyone knew that Jackson's parents owned Winters Sporting Goods, so Oliver ordering a hot new pair of sneakers and Jackson being the bearer of the news of their arrival had the vague ring of truth.

"Yeah, they're totally rad, flying off the shelves," Jackson added for dramatic effect.

Still, Coach Lurrell didn't seem convinced. "Is that so?" He stared at Oliver, waiting for him to crumble. Beads of sweat formed on Oliver's forehead as he nervously glanced over to Jackson, silently pleading, *Now what?* Jackson's cool eyes slyly scanned the area, obviously concerned about me reappearing, as was I.

I crept back from where they all were standing, praying that Coach Lurrell would not hear my footfalls softly crunching on the dirt. Making noise was the least of my worries, because I started feeling that warm, spine-tingling sensation emanating from my lower back. I may have been new to the whole body-chemistry-change thing, but I knew enough to know that this feeling wasn't a good sign. My body would start reappearing. I tried not to freak out or panic. I just kept hearing Master Kru's voice echoing in my head, commanding me to *breathe*.

As I inched my way out from under the bleachers, I heard Coach Lurrell bark at Oliver and Jackson: "Monsalves, give me three laps. Winters, my office, pronto." Oliver obediently jogged back out to the track, knowing better than to complain about his punishment. Jackson, however, walked in the opposite direction from the office, when the coach blocked his path.

"You deliberately trying to screw up your life, Winters? Because you're doing a heck of a job."

"Glad to know I excel at something, sir," Jackson replied without a hint of sarcasm as he obediently turned and followed the coach back to his office.

I stole back into the empty lockerroom. Summoning all my powers of concentration I tried to will my body to reappear. Nothing happened. I tried a second time. Again nothing. I had less than five minutes before the rest of my class returned from the field. Frustration welled up inside me. What if I was stuck like this forever? I kept thinking, *Why me? What did I do to deserve this?* But the Nica pity party would have to wait.

Just then I heard the locker room door swing open. I instinctively hid inside one of the bathroom stalls, forgetting for a moment that no one could see me. Two girls stumbled in, their voices muffled. I couldn't tell who they were, but I prayed they'd stay out of the bathroom. No such luck. They hovered at the sinks, brushing their hair and checking their makeup in the mirror for any flaws. They were gossiping about Maya being Little Miss Perfect. Dishing about how she always got everything she wanted—cheerleading captain, class president, and Chase Cochran. So I wasn't the only one who had issues with her. Those bobble heads kept chattering on, enthusiastically trash-talking all the other cheerleaders. Instead of rushing off I hung around as they divulged inconsequential stuff, like how Emily supposedly shoplifted cosmetics. And how Maddie and Annie talked behind everyone else's backs. And how Jaden had gotten an awful nose job over summer vacation.

"I mean, have you seen her nostrils?" one of the girls asked.

"Oh my God! Someone could drive a Mack truck through them," the other one replied.

As I stood only a few feet away from them, I thought, *Actually, this invisibility thing has its perks.* I could find out more dirt and secrets about my classmates than I ever wanted to know. The blackmail possibilities were endless. Thankfully, none of them had to use a toilet, and they were too busy to notice the locked stall door.

But then I sneezed. Loud. The urge to do so hit me suddenly and without warning. There was no way to stop it from happening. The sneeze just flew out of me. And it was a double one.

The girls spun around, a bit startled. One of them

stage-whispered, "Someone's in the stall." She tugged at one door and it opened. Then she tugged at my stall. I'd locked it. I could see Amanda Morovich put her hands on her hips, pissed at being spied on. "Who's in there?" She was a tall girl with a frizzy mop of red hair who I knew from my Spanish class.

I was silent, not moving a muscle or saying a word.

Amanda stomped over to the stall and pounded her fist on the door. "Open up, chickenshit."

I quietly cringed. If I opened the door, I took the risk I might suddenly become visible before their eyes. Who knows whom they would tell and what they'd do if it suddenly became public knowledge that I could vanish and reappear in seconds. I sure didn't want to find out. Then I heard some rustling from the neighboring stall. Lisa Hooper, the willowy captain of the volleyball team, had stood up on the toilet, peering over the stall into mine.

"No one's here, Amanda," she declared.

"Yeah, and who sneezed? A mouse?" Amanda gruffly squeezed her way into the stall with Lisa and then hopped up on the toilet to look.

Fortunately for me, I was still the girl who wasn't there. From Lisa and Amanda's point of view the stall was locked and empty.

"Very weird." Amanda shook her head, definitely perplexed.

The two girls exited the adjacent stall and returned to the

sinks. I was suddenly struck with an overwhelming desire to do something crazy and impulsive. So I unlocked the stall door while I was still hiding in there. Then I watched the girls' stunned reactions as the door inexplicably swung open.

"What the hell did *that*?" Lisa muttered, unnerved, looking around the restroom like it was haunted.

The bell rang.

"C'mon, let's go," Amanda insisted, yanking Lisa's arm and dragging her out of there as quickly as possible.

Once they were gone, I started laughing and finally breathed easy again. Not for long, though, because within seconds a flood of chattering girls burst into the locker room from the field. They were eager to shed their gym gear and reapply their makeup. Amidst the clamor of clanging locker doors and piercing voices, I saw my hands again, then my legs, and finally the rest of me. Relieved, I quickly exited the stall and then mingled with the rest of the girls without attracting the slightest bit of attention.

"Have you seen Maya?" I was hurrying to Spanish when Chase suddenly appeared beside me in the hallway.

"Not since this morning." I motored on ahead, preoccupied by my situation. I was in no mood to chat with anyone, least of all Chase Cochran. But he kept walking beside me. "Why don't you text her?" I snapped, anxious to get rid of him.

"Already did," Chase replied. "And her girls haven't seen

her either. Which is unusual, since they all seem to be joined at the hip." He chuckled, flashing that winning smile. Why did he have to be so annoyingly charming? Yes, it did occur to me that she'd been acting weird when I'd last seen her, but honestly, I was way too preoccupied with my own problems to worry about whether Maya was having a postpulse breakdown. I had no intention of worrying about whether Maya was avoiding Chase, much less getting sucked into the middle of their romantic squabble.

"Maybe she's volunteering for Cosmetics for Cambodian Orphans or Chechnyans for Change," I responded flippantly. "Or organizing the next pep rally." I hoped my sarcasm would get him to leave me alone.

"No. She would've told me. She tells me everything," he insisted, pursuing me like a stray puppy. "It's not like her to blow me off. If you see her, will you let her know I'm looking for her?"

I detected a surprising note of concern in his voice, as if he might actually care for someone other than himself. I almost felt bad for him. Almost.

"Sure thing." Then I darted up the stairs, leaving Chase stranded in the middle of the hallway with an exasperated look on his face.

Spanish was a total blur. Between watching the minutes slowly tick by on my cell phone and worrying that I might suddenly disappear again, I didn't hear a word that Señora Gibbons said. Oliver and Jackson each texted me during class to make sure I was okay. I surreptitiously hid my phone in my notebook so I was able to text *OK* without drawing undue attention from Gibbons. Mercifully, I held it together and survived until the bell rang. Then I was out the door, racing to the nearest staircase. Fortunately, I had study hall next and planned on ditching it and hiding out in the library stacks until lunch.

No sooner had I exited the stairwell and started charging past the science labs then I heard a disturbing crash come from inside one of the labs. The unmistakable sound of glass shattering—a lot of glass. I heard a series of loud thuds followed by another even louder crash. And then I heard someone cry out. More like an animal wail. Then I realized it actually sounded like Maya screaming. I was tempted to walk on and avoid any Maya hysterics, but I had to peek in through the door to see what was causing her to make all that noise. What the hell was going on in there?

I looked through the glass to see all hell breaking loose. I pushed the door handle down and cracked open the door. As I poked my head into the room, a glass beaker whizzed by my face. I flinched back just in time and it barely missed me. That wasn't the only thing that was flying. Books, glass beakers, pens—anything that wasn't nailed down—were zipping around the room like a barrage of Scud missiles.

"Oh. My. God," I muttered, trying to comprehend what I was witnessing. My eyes then caught sight of a seriously freaked-out Maya huddled underneath a lab table. She was trapped in the middle of all this chaos—a virtual prisoner.

"Help me," Maya pleaded, tears streaming down her cheeks. "Make it stop!"

Me? How was I supposed to make it stop? I was pretty sure I wasn't also responsible for causing some *Wizard of Oz*–like twister to wreck the lab. Could there be some invisible people throwing things around the lab? Or was something else causing all this mayhem? I had a hunch what it might be and decided to test my theory.

I coolly urged her to "Breathe, Maya. Just breathe." I felt like Master Kru was speaking through me.

"I am *breathing*," she barked back. "What the hell do you think I'm doing?" I thought it looked like she was incredibly pissed. And I suspected that I had to get her to calm way down before I could help her.

So I started making my way across the lab, ducking and dodging the flying debris. Even though Maya was barely fifteen feet away from me, it wasn't easy navigating the short distance.

I was about halfway across the room when Maya shouted, "Watch out!" I looked up, not a moment too soon.

I saw a pair of shiny scissors flying toward my chest. I instinctively dropped to the floor in the nick of time, avoiding direct impalement. Still, the scissors sliced my sweater, ripping a hole in the right arm.

"Thanks," I shouted back as I crouched down on all fours. I was annoyed and didn't feel like I should be so grateful for her saving my life—I wouldn't be in harm's way if it weren't for her. No way was I going to stand up again until the situation was under control. I sucked in my breath and then scooted across the floor like a crab on the beach until I was safely underneath the table with Maya.

"Get me out of here." She clutched my arm, terrified, desperate to flee. But we couldn't risk trying to leave just yet. First I had to get Maya to relax, which wasn't going to be easy. It was the only way to tell if my theory was right— and keep us both from getting killed.

"Everything's going to be okay." I patted her hand, trying my best to reassure her. Just the way Jackson had done with me under the bleachers during phys ed earlier that morning. I wondered if he'd had as many doubts as I did right now. "I need you to focus, though. Can you do that?"

"Focus on *getting me out of here*." Her eyes darted around the room in a hundred different directions. And I could feel her body vibrating at warp speed, like she was about to bounce off all the walls.

"Just look at me, Maya." I steadied her head with my hands and forced her to look right at me. "Ignore everything else. Look at me. I'm going to get you out of here, but you've got to trust me and do exactly as I say. Okay?" Finally her eyes locked with mine. She sucked back her tears and nodded timidly.

"Good. Now take a deep breath," I coached. "And exhale slowly." I demonstrated exactly what Master Kru had taught me back in Bangkok. Breathing in and out. Calm. Focused. After a few nervous breaths, I could see the tension in her body begin to dissipate. "Close your eyes," I continued, my voice firm but calm. "Clear your mind. Let everything go." Letting go was difficult for a control freak like Maya, but she dutifully followed my orders. Maya's resistance slowly slipped away. Her shoulders relaxed; her facial expression went slack. I could tell by the serene look suddenly appearing on her face that she was no longer frightened. She slipped into "the zone," where one finds tranquility and inner peace.

Less than a moment later every single thing that had been whirling around the room at warp speed just dropped to the floor with a collective thud. It was as if Maya had flipped one giant off switch. Hearing the loud thudding stop, she opened her eyes and gazed at all the stuff strewn across the floor. Dead silence. She shook her head in disbelief. A moment before, everything had seemed incredibly threatening. Now it all looked harmless.

Maya turned to me, glassy-eyed, hair in disarray, wondering what had happened. She looked shell-shocked and bewildered, like she'd been on the most intense roller-coaster ride ever. Her mouth hung open, as if trying to say something. No words came out. I knew from my own experience that she was struggling to make sense of a senseless situation. A million thoughts had to be racing through her confused mind, none of which made any sense.

Finally I said, "You want the short explanation, or the long one?"

Maya stared back blankly. And that's when I started to laugh. I wasn't sure if it was the absurdity of us huddled under the table like a couple of scared rabbits that struck me as hilariously funny. Or just the accumulation of every bizarre event that had happened since I'd gotten out of bed that morning. Whatever triggered my burst of hysteria, I suddenly couldn't contain myself.

Maya's eyes narrowed as she shot me this panicked look. She'd been hoping I'd have some answers. Instead it seemed as though I'd gone completely crazy. Maybe I had.

## 9. SEVENTEEN

"Stop exaggerating," insisted Maya as she barreled through the cafeteria like a bull in a china shop. "You're saying that I caused everything to go crazy in that lab? You're just trying to scare me." I followed her out to the quad, where Oliver and Jackson were waiting for us.

"Maya, I'm not trying to scare you," I responded in a hushed tone so as to not broadcast what we were discussing to the entire school. "I'm just trying to tell you what I know."

Maya rolled her eyes. "Which is what? That some random green lightning bolt or—"

"Pulse," I reminded her.

"Or whatever is giving me ESP or tele-frickin'-shit and causing freaky things." Her voice was antagonistic and condescending. "Next thing you'll be telling me that aliens have landed in Barrington. I think you've been hanging around Jackson too much."

I gritted my teeth, trying to stop myself from blowing

my cool. Twenty minutes earlier Maya had been practically curled up in the fetal position underneath the lab table, fearing for her life. Now she was striding confidently through school, head held high, as if nothing had ever happened. In the intervening time, Maya had pulled herself together in the girls' bathroom while I gave her the lowdown on the events of the past few weeks. A fresh coat of lip gloss later and she acted like I'd imagined it all. Either I hadn't done a very good job of explaining things or she was trying to repress her panic. I opted for the latter explanation. Fear makes people do strange things.

"It's real, Maya," Jackson declared, not mincing words. "We all saw it last night." The four of us—Jackson, Oliver, Maya, and me—were walking through the quad, avoiding the other kids who were eating lunch.

"And now we're all affected," Oliver added.

Maya pursed her lips and crossed her arms. A telltale sign that she felt defensive and was shutting us down. I opted for a softer, less confrontational approach. "We're all afraid. Pretending nothing happened won't make it so. Important thing is that we stick together, protect each other, and keep quiet until we understand what's happening to us."

Maya nervously looked around at all the kids chilling and enjoying their lunches. They were happily oblivious to what we were experiencing. Or perhaps they were wondering what the four of us were doing together? In fact I was wondering the same thing myself. In what normal high school universe would Jackson, Oliver, Maya, and I ever have *anything* in common? Now we were like these mutant Four Musketeers, except without the lame feather hats and unflattering leotards. Talk about being different and not fitting in . . .

"Look, I didn't want to believe any of it either," Oliver interjected sympathetically. "Until I was suddenly leaping across backyards like I was Superman or something. It's scaring the hell out of me," he admitted. "Our bodies are suddenly doing things that shouldn't be possible."

"Whatever," Maya exclaimed with a dismissive wave of her hand as she charged toward the student parking lot. "I'm sure there's a logical explanation."

"Logical?" I laughed at her. I was done playing nice. "What's so logical about me suddenly disappearing? Or Jackson shooting lightning bolts from his fingertips? Or that twister you caused back in the lab because you were angry with Chase about something?"

"*It wasn't me*," Maya emphatically insisted. "It wasn't my fault. The windows were wide open. There was a strong breeze. I had nothing to do with what happened." She was digging in her heels, willfully denying reality like a smarmy politician. Maybe she was even starting to believe the lies herself.

"Fear and denial won't help you sleep easier tonight," shouted Jackson as Maya picked up her pace and charged away. "It won't change what's happening to you. We just want to make sure you don't get hurt. Or hurt other people. Come with us. We'll *show* you what we all can do."

Maya stopped in her tracks and whipped around. Her face was taut, bright red with anger. "I don't care if you can all leap tall buildings in a single bound," she barked back. *"This has nothing to do with me."*

"What doesn't, babe?" Startled, we all turned around to find a somber Chase striding over to us. It was the first time since arriving in Barrington that I didn't see Chase flashing his usual overconfident smile.

Oliver, Jackson, and I instinctively tensed up, our bodies becoming rigid. Exactly how much had he heard of our conversation? And with Maya such a loose cannon, none of us had a clue what she might say or do at that moment. Exposure could prove dangerous. Especially since we didn't know why this was happening, and whom we could trust.

"Nothing, baby." Maya swooped over to intercept Chase before anyone else could say anything. "Just some stupid science experiment Nica's working on."

Chase put his arm around Maya. "Where have you been hiding? You had me worried. I looked everywhere." Underneath his surface concern I detected a trace of resentment, maybe a little hurt.

"Sorry, it's been a . . . crazy morning." Maya gave him a forced, unconvincing smile.

"Crazy, *how?*" Chase scrutinized Maya's face as she froze like a deer caught in the headlights. His suspicions were definitely aroused. Maybe he had heard what we'd been talking about earlier.

Oliver shifted nervously, glancing at his feet. Jackson shot me an urgent look to help Maya as she fumbled for an excuse. Maya could not pull off the deception without major assistance.

"Weren't you helping Principal Hellinger with something, Maya?" I feebly interjected.

"Yeah, right . . . Hellinger." Maya's eyes lit up with relief. "He asked me to plan next week's pep rally. It was hard to text." She ran with my lie and actually sounded halfway convincing.

"I'm just glad you're okay," Chase responded with a bright smile, seeming to accept her story. "And you too, Winters." Chase's eyes settled on Jackson. "Been a while. To what do we owe the honor of your presence today?"

"Just clocking in," Jackson replied. "Like everybody else."

"Speaking of time," Maya interrupted, taking Chase's hand. "Walk me to my locker? I forgot my science book." Eager to get out of this awkward situation, she nervously smiled and brushed back her hair with her other hand, giving Chase the full Maya charm.

Chase nodded, then turned back to Jackson, Oliver, and me. "Don't play in traffic, kids." And then he and Maya split, leaving the three of us in the parking lot.

"Now that wasn't the least bit awkward," Oliver joked as the lovebirds walked arm in arm back toward the quad. "Think she'll tell him?"

"Nah," I replied confidently. "Too scared."

"What about you?" Jackson turned and looked right at me with his beautiful blue-green eyes. "Doing okay?" His hand touched my shoulder. I felt this jolt of electricity run through me. Not the painful kind of jolt that Jackson could shoot out of his fingertips. This was amazing and warm and made me go weak in the knees. Was this what it felt like to crave someone's touch so badly that it made you ache all over? I'd never felt this way about anyone before. Then I began to wonder: Was he just being nice and cordial? Or did his touch mean something more—that he really liked me romantically, the way I liked him? As if it were even possible that a hunk like Jackson would ever want an insecure mess like me.

"Depends on your definition." I tried to affect a casual tone to cover my nervousness. Jackson removed his hand from my shoulder, as if he knew exactly what I was thinking. "I'm back to my normal self, at least for the time being. Though I have to admit, invisibility does have its advantages." I shrugged coyly.

"I can imagine," Oliver quipped.

"Better watch what we say, Oliver," Jackson snapped with a sly smile. "Never know who might be watching."

"Don't worry. You're both safe," I countered, my eyes locked with Jackson's. "Anyway, it's the 'now you see me, now you don't' that's driving me crazy. I don't know if I can survive three more periods till the end of school."

"Maybe you can get your father to write a doctor's note," Oliver suggested, half joking, half serious. "'Please excuse Nica from school. She's not all there today.'"

"Very funny," I replied, not the least bit amused. "I can just imagine the conversation." Truth was, I didn't even want to think about having such a discussion with my father. Ever.

"Well, start rehearsing," Jackson said. "Because guess who's in the nurse's office now."

"My dad's in school? *Today?*" I stared at Jackson in disbelief, my mouth hanging open like I was about to retch.

He nodded sympathetically. "I saw him when I passed by the administrative offices before lunch."

That immediately got me thinking about why my dad had shown up at school today of all days. He'd never mentioned he was coming in during the car ride this morning.

"Maybe it's just a coincidence, but wasn't my dad here after the last pulse too?" I asked Jackson, recalling my run-in with Dad in the nurse's office the day after my ride on his bike.

"Yeah," Jackson nodded, looking at Oliver and me. "I think he was."

My stomach twisted into knots. I felt queasy. There was no way I could calmly make it through the rest of the day with the whole disappearing issue hanging over my head. Stressing about why my dad was there and whether he might summon me down to the nurse's office for another parental chat would probably push me over the edge. I didn't want to be poked and prodded and grilled by my father.

Oliver shook his head sympathetically and sighed. "And you thought your day couldn't get any worse."

I would soon find out just how much worse it could get.

Before lunch was over, Oliver, Jackson, and I agreed to reconvene at Jackson's house after school and figure out what to do next. There were so many unanswered questions. For instance, why no one in Barrington was publicly talking about the pulse at all. It was as if there was a conspiracy of silence. We also needed to figure out why it was affecting the four of us. It didn't seem possible that no one else was aware of what happened. They all seemed trapped in a kind of communal denial. This hanging in limbo was unnerving, especially now that we had these big secrets, which we were too afraid to discuss with our own parents for fear of being exposed.

In the meantime I had to figure out what to do about my

father. I cycled through my list of limited options. Ditch school and hide out until the whole disappearing issue disappeared that night. Not the best plan, since the school would notify my dad of my absence and then I'd be in even more hot water. Or I could pretend to be sick and hope they'd send me home to recuperate. An even worse idea, since my dad would insist on finding out exactly what was wrong with me. Which left me with one less than optimal solution: Face Dad head-on. A risky move, but at least I wouldn't be caught off guard and I'd hopefully have some control over my body.

As soon as the class bell rang, I headed directly for the nurse's office. I rehearsed exactly what I would say to my dad in my mind so as not to be rattled when I saw him. I planned on playing it cool and casual. Maybe even make a joke about him checking up on me again at school. But then I thought better just be direct and ask what he was doing here.

When I arrived at the nurse's office, I was surprised to find that my dad wasn't there. In fact no one was around. Not even the nurse. I felt relieved that I wouldn't have to face my father until dinner. I just needed to hold it together until later tonight when my newfound "ability" would hopefully disappear.

I turned on my heels and exited the empty office, when I nearly collided with my guidance counselor, Mrs. Henderson. I'd been dodging her for a couple weeks now, not really in the mood to discuss my future life plans when I was barely able to make it through each day. Today I wasn't the only one who had something else on her mind. Mrs. Henderson appeared distracted and upset. Her eyes were red, and it was obvious to me that she had been crying.

"Mrs. Henderson, I didn't see you."

"Sorry, Nica," she said, quickly wiping her eyes. "I should know better than to walk and text at the same time." She forced out a laugh and plastered on a bright smile while slipping the cell phone into her pocket. "By the way, I haven't seen you in a while. I sent several e-mails to you, but you never got back to me," she said, sweetly but pointedly.

"Sorry about that. I've just been really busy with school." I flashed a smile, hoping to conceal my nervousness. I wanted to flee, but I could sense she had no intention of letting me get away so fast.

"Is everything all right? Are you feeling okay?" I felt like she could see right through me.

I froze for a moment, trying not to panic. Did she suspect something? Then I realized she was referring to the fact that I was coming out of the nurse's office.

"Oh. Yeah. Fine. I heard my dad was visiting. Guess I missed him. Bye."

I started to walk away, when Mrs. Henderson said, "Actually, you're in luck. Dr. Ashley's still here."

"Oh. He is?" I bit my lower lip and turned around. My hope of a quick escape suddenly evaporated.

"Yes. In fact I saw him going into Principal Hellinger's office not more than five minutes ago."

"Thanks. I'll track him down." I really wanted to go, but Mrs. Henderson stepped in front of me and deliberately blocked my path.

"How are you doing otherwise? Still adjusting to this place?" She placed a hand on my shoulder and looked at me with deep concern.

"Me? I'm . . . fantastic." I shifted uncomfortably and felt unnerved by the way she was staring at me. Was this an intimidation tactic she'd picked up in guidance-counselor school?

"I remember when I first moved here from Chicago eighteen years ago, I wasn't quite prepared for the whole small-town experience," she confessed. "Your mother was very welcoming. She introduced me around."

*"My mother?"* I was thrown by this unexpected curve ball of information. "I didn't know you guys were friends." Much less that my mother had played Susie Homemaker and rolled out the welcome wagon to new arrivals. My world was shrinking by the hour.

"Friendly," Mrs. Henderson clarified. "But she went out of her way for me nonetheless. And I'd like to do the same for you."

"Thanks. But I'm okay. Really." Truth was, I felt distinctly uncomfortable.

"Listen, Nica," Mrs. Henderson said, not giving up. "I know you're a sophisticated girl. You've traveled around the world and lived in many places. I did the same after college. Europe, Africa, and Asia. Then I married my husband, Ben, and settled down here. It was a major *adjustment*." Her expression visibly darkened as she scanned up and down the hallway to make sure we were alone. She then looked back at me and spoke. Her voice was soft and low, like she didn't want anyone else to overhear. "Barrington isn't like other towns. It's . . . *different*."

Her voice reminded me of the way my father had spoken to me about Barrington that first night I'd arrived. Except that the look I saw in Mrs. Henderson's eyes was one of unmistakable fear. As if she *knew* something that scared her. Maybe I was reading too much into her behavior, but the way she acted was extremely disconcerting. Still, I'd feel incredibly relieved to have an adult I could talk to and confide in. Someone who would acknowledge and understand all the weird shit that I was going through. But maybe Mrs. Henderson's pushiness was about something else. Maybe she was just one of those needy adults who wanted to prove they were still hip and cool by "relating" to a teenager. Maybe all she wanted was a girlfriend she could tell her marital woes to—as if I really wanted to hear any of that. Or maybe her motives were more nefarious? She might be trying to lure me into her confidence.

"You know, I really better get going," I replied, stepping around her, definitely in no mood to spill my guts. "Hate to miss my dad again."

And off I hurried down the hallway, feeling Mrs. Henderson's eyes watching me the entire time until I circled the corner. Once safely out of her view I slipped into the nearest stairwell, avoiding Principal Hellinger's office and my father.

As I dashed up the stairs, I paused to text Oliver about my close encounter of the strangest kind with Mrs. Henderson. ". . . based on the test results . . ." I heard a familiar voice coming from the floor above me. I stopped to listen. It sounded like my father. He was talking in a hushed tone with another man who had a deeper voice. Principal Hellinger? I wasn't sure. They were having a private conversation—more of a disagreement, actually. I hung back to listen, staying out of view. Then I crept up a couple more steps and peered up through the railing, keeping hidden. I saw that my dad was in fact talking to a trim businessman in a jet-black designer suit. The man had a full head of dirty-blond hair that was beginning to turn gray. He looked like an aging prepster from one of those fancy Ralph Lauren ads: an older, more distinguished version of Chase Cochran, which made perfect sense when my father called him Richard. I realized that he must be Richard Cochran, Chase's father. The apple didn't fall far from that tree.

Chase's father kept pressuring my dad for access to "all

test results." I couldn't imagine what kind of tests they could be referring to, but my dad balked at Cochran's request. He insisted on analyzing the blood tests first himself before sharing the results with Cochran.

Blood tests? Whose blood tests were they talking about? And why would my dad be sharing *any* blood-test results with Richard Cochran, CEO of Bar Tech Industries? I stood there in shock, trying to comprehend the implication of their discussion. My own father, a respected cardiologist, seemed way too tight with Richard Cochran, arguably the most influential man in Barrington. Besides running a Fortune 500 megacompany, Cochran was also a generous benefactor to our high school and numerous worthy causes. And my father was possibly sharing private medical information with him. Private information about students at school, some who were my friends—maybe even about me. I was utterly confused.

The class bell rang. In a matter of seconds the stairs would be flooded with students, which meant an abrupt end to Dad's conversation with Richard Cochran, not to mention my eavesdropping. As their secret meeting broke up, I darted back down the stairs to avoid detection.

"Maybe it's just a freak coincidence?" I was arguing with Jackson and Oliver while pacing around Jackson's garage. "Like lightning striking twice in the same place." I was seriously groping for a reasonable explanation of why my father might be violating the Hippocratic oath.

"A coincidence that a day after the pulse hits, your dad is back at school drawing blood from students again?" Jackson pulled his head out from under the hood of his prized Mustang long enough to shoot me a skeptical look. "It's got to be connected to Bar Tech. As does Cochran's extreme interest in those blood tests." He wiped the sweat off his brow with a rag and then turned his attention back to tinkering with his engine. I had to admit he looked kind of hot in just a tight tank top and his trademark faded jeans.

"I kind of agree, Nica," Oliver said. "You need to look at the facts."

"I can't believe my father would do something so awful like betray patient confidentiality," I exclaimed, defensive and still more than a little distressed by what I'd overheard in the school stairwell that afternoon.

"I'm just glad he hasn't gotten around to taking mine yet," Oliver muttered, looking visibly relieved.

"Mine either." I felt an incredible sense of relief as well.

"And I just never showed up," admitted Jackson. "But it's only a matter of time before they force us to comply."

"What would Bar Tech care about blood tests, anyway?"

"They're into all sorts of top-secret stuff," replied Jackson. "High-tech medical equipment. Satellites. Who knows what else?"

"Okay. Maybe I'm missing the obvious," Oliver said, trying to process this latest wrinkle, "but what's Cochran's connection to all this exactly? And what's your dad looking for in the blood samples?"

"There must be something detectable in the blood," Jackson conjectured. "A marker."

"Like a special gene," I added. "Or something in our chromosomes. Proof that we've changed. And that maybe other kids have changed too."

"How's that even possible?" Oliver asked, shaking his head in confusion. "I mean, it's not like we were *born* with these abilities. The pulse just made them happen."

"Maybe the pulse left a scar on us," I theorized.

Oliver nodded and joked, "You mean like the lightning bolt branded on Harry Potter's forehead?"

"Only it's *inside* our bodies," I countered. "*In our blood.*"

"Which means *they* must already know about the pulse," added Jackson, as he slammed his car's hood shut and wiped the grease off his hands. "And what it's capable of doing." His eyes sparked as if he'd just had a revelation. Before I could even ask what it was, he was hurrying back into his house, leaving Oliver and me standing in the garage without a clue as to what had just happened.

"I swear." Oliver audibly sighed, shaking his head, hands thrown up in exasperation. "That dude annoys the hell out of me sometimes."

"Yeah." I nodded, not wanting to admit to Oliver how much I was into Jackson. "Always ten steps ahead."

It was true that Jackson could be infuriating. He was cagey and guarded, never revealing too much, though I suspected he knew way more than he let on. Even more frustrating, I never knew exactly where I stood with him. Or how he felt about me. There were moments when he'd touch my arm or look me in the eye and I felt like we were connected. Then there were other times when he'd barely acknowledge my presence and push me away. Still, all that mystery and uncertainty drew me to him. I couldn't control my feelings. When I was around Jackson, I felt electric, alive. So while I was irritated by all his secrecy, I started to follow him through the door into his house, hoping to peel back yet another layer of the Jackson mystique.

"Where are you going?" Oliver asked.

"Inside."

"He's gonna get pissed." Oliver sounded annoyed at me.

I imagined Jackson being startled—and then like in some cheesy movie I'd grab him and give him a soulful kiss. I can dream, can't I? But all I said to Oliver was, "Oooh, I'm scared."

Oliver trailed behind me, grumbling how he hated being treated like a kid brother.

I found Jackson upstairs in his bedroom. "That's colorful. Why are we looking at last night's weather conditions?" I inquired, impatiently staring at a large computer monitor, which sat atop a long glass table. The screen displayed an array of US satellite weather maps detailing humidity percentages, precipitation, temperature readings, barometric pressure, wind velocity, and electromagnetic radiation calculations.

"Eleven thirteen p.m., to be exact." Jackson pointed to the huge spike on the EMR graph I had e-mailed him earlier. He was standing next to me while Oliver (ever the nerd) manned the Bluetooth keyboard. Jackson had the latest-generation Mac Pro. Faster, bigger, and more powerful than any computer Oliver or I owned.

"That's when the pulse hit," I responded, stating the obvious, as I finally got a good look at Jackson's bedroom. I half expected the walls to be plastered with photos of Dana Fox and crazy news clippings like a paranoid stalker might have. Instead Jackson's inner sanctum was unnaturally neat and resembled a tastefully decorated hotel room—all browns and beiges. Not your typical teenage boy's pigsty of dirty laundry, smelly sports gear, and posters of half-naked swimsuit models named Alyssa or Kenza. Except for a half dozen snowboarding trophies crammed on the top shelf of a bookcase, Jackson's bedroom was devoid of personality. Weird. As if Jackson didn't want to leave anything personal or incriminating lying around. Which I realized was pretty paranoid as well.

"EMR is way off the chart, as expected," shrugged Oliver, hoping for something more illuminating from Jackson.

"Check out October twenty-third." Jackson peered over Oliver's shoulder as Oliver dutifully entered the data. An array of graphs flashed on-screen, which Oliver scrolled through.

"The night I took dad's bike for a little spin," I muttered sarcastically. "How could I forget almost getting arrested? Not to mention my first pulse."

"EMR spike appears identical to the one from last night." Jackson restated what we already knew.

"Probably because they are," Oliver replied, rolling his eyes, a bit exasperated by all the Jackson intrigue. He dragged and clicked until both graphs appeared side by side. "Listen, show us something we don't know."

"Go back to April sixteenth." Jackson was unfazed by Oliver's irritability.

Oliver did as he was told and performed another quick search. A third graph appeared on screen. It also displayed that unique spiking pattern we had come to know.

"Bingo, sports fans," Oliver piped up like a game-show emcee. "We have a winner."

"So that's when the pulse began? April sixteenth?" I looked directly at Jackson, expecting some kind of confirmation. Instead Jackson hesitated a beat before answering.

"Maybe not."

"You're saying there were others?" That was news to me. "When? How far back should we go?" I pressed Jackson, eager to get to the bottom of when the pulse actually began. He didn't answer my question.

"Oliver, plug in the exact coordinates for the spike," commanded Jackson.

"Great. Just what I feel like doing: solving math problems," Oliver sniped while begrudgingly inputting the data.

"Now search for all possible matches." Jackson stared intently at the screen, expecting Oliver to follow instructions.

"Aye, aye, Captain." Oliver saluted, then obeyed Jackson's order.

We watched as the search quickly retrieved 5 MATCHES FOUND. The first four matched the dates we already knew about including July twentieth. Which left one other date.

I looked at Jackson with anticipation. He stared at me and then leaned over Oliver's shoulder and hit the enter key. An electromagnetic radiation chart filled up the entire screen with dozens of zigzagging colored lines.

"It's not recent," announced Oliver, quite surprised by what he saw. "It's not even from last year."

"June seventh, 1996," Jackson announced unemotionally, as if he had a hunch about what we might find.

"That's more than *seventeen years ago!*" I was stunned.

Oliver shook his head, more confused than ever. "Why

are our bodies freaking out when we weren't even born back then?"

He wanted to know and so did I. I looked to Jackson for an explanation. I could tell by his poker-faced stare that he wasn't the least bit surprised by what we had just discovered.

# 10. SILENCE IS GOLDEN

We cruised through town in Jackson's Mustang. I sat in the front seat next to Jackson. Oliver was unhappily wedged in the backseat, muttering how he was starting to feel like the third wheel. It was nearly six p.m. and getting dark. Businesses were preparing to close for the night. Shoppers were heading home from the market with food for dinner. By all appearances it looked just like the end of another typical day in Barrington.

Jackson had insisted on driving Oliver and me home. I wasn't sure what he thought might happen between his house and our own, but Jackson didn't want us on the streets alone. Oliver was relieved—he said he was too exhausted to walk home. And I took any excuse to ride up front next to Jackson. I kept staring at his muscular thighs, which looked like they were about to rip through his worn jeans.

And it wasn't even over yet. There were still several hours to go before the effects of the pulse wore off. I planned on locking myself in my bedroom until morning. By then it would hopefully be safe enough to face the world without the risk of disappearing. Even though I had managed to keep myself "whole" since school had ended that afternoon, I knew I wasn't fully in control of my body. In addition, there was also the not-so-insignificant matter of our recent discovery, which we vowed to keep quiet.

"Seventeen years seems so random," I declared, abruptly breaking the silence, trying to make some sense of everything.

"Maybe that's just because we don't see the full picture yet," Jackson countered.

I knew he was probably right. Despite hitting a brick wall as to knowing what caused the first pulse seventeen years ago, we weren't through digging. Not by a long shot. We also needed to figure out why the pulse had been suddenly reawakened six months ago.

"Notice anything strange?" Jackson asked. His eyes darted back and forth between looking out through the windshield and up to the rearview mirror.

Wondering what he meant, I peered out the passenger window and looked up and down the street. It took me a few seconds to notice what Jackson was talking about.

"Bar Tech Security," I replied, counting four patrol cars cruising along the street.

"They're everywhere," Jackson declared. "I counted three additional cars in just the last two blocks."

"Now that you mention it," Oliver concurred, turning around and staring out the rear window, "there were several cars hanging around school today. It didn't even register."

"They're like the Russian KGB. Lurking around every corner," Jackson proclaimed ominously. "Watching our every move."

"Not that you're being overly paranoid or anything . . . ," I retorted somewhat jokingly, hoping to lighten the mood and maybe my own apprehension. "What do you think they're looking for?"

"The question isn't *what*," Jackson answered back, firmly. "It's *who*."

After depositing Oliver at his front door, Jackson took me directly home. Normally I'd be thrilled to have some quality alone time with him. Just the two of us seated side by side in his cozy sports car. Unfortunately, today was not the ideal day for flirting. I was a bit preoccupied. We both were.

Along the way to my house we passed six more Bar Tech Security vehicles. Jackson didn't mention them and neither did I. There was no need. After each one drove by, he'd glance over at me. I'd feel his intense stare. It gave me goose bumps. When I'd look back at him, he'd abruptly turn away. Was he just concerned about me like a big brother? I had no idea what was going on inside his head.

We made it all the way to my street without incident.

Jackson pulled the Mustang into my driveway. I started to unfasten the seat belt when I felt Jackson grab my hand. I became flustered, not knowing how to react. He'd never done that before—touch me so forcefully like that. Was he trying to stop me from leaving? I felt my face burning up, turning bright red. I wanted him to kiss me. Did he want to kiss me? I had no idea what it meant.

Until Jackson said, "Looks like you have a visitor."

I shot him a befuddled look, not sure I heard him correctly. Then I followed his gaze out the windshield. Maya was sitting on my front steps, waiting for me to come home. I felt so deflated.

"What's she doing here?" I muttered, completely thrown to see her at my front door after the confrontation she and everyone had had in the school parking lot that day.

"I'm sure you're about to find out. Want me to hang around?"

Although I wanted him to stay, I shook my head and lied. "Thanks. It's probably better if I talk to Maya alone, given how she feels about you." Having Jackson there might complicate matters, not to mention be a major distraction for me. I was still too worried about what he thought of me. I needed to focus and be on my game when dealing with Maya.

"Right," Jackson replied. Was he disappointed or relieved? I had no clue.

227

I opened the car door and got out of the Mustang. "I'll text you later," I promised, peering in the window.

Jackson nodded, then backed out of the driveway and drove away.

I took a deep breath before proceeding up the front path. Maya stood up. Even from twenty feet away I could see her eyes were bloodshot. She'd definitely been crying.

"Sorry to show up like this," Maya said sheepishly, wiping her eyes as I approached the front door. "I didn't know where else to go." Despite her put-together appearance, the girl was seriously unraveling.

"Want to come inside?" I took out my house keys and unlocked the door. "My dad won't be home till seven."

She nodded. "Thanks." Then we stepped inside the house.

Maya followed me into the kitchen. "You want something to drink?" I opened the refrigerator. Dad had filled it with fruit and vegetable juice concoctions, various flavors of diet Hansen's, and liter bottles of mineral water.

"Water's fine," she said, looking around the house.

I poured two glasses and handed one to her. There was an awkward pause as we both sipped our drinks. I felt so self-conscious just sitting in my kitchen with Maya, acting like we were real friends yet neither of us knowing what to say. Maya was the first to speak.

"Chase and I had this huge fight. It was awful."

"Sorry." A pathetic response, but I really didn't know what else to say.

"We went for pizza after school," Maya continued. "On the way home he kept asking if something was wrong. Pressing me about going AWOL at school. He thinks I'm cheating on him, which is so ridiculous. I told him it wasn't true. He wouldn't listen. I don't know what came over me. Everything was fine and then it wasn't."

Maya's left hand balled up into a tight fist. I could tell she was wound even tighter than usual. So I trod carefully, fearing she might fly off the handle. I didn't need my father's kitchen to look like a tornado hit it. "What happened?"

"I'm not sure. All of a sudden there was this explosion of anger inside me. Out of nowhere. I felt like I wanted to rip Chase's head off. I ran out of the car before . . . I did something."

"Like in the classroom?" I gently reminded her.

She nodded. "I didn't want Chase to see me that way. I thought I could control it. My rage. But tree branches started snapping off, hitting his car. I even smashed his car window."

"I know how you feel," I declared. *"So do Oliver and Jackson."*

Maya sunk down into a chair at the kitchen table. "I'm really sorry about before. At school. I was a total bitch."

"Yeah, you were," I confessed with a little laugh, trying

to make a joke, as I sat down next to her. Fortunately, Maya laughed too. I quickly added, "You were also scared."

"I still am." She exhaled loudly.

"So am I," I admitted, touching her hand to let her know she was not alone.

"Truth is, I have been for a while," she admitted. "And I haven't been completely up front about everything."

"Up front about what?" I wasn't quite sure where she was going with this.

She took a deep breath before speaking. "This wasn't the first time all of *this* happened to me."

"You didn't just develop this ability today, did you?"

Maya shook her head guiltily. "It happened once before. I thought I was going crazy. But then it just . . . *went away*. The next day it was like nothing had ever happened. So I convinced myself that I had imagined it. That it was all just a bad dream. Instead of my body betraying me."

"Believe me: I know how that feels," I said with a reassuring smile.

"Well, that was then. And this is now. And now I'm ready," she declared, sitting up straight, staring back at me with a renewed sense of Maya purpose. As if she were preparing to perform at a cheerleading competition.

"Okay. What for?" I wasn't exactly sure what she meant.

"To join your crew," she proclaimed. "Become the Fourth Musketeer or X-Woman. Or whatever else you guys are doing. I mean, you want to find out why this is happening to us, right?"

This was a surprising turnaround. As Maya made her pitch, I thought that she could be a real asset to the team. She was in good with the school administration. Plus she could get us access to places Jackson, Oliver, and I might never be able to get into alone.

"Then the first thing you're going to have to learn how to do," I advised, "is control your ability."

"No way." Maya shook her head, adamant. "It freaks me out."

"You need to make friends with your power. *You can't let it control you.*"

"Thanks, Guru Nica," she snapped back, clasping her hands together and bowing her head as though she were praying. "You sound like one of those creepy self-help books. *Ten Days to a Happier Life.*"

I stood up, prepared to teach her a little lesson. "Watch and learn."

Maya sat back in her chair, arms crossed, waiting for something to happen.

That's when I disappeared right in front of her stunned eyes in about three seconds flat.

"*What the—?*" She bolted up out of her chair and looked around the kitchen in complete disbelief. "Nica? Where the hell are you?"

I decided to have a little fun with Maya. Just to prove my point, I snuck behind her and flicked her hair.

She yelped and spun around, looking for any sign of me. "Stop that! It's not funny."

"Yes it is," I replied, seemingly out of thin air. Then I began moving random objects around. Her chair. A glass. I even opened cabinets and the sliding glass door to the backyard, finally culminating with me whispering in Maya's ear, "Right behind you."

She turned around one last time as I reappeared. "Ta-da!"

"Okay, already. I get your point." Maya let out a reluctant sigh. "I'm in your hands."

I moved Maya's water glass across the kitchen table. "Okay, we'll start nice and easy. Concentrate on the glass and move it toward you."

"That's easy?"

"Yes. You can do it. It's all about focusing your energy up here"—I tapped her forehead—"and transferring it to the glass. The key is not to force it or *try too hard*. Remember how I had you do it at school?"

Maya nodded. "Breathe. Relax. And focus." Then she stared at the glass. Inhaled and exhaled slow, steady breaths.

I watched all the tension leave her body. One thing about Maya—she was the ultimate overachiever. So when she set her mind to a particular task, she performed it exceptionally well. After a few false starts she got the hang of it.

The glass glided slowly across the table, then moved around in figure eights.

"I did it. I moved the glass," Maya exclaimed giddily, completely surprised and excited by her ability. "What next?"

"Try opening the refrigerator door." I commanded.

Maya stared at the door and *whoosh*! It flew wide open like it was no big deal. She then looked at the chairs and tried rearranging them. First one at a time, lining them up in a straight line. Then shuffling them all around at once until they were back in the original positions where they started.

All of sudden Maya turned her head toward me. Before I knew what was happening, I had levitated off the floor. Thanks to Maya's power I was literally suspended four feet off the ground. Maya was giggling, having a grand old time playing with me.

"Okay, awesome display," I told her, giving her props. "You got the hang. Now put me down, girl." But Maya was intent on having her fun with me—maybe even teaching me a lesson. She spun me around a few more times for good measure before finally dropping me on my feet.

"That what you had in mind?" Maya asked, plopping in her chair, totally spent. "By the way, do you have any junk food in this health mecca of yours? I'm famished. And I don't want tofu or carrot wafers whatever."

I laughed. "How does caramel popcorn sound?"

"Like you read my mind." Her eyes lit up as I went over to the pantry and pulled out an unopened bag of caramel popcorn that was hidden behind the healthy snacks. As far as I could tell, it was my dad's only unhealthy indulgence. I figured he'd understand me consoling a friend in her time of need. "So, why us?" Maya asked, suddenly getting serious.

"No clue."

"And you guys have no idea what's causing it either?"

"No," I confessed. "We don't."

"What does your dad say? I mean he's a doctor and all."

"Nothing," I replied matter-of-factly, as we sat back down at the table with the popcorn. "I haven't told him anything yet."

"Why not? Shouldn't we be telling *someone* what's going on?" she wondered, ripping into the bag and grabbing a handful of the sticky caramel treat.

"It's probably best to keep a low profile for the time being," I answered cryptically.

"Why? What's gonna happen to us?" Maya challenged me with a raised eyebrow.

"You know those blood tests my dad does at school? I think he might be sharing the results with Richard Cochran."

"With Chase's father?" Maya reacted, really upset. "Are you sure?"

"Yeah," I nodded reluctantly. "Pretty sure."

"Your dad drew my blood. Why would Mr. Cochran care

about our blood tests?" Maya asked, genuinely baffled by the news.

"I doubt it's because he's looking for donors to the annual blood drive," I remarked. "Bar Tech is involved in all sorts of cutting-edge scientific research. Most of it highly secretive."

"What's he using the information for?"

"We don't know," I confessed. "But there are definitely strange things Jackson and Oliver have uncovered too. Going all the way back to Dana's disappearance." I filled her in on the specifics. And how our parents shut us down whenever we asked any questions. "When I tried talking to my dad about all those birds dying, he just dismissed it as if it was no big deal."

"I'm a terrible liar," Maya remarked. "My parents will know something's up with me. I talk to them about everything."

"Not anymore," I insisted. "Just be like other kids and keep your mouth shut. Not a word to anyone. Not even Chase. It's the only way."

"To what?"

"Find out what's really going on in this town."

Maya left my house a few minutes before my dad was due home. She hugged me and thanked me once more for being her friend and letting her into "the club," such as it was. Considering the wild events of the day Maya was in remarkably good spirits. Then again it might have just been a major sugar rush from all that caramel popcorn she scarfed down.

"Knowing I'm not totally alone . . . helps," she acknowledged appreciatively.

"Text me—if you need anything." I realized there was a genuinely cool girl underneath all Maya's intenseness.

Maya nodded, then walked out the front door down toward the sidewalk. I watched her until she turned the corner. As long as she could maintain her calm and not get upset or angry with anyone, she'd be okay until the effects wore off. Of course, that was true for all of us.

"I heard you were at school today," I brashly announced to my father while we were eating dinner. "Assisting the nurse again?"

My dad had picked up a roast chicken at the market along with couscous and green bean salad. I barely had much of an appetite (okay, I'd helped Maya finish off the caramel popcorn) but did my best to eat enough so that I wouldn't call too much attention to that—or to my prickly mood. I was annoyed before he said anything, because I knew he wasn't honest with me.

"I help out Mrs. Robbins when I can," he answered evenly, without a hint of emotion.

*Liar!* I couldn't believe my father could lie so easily. "Seems like the kids around here need an awful lot of checkups," I jabbed back.

"An ounce of prevention is worth a pound of cure," he responded with a knowing wink. "It's important to stay pro-active."

"Does it have anything to do with that research study you're conducting?" I asked, trying to play it cool and casual.

"Does what?" he answered, seemingly immersed in removing all the skin from his chicken breast before eating it.

"Whatever it is you're hoping to prevent," I replied. "What's your study about anyway? Sexually transmitted dis-eases?" I couldn't believe that I was being as direct as I was and confrontational.

"No, it's not about anything like that." My dad shot me an exasperated look, unamused. "Why the sudden interest, anyway?"

"I'm just curious why you need to take everyone's blood." I tossed out that hot-button question to see if it got a rise out of him.

"If you must know, I'm conducting a genomic cluster study. Not all the nucleotides within the human genome are part of our genes. In fact parts of our DNA don't serve any obvious purpose. This so-called 'junk DNA' may contain unrecognized functional elements."

"Functional as in what?" I wanted specifics. My father's explanation sounded plausible but also highly suspicious. Maybe there really was a marker in our genes indicating that the pulse had affected us.

Before I could press him further, his cell phone buzzed. He glanced at the display.

"Sorry, honey," he said, getting up from the table. "The hospital." And he exited the kitchen to take the call.

I crept into the hall to eavesdrop and see if he was lying to me again. But when I heard my dad ordering medication, I realized he was in fact talking to one of the hospital nurses.

I barely saw my dad the rest of the evening. He spent most of the night sequestered in his study on the phone. I tried to spy but could barely hear more than his soft murmuring behind the thick wooden doors. Okay, just my luck—my dad was a quiet talker.

Left to my own devices, I texted Maya to make sure she was okay and hadn't suddenly changed her mind or done something impulsive like blab to Chase or her parents. *Ty no problem w/rents*, she texted back. Maya had thankfully survived dinner with her parents and younger brother without any unwanted drama. Relieved, I reported the good news back to Jackson and Oliver. Jackson got annoyed that I'd made a unilateral decision to tell Maya what was going on. He thought she was unpredictable and untrustworthy. I apologized, not wanting Jackson to be angry with me. I reminded him that a few hours ago he'd made a big pitch for Maya to join us. I promised Jackson that I'd keep tabs on her. She'd be a valuable ally.

With everyone safe and sound for the time being, I plopped my head back on my pillow with an exhausted sigh. It was the first time all day I'd let my guard down. I glanced at the clock on the nightstand. It was nearly eleven p.m. In a few minutes I'd be back to "normal" (whatever that was?). Last night's pulse would be old news—ancient history. I held both my hands out in front of me and stared at them, focusing all my concentration on making them disappear for one last time. After all, there was no guarantee that there would ever be another pulse again.

My right hand began to shimmer as intense heat surged up through my arm into my fingers. I watched in amazement as my thumb disappeared. My other fingers then followed, evaporating into nothingness along with the palm of my hand, all the way down to my wrist. My right hand had completely vanished. It felt both scary and awesome to be able to control this ability, I had to admit. I couldn't help but smile.

My cell phone rang. I let out a tiny yelp I was so startled by the noise. My right hand instantly reappeared as I fumbled around my bed for the phone. The call was from a blocked number. I almost let it go straight to voice mail, but at the last minute I answered. Part of me hoped it might be Jackson.

"*Nica?* Is that you, honey?" The connection was awful, crackling with a lot of static.

"Mom?" I replied, totally shocked and flustered. Of all the nights Lydia could pick to call and check in.

"I'm using someone's satellite phone. So I only have a few minutes. How are you? Is school okay? How're you adjusting? How's your dad? *Tell me everything.*" She sounded unusually concerned, even worried.

"Everything's fine, Mom." I clenched my teeth together and lied even though I was dying to tell her the truth. "Though it's hard being in your shadow."

"What do you mean?" There was a trace of defensiveness in her tone.

"Believe it or not, everyone still remembers you," I quipped back. "My friends' parents, even my guidance counselor, Julie Henderson. You never mentioned how popular you were when you lived here."

There was a long pause before my mother responded.

"What can I say, honey? Your mother's a memorable person." She was trying to make a joke, but I detected a definite unease in her voice—an uncomfortable edginess.

"Apparently," I replied. "I'm surprised you ever left."

There was another uncomfortable pause.

"What's wrong, Nica?" My mother's voice suddenly took on a maternal, concerned tone. She knew me too well. "*Has something—?*"

"*Nothing,*" I blurted back, way too fast, trying to regain my equilibrium. "Nothing's wrong. I'm just still *adjusting.*

And I'm really tired. Long day. Too much homework. All thanks to you," I kidded, desperate to keep things light, even though my stomach was churning from lying to her.

"My little student. How are the kids? Any cute guys?" I heard an uncharacteristic urgency in her voice. She really wanted to dish—more than usual—but I refused to give her the satisfaction. I was still pissed at her for shipping me off here.

"How about *you*?" I deflected the question, throwing it back at her. "What's it like on the bottom of the world? Any cute scientists?"

"Seven months in this freezer with nowhere to hide? Dating's the furthest thing from my mind." She laughed and then so did I. Lydia might have dropped the ball on a lot of things—but she was always professional when it came to work and her writing assignments.

"Yeah. Mine too." I missed my mother's infectious laugh. Suddenly I found myself fighting back tears. I pinched my arm really hard so that I'd stop being weepy.

"Oh, honey. I miss you so much. Listen, I've got to go. Battery is running low. Call you when I can. Love you!" *Click*. And then Lydia was gone. That was my flighty mother.

"Bye. Love you too," I dejectedly muttered back to dead silence.

I hung up and tossed the phone across the bed in anger. Lydia's call didn't make me feel better. If anything I felt more stressed and upset than before. I knew I wouldn't be able to fall asleep for hours. *Thanks a lot, Mom.*

The next morning I woke up with a massive headache, just as Jackson had predicted. A dull, throbbing pain across my forehead.

Unfortunately the two aspirin I popped seemed to have no immediate effect on the pounding inside my head. Not feeling up to walking, I rode silently in the front seat of the Prius while Dad shuttled me to school. He didn't say much either, just stared out the windshield deep in thought. There we were, father and daughter, seated barely two feet apart and yet both retreating to our own private worlds. I suspected our silences might be connected. Did Dad think the same thing?

Halfway to school he finally spoke. "You know, I've been meaning to ask you how Jackson Winters is doing."

"What do you mean?" I was thrown by his question and suddenly on my guard. I didn't remember mentioning Jackson to my dad. Ever. Now all of a sudden he was quizzing me about Jackson.

"You guys are friends, aren't you?" my dad asked quite pointedly.

"I see him around school." My entire body tensed up. "Why are you asking?" And who was gossiping about my personal life to my father? A teacher? One of the kids?

"I don't know how much you know about Jackson," my dad responded diplomatically, "and his obsession with Dana Fox. But he's a *troubled* boy. And I just don't want you getting mixed up in something you can't handle."

"Like what, Dad?" I couldn't stop myself from feeling angry and defensive. I opened up my bag and pretended to look for something, not wanting him to know that he was pressing my buttons.

"Like breaking curfew again, for one," he reminded me. "Or getting into trouble with the authorities like Jackson does. Just focus on your schoolwork."

"No problem. I got it covered," I answered curtly, turning away from him and staring out the window, trying to will my throbbing headache into oblivion. But I couldn't stop my brain from obsessing over the fact that Jackson had been right.

*They were watching him. And they were watching me, too.*

By the time I entered my first class, I felt marginally better, the extra-strength aspirin finally working its magic on me. Maya, on the other hand, staggered into the room, looking like she'd had a sleepless night.

"Everything all right?" I asked as she walked unsteadily by my desk.

"Hardly. I've got this epic headache," she whispered in my ear. Fortunately, there were a dozen conversations going on simultaneously, so no one was paying any attention to us.

"Me too. Jackson says they're growing pains." I reached into my bag and handed her a couple of aspirin as she sat at the desk behind mine. "He and Oliver had them . . . *after*."

"Lucky us," she grumbled before chasing back the pills with a sip of water from her ecofriendly personalized bottle.

Just then the bell rang. All conversation ceased as everyone turned to face the front of the room. Mr. Ghiradelli launched into a lecture about the seventeenth-century English philosopher Thomas Hobbes and his "social contract" theory.

"All societies agree to abide by common rules and accept corresponding duties to protect themselves from violence and other kinds of harm," Mr. Ghiradelli pontificated as he strolled up and down the aisles. "Can anyone think of an example of how individuals give up some of their individual rights so that other people will cede theirs?" He looked around the room as Trent Hiroshi's hand shot up. Trent always had to be the first to volunteer and was definitely teacher's pet. "Trent?"

"Well, Mr. A. gives up his right to kill Mrs. B., as long as Mrs. B. does the same."

"Precisely. This results in the establishment of civilized society." Ghiradelli then blathered on about how the state assumed control of the police force and the military to protect us from anarchy.

It got me thinking. Was that what had happened in Barrington? Did something so awful occur (the pulse?) that made the town impose a curfew and round-the-clock private security, among other things? Were our lives being controlled by a secret social contract? The only way to know for sure was to find out what had happened here seventeen years ago. There must be someone in this stupid town who would talk—someone who would tell us the truth.

After first-period World History I went down to Mrs. Henderson's office instead of my next class. She was working at her computer and sipping tea out of a red-and-white Bar Tech mug. I remembered that at one time she'd been a newcomer like me. She wasn't born and raised here like so many residents. She had only lived in Barrington since marrying her husband eighteen years ago. I also remembered how apprehensive and cautious she'd seemed when talking about the town.

"Mrs. Henderson?" I politely knocked on the door, which was open.

She looked up, surprised to see me standing in her doorway. "Nica. What's up?" She glanced at the clock. "Don't you have English now?"

"Yeah, I just needed to talk for a minute."

"Okay," she said, setting down the mug, suddenly a bit guarded. "What's on your mind?"

"Remember the other day?" I asked, stepping into her office. "You said how this town was . . . *different?*"

At that moment I saw her entire body stiffen. "All I meant was . . . Barrington's a small town . . . with small-town values. *Why are you asking?*"

"Well, I guess I didn't realize how *different* things were here," I replied lightly, my mouth suddenly going dry. "And since we're both kind of like outsiders—not growing up here—I thought maybe you could give me an honest perspective. Answer some questions." I smiled even though my heart was practically racing I was so nervous.

Mrs. Henderson stood up. "Listen, how about we chat after school? In the meantime you really should get to class."

"Sure," I replied, quickly gathering up my things and leaving her office. Bewildered as to why she'd just blown me off like a frigid Antarctic wind.

Six hours later I stood in the corridor outside the administrative offices, pacing back and forth, waiting for Mrs. Henderson to return. It was 3:10 p.m. and school had finished twenty-five minutes earlier. After weeks of wanting to chat about my future, Mrs. Henderson suddenly seemed to be avoiding me. I was pissed at her for standing me up. And I was also annoyed with Jackson for appearing to be right once again about something else.

"What makes you think Henderson will ever fess up anything?" Jackson had challenged when we'd met underneath the field bleachers during lunch. "Or that you can even trust her?"

"I just have this feeling." Or maybe I was just a glutton for punishment.

"You ever think that maybe she's the one who's been playing double agent with your dad about us?" Jackson raised a valid concern.

"It could be any teacher, or even a student for that matter. Besides, I just don't think Mrs. Henderson would do that. I just don't think she's the informant type." I dismissed his concern with a wave of my hand. "Maybe I'm being naïve, but I believe that Mrs. Henderson wants to share something with me."

"Well, if you're so intent on talking to her, maybe I should go with you as backup," Jackson proposed. "I just don't like you meeting with her alone after hours."

Jackson seemed genuinely concerned about my safety—*about me*. Which thrilled me to bits and made my heart thump and legs wobbly, but which also kind of freaked me out. So instead of playing the vulnerable maiden who needed protection, I went into Nica's cynical I'm-too-cool-nothing-fazes-me insecure mode.

"She's a high school guidance counselor, Jackson. Not a CIA operative," I snarked. "What's the worst that could happen to me?" I glibly joked, not thinking.

"I'd hate to find out," Jackson snapped back at me, angrier than I'd ever seen him get before. He glared at me with those intense eyes that made me want to die.

"Sorry, I didn't . . ." But Jackson stalked off before I could sputter out an apology. I felt like such an idiot. Dana was still MIA, and I'd idiotically joked about getting whacked. I was so stupid; no wonder he had no interest in me.

As I waited for Mrs. Henderson to show up, I heard the squeaking of rubber soles on linoleum approaching. Mr. Garcia, one of the other guidance counselors, trudged over in his worn brown Rockports to inform me that Mrs. Henderson had already left for the day. Would I like to leave a message? *Yeah, next time don't stand me up.* Instead I respectfully said thanks but no thanks, and I went to the nearest exit.

"You were right. She stood me up. Big surprise," I confessed with a self-deprecating laugh, leaving Jackson a rambling message on his voice mail. I was halfway home, walking at a fast clip along Main Street. I noticed a Bar Tech Security vehicle cruising down the street. Slowly. I barely gave it a glance, all too preoccupied with getting out my inept apology. Besides, those guys were all over Barrington.

"Anyway, about before . . . ," I continued, nervously babbling on to Jackson's voice mail, "please just ignore what I said. I mean, I do most of the time . . ."

But I realized that this security car was different. *It was following me.*

"Jackson, listen." I took a breath, trying to keep cool and not panic while I picked up my pace. "I'm in town and I think I'm being followed. By one of those Bar Tech goon cars . . ."

I was about to make a run down a side street when I collided with a tall, well-dressed man in a suit. I dropped my phone on the sidewalk.

"Sorry." I muttered, making my excuses and trying to sidestep the guy and retrieve my phone.

But the man picked up my phone first. And held it in his hand as he spoke to me. "Are you Nica Ashley?" His voice sounded eerily familiar. That's when I really looked at him and realized I recognized the guy.

"What?" I replied, discombobulated, wanting to get my phone back from him, totally thrown off my game.

"Dr. Ashley's daughter." The commanding voice belonged to none other than Chase's father, Richard Cochran, CEO of Bar Tech. The man my dad shared private medical information with.

"The one and only," I quipped, a bit freaked out that he knew who I was. My heart was pounding, and I felt adrenaline pumping throughout my body. All I wanted to do was get away.

"I've been wanting to meet you for some time," Cochran

said charmingly, while his intense dark-brown eyes practically bored a hole right into my brain. "My son speaks very highly of you." He still had my phone in his hand. Jackson's name was illuminated on the screen. The entire conversation was being recorded.

"Oh. Well, Chase is an awesome guy. But then you probably know that already." I felt myself babbling, but I was desperate to get my phone back before he saw Jackson's name.

"I've been telling your dad he should bring you by the house for dinner," he pressed, moving closer to me. "I'd really like to know you better. Hear all about your world travels. And how you're adjusting to Barrington."

"Dinner sounds great." My eyes darted up and down the block for that security car, which was now idling across the street. Was it waiting to take me away?

A wave of intense paranoia washed over me. Suddenly this run-in with Cochran didn't seem so *random*. I had a sickening realization that Cochran might've been tailing me the whole time. Thoughts of all Jackson's Dana Fox missing posters filled my head. I might have had the ability to disappear, but I didn't want to vanish like she did.

I had to get out of there.

"Can I drop you somewhere?" He pointed to a sleek black Mercedes sedan with tinted windows parked near the Bar Tech Security vehicle.

"No, thanks. I'm actually meeting friends," I lied, completely unnerved by the situation. A lame excuse, but all I could think of in the moment. No way was I getting in a car alone with him. "But I'll need my phone back first." I reached out. He smiled and handed my phone back to me.

And then I hurried off, my phone clutched in my hand, trying not to totally lose my shit in the middle of town. I could feel Cochran's intense eyes watching my every move, as well as that Bar Tech car lying in wait for me. I had no idea how I was going to escape their watch until I remembered that Violetta's Pizzeria had a rear exit.

I made a beeline through the front entrance of Violetta's as if I were going there to meet up with my friends. Luckily, the place was hopping with kids ordering slices, calzones, and drinks. I rushed through the pizzeria without drawing much notice from anyone except for Mr. Bluni, who happened to be there again enjoying a postschool slice with his teaching cronies. Although I avoided his table, he still watched me racing like a bat out of hell toward the rear of the restaurant. I knew I looked suspicious, but I wasn't about to stop and make up an excuse to my biology teacher. I just had to get out of there. Once I reached the back door, I cracked it ajar and scanned up and down the alleyway. No sign of either Cochran's Mercedes or Bar Tech Security.

Weaving around overfilled Dumpsters and parked cars I maneuvered my way through the alley toward a side street with several smaller shops (locksmith and dry cleaner among them) that ran parallel to Main Street. I dashed down the block, head down, praying I wasn't being followed.

I quickly crossed the street at the intersection, then bolted down the next block and found myself hurrying down an unfamiliar residential street of newer split-level homes. Keeping up my pace but finally breathing a little easier, I redialed Jackson but got his voice mail again. I left a brief message that I was okay and then hung up. Frustrated and needing to talk with someone about what just happened, I started dialing Oliver, just as a deep-sea-blue BMW coupe pulled up alongside me. I glanced over, hoping it was just a random car driving up the street. But I got this sinking feeling in the pit of my stomach when I realized that the car was definitely following me. I hadn't escaped Bar Tech. My throat was suddenly so parched. I desperately needed some water, but more importantly I desperately needed help. My biological "fight or flight" response kicked in. I had to run. I scoped out the immediate neighborhood. The street was deserted. No one was around. As I was preparing to make a mad dash through the yard of this charmless brick colonial, I heard my name being called.

"Nica." It came from inside the car. The tinted passenger window rolled down, and I could finally see the mystery driver.

*"Mrs. Henderson?"* I was completely taken aback to see

her sitting there. Was this a coincidence? Or just a trap to lure me? Paranoia and suspicion washed over me.

"Get in the car," she demanded, looking up and down the street.

*CLICK.* She unlocked the passenger door with a flick of a switch.

"You wanted to talk, right?" It was a question but it sounded like an order. "Hurry."

I stared at her, hesitant and not moving, trying to read a hidden agenda. Dare I trust her? I stepped off the curb and grabbed the handle, opening the door. Maybe I was deluding myself, but I had a gut feeling that Mrs. Henderson wanted to talk too (perhaps as much as I wanted to talk to her?). So I slid into the soft gray leather seat and strapped myself in with the safety belt.

Mrs. Henderson gave me a serious, poker-faced look before rolling the window back up. Then she shifted the car into gear, turned right at the first intersection, then sped up a winding street toward the hillier part of town. Neither of us said a word.

All the while my heart was beating so rapidly I thought I might pass out from anxiety. Was this the smartest thing I'd ever done? Or was it the dumbest?

## 11. THE INCIDENT

Mrs. Henderson parked the car on a dead-end street that backed onto a secluded wooded preserve. We were all alone. Chances were no one was going to accidentally stumble upon us.

"Certainly is private here," I remarked, secretly wondering if I could make a quick escape if I had to run.

She shifted her body in the seat to the right so that she could face me.

"Sorry for standing you up earlier, but talking at school wasn't the best idea," she stated guardedly. "So tell me what's troubling you?" She asked it calmly as if she were counseling me in her cozy office rather than huddled in her car in the middle of nowhere.

"Troubling me?" I took Jackson's advice and played it cagey. "You mean other than terrorism, global warming, and the ballooning deficit?"

"Listen to me, Nica," she responded with a serious expression. "We don't have much time to talk." She glanced out the rear window. "Exactly what is it you *think* you know?"

I chewed on my lower lip. Time to get real. It was now or never.

"The pulse," I blurted out. "I know about the pulse."

Mrs. Henderson's eyes grew wide with apprehension. "I was afraid of that. I should take you home." She was about to push the ignition button.

"No," I snapped, grabbing her hand. "You can't get me to fess up and then go all radio silent."

"I'm trying to protect you," she countered. "The less you know the better."

"Right. Protect the kids. Impose a curfew. Pretend nothing weird is happening in this town." I was really pissed. "Well, the train's already left the station, Mrs. Henderson. It's too late to bury my head in the sand."

She shut her eyes for a moment and exhaled before settling back into her seat. "What did your father say about it?"

"Nothing. I'm afraid to tell him anything. Or even my mother." She looked surprised by my admission.

"So why are you telling me?" Now she sounded angry.

"Because. You know what it's like moving here and trying to fit in. You know there are things about this town that are different from other towns. Like having the mandatory curfew, and all that private security. What are people worried about? What are they afraid of? It's the way people are not talking that's so suspicious. *You understand.*" I watched her expression soften considerably. I could tell I was getting through to her.

"Does anyone else know what you know?" She leveled her gaze at me.

"No," I replied, lying through my teeth. I wasn't about to incriminate Jackson or Oliver or Maya or tell her anything more before I knew more about her.

"Tell me what happened, everything," she ordered, clearly concerned. "I can't help you if you don't tell me."

"It was a few nights after I arrived," I said, reliving the experience in my mind. "My dad had to go back to the hospital after dinner. I had a bad case of cabin fever so I snuck out. I wasn't planning on staying out long. Next thing I knew it was after curfew." Mrs. Henderson listened attentively as I told her about my joyride culminating with the pulse. No mention was made of Jackson.

"How have you been feeling? Since the pulse." She was scrutinizing me.

"A little strange," I said, lying with an evasive shrug. "Mostly scared."

Any other time I might've been a little freaked out by how good I was getting at lying. At that moment my conscience was taking a backseat to my curiosity and self-preservation.

"Everything's going to be all right," she declared, doing her guidance-counselor best to reassure me. It wasn't exactly working.

"What's causing it? The pulse?" I pressed for more answers.

"No one knows for sure."

"Is it connected to what happened here seventeen years ago?" This was the moment I'd been waiting for, and it provoked a big reaction from her.

Mrs. Henderson silently sat there. Her mouth hung open in surprise and astonishment until she gathered her thoughts and finally spoke.

"Who told you about *that*?" She barely talked above a whisper, and I caught her looking through the rearview mirror. It was evident that our conversation was making her feel uneasy.

"No one told me anything about it." I perched on the edge of my seat.

"Then how did you find out?" She locked eyes with me.

"Weather charts," I replied. She looked confused, so I spelled it out for her. "I discovered an anomaly in the electromagnetic radiation index from the nights when the pulse struck. Four separate incidents in seven months. I searched back further. The first anomaly occurred seventeen years ago."

"June seventh." She nodded, corroborating what Jackson, Oliver, and I had discovered.

"What happened that night?" I was not going to leave until I had some hard answers.

Mrs. Henderson took a deep breath and exhaled before

she spoke. "I'd met my husband, Ben, while vacationing in Italy after college. We had one of those whirlwind courtships. Next thing I know, I'm married and living in Barrington. He worked for the US government as an aerospace engineer. He helped me get a job in human resources."

"You worked for the government?" I was surprised to hear this fact.

"Yes. They had a top-secret research facility just outside town. Anyway, at 10:37 p.m. on the evening of June seventh, something went terribly wrong. There was an accident at the facility."

"Like an explosion?"

"No, not exactly. In fact I never heard a blast. Neither did my husband, or anyone else for that matter. There just was this *unexplained* spark of greenish light over the town. It only lasted for a few seconds and then abruptly disappeared."

"That must've been the first pulse." This confirmed what Jackson, Oliver, and I thought.

"I didn't know what it was. No one did," Mrs. Henderson continued. "Only that it felt as if a powerful charge had passed through my body. Everyone was terrified. Was this pulse a vibration from beneath the surface of the earth? A meteor? Alien contact?"

"So what did you do?" I wanted her to keep talking.

"Emergency workers in hazmat suits descended on the

town. The government facility was immediately shut down. The town was quarantined." She paused, and then lowered her voice to almost a whisper. "Six employees who worked in the lab vanished."

"You mean they just disappeared?"

"Without a trace," she nodded. "No one—not even their families—ever knew if they died in the incident or were horribly injured. They were just gone. A few months later Bar Tech took over the facility." Her left hand gripped the steering wheel so tightly that her knuckles were practically white.

"And now it's their headquarters," I acknowledged. "With Richard Cochran in charge."

"He's rebuilt and expanded Bar Tech through the years to accommodate their growing businesses. They manufacture everything from scientific satellites to medical equipment. They do business on every continent. Their influence is truly global."

"But why didn't anyone ever talk about it? Why didn't the media report what happened?" I was completely baffled by the lack of coverage.

"Because the media never knew about it. We were all paid a lot of money to keep silent and never speak of what had happened," she ashamedly confessed.

"And if you didn't comply?" I asked, unnerved by this disturbing tale.

Mrs. Henderson paused before answering. "The few who

protested or refused to go along vanished with no forwarding addresses. A matter of national security, we were told. But my husband and I got the message loud and clear: Keep your mouths shut and we'll take care of you, or else." I could see the fear was still in her eyes after all these years.

"So you were all bribed to go along with it and keep quiet just so you could live the good life." I was horrified by what she was telling me.

"You have to remember, we were all living in fear back then. It seemed a small price to pay for peace of mind," she insisted. "Jobs in Barrington were suddenly plentiful. A curfew was imposed and security tightened. We all tried to go on with our lives, most choosing to forget. Others had a harder time."

"Like my mother, who left town," I remarked, suddenly understanding why Lydia had been so eager to leave when I was a child.

"Years went by. There seemed to be no harmful after-effects—medical or otherwise. The pulse never happened again. Life returned to normal. So much so that I . . . we forgot there ever was a pulse."

"Until one night seven months ago when the pulse mysteriously returned," I interjected. *And Jackson's girlfriend, Dana Fox, disappeared*, I thought. For some reason I sensed that it would be dangerous for me to say that aloud.

Mrs. Henderson suddenly sat up in her seat and pressed the ignition button. "We need to go."

I turned around and saw what had suddenly spooked her. A Bar Tech Security vehicle was cruising up the street. Mrs. Henderson quickly turned the car around the cul-de-sac and then proceeded down the road, passing the security car along the way. The uniformed driver glanced over in our direction but decided not to follow us. Mrs. Henderson kept her cool and drove toward the nearest intersection.

All the while, I tried not to flip out. My mind struggled with the awful knowledge that the town had not only sold us out but our futures, too. We were left with a dark legacy that was not our fault.

We arrived at my house a few minutes later. Mrs. Henderson seemed down, almost depressed. There was more I wanted to know, but I knew it would have to wait for another time. Still, I couldn't get out of the car without at least asking if she had a theory.

"So why is it happening again now? After all these years?"

Mrs. Henderson shook her head and looked at me. "I don't know. My husband refuses to discuss it with me," she admitted with trepidation. "Just told me not to worry. Said Bar Tech has always done right by this town. So I'm trying not to worry, like everyone else." No matter how much she claimed otherwise, it was obviously weighing as much on her mind as it was on mine.

As I reached for the door handle to exit the car, Mrs.

Henderson touched my shoulder. I turned around to face her.

"You won't say anything about all this," she said, almost pleading with me. "To anyone. *Especially your dad.*"

"Not a word," I vowed, knowing I would violate this promise as soon as I got in the house. I knew I had to tell Jackson and Oliver. They had a right to know what I had found out. It impacted all of us. And I also knew that if the situation were reversed, they would definitely confide in me.

The question I wrestled with was how to tell them. Mrs. Henderson's paranoia had started to affect me. I started dialing Jackson's phone number on my cell when I abruptly ended the call. No way could I risk saying anything that might expose our secrets. Who knew if we were being watched or taped? If only we had a secret code or way to communicate that no one else understood.

I pondered my options while I nuked a chicken burrito. All this deception made me incredibly hungry. I wondered if it was just my teenage metabolism, or did all spies have huge appetites? As I wolfed down the cheesy mess, I had an epiphany.

I immediately texted Jackson: *Science project crisis. Meet at overlook? Tell Oliver?* Not the most brilliant encryption ever, but I had a feeling Jackson would catch on. Less than a minute later he replied: *On my way.*

• • •

The three of us met up thirty minutes later at the same remote overlook where I'd run into Jackson the night of the pulse. It was the perfect hideaway. No annoying Bar Tech Security vehicles roaming around or getting up in our business.

"Why the 911?" Oliver asked as he hopped out of Jackson's Mustang. "I was in the middle of an awesome Gears of War match."

"Sorry to spoil your geek-out, but I just had a very enlightening tête-à-tête with Henderson," I announced, much to Oliver and Jackson's surprise. "You won't believe the secrets she told me."

"Enlighten away," Jackson responded, in a much better mood, eager to hear my report. He had a little grin, as if he was proud of my work.

Barely taking a moment to breathe, I spewed out all the secrets surrounding "the incident" and Bar Tech and its cover-up that Mrs. Henderson had confided to me that afternoon. Neither Jackson nor Oliver made a sound while I spoke. They listened with rapt attention, absorbing even the smallest detail. I finished recounting the conversation, and we all just looked at each other.

"Holy shit," Oliver muttered, in total shock. "It's like we're living in some toxic dump."

"Except without any evidence," I reminded them. "No physical proof that anything ever happened."

"Who'd ever guess that the safest town in America is a virtual prison?" Jackson angrily observed, staring out at Barrington down below.

"Our own parents knew all this and kept silent." Oliver cringed.

"Money makes the world go round, guys," I cynically stated, thinking about my dad. "Depressing, but true." Was that why my dad cooperated with Cochran? Just for money? That didn't seem like the dad I knew and loved. Or did he have some other reason? Whatever the truth, I felt sick and betrayed.

"Why us?" Oliver shook his head, clearly undone by all the revelations. "Why are we the *only ones* who've changed? I mean, Nica just moved here. It doesn't make sense."

"Actually, I was born here too," I confessed. "My mother moved away with me when I was two."

"Even so. Most kids in this town were born here," refuted Jackson, "and except for Maya, I think we might be the only ones."

"We may not know why it's happening to us," I interjected, "but it seems more than possible that Bar Tech is involved." I then turned to Jackson. "But you've suspected that for a while, haven't you?"

Jackson nodded and ran his hands through his hair, obviously struggling with something.

"Does it have to do with Dana's disappearance?" I asked

delicately, hoping it would open the door for Jackson to confide in us.

"Yeah, I think it does," he admitted somewhat reluctantly. "Dana had been interning at Bar Tech for a few months. Thought it would look great for college, working at a big Fortune 500 corporation. Anyway, next thing she's hanging out in Cochran's office a couple days a week after school."

"How did that happen?" I asked, taking a seat next to Oliver on top of a large rock outcropping.

"Apparently, Chase mentioned something to his dad about Dana interning at Bar Tech. He called her in for a general meet and greet. She wasn't expecting anything other than a hello, but she obviously impressed him enough that he gave her a shot."

"To work in his office?" I sounded a bit skeptical.

"Dana was like that—she impressed everybody," Oliver interjected.

*Of course she did*, I thought, as a little mocking voice snarked in my head. It was obvious that Dana had been Miss Perfect. Everything I was definitely not, nor could ever be. Suddenly I felt ashamed. I couldn't believe I was feeling jealous of a missing girl I'd never met. I tried to redirect my focus to the here and now. "So what exactly was Dana doing for Cochran?"

"Mostly bullshit office stuff. E-mails, phone, answering correspondence. Nothing major. But then one day something happened. She wouldn't say what it was, but she was acting really weird. Paranoid. When I pressed her about what was wrong, she shut me down. Insisted she couldn't talk about it."

"But you're positive it had something to do with Bar Tech." I always had the feeling Jackson knew more than he was letting on. And now he was finally coming clean with us.

"Absolutely," Jackson affirmed without hesitation. "All Dana would say was that she'd been in the office late. Cochran had just returned from some secret Asian trip. She accidentally overheard him talking to someone about some classified government research project."

I locked eyes with Jackson. I didn't need much prompting to believe that the secret project Dana had found out about was connected to what was happening to all of us.

"What happened then?" Oliver chimed in, perched on the edge of the rock, riveted.

"The pulse happened," Jackson replied sadly. "Dana showed up at my house late that night, after curfew. She was a mess. Had skipped school that day and hadn't been able to eat or sleep. She was convinced that Cochran knew about what she'd overheard. Because he'd been asking her all sorts of questions that day."

Jackson paused a beat, steeling himself with the memory of that night before continuing with his story. "Dana and I were in my car. I was trying to calm her down. I thought she was exaggerating. Then all of a sudden . . . *wham* . . . it hit. Like a sonic boom, only so close my body was literally vibrating from the force of energy."

"What did you guys do?" I pushed, wanting to hear the full story.

"Nothing at first," Jackson said. "We sat there, stunned. Not saying a word. Then, after a few minutes, when there were no alarms or fire trucks or sirens, I assumed it was just some weird lightning storm. So I drove Dana back to her house. Then I came home and went to sleep. Next morning everything seemed okay. Except for the frantic message I got from Dana on my way to school."

"What did she say?" Oliver inquired with an awful sense of foreboding.

"Just that she was freaked out because Bar Tech Security had shown up at her house, wanting to question her. But that I should meet her in the quad at school before first period."

"And she never showed," I added somberly.

Jackson shook his head, confirming the fact. "I should've taken her more seriously. I should've done something."

I really began to comprehend how much pain and guilt Jackson had been carrying around the last seven months.

"When did you know that Dana wasn't making things up?" I asked. "What changed your mind?"

"When bolts of electricity shot out of my fingers and

nearly killed my neighbor's dog," he admitted solemnly, looking at his hands as if they were deadly weapons. "The day that Dana . . . *disappeared* . . ." Jackson continued, "I went down the rabbit hole and didn't want to come out. The next time the pulse hit, I became angrier and angrier and my powers grew stronger and stronger. Which only left me feeling more and more isolated and out of control. Then you arrived." He stared at me meaningfully, as though he really cared about me.

Oliver noticed the look. I looked away, my face burning up from embarrassment, not knowing what to say or if this was the right moment to say it.

"Is there any doubt now that Bar Tech's fingerprints are all over this? That they're deeply involved in what's happening here?" Oliver asked, looking at Jackson, then at me.

"None," I responded, secretly thanking Oliver for changing the topic. "And that's the reason you both have to promise not to say anything to anyone. We've got to protect Mrs. Henderson."

"What about Maya?" Oliver asked. "Doesn't she need to know?"

"Eventually," Jackson asserted. "She's dealing with enough crap right now."

"Yeah. Chase is suspicious enough as it is," I concurred. "No need to make it any harder on Maya than necessary."

We all nodded and silently agreed to keep things confidential. What we had discovered was incredibly explosive. Who knew what the repercussions might be if it the truth got out? Or what might happen to us?

My dad came home early from the hospital that night. Luckily, I'd made it back from our clandestine rendezvous minutes before he walked through the door. I was already holed up in my bedroom pretending to be doing homework when Dad appeared at the door.

"Hey," I said, barely looking up from my books.

"Feel like sushi?"

"Sure," I replied with a tight smile. "You know what I like." Then I buried my head back in my books, not wanting to reveal how disappointed and betrayed I was really feeling about him.

Dad suddenly tossed my coat at me. "C'mon, we're going out. My treat."

I hadn't planned on this. "Can't we just get takeout? I've got so much work." I was in no mood to have to go out and be social with my dad. I didn't think I could cope with my paranoia and with his prying questions.

"Nonsense," he said, grabbing my hand and pulling me up to my feet. "An hour won't kill you."

My father gave me no choice. I had to go. I swallowed down my anger and got into the Prius, hoping I could make it through dinner with my dad without making a scene.

• • •

Dinner at Sushi Roku surprisingly turned out to be a welcome distraction: an island of family normalcy in an otherwise crazy universe. We sat at the sushi bar with a dozen other people, enjoying delicious sashimi and green tea ice cream. Dad was in a particularly talkative mood, asking all about how school was going. He was so sweet and caring that I couldn't reconcile that this was the same man who was sharing medical secrets with Chase's father. I'd been feeling so distant from him and upset that it was actually comforting to just be his little girl again and let him be my father again. If only for one night.

As we left the restaurant and walked out to the car, my dad started asking me about Chase. I was thrown. It was completely out of the blue.

"What about him?" I replied warily, wondering where this line of questioning was headed.

"Are you guys hanging out at all?"

"Me and Chase?" I laughed. "Hardly, Dad. What made you ask?"

"His father invited us over to dinner in a few weeks," he responded pointedly. "Said you two met in town."

"Oh, yeah. I'd almost forgotten." I played it down, when the truth was I hadn't forgotten a thing about my disturbing run-in with Chase's dad that afternoon. "What did you tell him?"

"That I had to check my schedule," he answered evasively as

he got into the car. "Anyway, I thought you didn't like Chase."

"He's okay," I answered noncommittally, sliding into the passenger seat. I wasn't about to tell my dad what I really thought about Chase and his creepy father.

"Then you won't mind if I put it off for a while," he announced as he started the engine.

"No," I answered, relieved but also troubled by the conversation. Was my father deliberately trying to keep me away from Chase and his family? I hadn't a clue, which only fueled my already simmering paranoia.

When we got home, I discovered that I had left my cell phone on the floor. A phone call had come in when I was out to dinner. It was from a number I didn't recognize. I checked voice mail, but whoever called hadn't left a message. Curious, I called the number back, and it went directly to Mrs. Henderson's voice mail. I wondered what she wanted and started to leave a message but decided not to. Better to talk to Mrs. Henderson in person the next day at school.

I had forgotten that there was a big football playoff game the next afternoon, so the entire school was energized and focused on winning. First thing in the morning, the marching band was assembled in the quad playing a hip-hop version of the school anthem, cheered on by the student body. It was altogether too loud and too much spiritedness for me to deal with at seven forty-five a.m.

Especially since my mind was still replaying the disturbing details of what Mrs. Henderson had told me the day before. The more I thought about it, the more I realized I felt a bit guilty about breaking my promise to her and telling Oliver and Jackson about the incident. Not that I didn't think they had a right to know, because they did. It was just that Mrs. Henderson had gone out on a major limb to confide in me. Maybe I was being naive, but I trusted her. I wanted to come clean and tell her the truth.

As soon as the lunch bell rang, I hurried down to Mrs. Henderson's office. I was prepared to make a full confession and reassure her that we'd protect her identity and never betray her. I was also more than a little curious to find out why she'd called me last night. Her door was open, and I poked my head in, but she wasn't at her desk.

"May I help you?" The voice came from behind me.

I spun around to see a pleasant but frumpily dressed woman in her fifties standing before me. "I'm looking for Mrs. Henderson. Is she at lunch?"

"Mrs. Henderson is not in today," the frump said, as she walked right into Mrs. Henderson's office.

"Oh? Is she sick or something?"

"Actually, Mrs. Henderson is no longer here."

"*What?*" I stared at her, confused and thinking that I must've misheard what she said.

"Family emergency or something." She revealed this fact

with just the right touch of compassion. "I'm Mrs. Balato, by the way. I'll be taking over for Mrs. Henderson."

"Taking over? How long will she be gone?" I leaned against the door, trying to steady myself and process the information. My stomach felt queasy. I was afraid I might be sick on the frump's clunky olive-green pumps.

"Not to worry. I'm a quick study," the frump replied, confidently patting the stack of student files piled high on the desk. "I'll be up to speed in no time."

I turned and staggered out of the office as Mrs. Balato called after me: "Wait, dear! What's your name?"

Next thing I knew I was aimlessly wandering the school halls, trying not to let my paranoia take over and cause me to flip out. After all, maybe Mrs. Henderson really did have a family emergency. That could have been the reason she called last night—to tell me why she wouldn't be in school today. Before I jumped to any whacked-out conclusions, I needed to find Jackson and Oliver and tell them what happened.

No sooner did I reorient my internal GPS and head directly for the quad than Chase came barreling down the stairs.

"Nica, hey," he shouted with a big smile, stopping in front of me. "Just the girl I'm looking for."

"Sorry, Chase. I don't know where Maya is," I barked back, charging up the staircase past him.

"No problemo," he replied, using the full extent of his

Spanish-language skills. "'Cause I was actually looking for you." Chase stayed on my heels, taking two steps at a time.

"Can't this wait? I'm kind of in a rush," I answered back, barely holding it together.

"It's about Maya's surprise party," Chase announced. "Annie said you volunteered to help out."

"Yeah. Whatever. Just text me what you need me to do." What I needed was for Chase to leave me alone so that I could find Jackson and Oliver and tell them about Mrs. Henderson's mysterious departure from school.

"Why is it I always get the feeling that you don't like me?" Chase suddenly had this hangdog expression on his face.

"I like you," I responded, wondering why the most confident guy in school needed reassuring. "I just don't have time to soothe your wounded ego right now."

"Ouch!" He snickered. "Guess I deserved that." He politely held open the stairwell exit for me.

"Sorry," I relented, acknowledging that he was trying not to be so intolerable. "Didn't mean to be so harsh." I breezed through the door past him outside to the quad.

"Prove it," Chase challenged, like we were about to have an old-fashioned duel.

"Prove what?" I scanned the courtyard, half listening, hoping to locate Oliver or Jackson among the lunch crowd.

"That you like me," Chase declared, flashing a flirtatious smile. "Make it up to me."

"What are you talking about?" I snarked dismissively, when I saw Oliver waving me over to an empty table.

"Come over to my house after today's game," Chase said suggestively. "So we can get to know each other better."

I stopped in my tracks and shot him an incredulous look. "You're not really dumb enough to be hitting on me, are you?" Then I waved back to Oliver.

Chase shrugged audaciously, exuding a hefty dose of jockish swagger. "Is this 'cause of Jackson? 'Cause FYI: Dude's still hung up on Dana, in case you hadn't noticed."

"No. Actually it's because you're a total jerk," I proclaimed with a sweet smile. "Not to mention Maya's my friend."

"She won't mind," he asserted.

"Well, I do." I shook my head in disbelief and anger before marching away from Chase and heading directly over to Oliver.

"You stood me up for Mr. Perfect?" Oliver quipped as I arrived.

"Don't even go there," I snapped back in a foul mood.

"Easy does it, Cujo," Oliver chuckled, throwing up his hands defenselessly. "Don't bite my head off." He could see I was about ready to boil over. "What's going on?"

I grabbed his arm and dragged him into the parking lot, far away from the other kids. Once we were safely out of everyone's earshot, I let loose.

"Mrs. Henderson is gone," I announced ominously.

"What do you mean, *gone*?" Oliver looked at me expectantly.

"No longer working here as of this morning," I announced skeptically. "Some kind of family emergency."

"Holy crap," Oliver murmured. "Does Jackson know?"

"Not yet," I replied, shaking my head. "I just found out myself."

"Have you tried calling her?"

"No," I confessed, feeling a bit foolish. "I was so spooked I didn't know what to do."

Oliver was right. I had to call Mrs. Henderson directly and find out what happened. I took out my cell phone and quickly dialed Mrs. Henderson's number. I immediately got an automated recording: "This number is no longer in service . . ."

I hung up and stared at Oliver, pretty shaken.

"Well? Did it go to voice mail?" Oliver asked hopefully.

"No. Her number has been disconnected." I was practically trembling, and I could see that Oliver was now worried too.

"How could anyone know she talked to you?" He looked around the lot nervously. The usual contingent of Bar Tech Security vehicles patrolled the school grounds.

"We passed a security car yesterday," I whispered, as the blood drained from my face. "I didn't think anything of it at the time, even though Mrs. Henderson got anxious. Then she tried calling me last night. But I was out to dinner with my dad."

"Did she leave a message?" Oliver's eyes grew wide with worry.

I shook my head. "I didn't leave one either. I figured I'd see her today. Oh my God, Oliver . . ."

"Let's not go crazy just yet," he commanded as if suddenly he were my dad. "Maybe she really did have a family emergency. Maybe her husband got sick."

"It's possible," I nodded, desperately wanting to believe Oliver.

"Yeah, totally." Yet Oliver's strained smile betrayed his own deeper concern that Mrs. Henderson's abrupt departure wasn't just a coincidence.

Needless to say I couldn't concentrate on much else the rest of the afternoon other than worrying if something awful had happened to Mrs. Henderson. There had to be a way to find out. I tried calling the ever-elusive Jackson several times to get his advice, but once again he was MIA. I left several increasingly cuckoo-for-Cocoa-Puffs messages for him but never heard back. Oliver mentioned receiving a cryptic text from him—something vague about "connecting the dots," which made it sound like he was doing art therapy.

Maya, meanwhile, tracked me down in the crowded hallway

after eighth period. She was colorfully outfitted in her finest cheerleader ensemble.

"Hey, you," she chirped brightly, slipping her arm through mine like we were best girlfriends. A far cry from how PMSing she was the day before.

"Someone's feeling chipper," I remarked, noticing her cheerleading posse trailing ten feet behind us.

"Totally," she replied with a sly grin. Then she leaned in and whispered so her girls couldn't overhear: "Is it always like this? Psycho bitch one day, normal the next?"

"Define normal," I quipped. Maya laughed. I wondered whether I should say anything about Chase or Mrs. Henderson or keep it all to myself.

"By the way, you're coming, aren't you?" Maya asked hopefully.

"To what?" Between my awkward Chase encounter and Mrs. Henderson's disappearance, I felt so rattled that I had no idea what she was talking about.

"The pep rally in five minutes," she urgently reminded me.

"Sorry, I can't." The playoff game had completely slipped my mind.

"What? Why not?" Maya's smile vanished. She was visibly deflated. "It's kind of a big deal for Chase if we win this game. And our school. *Please?*"

"I really need to be somewhere. It's kind of important." I

knew I had to tell her all about the incident and Mrs. Henderson, but not right then in the school hallway.

"Something bad?" She touched my arm, genuinely concerned, waving her posse on ahead to the gymnasium so that we could be alone.

"I hope not." The look in my eyes urged Maya to drop the matter. She nodded, catching my drift.

"Call me later," she implored, looking worried. "Okay?"

"Okay," I agreed before hurrying off.

I rang the bell and anxiously waited for someone to answer the imposing brown front door. It was the entrance to a stately stone Tudor residence with leaded glass windows, probably built back in the 1920s. I knew someone must be home, because a silver Mercedes sedan with a Bar Tech decal on the windshield was parked in the driveway. I guessed it was Mrs. Henderson's husband's car. A dog was barking loudly somewhere inside as footsteps approached.

An unkempt-looking intellectual with spiky hair and tortoiseshell eyewear opened the door in a huff. He had a dazed, lost expression. His yellow Ralph Lauren dress shirt was haphazardly buttoned. "Yes?"

"Hi. Mr. Henderson?" I asked, very politely.

"What do you want?" he responded, quite impatient, before turning back to the front hall and shouting, "Bruno, quiet!" But the dog continued his incessant yapping.

"I'm Nica Ashley. Mrs. Henderson's my guidance counselor. Is she home?"

Mr. Henderson turned visibly pale. "No . . . she's not . . . ," he said, shaking his head as he fought back emotion.

"When do you expect her back?" I asked solicitously.

He faltered and grabbed hold of the door for support. *"She's . . . gone."*

"What do you mean, *gone?*" I felt queasy and had an awful premonition.

"There was . . . *an accident.*"

"Oh my God . . ." I tried to process the news but was in complete shock and disbelief about what he was telling me. Mrs. Henderson was dead. "What happened?"

"I can't talk about it. Please leave. You've got to go." He tried to shut the door, but I stood in the way. His eyes darted up and down the street, slightly paranoid, as if he was looking for someone or was afraid of being watched.

"Please, just tell me what happened." I was practically begging him. "Is Bar Tech involved?"

Mr. Henderson's face flashed red with anger and hostility. *"You need to drop all this."* Then he slammed the door in my face, leaving me trembling and breathless on the front stoop—and feeling horribly guilty about what had happened to Mrs. Henderson.

I staggered down the steps and made my way back to the sidewalk. Mr. Henderson was definitely frightened and also hiding something about the accident—if it even really was an accident. Or was I just being melodramatic and reading too much into things? I glanced back at the house and caught him staring at me through the window. He was talking to someone on the phone. He shut the drapes as soon as he saw me looking at him.

I picked up my pace and walked away from the house just as a Bar Tech Security vehicle suddenly turned the corner. As soon as I was down the block, I broke into a jog and began running as fast as I could back to school.

## 12. CIRCLE GAME

"Are you all right?" Jackson urgently asked as he steered his black Mustang into the crowded student parking lot where I was waiting for him. Even though the football game was still going on, no one was around. I could see the worry in his eyes as I hopped into the passenger seat.

"I'm fine," I lied, as I held back my tears. I was incredibly relieved to see him. "Just a little spooked is all." Actually a lot spooked, but I didn't want to come off sounding like a terrified little girl. I had texted Jackson after leaving the Henderson house not ten minutes earlier. He'd texted me back immediately and said he'd meet me in the school parking lot, which was only five blocks away. As far as I could tell, no one had followed me. But how could I know for sure?

"It's not your fault," declared Jackson. He could tell I was barely holding myself together. "Don't blame yourself. Accidents happen."

"You really believe that?"

"No," he admitted, shaking his head. Neither did I for that matter.

"If they knew *she* talked," I sputtered, as my imagination ran wild, "who knows what else they know? *Even about us.* I mean, they *murdered her.* An innocent woman."

"We don't know that it's murder for sure," Jackson calmly replied, trying to defuse my fear. "What did Henderson say?" I'd never seen him looking so concerned about my well-being before. Not that I was going to complain. All his attention made me feel special. Like he really cared about me.

"He warned me to leave it all alone," I said no longer feeling like Jackson's paranoia was all in his head. *"To drop this."*

"Next time, don't be so crazy brave, going off without telling anyone. It's more important than ever that I know where you are." Jackson then reached out and touched my hand lightly. "I don't want to lose another . . ."

My heart began to flutter, and my skin broke out in goose bumps. I impulsively reached out and placed my hand on top of his. He then turned his hand over and clasped mine. I looked at Jackson, feeling the warmth of his hand. He looked back at me with that intense, burning stare. I felt excited and exposed, as if he could see right into my soul and know exactly how I was feeling.

I gazed deep into his eyes, expectant and hopeful, wondering what he might say. Instead of speaking he leaned in toward me. I leaned forward. Our lips met. His were soft and full. He kissed me. I kissed him back, shutting my eyes and feeling as though I might melt into the seat. I'd never felt so alive before—like every nerve in my body was on fire. And I didn't want that feeling to end.

But it did. All of a sudden Jackson pulled away from me, abruptly and unexpectedly. I opened my eyes, looking at him in total confusion. "Is something wrong?" I asked, concerned, not knowing what had happened.

Jackson looked back at me with this contrite, almost regretful expression but didn't say anything. Desperate to fill the awful void of silence I just blurted out the first thing that came into my mind: "Was I that bad?" I was hoping a bit of levity would break the tension.

The only thing Jackson could say was "Nica." His tone was sympathetic but also slightly patronizing, like the way a shrink talks to a delusional patient.

Which only made things worse and me feel even more humiliated, like I was the world's biggest loser. A thousand thoughts raced through my mind. Had I done something wrong? Was I such an inept kisser that he couldn't stand it a moment longer? Was I too self-involved? I wanted to bury myself alive and never see Jackson again. On top of the mess of insecurities I was fighting off, I had to face the awful reality that Mrs. Henderson was dead and possibly murdered . . . because of me.

Before either of us could say another word, a loud roar

came from the direction of the football field, followed by raucous cheering. Judging by the noise I knew that Barrington High had just won the division playoff game. In no time at all the parking lot would be overrun with people celebrating yet another victory for quarterback Chase Cochran. As if the jerk needed any more affirmation that he was God's gift to Barrington.

"We should go." Jackson immediately gunned the Mustang's engine. "And let's not say anything about Mrs. Henderson to anyone."

I nodded and sank back in the car seat, crushed and mortified. If he read my humiliation, he didn't say. In fact he didn't speak to me the entire car ride back to my house. He was like a block of ice. Which only made me feel even more paranoid and insecure. Was he upset with me for being so hopelessly lame? I sat there staring at my hands, angry with myself and consumed with regret. But I was also more than a little angry with Jackson for going from concerned to dickhead in a matter of seconds.

"Thanks for the ride," I muttered as Jackson pulled up to my house. I didn't know what else to say; I was still so puzzled by what had happened in the parking lot.

Jackson nodded as I opened the car door to leave. Before I got out, he looked up and finally spoke. "I'm sorry. I just can't do this now. *With you.*"

I was so caught off guard that I just stared blankly and mumbled back, "No problem." Meanwhile all I wanted to do was run and hide. I got out of the car and slammed the door, hurrying up the front walk toward my house.

I heard the Mustang zoom away as I unlocked my front door. By the time I turned around, Jackson's car was gone. I was left standing there, feeling pathetic and wondering what I'd done wrong. I was incredibly upset with Jackson and also worried about him at the same time. Crazy, I know. But he was obviously going through some private torment.

No sooner had I entered my house than my cell phone started buzzing. It was six fifty p.m. and I was in no mood to chat, still wounded by Jackson's rejection and abrupt cold shoulder. Still, it might be my mom or dad. Exasperated, I fished the phone out of my cluttered bag and glanced at the display. Oliver's name appeared on-screen. That's when I also saw that I had three unread texts from him. I realized that I had never texted him after disappearing from school that afternoon. Oliver was probably worrying about what had happened to me.

"Hey, sorry. I just saw all your texts," I blurted into the phone, as I fumbled with my books. "I've had quite the afternoon."

"You're not the only one," Oliver retorted, all too mysteriously. "You hear about Mrs. Henderson?"

"Yes," I replied softly. "I heard. Who told you?"

"My mother," he answered, before pausing a beat. "Do you think—?"

"I don't know," I interrupted, not allowing Oliver to finish his chilling thought. "Can we discuss this some other time?"

"Right," he agreed, and swiftly changed the subject. "Anything else going on?"

I sighed and then proceeded to download the CliffsNotes version of my distressing afternoon, starting with Chase hitting on me, which elicited a sympathetic sigh of concern from Oliver and finished with an offer to defend my honor. "Want me to kick his ass for you?" Oliver said, half serious.

That elicited a much-needed laugh from me. "Now *that* I'd like to see." But I was in no mood to wallow in self-pity a moment longer than I had to. "Enough about my little melodrama," I declared, eager to move on. "Were you texting me about Mrs. H. or something else?"

"You sitting down?"

"Cut to the chase, Oliver," I replied suspiciously as I headed toward the stairs. I was in no mood for a game of twenty questions.

"Guess whose mom worked at that government lab seventeen years ago," Oliver announced with great drama.

I stopped on the first step, trying to absorb what he was saying. "You mean the one that had that accident? *Are you sure?*"

"Positive. She told me."

"Are you crazy? What did you tell her?" I was ready to bite his head off for violating our promise not to say anything to our parents.

"Nothing. I didn't tell her a thing," he snapped back. "Not a word."

"Then how did the subject come up? What did you say? 'Hey, Mom. School was great. You ever work at that secret lab in town?'" My voice dripped with derision.

"My mom enjoys her chardonnay. Usually has two glasses after five p.m. to take the edge off after a long day."

"And you encouraged her tonight," I conjectured with a raised eyebrow, hazarding an educated guess.

"Let's just say I didn't *discourage* her." Oliver's voice suddenly got a bit coy. "Anyway, that third glass made her way more chatty than usual. So I nosed around about my dad," Oliver retorted, trying to diffuse my anger. "You know, where they met. What was he like? Stuff like that." He continued, "She didn't want to talk about him, but I kept pressing and throwing a big guilt trip how she owed me until Mom let it slip that she met him at work. Which was the first time I ever heard that they worked together. We're talking inter-office romance. Pregnancy. Anyway, Mom demands I not say anything to anyone. I tell her no way unless she tells me *everything*. By now she's so upset and flustered that she confesses how she was a secretary and my father was a scientist for the US government, which must be how I got my brilliant mind."

I sat down on my bed. Oliver had my undivided attention. *"And?"*

*"And.* As far as I know, the only US government facility Barrington ever had was that secret lab."

"Oh my God," I muttered as I sank down on the stairs, knowing Oliver was right, my mind spinning with theories of what that might mean. "Do you think it's possible that—?" I couldn't complete my thought because just then my dad walked through the front door with take-out dinner from Thai Smile.

"Get it while it's hot and spicy," Dad loudly declared with a big grin, waving the bag.

"Yikes. I hear trouble," Oliver said warily.

"Yeah. Listen, I'll call you later," I announced as I abruptly hung up on Oliver and welcomed my dad home.

Oliver got me thinking: How much did *I* really know about *my* parents? Truth was, there'd always been gaps in their story. Like how they'd ended up in Barrington when they didn't know anyone here. Or why my mother was so reluctant to talk about her life here. Or why my dad had let my mother leave town with me when I was still a toddler. Or why my dad had stayed in Barrington and never remarried. Little inconsistencies I'd never bothered to think about.

That was until Oliver told me about what he discovered about his parents. It was becoming clear that the adults in our world hadn't been totally candid.

"I heard you guys had quite the day today," my dad stated somberly as we consumed the kaeng som and pad thai at the kitchen table.

"What do you mean?" I replied evasively, all the while trying to keep my cool, not exactly sure if he was referring to Mrs. Henderson's accident or something else.

"The football game," he answered with a smile. "You guys won the playoffs."

"Right. The playoffs." I heaved a sigh of relief. "All hail the great Chase Cochran," I scoffed, rolling my eyes as I sipped my soup. Meanwhile I wondered if my dad was testing me to see what I knew about Mrs. Henderson, if anything.

"Do I detect a note of sarcasm?" He shot me a bemused look, sensing there was a story there.

I shrugged. "Dude's an arrogant dick."

My dad chuckled. "Sometimes the arrogant dick is really just an insecure boy."

"Is that how it was with you and Mom?" I slyly asked, using my father's comment as an opening to delve further into my parents' relationship.

"Guess I was a bit full of myself back in the day," he admitted wistfully. "Until your mom put me in my place."

"How did you guys meet again?" I asked innocently, hoping to lure him into opening up more. Dad wasn't a big wine drinker, so I had to resort to old-fashioned methods—direct questioning.

"On the subway," he responded, a bit embarrassed. "I was doing my cardiology residency at Columbia. Your mom was working as a freelance writer. We were riding in the same car. I kept smiling at her, hoping she'd smile back. Of course she wouldn't give me the time of day. She dropped her notebook as she got off at Columbus Circle. I picked it up and ran after her. Wouldn't give it back to her until she agreed to have dinner with me. The rest, as they say, is history."

"Why did you end up here? It's not exactly like Barrington is a natural jump from New York City."

"I had a job opportunity. At the hospital," he replied somewhat ambiguously, looking away from me. "You want the rest of the pad thai?"

I shook my head no, more focused on not letting this opportunity to discuss the past slip away. "What about Mom? How did she feel about moving to the middle of nowhere?"

"She had her issues," he admitted reflectively. "But we were young and in love."

"So while you were busy at the hospital, Mom was writing press releases with Mrs. Winters, right? You know before I came into the picture."

"Yeah, long time ago. More than seventeen years," he said with an unusual hint of nostalgia. "Time flies."

"By the way, who did Mom work for back then?"

My dad got up from the table and started clearing the dishes before answering. "This government research lab. She wasn't there very long."

I tried not to react or show how stunned I was. "Mom worked as a publicist for the government? I never knew that." It seemed inconceivable to me that my mother ever worked for the government or any kind of big bureaucracy. She was always so antiestablishment anything. "How come no one ever told me?"

"We didn't? I figured your mother must've mentioned it." My dad tried to act detached about the whole matter, as if it were no big deal.

"Nope. She never said a word," I responded, looking right at him. But the way he wasn't really looking at me made me suspect there was more to this story. What else didn't I know? I got up from the table and handed him my plate to rinse off. "Why did Mom leave the job?" I stood next to him, waiting for an answer.

Finally my father's answer came: "The government shut the place down. Budget cuts as I recall. That and your mom was pregnant with you."

*Oh my God.* I stood there, unable to move, feeling like I'd been kicked in the gut. I tried not to visibly react, but the revelation shook me. My head was spinning. *My mother was pregnant with me when she worked at the government facility, just like Oliver's mother was pregnant with him when she worked there. Which meant they must've been pregnant when the incident occurred! And since our birthdays are only a few months apart . . .*

I couldn't help but think that if my mother and Oliver's mother had both been affected, then maybe Jackson's mother had been affected as well, since she had worked with my mother. What if Maya's mother worked there and was pregnant when the incident occurred, too? This could be the missing link we'd been searching for, which might explain why we four had been affected by the pulse.

"I better go upstairs and hit the books," I said to my dad, quickly excusing myself, wanting to get out of there and alert everyone about my shocking discovery.

"Before you go," my dad said, "I don't know if you heard the news about Mrs. Henderson."

"What news?" I played dumb.

"She was in a car accident," he stated without much emotion, like a veteran doctor. "It was fatal."

"Oh my God, that's terrible," I responded sympathetically, hoping that he didn't see through my charade.

"Yes, it's tragic. Anyway, I thought you should know before school tomorrow."

"Thanks," I replied, wanting this conversation to end but also anxious to know more.

"By the way, she was your guidance counselor, wasn't she?"

"Yeah . . . she was." I nodded, not realizing he knew that. "But I really didn't know her all that well."

*"For some reason I thought you did."* He shot me a probing look, as though he doubted my story. How much did he know?

"Not really, other than running into her a few times in the hallway."

"Well, she promised me she'd look out for you. Being the new kid and all. Not to mention she was fond of your mother."

"Yeah, I remember she mentioned that once." I wanted to know more about her "accident." And I wanted to find out exactly what my dad knew, but I didn't want to appear too pushy. "Do they know what happened?"

"Apparently she was out driving alone. Skidded off one of the back roads and crashed head-on into some trees." He shook his head empathetically. "By the time they brought her into the hospital, it was too late."

I listened dispassionately to my father's explanation without breaking down or losing my composure. "I guess accidents happen."

"Yeah," he replied. *"They do."* The way my father said it chilled me to the bone.

• • •

As soon as I shut the door to my bedroom, my fingers furiously tried texting Jackson and Maya, asking them to discreetly confirm that their mothers had worked at the Barrington government facility over seventeen years ago. It actually took me several attempts to get the texts right; I was trembling so badly because I was so freaked out by what my father had told me, not to mention the sketchy details about Mrs. Henderson's "accident."

I managed to get hold of myself long enough to also text Oliver: *Mine 2!*

A bit cryptic but I hoped he'd understand exactly what I meant.

Less than a minute later Oliver answered: *OMG.*

It was clear that he understood perfectly. In the meantime I received a text back from Jackson, which only said: *Talk tomorrow.* I knew he was paranoid about texting anything incriminating, as was I, so I was about to respond *OK* when my phone rang. It was Maya.

"Hey, girl. Missed you at the game." She sounded super perky, but I could hear a distinct edge in her voice. It was one of concern.

"Yeah, sorry. I heard it was epic."

"Chase was awesome. As usual. By the way, I'm in the middle of that *assignment* you asked me about. It's tricky, but I think I can figure it out by morning." She was cautiously speaking in code, clearly referring to my text about her mother working for the government.

"Excellent," I replied. "We'll compare notes at school tomorrow."

"Speaking of school," Maya interjected, "isn't it *awful* about Mrs. H.?" Her tone implied that she was as suspicious as I was about the supposed accident.

"Yeah. Really awful."

What followed was a moment of silence between us, and then we both hung up, neither of us saying another word.

The next morning Jackson arrived at my house promptly at seven thirty a.m. to drive me to school. I was relieved to find Oliver and Maya already in the backseat of his car, as I was eager to put the entire awkward kiss incident behind me. Jackson seemed to feel that way too, as he acted quite cool— like nothing weird had happened between us. Which truthfully only made me feel worse. Luckily, there were more important things to obsess about at that moment instead of how Jackson felt about me. Specifically Mrs. Henderson's suspicious accident and exactly how our mothers were connected. And Jackson's Mustang seemed to be the safest place for us to talk openly without drawing too much unwanted attention from fellow students, teachers, or parents.

"FYI," Maya announced as soon as I hopped into the car, "apparently, my mother worked for the government way back when."

"Doing what?" I asked with great interest, hoping that my theory about how we were all connected would prove true.

"Maya's mom's a rocket scientist," Oliver chimed back.

"Yeah, and mine's the queen of England," I snarked, thinking he was joking. "Seriously, what does she do?"

Maya nodded, embarrassed. "Actually, she's like a physicist or something. Met my dad at MIT."

"Nerds of a feather," Oliver quipped. I have to admit I was kind of impressed.

Finally Jackson interjected: "Now they both work at Bar Tech."

Here was yet another connection between the government facility and Bar Tech. I shot Jackson back an uneasy look, which Maya picked up on.

"Why does any of this matter?" Maya asked, looking at all of us with concern.

"Because I think we all share one special thing in common." Then I turned to Jackson. His mother was the last piece of the puzzle. "What about *your* mom?" It was my first verbal communication with him since the day before.

Jackson took a beat before responding. "She claims she's worked with my dad at the family store ever since they got married twenty years ago."

"So much for your brilliant hypothesis," remarked Oliver with a sympathetic shrug. That seemed to poke a major hole in my theory that all four of our mothers worked at the facility when the incident struck.

I turned to Jackson unfazed by what he said. "Your mother's lying. She told me she worked with my mother. My dad said they wrote press releases."

"I know," Jackson admitted with a validating smile.

"Big surprise. They're all liars," Oliver mumbled, discouraged at the prospect that he couldn't trust his own mother.

"After my parents went to bed, I did some sleuthing," Jackson continued. "Fortunately, Dad's a bit OCD. Found all his financial records dating back to college. Appears my mom briefly moonlighted as a freelance writer at the facility to make extra cash because they had just opened up the store."

"Looks like Nica wins the gold ring then," Oliver proclaimed, suitably impressed.

"Somehow that doesn't give me much comfort." This was one time being right felt awful. To know your own parents lied to you was not something I wanted to celebrate.

Maya looked confused. "So all our mothers worked at the same government facility?" She was still not putting everything together.

"*While they were pregnant,*" Jackson added.

There was a moment of silence while Maya absorbed the implications. "That's how we're all connected?"

"Yeah," I said softly, nodding. "They all worked at the facility when the original pulse occurred seventeen years ago."

"I think I'm going to be sick," Maya muttered, looking less than thrilled by all the revelations.

"Should I open a window?" Oliver asked, cringing at the thought of Maya spewing all over his pants.

"Don't do a thing," Jackson announced, abruptly shifting gears and slowing down. "I think we're being followed."

I immediately looked out the passenger side view mirror and saw a Bar Tech Security vehicle about a half block behind us. "Big deal. We're just going to school."

"Yeah. It's not like we're doing anything wrong," Oliver agreed, peering out the rear window.

"Other than exposing murder and a major conspiracy," Jackson countered solemnly, driving at the speed limit so as to not attract any further attention from our Bar Tech pursuers.

"As if my morning needs any more drama," Maya groaned, finally grasping how vulnerable we all were and how we'd just uncovered the tip of a treacherous iceberg.

## 13. SHE CAME IN THROUGH THE BATHROOM WINDOW

Five minutes later we arrived at school with our Bar Tech escort thankfully driving on. The student parking lot was jammed with the usual morning traffic, but Jackson found a spot. Word had broken about Mrs. Henderson's death. All around us I heard kids talking about how cool she was and also how sad it was that she was gone. The school was planning to hold a memorial after the Thanksgiving holiday break.

"What do we do now?" Maya asked apprehensively as we all got out of Jackson's Mustang, preparing to face another day of school.

"Act normal," Jackson responded coolly, marching on toward the entrance.

"Hmm, normal. I don't think I've ever done *that* before," Oliver joked, trailing right behind Jackson.

Maya turned and looked at me for support, seeming a little lost and burdened by all the secrets she had to carry. I shrugged and smiled reassuringly, indicating I felt as adrift as she did.

Try as I might, I still couldn't shake off this nagging feeling that something bad was about to happen, particularly in the wake of Mrs. Henderson's fatal accident. I had no idea exactly what might happen or even what I was afraid might occur. All I knew was I felt this terrible unease down to my bones.

At first I wondered if it might be some sort of spooky premonition. Or perhaps I was suffering from post-traumatic stress disorder because of what I'd discovered about my parents. Whatever was causing this agitation, I drifted from class to class without any memory of what I'd just sat through.

Making matters worse, I became convinced that Chase was following me around school. At first I shrugged off the coincidence that he always seemed to be appearing around a corner just as I was coming from the opposite direction. Or standing behind me on the cafeteria line. He passed by my locker just as I was heading off to English. Then he suddenly bumped into me just after I exited the restroom.

"We've got to stop meeting like this," Chase razzed. "One might think you're actually stalking me." He flashed his twinkling smile.

"I could say the same thing about you," I sniped back, walking around him, in no mood to talk—especially to him.

He trailed alongside me, refusing to leave me alone. "You missed an awesome game yesterday."

"Did I?" I shrugged, not giving him props for his big win because he was annoying the hell out of me.

"Yeah. I was a little hurt you weren't there," he replied. "To help me celebrate." He had this downcast expression.

I shot him a dubious look, not buying his sad-boy routine for one second. "I'm sure you had plenty of adoring fans cheering you on to victory. Not to mention Maya." His arrogance and self-importance made me angry.

"I guess we can celebrate when you come over for dinner," he grinned.

"Who told you I was coming over for dinner?" I flashed a dismissive look.

"My old man," Chase replied. "You made quite an impression on him. And that's not easy."

"Yeah, right," I responded mockingly, even though I was more unnerved by the mention of his dad.

"So have you reconsidered my proposition?" he brazenly said with a smug smile, suddenly cornering me. "We'd be really hot together." He was insistent and overbearing. "You can't fight the inevitable."

"You're dreaming." I clenched my jaw, overcome with rage and an overwhelming urge to kick him in the balls. Before I could do or say anything I might regret, I realized that *my left hand was starting to disappear!*

*OH MY GOD! Why the hell is this happening to me now?*

Chase continued chattering, but I never heard a word he

said, because my mind was racing. Could there have been a pulse the night before that I didn't know about? That none of us knew about? I hadn't seen anything. And Oliver, Maya, and Jackson had never mentioned anything on the ride to school. I quickly shoved my disappearing hand behind my back so that Chase wouldn't see what was happening to me.

Chase pressed in closer, oblivious to my turmoil. "Don't tell me you're not into me. I see the way you're always checking me out."

I was panicking, trying not to totally flip out. Kids streamed by, whispering and definitely noticing us together. They must've been wondering what was going on between Chase and me. Meanwhile that warm tingling sensation was shooting up from my hand to my elbow. I knew if I didn't get away from Chase immediately, he'd see that something was seriously wrong with me when I completely disappeared before his eyes.

"Get lost," I barked, plowing past Chase, racing down the hallway as my left arm was vanishing.

I cut gym and made it safely into the school library and hid among the nonfiction stacks. Regaining command of my mind and body, I managed to calm myself enough so that my left hand and arm slowly returned to their normal state. Then I texted Jackson, Oliver, and Maya, alerting them how we were vulnerable because the pulse must've happened overnight. This set off a flurry of anxious coded texts speculating how it happened without our knowledge, ending with Jackson ordering everyone to meet during lunch.

Once I finished texting, I noticed that I'd taken refuge in the science section. The irony wasn't lost on me. One fat volume on genetics caught my eye. I pulled it out and thumbed through the dense text, wondering if I might find some answers about my own strange predicament. As I tried to decipher some complicated scientific mumbo jumbo about genetic mutations that occurred after conception, I became aware that someone was standing behind me. Watching me. Before I could make sure that all my limbs were still visible and intact, I heard my biology teacher, Mr. Bluni, speak to me.

"Somatic mutations? That's pretty advanced stuff," he remarked in his usual snide tone as he snooped at what I was reading.

"Yeah, way over my head," I answered as I closed the book and slid it back onto the shelf, desperate to get away from him.

"Don't undersell yourself," he replied. "You're a smart kid. I could explain it if you weren't always running off somewhere." Mr. Bluni stared me down and blocked the aisle so I couldn't leave. "Nica Ashley, mystery girl. So many secrets."

"Not really." Despite my unease, I tried to think on my feet and not panic too much. "Just thinking about a cool topic for my bio term paper."

Mr. Bluni seemed to perk up with that tiny bit of ego stroking. "Well, a somatic mutation is also called an *acquired* mutation, which occurs in utero."

"Acquired?" I asked, not sure I followed.

"Meaning it was acquired after conception and wasn't inherited from a parent," he explained.

"And how does *someone* or *something* acquire these mutations?" I knew I was taking a big risk talking to my biology teacher. However, I sensed I had a window of opportunity to find out how I might have been affected when my mother was pregnant with me.

"Some are spontaneous," he elaborated, "a random error. Others appear to be the result of exposure to toxins or radiation."

"*Radiation?*" Now I was the one who perked up. So it was possible and very likely that the first pulse had affected my genetic code.

"Yes. It interferes with cell division and genetic structure." He then gave me one of his intimidating stares, which made me uneasy. "Is that why you and Oliver were reading all about bioelectrical energy and electromagnetic radiation?"

"Yes," I muttered, realizing he'd made the connection. How much did he know or even suspect about Oliver and me? I hadn't a clue, but I felt like I was skating on thin ice.

The bell rang.

"I should go," I said, feeling my heart thumping like crazy as I gestured toward the door. "Spanish."

Mr. Bluni just stared. "To be continued."

"Thanks." Then I got the hell out of the library as fast as I could, leaving Mr. Bluni behind in the stacks.

"Nica, wait up." Maya chased me down the hallway, breathless.

"Hey. Can we talk after school? I'm late for Spanish." My unpleasant encounter with Chase suddenly came thundering back. I knew I had to tell Maya about it, but I didn't want to get into it right then and there. We were alone in the corridor.

"What's going on?" she responded, not letting me go, clearly distressed.

"You mean about the *pulse* last night? I'm as mystified as you are." I was also still flustered by my run-in with Mr. Bluni.

"*No. With you and Chase?* Everyone saw you in the hall." I saw the hurt in her eyes.

"Maya. It's not what you think." No matter how I tried to explain what happened, I knew it would sound like I was making excuses.

"I thought you were my friend!" Maya was trembling, near tears. An insecure mess. I felt horrible.

"I am your friend. Chase cornered me. Wanted me to

come over. I told him no. But he wouldn't leave me alone."
Moving around so much since I was five, I wasn't used to
navigating these kind of messy emotional dramas with
girlfriends. On top of that, I'd been totally blindsided to
discover that another pulse had hit the night before. High
emotions plus the pulse were a recipe for disaster.

"Liar. Chase loves me. You're just jealous and trying to
steal him." Maya was really working herself up into an agitated state. "I've been nothing but nice to you since you got
here."

Suddenly the glass panes in all the classroom doors
started vibrating and rattling. I worried that Maya would go
ballistic in the school hallway and smash all the glass.

"Maya, listen to me. Chase is a snake. You can't trust
him." Painful as it was, I had no choice but to be honest
with her.

"You don't know him," she insisted, terribly upset, her
voice raised. "He wouldn't do that. We're perfect together.
Perfect!" Her body was practically trembling with rage.

Lockers shook and rattled all around us. Doors burst
open. Ceiling tiles were bending and buckling, causing a
deafening racket. If Maya's anger wasn't curtailed, I was
afraid the entire hallway would explode into a tornado of
metal, glass, and tile.

Classroom doors swung open as concerned teachers and
startled students poked their heads out into the hallway,

fearful that an earthquake was hitting the school. Their wide eyes and shocked stares riveted on a very emotional Maya shouting at me. I could read their stunned expressions. They'd never seen Miss Cool, Calm, and Normally Collected lose her shit like this.

I knew if I didn't react quickly to defuse this situation, not only would Maya be exposed before the entire school, but ultimately so would Oliver, Jackson, and I. I grabbed Maya in my arms and wrapped her in a tight embrace—the way parents sometimes do a toddler throwing a temper tantrum.

"Don't lose it," I commanded Maya, whispering in her ear. I hoped she wasn't too far gone to come back from the brink.

Maya glared at me with her wounded-doe eyes and then at everyone else in the corridor, realizing the precariousness of the situation. I felt her take a deep breath.

And then all the shaking and rattling ceased. Just like that. Drawing looks of bewilderment and confusion from students and teachers gathered in the hallway.

Maya broke free from my embrace and rushed off in tears. I felt awful about hurting her. But this was no time to wallow in regret and self-pity.

I blurted out: "Did you all feel that tremor?" I desperately hoped that I might convince at least a few people that what they'd experienced was an earthquake and wasn't caused by Maya.

● ● ●

Oliver and Jackson were already huddled at a table in the quad by the time I arrived during lunch. They both looked unusually serious.

"Our girl Maya had a bit of a meltdown," Oliver glumly declared, glancing at Jackson.

"So you heard," I replied concerned. "I knew too many people saw what Maya did in the hallway for word not to spread like wildfire."

"Hallway?" Jackson asked, a bit confused. "Everyone's talking about her nearly destroying a classroom." He locked locking eyes with me.

"What classroom?" I looked back and forth between Oliver and Jackson, trying to read their expressions. "What are you both talking about?"

"She had a huge fight with Chase," Jackson continued, unemotional.

"*About you*," Oliver added sheepishly. I knew he wasn't trying to embarrass me in front of Jackson, but it was painful to hear nonetheless.

"Oh no. Is Maya okay? I can explain everything." I was anxious to get out my side of the story of what had gone down between Maya and me in the hallway—especially to Jackson. Not that he and I were dating or anything, but I couldn't help feeling incredibly guilty. I'd never been accused of being the "other woman" before. It wasn't fun.

"She went home. Doesn't want to see anyone," Jackson said, looking at me with what felt like accusatory eyes. What it really seemed like he meant was that Maya didn't want to see me.

"Chase is a liar. Nothing happened between us," I asserted defensively, intent on telling my best friends the truth. More to the point it was important to me that Jackson know.

"We've got bigger problems," Jackson interjected, shutting me down. "*Now that Chase knows.* He saw Maya nearly destroy that room. She told him about the pulse."

"How do you know?" Now I was the one trying not to freak out.

"I ran into Maya as she was leaving school." Oliver answered. "She was nearly hysterical. Blurted out everything that happened."

"Holy shit." As if it weren't bad enough that half the school had witnessed Maya's wrath unleashed, this was potentially even more threatening. "If Chase knows about Maya and the pulse, it won't be long before he figures out about the three of us. And the reason we've all been hanging out together."

"He promised Maya he wouldn't tell anyone about her ability," Oliver exclaimed, rolling his eyes, obviously not buying that Chase would keep his mouth shut.

"I wouldn't count on his silence," I replied, afraid of what

Chase might do with such explosive information about his girlfriend.

"He's going to sell us out," Jackson affirmed, knowing Chase all too well. "The bigger issue is: *What do we do?*"

"Stop him," I insisted, my blood beginning to boil with rage. "We've got to do a preemptive strike."

"What? Kidnap him and hold him forever?" Oliver asked, making a valid point.

"I don't know. But I'm certainly not going to sit around and twiddle my thumbs. I'm going to find out what that creep's up to," I proclaimed, grabbing my books and getting up from the table.

"Just how do you plan on doing that, *Jane Bond?*" Oliver asked, intrigued and more than a little worried about my declaration.

"I'll figure something out," I countered, walking away from them and back into school. No way was I going to sit idly by waiting for Chase to expose my friends and me.

My initial impulse was to track Chase down and use my Thai kickboxing training to whip his pathetic ass out in the quad. But I knew that wouldn't stop Chase from blabbing. In fact it would probably only spur him on. I had to be shrewder and turn the tables on that pompous jock. That was when I realized I had the perfect weapon right at my fingertips.

*I had the ability to disappear.*

True, it was risky and dangerous. And my control over my power sucked big time. But desperate times called for desperate measures. If I didn't do something before the evening, my advantage over Chase would vanish when the twenty-four-hour window passed. And there would be no predicting exactly if and when the next pulse would occur. Now was the time for me to act.

I dumped all my books in my locker, then went directly to the nearest restroom. I locked myself in a stall and waited for the place to clear out as the class bell rang. Utilizing Master Kru's breathing techniques I slowly relaxed my mind. Harnessing all my energy I focused it on making my entire body disappear. In seconds my limbs vanished, but the rest of my body was still visible. I shut my eyes and kept breathing steadily. The familiar tingling began to spread up my arms and legs and into my stomach, up along my torso and neck, and into my head. By the time I opened my eyes, I had evaporated into thin air.

After emerging from the stall, I cracked open the restroom door just wide enough to slip out into the hallway. I snuck along the corridor, carefully passing the occasional teacher and student without incident. Once or twice I nearly collided with someone but managed to sidestep them before impact. Luckily, they seemed totally unaware that anyone was in the hallway with them.

I caught up with Chase after sixth period and followed

him to his next class, eavesdropping unobserved on all his conversations with his friends. It was kind of trippy at first getting a real inside view of BMOC jockdom. Kyle, Vox, Alex, and Chase argued heatedly about who had the hottest girlfriend. I kept waiting for Chase to spill the beans about Maya, but he never said a word to anyone about what he'd witnessed. By the time eighth period rolled around, I'd gotten the hang of this disappearing and reappearing at will. Unfortunately, I was bored out of my mind with spying on Chase. His conversations were dull and totally self-centered—he always managed to be the main topic no matter whom he talked to. Usually the talk was about how awesome he was.

Meanwhile he never once let anything slip about Maya.

I wondered if I might be wrong in my assessment of Chase Cochran. True, he was obnoxious and egotistical, but that didn't necessarily mean he was also a slime bucket who'd rat out his girlfriend. Perhaps he really would stand by his promise and keep Maya's secrets. However, before I could be absolutely certain what his intentions were, I had to follow Chase home to see how he acted behind closed doors.

Chase lived in an enormous house in the same upscale neighborhood as Dana Fox. Except the Cochran house wasn't some new monstrosity designed to look like a European château. Theirs was a sleek midcentury glass-and-steel fortress. The house was meant to impress and intimidate, and that it did.

I slipped inside through a rear entrance, trailing closely on Chase's heels through large, expansive rooms with soaring ceilings. The place was beautiful but also austere and cold. Few photos or personal memorabilia were displayed anywhere. The floors throughout the house alternated between blond wood and polished concrete. I did my best to keep in step with Chase's movements so as to not betray my presence. Every sound and footfall was amplified and echoed off walls of glass overlooking hundred-year-old towering pines and aspens. All that nature was breathtaking. I couldn't help but pause for a moment to take it all in, transfixed. But when I looked around, Chase was gone.

I was suddenly lost in a maze of interconnecting rooms. I wandered through a vast kitchen and family room into a music room with a grand piano. How had I gotten so turned around? *Where did Chase go?* I felt myself get agitated. My blood pressure started to rise, which caused my right foot to suddenly reappear. I stopped moving, closed my eyes, and regulated my breathing so that I regained control of my body.

As my right foot disappeared safely into the ether with the rest of me, I heard several voices coming from the far end of the house. I tiptoed through a vast library with floor-to-ceiling bookcases, which finally deposited me at the double-door entrance to Richard Cochran's home office and private sanctuary. There I discovered Chase meeting with his father and another man. As I crept into the room and discovered this other man's identity, I had to stifle myself from crying out.

The third person in the room was my own father. And he was questioning Chase—about Maya's meltdown at school. I stood behind the low-slung sofa, unseen, quietly listening in total shock.

"Tell me exactly what you saw," demanded my dad, hanging on Chase's every word.

"Maya was ragging on me about something stupid. I tried calming her down, but you know how girls get." Chase smirked. "Anyway, all of sudden she's flipping out, doing emotional one-eighties. Then everything in the room is freaking whirling around my head. And I'm like, 'whoa, this is some serious whacked-out bullshit; what the hell happened to you?' Afterward she's crying and begging me not to say anything about what she did. Saying it's not her fault. Blaming it on some mysterious green pulse that lights up the sky."

I was horrified at how easily Chase betrayed Maya, eagerly divulging everything he knew. It took every ounce of willpower to stifle my rage and stop myself from kicking his bony ass.

"Did she say if anyone else was affected?" Richard Cochran grilled his son, wanting details.

Chase shook his head. "No. Claimed she was the only one. But Maya's a bad liar."

"Stick close to her." Chase's dad patted his son on the shoulder. "See what else you can find out. Remember— you're my eyes and ears."

"I'm on it, sir," Chase replied enthusiastically before exiting the room. He acted as if spying on his friends was as easy as throwing a football.

Once Chase was safely out of earshot, Richard Cochran turned to my dad. "There must be others by now."

"Blood tests are still inconclusive. I haven't taken samples from everyone yet." My father stated this with a slight hesitation—which made me wonder if he was holding something back.

Cochran must've felt this too, since he pressed him harder: "But you've identified a *positive marker*."

My father nodded his agreement. "That doesn't mean everyone that has the marker has converted like Maya. Or that they ever will." He took a beat before continuing. "As with any genetic mutation, some develop the disease or condition while others stay carriers. I have no way of predicting which ones will exhibit enhanced abilities and which will remain dormant."

"Then it's time to accelerate the progression," insisted Cochran. "Step up our timetable."

My father balked. "And risk overexposing these kids? There's a precarious balance between just enough radiation and too much."

"Marcus, we're on the verge of a major discovery Darwin never imagined." Cochran was speaking with an almost religious fervor. "Who could've predicted that a spy-satellite explosion seventeen years ago would ignite the greatest leap in human evolution?"

I knew they were talking about the incident. The first pulse had been an accident. The explosion must have irradiated our pregnant mothers and somehow mutated our DNA. It was a somatic mutation, just like Mr. Bluni had explained. And now Bar Tech was deliberately setting off the pulse to bring out our abilities. They were using us as scientific guinea pigs. Or worse . . . I was so spooked and freaked out by what I was hearing that I lost my footing and stumbled back.

"Still, we need to proceed with caution until we know how many we're dealing with and who they are," my father admonished Cochran. "These kids are still developing, maturing. Their powers are erratic and unpredictable. Maya's a perfect example. She could've inflicted serious harm today."

"You focus on the science. I'll worry about the rest," Cochran pointedly instructed my father. "Our timeline has accelerated considerably. Bar Tech is on the verge of closing one hundred billion in technology deals."

Before I realized what was happening, I actually started to rematerialize in the room. I could see my feet! I gasped, in a panic, losing control over my own body, my own power. If I didn't act quickly, in a matter of seconds I'd be exposed.

Cochran, having heard me, raised his hand and silenced my father. "Chase? Is that you?" He looked around the room, suspicious, sensing my presence. My dad looked around too, unsure what Cochran had heard.

Not hanging around to get caught red-handed, I escaped out the door and booked the hell through Chase's house before I completely reappeared. I raced out the back door and across the yard as the lower half of my body started materializing. I was desperate to make it to the safety of the woods. By the time I found cover among the trees, I was nearly back to myself again. But I didn't stop running. Adrenaline coursed through my body.

My mind reeled as it hit me full force that my dad was actually in league with Richard Cochran. I couldn't deny the truth any longer. My impulse was to run as far away as I could and never look back. But where would I go? Home? I didn't have another home to go back to, thanks to my mother. Lydia was holed up in Antarctica for the next six months. Even if I could reach her by phone, which was doubtful given the spotty service down there, what could she do? What *would* she do? After all, she'd sent me to live with my father. I was a virtual prisoner in Barrington.

I finally stopped running in the middle of the street, nearly ready to collapse from exhaustion. I looked around and discovered I was standing in front of Jackson's house. How the hell did I get there? Was it on instinct? Whatever it was that had led me there, I had to tell Jackson everything I knew.

I hurried up the walk and rang the doorbell. No answer. Jackson must be home. His car was parked out front. I pounded on the front door. I started to freak, worrying that something awful had happened to him. *Maybe my dad and Cochran already know about Jackson?*

I ran around to the back of Jackson's house, peering in through every window and door, trying to find out if Jackson was all right. But there was no sign of him. Anywhere. I called his cell, but it went straight to voice mail. I feared the worst.

Next thing I knew, I was yanking out the screen to a bathroom window. It had the same lock as my dad's house. Using my trusty Swiss Army knife I wedged and pried the small wood window open and squeezed inside. The house was eerily silent.

"Jackson," I called out, creeping into the long hallway between the bedrooms. There was no response. I made my way down toward Jackson's bedroom, hearing sounds the closer I got. They were the sounds of running water.

I stood in the doorway, looking around Jackson's room.

The clothes he'd worn to school were strewn across the floor—jeans, T-shirt, boxer shorts, and socks. I hadn't intentionally snuck in. Well, I had, but I was honestly so concerned about him. I didn't mean to stay when I discovered that the real reason Jackson hadn't answered the front door or taken my phone call was because he was taking a shower. Not only that, he was singing to himself!

I was so overcome with relief that Jackson was all right that I had to stop myself from laughing. What an insane day it had been. I knew I should just leave the house immediately, but I couldn't help but sneak a peek at Jackson's naked body. I was an awful person, I know. A Peeping Tom. But I was also only sixteen and wildly curious. I told myself that I'd just take a quick peek and then leave. Jackson would never know I was there.

I slunk toward the bathroom door like a kitten and caught Jackson shampooing his thick mane of hair. His muscular back was facing me, so he didn't see that I was spying on him. My eyes scanned down his body, taking in his powerful physique. If these were biblical times I would have probably been struck down by lightning or gone blind for my lustful sins.

As Jackson rinsed the suds out of his thick, lustrous hair, he turned around unexpectedly, and I suddenly saw everything. And I mean *everything*. He was naked. Completely exposed. I fantasized about stripping naked right there and joining him in the shower, where we'd have wild sex. But the truth was, I was so flustered and embarrassed—not to mention inexperienced—that I just stumbled back on my feet and almost fell. I prayed he didn't hear me.

Before I could make my escape, Jackson stepped out of the shower. After wrapping a towel around his waist, he was checking himself out in the mirror while combing out his wet hair. Meanwhile I was trapped on the far side of his bedroom. There was no way I could slip past him unnoticed. He would undoubtedly spot my reflection in the mirror trying to flee.

My only option at that moment was to go stealth (aka invisible) and then get the hell out of there. This time I managed to disappear in less than three seconds. My skill had definitely improved.

Jackson exited the bathroom into his bedroom. He fished a clean pair of boxer shorts out from a dresser drawer. Then he dropped his towel. And he just stood there, naked, not putting on the boxers. I tried to regulate my breathing, slow and silent, so as to not give myself away.

But something about the way Jackson was acting made me suspect that he already knew I was there. Maybe he'd caught a glimpse of me when I wasn't looking? Or maybe he just sensed my presence. In any case, he kept glancing around the room. It almost seemed like he didn't mind.

I admit that I also got into the whole voyeuristic thing

for a brief moment, until Jackson's parents suddenly arrived home. As the front door slammed shut, I heard them call out for him. Jackson quickly threw on his clothes, while I used the distraction to escape. I darted down the hallway and slipped into the green-tiled bathroom, sneaking out the same window that I'd climbed in through only minutes earlier.

## 14 FATHERS' DAY

I needed some serious help. Bad enough I spied on my own father. Now I was spying on my friends too—on Jackson—the boy I couldn't stop thinking about. The boy I dreamed about every night when I went to sleep. And I enjoyed having my ability way too much. What might I be driven to do next? I was afraid to find out.

By the time I arrived back home, it was nearly dark. My father was already there, surprising me as soon as I breezed in through the front door.

"Where have you been?" he prodded, more intense than usual. "I was about to send out a search party." I couldn't read whether Dad was pissed at me for something or concerned.

"Sorry. I was . . . at the library working on a project," I lied. "Just lost track of time."

"Not to mention your books," Dad remarked, astutely noticing that I had come home empty-handed. No bag, no books.

"Yeah. Ditched them in my locker." I sighed. "Carrying them back and forth is such a hassle." I didn't know if my excuse sounded plausible or if he suspected what I'd been up to that afternoon. But I was in no mood to find out. I whisked past him, about to head up the stairs to my bedroom, wanting to avoid getting the third degree.

"Hey. Not so fast," my dad declared, stopping me dead in my tracks. I braced myself, fully expecting the grand inquisition. Instead my dad then said, "You've got a visitor." He gestured back toward the kitchen.

"I do?" Totally flustered, I glanced toward the kitchen, having no clue about who my mystery visitor might be.

I entered the kitchen and breathed a sigh of relief when I found Oliver seated at the table.

"Hey, sorry to barge in like this." He stood up, looking unusually pale. No jokes, no smile. I immediately knew something was wrong.

"No problem," I replied awkwardly, aware my dad might be listening from the living room.

"I could really use your help on that English paper." Oliver tilted his head at an angle, indicating he needed to talk to me in private.

"Sure." I nodded my understanding. "C'mon upstairs." I turned and walked out of the kitchen with Oliver tight on my heels.

• • •

"Where have you been?" Oliver exclaimed, anxiously pacing around my bedroom like a caged puppy, as I shut the door. "I'm like totally freaking out."

"Sorry. I was doing some reconnaissance," I replied cryptically, turning on some music for maximum privacy. "What's wrong?"

"Nothing other than my entire life being upended in one afternoon," proclaimed Oliver very dramatically.

Although I felt the same way about what I had discovered at the Cochran house that afternoon, I let Oliver vent first. "Care to elaborate?"

He finally stopped moving, then sat on my bed. "It's about my dad."

"What about him?" I knew his dad's identity was a hot-button issue for Oliver. Despite the fact that he professed it didn't matter to him.

"I know who he is," Oliver announced gravely, preparing to drop a major bombshell.

"Wow." I hadn't seen that coming. I sat down on the bed next to Oliver, bracing myself for something big.

Oliver took a breath and then blurted out, "It's *Richard Cochran*."

"Yeah, right." I laughed, convinced he was trying to punk me. "You almost had me there."

"No joke, Nica." He stared back at me, dead serious, not laughing.

"*Seriously . . . ?*" I said, my mind processing this stunning revelation. "Chase's dad is your dad too?"

He nodded affirmatively. "My mom finally confessed."

"Why? After all these years?" I probed, shocked and wondering what had compelled Oliver's mother to spill her darkest secret. I cranked the music volume up a little louder to drown us out.

"We got into a huge fight. I demanded she tell me the truth about how my dad died."

"What did she say?" I asked, still trying to wrap my head around the fact.

"She lied at first, like she always did. But I told her I knew things," Oliver continued, still pumped up from his run-in with his mom. "That there'd been an accident at the lab seventeen years ago when she worked there. She freaked out. Told me never to mention it. It was too dangerous."

"Then what happened?"

"I told her it was too late. That I wouldn't stop asking questions until I knew everything about my father. Things escalated. She cried but I held my ground until she finally admitted he was still alive. And living in Barrington."

"That must've been the reason why she never told you his name."

"Yeah. Then she confessed and made me swear never to tell a soul. So of course I came here right away to tell you."

Oliver grinned in spite of being unsettled by the news, as if to show he hadn't totally lost his sense of the absurd.

"Your secret's safe with me," I vowed, wrapping my arm around his shoulder for solidarity. "I won't tell anyone."

"Creepiest thing about it . . . that means Chase is my half brother." Oliver winced at the thought.

"That is creepy," I concurred. "Especially after I tell you what that Benedict Arnold did today."

"I'm all ears, Mata Hari." Oliver's eyes widened, eager to hear the latest dirt.

"Well, I kind of followed the jerk home after school," I confessed to Oliver, who was now perched on the edge of the bed with anticipation.

"And I'm betting he never saw you." Oliver raised his eyebrows, shooting me a look that said he knew I had used my power to be invisible.

"Neither did my father or Richard Cochran for that matter." I shot Oliver a sheepish grin, as if I'd done something very naughty. And then I proceeded to fill him in about my run-in with Mr. Bluni in the library and my afternoon surveillance mission, including the very upsetting news that my dad was in cahoots with Richard Cochran.

"So all this stuff is happening to us because a random satellite exploded seventeen years ago?" Oliver asked, trying to wrap his head around the implications of what I'd found out.

"Except now Cochran has found a way to duplicate the original pulse," I added.

"Which he's deliberately setting off to strengthen our abilities and smoke us out into the open." Oliver understood the ramifications and the danger we were all in.

"And then what? *What does he want from us?*" I asked, fighting back my fears of being turned into a caged lab rat and the overwhelming urge to run and hide under the covers.

Oliver shook his head, equally scared, having no idea what their ultimate end game was. We sat on my bed in silence, pondering the great unknown.

Later that night there was a knock at my bedroom door. My dad stood in the hallway, wanting to chat with me. And he refused to take no for an answer, lamenting that we were becoming like two ships passing in the night. He insisted that wasn't the kind of dad he wanted to be with his only child. So I had no choice but to let him in.

"Tell me what's going on with you," he probed, sitting on my bed, intending to stay for a while.

"You know, the usual. Classes, friends, homework. Blah, blah, blah." I shrugged, playing it cagey. I wasn't sure what he was fishing for, so I kept things light. "It's a vicious cycle."

"Interesting . . . ," he said, and then exposed the real

agenda behind our little chat: "Because I heard there was a bit of a ruckus at school today."

"*Ruckus?*" I furrowed my brow, feigning ignorance.

"Something about Maya Bartoli having a major meltdown with you in the hallway."

*Oh, shit.* I should've known there were too many witnesses for Maya's near explosion over Chase to go unmentioned around school and town.

"It wasn't exactly a meltdown, Dad," I replied, rolling my eyes and shaking my head dismissively as if it was no big deal. "More a misunderstanding between Maya and me."

"Is that what you call yelling so loudly that windows shatter?" I couldn't remember my father ever grilling me this intensely.

"Kids exaggerate," I scoffed. "Glass didn't break. Maya got upset. Voices were raised but nothing was thrown."

"Just as long as *you're* all right." My dad gave me a hard stare. "These years can be challenging. Emotionally as well as physically."

"Yeah, they can," I answered, trying not to squirm or look away and betray my secret. Just trying to figure out how much my father knew about what was going on with me.


"Weapons," proclaimed Jackson the next morning as he drove Oliver and me through town on our way to school.

329

"Bar Tech wants to turn us into human weapons."

"Seriously?" Although I was horrified by the thought, I also couldn't help but laugh at the crazy idea. "*We're* the cutting edge in stealth warfare?"

"Absolutely. Think about it," Oliver chimed back, excited. "Jackson's electrical power. Your invisibility. My physical prowess. Not to mention Maya's telekinesis. Innocent-looking students by day. Awesome superpowers by night. Who'd ever guess? It's genius."

"Madness is more like it. And also a hundred billion in technology deals for Bar Tech according to Cochran," I retorted, rolling my eyes, appalled by the prospect. "I certainly hope the security of this country never depends on me." I glanced over at Jackson as he stopped at a red traffic light on Main Street.

"One hundred billion is a big incentive," Jackson said as he looked back at me with a sly grin, which made me feel incredibly self-conscious. Was he just reacting to my somewhat amusing comment? Or was he letting me know that he knew I had broken into his house the day before? One thing I did know for sure—I wasn't going to ask him why he was grinning.

"By the way," I said, quickly changing the subject, "has anyone heard from our friend Maya?"

"Not a peep," Jackson replied, shaking his head no.

"Me neither," Oliver added. "I texted her last night but never heard back."

"Same here," I acknowledged, feeling a twinge of anxiety that none of us had heard a word from Maya. "I just assumed she was still mad at *me*."

"Maybe she's mad at *all of us*," Oliver speculated, throwing off his concern with a shrug.

"Maybe . . . ," I muttered back, not really believing that was the reason we hadn't heard from her, yet not wanting to worry needlessly.

"Ask her at school," Jackson said matter-of-factly, looking over at me.

Our eyes locked. I could tell Jackson was troubled as well that no one had heard anything from Maya, given what had happened yesterday at school. I knew in my gut that it just wasn't like her to go radio silent.

Still, I wasn't quite prepared for the major shit storm that we were about to fly into.

As soon as Jackson pulled into the school parking lot, I knew something major was going down. First of all, the place was more crowded and chaotic than was usual for early morning. Kids, looking dazed and confused, were getting corralled into the quad by Bar Tech Security. The campus was crawling with guards. More than I'd ever seen before. They were stationed everywhere I looked—throughout the quad, at all the entrances, even on the school roof—swarming like ants at a summer picnic.

"Maybe coming in today wasn't the best idea," Oliver remarked with concern as Jackson parked the Mustang.

"Nothing we can do about that now," Jackson responded. "Without drawing unwanted eyeballs." He was referring to Bar Tech Security.

"What do you think's going on?" I asked Jackson as I exited the car.

"I've got a feeling we're about to find out," muttered Jackson forebodingly as he locked the Mustang and scanned the parking lot.

I took a deep breath, then started walking toward the main entrance with Oliver at my side. Jackson ambled behind us on full alert. I kept glancing over my shoulder and noticed that his eyes never stopped scanning the school grounds. He seemed to be clocking the position of every security guard. Was he cataloging this information for future reference? Or was he calculating an emergency escape route?

As soon as Oliver, Jackson, and I strode through the main doors into the lobby, we were immediately herded into the school auditorium along with rest of our fellow students. The hall was jam-packed. More than I'd ever seen it. I looked around at people's faces. They appeared to be as bewildered and panicked as I felt. Rumors were running rampant. I overheard snippets of conversations as I proceeded down the aisle, scanning about for seats: "... searching for drugs?" "... someone died ..." Truth was, none of us had a clue why we were sitting there or what was going on.

The only thing I knew for certain: Fear was in the air.

I spotted three seats together toward the back. Jackson and Oliver followed me as I made my way into the middle of the row and sat down. Jackson took the seat to my left, Oliver to my right. We barely had time to settle into our chairs when the entire faculty filed into the auditorium. They looked like a funeral processional, except it wasn't for Mrs. Henderson. There was a great deal of whispering among the audience as the teachers silently filled up the first two rows of seats. They barely acknowledged our presence, except for Mr. Bluni, who spotted me sitting with Jackson and Oliver. The entire scene seemed surreal to me, like a strange dream.

"Who died?" Oliver quipped, referring to the teachers' somber expressions.

Jackson shot Oliver a harsh look, which made him clam up and contritely sink back into his seat. Oliver realized it was too soon after Mrs. Henderson's accident to make such a flippant remark.

"Anyone seen Maya?" I asked, scanning up and down each row, searching for her.

"Maybe she took a sick day?" Oliver suggested, clearly wishing he'd done the same.

Before Jackson could weigh in on Maya's whereabouts, the auditorium suddenly got quiet. Principal Hellinger strode up the steps to the main stage and approached the podium. He adjusted the microphone and cleared his throat, then gazed out at the audience before speaking.

"Good morning," he said without any of his usual cheerfulness. "You all must be wondering why you've been assembled here so early in the morning."

I sat there and didn't utter a sound. And neither did Oliver or Jackson or anyone else in the audience for that matter. Everyone just wanted Hellinger to get to the point. Enough suspense. Was an asteroid about to collide with the earth? Or was all this drama being orchestrated for some other reason?

"Unfortunately, I have some bad news," Hellinger announced. "There's been an accident. One of your classmates is in the hospital in a coma."

A murmur swept through the crowd like a forest fire. "What happened?" "Who was it?" "Will they be okay?" Hellinger raised his hands to quiet the assembly. After the audience settled down, our principal dropped the biggest bombshell of all.

"It's Chase Cochran."

Loud cries and incredulous gasps erupted throughout the hall. I glanced over at Oliver and then at Jackson in shock. We now knew the "who" in this mystery. The major unanswered question still remaining was: What had put Chase in a coma? I had my suspicions.

Before any questions could be answered, Richard Cochran appeared on stage beside Principal Hellinger. Hellinger stepped away from the podium as a grim-faced Cochran took center stage at the microphone. He paused before speaking.

"My son, Chase, was brutally beaten yesterday afternoon by an unknown assailant. He's in a coma, fighting for his life. Bar Tech Security is leading the investigation." Cochran took a breath, scanning the faces of the audience.

"Hey, Dad," Oliver muttered softly, barely audible but loud enough for me to hear.

I looked at Oliver and gently squeezed his arm in support, knowing how painful this moment must be for him. Seeing the man he'd just discovered was his dad standing up there, talking about his son.

Cochran meanwhile continued: "I'm offering a hundred-thousand-dollar reward for any information on who was responsible for this heinous attack. If you know anything, please come forward. All tips will be kept confidential."

Cochran then turned on his heels and walked out of the auditorium without saying another word. The audience was left momentarily thunderstruck.

Principal Hellinger quickly returned to the podium

and was inundated with a barrage of questions. Students stood up, shouting over one another. Who'd do such an awful thing to "wonderful" Chase? Was it a random attack? Another student?

"Please! One at a time." Hellinger tried responding in an orderly fashion but was drowned out by the chorus of angry voices.

Meanwhile my mind was working overtime formulating its own theory about what might have happened to Chase. And it all led me back to one obvious conclusion about who was involved.

"You think Maya did this?" I whispered to Jackson, voicing my growing suspicion that her absence from school wasn't coincidental. Especially after what had gone down between Chase and Maya the day before.

"I don't know," Jackson replied, trying to wrap his head around my hypothesis. "But it sure is a great excuse to launch a witch hunt. Flush us out."

I could tell Jackson was disturbed by what was unfolding in the auditorium.

"This whole thing is creeping me out," Oliver whispered, huddling closer, visibly nervous.

I nodded in agreement, unable to deny that I was also feeling an unsettling brew of fear and dread. That's when I realized that students all around us were staring and pointing accusatorily . . . at Jackson. Including Chase's boys, Kyle,

Alex, and Vox, who were seated a few rows ahead of us.

"What about Winters?" ". . . always been jealous . . ." "Where was he yesterday?" I couldn't believe Chase's friends were scapegoating Jackson, blaming him for Chase's injuries. They actually thought he was Chase's attacker. I knew it was completely crazy. After all, I had been with Jackson yesterday afternoon, which meant he couldn't have attacked Chase. True, I'd been *invisible*, and Jackson hadn't exactly known I was hiding in his bedroom. But that was beside the point.

*Jackson was innocent.*

Of course I couldn't exactly tell everyone in school the reason I knew this for sure, for a couple of reasons. First, it would betray my secret. *Our secrets.* And second, it would make things even weirder than they already were between Jackson and me. Which left only one thing for the three of us to do.

"Time to go," I whispered, grabbing Jackson and Oliver's arms as I stood up.

The mood in the auditorium had shifted and turned ugly. Principal Hellinger left the podium, giving up trying to control the crowd. Everyone's confusion and anger suddenly seemed to be directed at Jackson. His outsider status put him squarely in the blame-game crosshairs. All Jackson's former pals from the football team—like Kyle and Alex—not to mention his fellow students who had known him their whole lives, were vilifying him. They were ready to string Jackson up as if he were a terrorist or something. I was afraid of what might happen to Jackson if we didn't leave the hall immediately.

I forced my way through the row toward the aisle with Jackson and Oliver close behind me. From two rows ahead I heard Kyle shout, *"We know it was you, asshole."*

*"What did you do to Chase?"* Alex yelled angrily, pointing directly at Jackson.

"He didn't do anything!" I snapped back at them, pissed as hell.

"Don't waste your breath, Nica," Jackson insisted. "No one's listening."

"Can we discuss this later, guys?" Oliver nervously interjected. "When we're *not* fighting off an angry mob?"

"Good point," I retorted, barreling up the aisle toward the nearest exit.

"Remember. Whatever happens . . . ," Jackson whispered to Oliver and me, *"don't* expose your power."

"Believe me," I snapped back, "that's the last thing on my mind." I had absolutely no intention of doing anything so crazy as exposing myself in front of the entire school.

Oliver and Jackson swiftly followed my lead toward the exit doors, practically on my heels. Kids were already spilling out from the rows and jamming the aisles. The three of us hustled out of the auditorium and through the lobby, while the rest of our classmates remained inside.

"Where are we going?" Oliver asked, nervously glancing over his shoulder.

"Anywhere that's not here," proclaimed Jackson. "Remember: No matter what happens . . . *don't* use your power."

As I shoved open the exit doors into the quad, I immediately noticed that it was dark outside, as if an enormous thunderstorm were about to blow through town. Except that there weren't any threatening clouds in the sky above us.

In fact there wasn't a cloud anywhere in sight.

"That's weird," I muttered, gazing up at a blue sky, confused as to why it was suddenly so dusky at only nine in the morning. And it was quickly growing darker by the second.

Jackson and Oliver both looked up at the sky. Oliver was as perplexed as I was. Jackson's face, however, registered immediate alarm.

"Grab something!" Jackson barked to us as he reached out for a nearby bike rack.

Before Oliver or I could react, let alone process what Jackson meant, a blinding flash of phosphorescent green light blazed up the sky.

*Oh my God*, I thought. *The pulse is happening again. We're totally exposed.*

I instinctively shielded my sensitive eyes from the intense glare as the most forceful *WHUMP* of energy I'd ever experienced in my life hurtled me back against the large oak tree . . . *WHAM!*

A searing jab of pain exploded throughout my entire body as I ricocheted off the tree like Dorothy in that Kansas tornado . . . plummeting to the ground in the middle of the quad with a deadening thud. . . .

I was completely dazed and in excruciating pain . . . with no idea what had happened to Jackson or Oliver . . . or whether they were seriously injured.

## 15. HIDE AND SEEK

"Ow . . . ," I groaned, rubbing my throbbing head. Although barely a few seconds had passed since the pulse hit, I felt extremely groggy and disoriented. As though I'd been unconscious for hours.

I opened my eyes, squinting in the light. Trying to focus on something . . . anything.

*"Nica? You okay?"* a distressed voice asked with some urgency.

I looked up as a blurry figure came toward me. I started to make out the details of Jackson's face. "Think so . . . ," I muttered, incredibly relieved that Jackson was all right.

But then I saw he was frowning, looking as disturbed as I'd ever seen him. Deep concern flashed in his baby blue-greens. He extended his right hand toward me and I latched on to it, never wanting to let go.

As he helped me to my feet, I noticed a thin stream of blood running down his face.

"Oh my God. Your forehead . . ." A nasty two-inch gash

ran along Jackson's hairline. Now I was the one who was alarmed.

I gently touched his wound, wiping away the thin trail of blood running down to his eyebrow. Our faces were only inches apart.

"I'm fine," Jackson insisted, brushing my hand away from his face as if he were swatting away an annoying fly.

"Hey, O. You alive?" Turning away, Jackson shifted his attention to Oliver, who was splayed across the courtyard at least thirty feet away from us. We'd been the only ones out in the quad when the pulse hit.

"And kicking," Oliver quipped back, flashing an enthusiastic thumbs-up. I was thankful he hadn't lost his biting sense of humor, even in the face of adversity.

It was then I heard screaming and shouting emanating from inside the school. I turned toward the front entrance, my senses on full alert as . . .

. . . a barrage of panic-stricken kids charged out through the doors. Scores of students flooded the quad like a giant tidal wave . . . pushing and shoving and fleeing in every direction . . . yelling for help. Driving Jackson and me apart.

It was complete chaos. A massive teenage freak-out, unlike any I'd ever seen.

Momentarily stunned by the onslaught, I suddenly found myself stranded in the middle of all this pandemonium. I was frozen with fear, unable to move an inch. Scores of terrified kids rushed by me, nearly trampling one another, desperate to escape the school grounds. The running of the bulls in Pamplona, Spain, would have seemed tame by comparison.

Fights began erupting all over the quad like flash fires. Best buddies Kyle and Alex were throwing serious punches at each other, going at it like they were mortal enemies. And BFFs Lisa Hooper and Amanda Morovich were suddenly kicking and scratching and yanking each other's hair. It seemed like the entire student body had lost their collective minds.

"Nica! *Nica!*" Jackson shouted at me, shaking me out of my trancelike confusion.

My eyes found him trapped across the yard with Oliver. They were yelling and waving for me to come over. But I couldn't hear much more over everyone else's crying and shouting.

I fought my way through the dense crowd, desperate to reach Jackson and not lose my shit in the process. At the same time, Jackson was pushing and shoving his way across the quad toward me. Luckily, somewhere in the middle of the crush of people he snagged my arm. Jackson didn't let go of me until I was standing safely beside him and Oliver, protected by some trees.

"Now what?" I asked, watching in utter disbelief as kids mobbed the parking lot and spilled over to the surrounding streets.

"We get the hell out of here," Oliver snapped back, eager to get going.

"Easier said than done," Jackson responded, staring at the jammed parking lot with an uneasy expression. "It'll take twenty minutes at least."

Car horns honked and blared, as agitated students tried navigating their vehicles out of the gridlocked maze. *Bam.* Jaden's red BMW coupe rear-ended a scrawny mathlete's new black Ford Focus. Doors were kicked open as Jaden and the mathlete got into a fever-pitched screaming match, angrily waving accusatory fingers into each other's faces.

Elsewhere in the parking lot random kids were hopping out of their cars and getting into ridiculous brawls with each other. Others simply abandoned their vehicles and hoofed it. Creating even more havoc.

"Why isn't security doing anything?" I exclaimed, pointing at the more than two dozen Bar Tech Security guards scattered around the yard along with various members of the school faculty, including Mr. Bluni. They were just standing there and hanging back, watching the frenzy unfold. But they were most definitely not getting involved. "It's like they're deliberately not intervening," I observed.

"Not all of them," Oliver countered ominously. He discreetly nodded toward something that was happening across the quad.

My eyes followed Oliver's gaze to find Officers Korey

and Lorentz jostling their way through the crowd. They were the very same two officers who had stopped me during my motorcycle joyride soon after I arrived.

*They were heading straight toward us.*

"Am I imagining things, or are they heading this way?" I questioned aloud, my body tensing up with apprehension.

"I doubt they're coming over to see if you got your license," Jackson declared caustically, shaking his head. "This can't be good."

"Let's split before we find out." Oliver looked over at me and could read the anxiety in my face.

It was clear to me that we had limited options. The quad was still thick with kids pushing their way out. The three of us were as vulnerable as a flock of sitting ducks.

"Follow me," Jackson ordered, whipping around and taking off, bulldozing his way through the crowd. I followed in his wake, clutching on to his jacket so I wouldn't lose him.

I kept glancing over my shoulder to check on Oliver and saw Officers Korey and Lorentz barreling after us. They were maybe three car lengths behind us. No doubt about it—we were the target.

"Don't look at them," Oliver admonished me. "Just keep going." His hand pressed firmly against my back so that I'd have to keep moving forward with Jackson.

"They're gaining on us," I warned Jackson as he pushed ahead, forcefully shoving kids out of his path. He was avoiding the parking lot and heading directly for the nearest street instead.

All of a sudden this hysterical girl with a mane of wild red hair crashed into me, almost knocking me off my feet. I held on to Jackson so as to not fall and get trampled underneath the crush of kids. Once I regained my footing, I became aware that Oliver wasn't holding on to me. I glanced over my shoulder to make sure he was still following us.

Oliver wasn't behind me anymore. But those persistent officers still were. And they were quickly closing the distance gap.

"We lost Oliver," I shouted to Jackson in a growing panic. The last thing I wanted was for Jackson to have to zap Korey and Lorentz or for me to go stealth invisible so that we wouldn't get caught. But we were running out of time and options.

Just then I heard someone shouting. I scanned the crowd and was shocked to discover Oliver leaping thirty feet over the astonished crowd like a puma in the wild.

"Over there." I tapped Jackson on the shoulder, pointing at Oliver across the quad.

"Catch me if you can!" Oliver giddily taunted the guards. He was purposefully sprinting in the opposite direction toward the parking lot. Obviously hoping that our pursuers would take the bait and follow him instead of Jackson and me.

"So much for keeping a low profile and not exposing ourselves," I remarked, amused and impressed by Oliver's newfound fearlessness.

"Classic military strategy. Create a diversion," Jackson quipped back, nodding approvingly with enormous respect.

Sure enough, Oliver's plan seemed to be working. Drawn by his extraordinary display of agility, the storm troopers temporarily forgot about Jackson and me. They were now hot after the leaping geek, along with the more than two dozen other Bar Tech guards who'd suddenly been alerted. In seconds the entire security force had mobilized and was chasing Oliver as he loped through the school parking lot like a gazelle on the African savannah. Meanwhile the rest of the students pointed and gaped in awe as the once-nerdy Oliver vaulted over their heads like an Olympian God.

Which gave Jackson and me just enough time to flee the school grounds and escape Bar Tech Security undetected.

I was shaken by the morning's events and hoped to stay off the Bar Tech Big Brother grid until Jackson and I figured out our next move. Luckily, the towering ash-white aspens in South Mountain Park and Preserve hadn't yet shed all their golden leaves, providing just enough cover so Jackson and I could lay low and think. Unfortunately, it was also a total dead zone as far as any cell-phone service. Which meant no sending or receiving texts. No way to contact Oliver to find out if he was okay. I felt isolated and alone—like Jackson and I were the only human survivors in one of those gruesome zombie flicks.

"I don't understand—how could there have been another pulse so soon?" I questioned Jackson, as the two of us trudged through the dense woods. *"In broad daylight?"*

*"They* caused it, Nica," Jackson asserted, glaring at me, his eyes brimming with rage. "To see *exactly* who'd be affected." His downcast expression suggested that he was as unnerved as I was by the morning's dramatic events. But that didn't stop him from constantly scanning the area to see if we were being followed.

"And Oliver took a bullet so *we* could get away," I apprehensively countered, not feeling any relief at evading capture when my best friend's fate was so . . . *uncertain.* "Think he's all right?" I begged, my voice cracking with emotion. I desperately tried to fight off this overwhelming hopelessness rising up from the pit of my stomach, without success.

"No way they could catch him," Jackson proclaimed optimistically, softening his tone. "Not even a cheetah could," he quipped with a quiet chuckle, trying to placate me as much as himself.

"You really believe that?" I snapped back, refusing to buy into his delusion that we'd somehow prevail over the forces of darkness. "We're not in some stupid-ass video game where we can take down the bad guys in a few hours and progress to the next level. This is the real world—with real-world consequences. And in the real world, *kids get screwed*." I was so worked up and upset that I was practically breathing fire.

Jackson grabbed my arm, pissed. "Stay focused. I need you to stay focused. Otherwise we *will* be screwed."

"Why don't we just face facts?" I lashed back at him, getting even more riled up. "We're outmatched by Bar Tech. And by whoever else is behind all this shit. We've been outmatched from the beginning." I yanked my arm free and broke away from him. "If they killed Mrs. Henderson, who knows what they've done to Maya or Dana?"

"Then what do you suggest we do?" Jackson charged after me, pissed as hell. "Let them use us?"

"*No.* We leave town. Go to Denver. Then spill our guts about the whole conspiracy to the police or the FBI or the CIA or the CDC. Whoever the hell we can get to listen. Before it's too late."

"Really think they'll believe a couple of hysterical kids?" Jackson shouted back, dismissive. I'd never seen Jackson that upset with me before. "Besides, it's not even like we really know the full story."

"I know *enough*," I proclaimed, determined to get out of Barrington as soon as possible.

"*So do I*," Jackson shot back at me, abruptly turning and walking off in the opposite direction.

"What's that supposed to mean?" I asked, charging after Jackson, refusing to let his cutting remark just fly by unchallenged.

"That Nica always takes off and leaves when the going gets tough. *Just like her mom.*" He turned to look at me. His steely blue-green eyes stared disapprovingly.

I stopped dead in my tracks, blinking back tears. Jackson's stinging insult had wounded me and I wanted to run away. But then I looked around the seemingly endless landscape of forest and realized I had no freaking clue where the hell I was. The woods were dense with thicket and had no real trails. I'd be completely lost without Jackson.

Silently repeating Master Kru's mantra to myself, I focused on the bed of dry, decaying leaves lying on the ground beneath my feet. No way was I going to let Jackson see me lose my shit. No way was I going to let him see me cry. I didn't want him to know how stung I was by his hurtful appraisal of my character and my mother's. I felt crushed. No one—not even my mother—had ever said anything that harsh to me . . . or that truthful.

"You can leave and do whatever the hell you want," Jackson scolded, continuing to let his anger rip. Clearly determined to speak his mind. "But no way will I ditch Oliver. Or even Maya. They're my *friends.*"

"They're *my friends* too," I snapped back, feeling my rage bubbling to the surface. "Think I don't care about what happens to them?" I was now so furious that I felt my whole face flush hot and turn bright red. My hands were even starting to disappear, and I couldn't have that.

"It's not the same," Jackson blurted back. "You weren't raised here. Barrington's my home. My family has lived here forever."

"And what? Growing up here gives you authority?" I was so upset with Jackson that I hadn't even realized I'd started to cry until I felt a warm, salty tear roll down my cheek and hit my lips. I wiped it away with the back of my right hand, determined to not be the girl who wept when the going got tough. "This affects me as much as it affects you."

"No. It doesn't," he replied, quickly tempering his attack on me. "It just means . . . I can't pick up and leave. Not when Dana's still missing." His eyes flashed with regret and vulnerability.

I nodded absently while a sharp pain jabbed my already tender heart. I felt as though all the air had been punched out of my lungs. I took in shallow breaths and felt lightheaded. But I refused to collapse into a blubbering ball of self-pity. Despite how wounded I felt by his brutal honesty, I managed to hold it together and not disappear.

"We better keep moving," I said, trying to deflect my emotional state. "Get out of this dead zone." I waved my cell phone and picked up my pace, walking on ahead of Jackson, not wanting him to see my pain.

"Follow that path," Jackson advised. "There's a clearing not too far off. Service should be better."

I followed the narrow dirt trail, my mind still reeling from what he'd said. So that was what this fight—if not our entire relationship—was *really* about: Dana Fox. Even though Jackson hadn't mentioned her in some time, it was clear she was *always* in his thoughts. I realized that was why whenever things threatened to get too dangerous between us, Jackson would deliberately push me away. The tremendous guilt he obviously suffered over Dana's disappearance would never allow him to be with me. Not as long as she was still missing. He needed to keep me at a safe distance—physically and emotionally.

Deep down I'd always suspected that until Dana's whereabouts were definitively known—whether she was dead or until she'd been found—she'd be the wedge between Jackson and me. Dana would always be first in his heart. And I'd always be the proverbial gate crasher in the relationship. That was a painful truth for me to accept.

Jackson and I silently made our way through the brush. The only sounds were from the cracking and snapping of small twigs beneath our feet as we walked. I felt Jackson's eyes on my back as I led the way, but I wouldn't turn around to look at him. I was afraid I'd lose what little composure I had remaining and say something stupid I'd regret.

"Sorry," Jackson mumbled as we finally emerged from

the woods toward a sloping hillside clearing, which led to the edge of town.

"About what?" I replied, acting like I didn't have a clue what he was talking about.

"*Before*. I didn't mean to be so harsh." He couldn't get out the rest of his words, so I jumped in to fill the void.

"You were right." I shrugged. "I was being a jerk. About everything." I eagerly took the blame, desperate to leave all my messed-up feelings behind in those woods.

"No. I was the jerk." Jackson's voice was insistent but also tinged with regret.

I turned around, feeling incredibly remorseful. "You were just being a friend."

All the steeliness had drained from his face. What remained was vulnerability and sadness in his eyes. I wanted to take his hand, to touch him. But I held back and kept my distance, just nodding instead.

Suddenly my cell phone beeped, pulling me back to the crisis at hand. Cell-phone service had finally returned. We were back on the grid. I quickly dug my phone out of my back pocket. Five missed text messages from Oliver flashed across my screen.

"Oliver?" Jackson asked, angling next to me to sneak a peek.

I nodded, showing Jackson the screen as I scrolled through Oliver's numerous texts. "Says he's okay. Wants to meet us."

"At his house?" Jackson asked, already hurrying ahead through the field toward a one-lane fire road that would lead us back to town.

"No," I called out, charging after him. "At Maya's."

Jackson shot me a troubled look as I caught up to him. I could tell he was wondering why Oliver would go to Maya's unless she was in trouble or something had happened to her.

I marched alongside Jackson with a fresh sense of purpose and resolve. Humbled by his fierce determination and loyalty to his friends, I realized that I would not be leaving town either. Not that day, at least. No way would I let my friends down. Not when they needed me.

# 16. PLAN B

Keeping mostly to the back roads, Jackson and I avoided passing through the center of town, which appeared to be on major lockdown. Shops and businesses were all shuttered. Signs in the windows blatantly lied: CLOSED DUE TO EXTREME WEATHER. Sidewalks were mostly empty. Gone was the normal hustle and bustle of people going about their daily business. The only signs of life were Bar Tech Security patrolling the streets. I didn't know if they were still looking for Oliver or for Jackson and me, but I wasn't going to risk exposure to find out.

Anyway, my mind was focused elsewhere. I felt awful. In all the confusion of the pulse hitting and the emotion of the morning, I'd almost forgotten that Maya had been a no-show at school. Then I remembered that the day had started badly with the unsettling news that Chase was lying comatose in the hospital. Had Maya really been responsible for almost killing him?

Fortunately, Jackson was already an old pro at lying low

and sneaking around town. He and I managed to dodge the patrol cars and weave our way over to Maya's house without tripping any alarms or alerting Bar Tech Security to our whereabouts. Still, it was a surreal experience for me. In all my travels to unfamiliar countries I'd never had to worry about being hunted down by the authorities. Here in my home country I suddenly felt like a fugitive because of who I was and what I'd become. I was even afraid of letting my own father know where I was hiding. He'd been calling and texting and leaving me messages, but I hadn't called him back. If my darkest fears and suspicions about his collaboration with Cochran and Bar Tech were true, then I certainly couldn't trust him.

The unpretentious, cream-colored ranch house was less than two blocks away from where Dana Fox lived. A large, Tuscan-inspired residence, Maya's house was comfortably set back from the road. It had a beautifully manicured lawn studded with pink and white rosebushes and perfectly trimmed shrubs. And it looked like one of those upscale home-magazine covers presenting the ideal American home. It cried out perfection. No surprise that this was where Maya Bartoli lived.

But curiously, there was no sign of her, or anyone else at the house for that matter. Not even Oliver. In fact the house projected an eerie, vacant feeling . . . a stillness that I found worrisome.

"He did say to meet him at Maya's house?" Jackson asked, scanning the vicinity, as we hid among the orange and red maple trees that ran up the long brick driveway.

"In black and white," I whispered, showing him Oliver's most recent text on my cell-phone screen.

"Let's check around back," Jackson whispered, motioning toward the rear yard.

Using the trees for cover, Jackson and I crept up the driveway toward the garage, always keeping our eyes on the street, too, in case any Bar Tech guards were lurking around. Just as we were circling around the side of the house, something leaped down thirty feet from the top branches of an enormous oak tree. Jackson whipped around upon hearing the noise. I flinched and muffled a scream as a figure landed in front of me.

It was Oliver, his arms spread wide, with a theatrical "ta-da!" for maximum effect. "Hey, bitches," he said, grinning proudly over his nimble feat.

"Oliver! You trying to give me a heart attack?" I snapped back, punching him in the right arm.

"Ow! That hurts," Oliver responded, grimacing and rubbing his arm.

"Lucky I didn't throw you," I replied, shaking my head, relieved but annoyed.

"And you're both lucky I didn't zap you across the street," Jackson interjected, stepping between Oliver and me. "Can we get down to business?"

"Right. Sorry. Reboot," Oliver responded, taking a deep breath.

"So? Tell us what happened," I pressed, anxious to hear exactly what had transpired since we'd fled school a few hours earlier.

"Well, as you both recall, yours truly was being chased through town by our good friends at the Bar Tech goon squad," Oliver began quite dramatically.

"Yes, we remember it well. Mind fast-forwarding?" Jackson gestured wheels spinning, stressing the urgency of our situation and the moment.

"Absolutely." Oliver nodded, continuing: "Anyway, I'm literally flying over people's backyards and through trees. Yada, yada. Even racing after me in their souped-up squad cars these bozos were having a tough time keeping up. It was actually kind of awesome. Well, I didn't want them following me home, so I circled back through town, when all of a sudden I get this urgent 911 text from Maya. I mean, I couldn't exactly reply midair—"

"And what did she say?" I nudged him along, hoping he'd get to the point.

"Just this." Oliver fished his phone out of his pocket and showed Maya's text to us. Jackson and I looked at the screen.

"*Bar Tech*," I uttered, reading the two-word message aloud and exchanging worried glances with Jackson before looking back at Maya's house.

"That's exactly what Dana texted me. *They* were here," Jackson added, walking toward the house. *"They knew about her."*

"How?" Oliver asked, looking at Jackson and me.

"Her wig-out with Chase yesterday morning at school," I reminded him. "Chase narced on her to his father and *mine*."

"Think they're watching us?" Oliver questioned, looking around the property and brazenly flipping the bird for the imagined cameras.

"I think they're long gone," Jackson responded, already peering in through the first-floor windows to see what was happening inside the Bartoli residence.

"They were long gone by the time I got here," Oliver responded, following after Jackson. "I tried texting and calling Maya, but . . ." And then he shook his head gravely, indicating he had never heard back from Maya and didn't know much else.

"They could've taken Maya anywhere. Or worse," I reflected solemnly, trying to fight off my increasing frustration at not being able to do something about Maya's disappearance.

"I don't think they did," muttered Jackson, his eyes gazing far off into the distance. I watched him and could almost see the gears spinning in his brain. He knew something.

"Meaning . . . ?" I asked, curious to hear his theory about where he thought they might have taken Maya.

"Meaning I don't think they moved her too far away. Too

much could go wrong. Not to mention too many prying eyes. I think Maya's still in town. Somewhere close by," Jackson declared with conviction. Which got me wondering . . . where would I take someone if I wanted to hide her in Barrington?

"The city jail?" Oliver speculated with a shrug.

"No. Too public," I interrupted, studying Jackson's determined expression. I thought I knew him well enough by now to be able to decode his thought process. "Somewhere right under our noses. *Like Bar Tech headquarters.*" I blurted out my epiphany as if I'd stumbled across a treasure map.

"Yeah." Jackson nodded, surprised that I'd arrived at the same conclusion that he had but giving me props. *"Like Bar Tech."*

Jackson shot me a half smile, impressed by my perceptiveness. I looked back at him, acting all nonchalant and cool, while inside I was beaming.

"Genius," Oliver remarked, nodding as he absorbed the inherent logic of Jackson's and my claim.

"You know," I piped up very matter-of-factly, "I've always wanted a tour."

"No time like the present," Jackson responded glibly, shrugging *why not.*

I looked back at Jackson and cracked a big smile. He smiled back, then began walking toward the driveway and the street. Was he thinking the same thing I was thinking?

"Well, what are we waiting for?" Oliver chimed in, following Jackson back toward the street. "Maya needs us."

Oliver gestured for me to follow him, which I eagerly did. I knew our mission was completely crazy. Maybe it was even what the Navy SEALs call a suicide mission. What made us ever think we could take on a powerful corporation like Bar Tech? They were secretive and dangerous. Not to mention they might actually be responsible for people disappearing—like Maya and Dana. And yes, maybe even for killing Mrs. Henderson. But for once I wasn't second guessing myself or doing the rational thing. I was throwing all caution to the wind. I was trusting my gut instinct, as well as trusting Jackson's. Logic and reason didn't concern me. Because I was with my friends, and I wasn't afraid.

Oliver, Jackson, and I spent the rest of the afternoon hiding out in some random family's garden shed in their backyard on the outskirts of town, not too far from Bar Tech headquarters. We were strategizing and planning our assault on the fifty-two-acre Bar Tech compound. Jackson knew it was protected by an extremely high-tech security system.

"Which means they're protecting some pretty big secrets," Jackson emphasized for effect.

"So what you're saying is, all we have to do is infiltrate one of the more sophisticated security systems imaginable," I stated, amused that we were even discussing something so outlandish.

"Every system has its weaknesses," Oliver chimed in, agreeing with Jackson. *"Vulnerabilities."*

"Trick is to just figure out what they are . . . and *exploit* them," Jackson stressed. "We've got a precious few hours remaining before our collective powers disappear. What better use than to break into a high-security compound?"

Meanwhile my father had sent several increasingly insistent texts to find out where I was and if I was all right. He never directly mentioned the pulse or what had happened at school but demanded I come home immediately.

I ignored his demands and wasn't about to go home—not yet. Instead I sent back an ambiguous but hopefully reassuring text: *All well w/friends.*

I had no idea whether my dad would believe me or flip out for defying him, because then Jackson ordered Oliver and me to power off and disable our phones. He worried that Bar Tech might be able to track us using their sophisticated GPS. Not to mention other more sophisticated technology that we didn't even know about. But at the very least we could prevent our phones from betraying us.

*"Seriously?"* I asked, slightly skeptical.

"Seriously," Jackson replied decisively.

As if to prove his point, he then removed the SIM card from the back of his phone and smashed it on the floor of the shed with the heel of his boot.

"It's the only way to be sure," Jackson said.

Oliver looked at me and shrugged. He popped out his SIM card and smashed it too.

Which left me standing there, hesitant and alone. I was the only one whose phone was still activated. No matter where I traveled, I never went anywhere without my trusty smartphone. It had always been my connection to the outside world, my communication lifeline. No matter where in the world I was living, it was my constant companion— the only thing that never changed. Whenever I was lonely or bored, I could always whip it out, text Lai or other friends, or find a thousand other activities on it to entertain me. And now Jackson was asking me to actively cut off my sole means of communication outside Barrington. It was like asking me to go without clothes. Still, I knew Jackson was right about this, as he had been right about so many other things.

I stared at my phone and sighed in resignation. Even though I knew I could always purchase a new SIM card (exactly when, I didn't know, since I was on the run . . . but theoretically I could), it was the act of severing my connection with the outside world that filled me with anxiety. On the other hand being with Jackson and Oliver gave me strength. It meant I was a part of something that mattered more to me than some stupid phone.

So I popped out the SIM card, tossed it to the ground,

and then smashed it to smithereens with the heel of my shoe. And I was pleasantly surprised that I actually felt pretty good destroying it.

"Okay, now what?" I asked Jackson, prepared to take on the world. Or at least Bar Tech.

"We wait until dark," he answered somberly.

It seemed like an eternity before darkness finally descended upon Barrington. Jackson, now confident that Bar Tech could no longer track us with our phones at least, gave the go-ahead. It was time to move on. And so the three of us left the relative safety of our hideout to rescue Maya and maybe even take down Bar Tech.

# 17. BAR TECH

The ultrasecretive Bar Tech headquarters sat atop the high-est point in Barrington. I'd never paid much attention to the building before. A sprawling, modern steel-and-stone corporate behemoth with very few windows, it loomed over Barrington like an ancient castle or medieval fortress.

Formidable. Powerful. Impenetrable. An electrified, barbed-wire fence was a none-too-subtle warning to all would-be gate-crashers to KEEP OUT. It was definitely intimidating.

Jackson, Oliver, and I silently crept up the hillside, ven-turing into enemy territory. I was undeterred by the inher-ent risks and the danger I was putting myself into. I felt a little like a modern-day Joan of Arc—except without the fancy armor and visions of God talking to her. At seven-teen, despite daunting odds, Joan had fought to help fif-teenth-century France regain control of its country from the English during the Hundred Years' War. Not that I was anything like a future saint, but thinking about what Joan had faced did inspire me to press on with our mission.

The three of us stood outside the Bar Tech compound perimeter fence and stared at its threatening sign: NO TRES-PASSING.

"I can hop over it," Oliver offered, eager to do his whole leaping-lizard thing, which he was getting amazingly good at.

"No need," Jackson said, suddenly extending his hands to grab more than ten thousand volts of high-tensile wire.

"Wait! What are you—?" I momentarily panicked, expecting Jackson to be zapped into oblivion. Until I remembered that he was actually like a power station. He could emit plenty of voltage himself. I shrugged, feeling my face flush, a bit embarrassed.

Ignoring me, Jackson gripped the fence with both hands. I heard horrible, sizzling, zapping sounds. They were fol-lowed by a flurry of blindingly bright blue-white sparks.

Oliver and I dodged the flying embers, not wanting to get scorched, as Jackson blew out the electrical circuits and the entire Bar Tech power grid. After a few seconds Jackson let go of the fence and there was quiet. A moment later he magically whipped out a pair of wire cutters from his coat pocket.

"Swiped them from the shed," Jackson slyly admitted, reading my surprise at the sudden appearance of the cut-ters. "Figured they'd come in handy." A few quick snips and Jackson easily cut through that wire fence like it was a sheet of paper.

"He was an Eagle Scout," Oliver quipped to me, explaining Jackson's dexterity and fondness for gadgetry and tools. "I never even earned my Wolf badge."

"Be prepared," Jackson glibly responded, quoting the Boy Scout motto, as he pried apart the rigid wire fence and waved Oliver and me onto Bar Tech property.

"Won't they know? About the fence being breached and all?" I asked, voicing my concern that the Bar Tech cavalry would no doubt come charging over and round us up like prize cattle.

"They'll need to figure out what's wrong first," Jackson replied, leading our offensive up the hillside. "They'll think their security system had a glitch. Which gives us just enough time to locate Maya before they realize what the hell happened."

"And if we don't find her in time?" Oliver asked.

"We do what we have to," answered Jackson coolly, resolute in his mission.

To me that meant we'd use our powers and get out of there at all costs. I shot Oliver a harsh look, indicating my tacit approval of Jackson's declaration. I was impressed by how Jackson had thought through every last detail. Oliver shrugged apologetically. He was obviously contrite for casting any doubt on our operation. I nodded empathetically— having suffered my own doubts—and then gestured that we should proceed. After all, time was of the essence.

As Oliver and I followed Jackson up the rugged, rocky terrain, I began to wonder just how long Jackson had been planning this assault on Bar Tech. This didn't seem to be a whim or spur of the moment decision by him. Had he started planning this immediately after Dana went missing? Had he connected her disappearance to Bar Tech even back then? Before I had ever arrived in Barrington? Before he even knew about the pulse?

It took the three of us several minutes to scale the steep hillside. We moved in unison, clambering low to the ground to avoid detection from the spotlights that randomly scanned the area. I felt like a wannabe Navy SEAL on some top-secret mission in Pakistan, except for the minor fact that I was untrained, unarmed, and had no night-vision goggles.

We made it to the crest of the hill without being noticed and finally reached the darkened Bar Tech headquarters. The facility was called the Integration and Testing Complex. Radiating off the sprawling central building like spokes of a wheel were six warehouselike rectangular structures. They were numbered plainly—BLDG 1 through BLDG 6—with no other identifying signage or markings.

"What do you think those are?" Oliver whispered, pointing to the seemingly ordinary buildings.

"Research labs?" I conjectured, glancing over at Jackson, who was wedged close to me as we were lying on the ground.

"We'll find out soon enough," Jackson replied quite cryptically, silently sizing up the structures. I admired how skilled he was at reconnaissance and surveillance.

Fortunately, the electricity was still out across the entire compound, courtesy of Jackson blowing the electrical grid earlier. I heard guards off in the distance shouting and scrambling around the grounds as they attempted to restore power and check for possible intruders. It was an effective distraction, hopefully providing us with just enough time to find a way inside and locate Maya.

Jackson got up and gestured for Oliver and me to follow him. He darted across the walkway between Building 2 and Building 3. Half crouching, I hurried after Jackson and prayed that I wouldn't stumble or make any unwanted noises. Oliver followed me, light on his feet. We made it to the side of Building 2 sight unseen and huddled close to the wall. Jackson tried opening the first door we encountered. It was locked and protected by a coded security keypad.

"Don't suppose anyone knows the code off the top of their heads?" I dryly quipped.

Oliver examined the keypad and announced: "It's a CypherLock."

"What's the deal with it?" Jackson whispered, turning to Oliver in hope that he had some answers.

"Popular with the military and government and other high-value targets," Oliver explained. "Requires a four-digit entry code, which usually changes several times a day for added safety. Simple but highly effective."

"Don't tell me you learned all this playing video games," I teased, despite being suitably impressed with his knowledge.

"Like I've been telling my mother for years: They're not a waste of time," Oliver replied irreverently with a little smile, pulling out his cell phone and logging on to the Internet.

"Don't you need your SIM card for your phone to work?" I reminded him of our ritual smashing of the SIM cards not that long ago.

"Actually, only our phones and the GPS have been disabled," Jackson enlightened me. "The device still has Internet capabilities."

"Well, according to this hacking website," Oliver interrupted, scrolling through his phone, "there's a default code that might allow us to reprogram the system."

"Great, hurry. What's the code?" I pressed, worried that some guards might pass by at any moment.

"Not that simple," Oliver responded. "We need a power source to activate the system."

"Why didn't you say so in the first place?" Jackson replied, holding out his hands and rubbing his fingertips like an expert safecracker.

Oliver and I crouched back as a bright jolt of electricity

surged out of Jackson's fingers to the keypad. The solid red light suddenly started flashing intermittently. Oliver hurried over and entered the four-digit default code. The panel light changed from flashing red to flashing green. Then he quickly entered another four-digit number before the light switched back to solid red.

"Care to do the honors?" Jackson asked, looking directly at me.

"My first industrial break-in. How romantic," I remarked, half joking but also half serious, as I stood next to Jackson at the keypad waiting for Oliver to tell me the code.

"Six, seven, nine, six," Oliver whispered.

*The date of the accident.* I nodded, having an "aha" moment, impressed by Oliver's ingenuity. I entered the code and was pleasantly surprised when I heard the door click loudly. Amazingly, we'd unlocked the door.

"Now that's what I call teamwork," Jackson declared proudly. Then he opened the door slowly and carefully, being as quiet as possible. He peered inside, scanning around the darkness in all directions. He then nodded to Oliver and me that the coast was clear and hurriedly waved us in behind him. We entered a long, dark corridor and let the door swing shut behind us.

I was immediately struck by how incredibly cold it was inside the building—almost like the inside of a refrigerator. Goose bumps ran up and down my arms as I zipped up my jacket. I looked around and tried to get my bearings. It took several seconds for my eyes to adjust to the lack of light.

I crept down the deserted corridor behind Jackson. It led us into a cavernous warehouse filled with at least half a dozen intricate steel structures in various stages of development. They looked like giant mechanical creatures resembling mutant spiders, straight out of a science-fiction film.

"Holy crap." Oliver muttered in amazement, his wide eyes taking it all in. "It's like World of Warcraft come to life."

"Doesn't look like Maya's here," I remarked, stating the obvious. I felt both a bit awed and a bit frightened by what we'd discovered. *What exactly were these things?*

"We'll just work our way through each building until we do find her," Jackson stated, seemingly unfazed by the huge skeletal structures that were looming over us.

"What're they building? Space ships?" I asked, cocking my head sideways, not having a clue exactly what I was looking at.

"Satellites," Jackson answered. "The kind that get launched into outer space. This is where they build and test them."

"What do they do up there in space?" I responded, stunned to actually be standing beneath such amazing machines or whatever they were.

"Not only do they track weather systems, they also track

our every movement using GPS," Jackson replied threateningly. "A perfect way to spy."

"They're made of aluminum, titanium, and steel," Oliver said, walking underneath each one, closely checking them out. "Though there's also some sort of graphite fiber-polycyanate face sheet over aluminum honeycomb core here."

"Thanks, Einstein," I kidded Oliver, despite my growing uneasiness at how Bar Tech was using its awesome technology against kids like Jackson, Oliver, and me.

"That's probably the thermal stress facility," Oliver added, pointing to an enormous freestanding Plexiglas chamber—like one of those stand-alone isolation booths. Except this one was so large an elephant could have easily fit inside it.

"Thermal stress? Now you've really lost me," I had to confess. Science and cutting-edge technology never were my strong suit.

"Where they test these babies before launching them into outer space," Oliver responded, really getting into all this geek-speak.

Just then we heard raised voices and hurried footsteps entering the building. Oliver and I looked at each other and froze in place as the footsteps charged down the corridor. It sounded to me like they were heading right toward us.

Jackson quickly crept over and whispered, "Time to split and find Maya before they find us."

I nodded, trying to contain my fear despite my heart

beating a mile a minute inside my chest. Pulling myself together, I hastily tiptoed after Jackson as he led Oliver and me to an exit at the rear of the building—just as two security guards were rushing in through the front door of Building 2.

"They must suspect we're here," murmured Oliver, a bit winded. He kept nervously glancing over his shoulder after our hasty departure from Building 2.

Darting past Building 3 in complete darkness, we slipped around the perimeter of Building 4, our bodies pressing close to the exterior wall. We had narrowly evaded capture and detection by the goon squad, who were now on the opposite side of the compound, busily turning Building 2 upside down, looking for the mystery invaders.

"What if this whole Maya abduction was just a setup?" I speculated. "A trap to lure us here."

"Of course it was," Jackson replied definitively, gesturing for us to keep low to the ground as we crept toward the nearest door. "But that doesn't mean they'll get us."

Jackson suddenly held his hand up, holding me back behind him. I held my hand out and silently cautioned Oliver not to move a muscle either. Jackson pressed his ear to the door, listening for any voices or sounds of people waiting inside.

Suddenly the headlights of a gleaming black SUV flashed out of the darkness, brightly flaring in our direction. The oversized vehicle was zooming up the road, and the three of us were directly in its path. *Oh, shit.* We dropped down to the ground in unison.

I was silently praying that the glimmering headlights wouldn't betray our presence, when I felt something gently touch my hand. It was Jackson's hand. Concerned at first, I glanced across the pavement, and my eyes met Jackson's, thinking he wanted to warn me about something. Instead he gave me this tender, caring look as his hand clasped mine. Jackson and I lay side by side, our hands entwined for a few brief seconds. Neither of us knew whether these were going to be our final moments together or not. I was a jumble of emotions. I felt elation at having such an intimate moment with Jackson and also abject terror that we were about to be exposed and locked up.

Luckily, the headlights just missed revealing us. The SUV whooshed by the building, speeding off to another area of the compound. Once the vehicle receded from view, Jackson pulled his hand away from mine and rose to his feet. Our moment was gone. It took me a second to catch my breath and pull myself together before I stood up too. By then Jackson, now back to all business, had cracked open the door, and we all slipped inside Building 4.

No one made a sound. But there definitely were other people lurking inside that facility besides the three of us. Their presence was felt. Ambient noises. Like heels clacking on tile, perhaps? And possibly a few muffled voices. It was difficult to know for sure what kind of situation we were walking into.

I skulked along the narrow, winding corridor in between Jackson and Oliver. The three of us moved like a pack of feral cats stalking their prey. Except in this instance we didn't know if *we* were potentially the prey for Bar Tech. Still, we forged ahead, creeping through the tubelike passageway, which resembled a New York City subway tunnel: cramped, dark, and windowless. All my senses were on high alert, and so were Jackson's and Oliver's. I was aware of an overpowering chemical smell, which almost made me sick to my stomach. It reminded me of a strong disinfectant or antiseptic.

We reached a set of double doors at the end of the tunnel. They were solid steel, with no window to see through. Jackson was about to open the doors when I grabbed his arm and stopped him. He shot me a puzzled look. I didn't say a word. Instead I just pointed to myself and then at the door. He nodded his understanding. Oliver then nodded too.

I took a deep breath and shut my eyes. Then I channeled all my anger and rage and how majorly pissed off I was feeling at that moment. Over being betrayed by the adults in this town and in my life. By my own father, no less. That now-familiar warmth quickly infused my body from my toes up to my scalp, followed by that red-hot tingling up and down my spine. And by the time I opened my eyes, I could see by Jackson and Oliver's captivated expressions that it had worked. Mission accomplished. I had successfully become invisible in just a few seconds.

"You're really getting the hang of this disappearing thing," Oliver said, nodding, quite amused.

"Not exactly a skill I can list on a college application," I kidded. "But it's definitely coming in handy."

"Nica," Jackson interjected. "Remember to tap on the door if everything's okay in there." He was determined to keep Oliver and me on track.

"Copy," I replied, adopting Navy SEAL lingo like I was an old pro instead of a terrified sixteen-year-old.

Jackson then juiced the digital entry pad with his index finger, zapping it with just enough electricity to disarm the door locks. I gently pushed the doors open just wide enough for me to sneak inside the vast warehouse space without alerting attention. True, I was completely invisible, but a door magically opening and closing would definitely raise a few eyebrows.

I navigated that move as smoothly as if I had been doing industrial espionage my whole life, instead of just the last few days. I had no sooner crossed the threshold into the main warehouse than suddenly I encountered a pair of high-beam flashlights. Two very large and very imposing Bar Tech guards were heading right in my direction.

My immediate impulse was to grab hold of something really big and heavy and whack both of these brawny linebackers across the head. But then I had to remember that I wasn't there to act out my anger or frustrations on them, as good as that might feel in the moment. This mission was about being stealth and locating Maya. So I deftly stepped out of their direct path as they barreled toward me. Last thing I wanted was to get mowed down—invisible or not.

The bigger of the two thugs, a freckled, redheaded hulk with no neck, was talking on a Bluetooth headset.

"Yeah, everything's locked down. Over," he confidently reported back to central command.

As soon as he clicked off his Bluetooth, Jackson came charging through the double doors like Iron Man with both hands blasting on all cylinders.

*CRACK! WHAM!* Blinding bolts of white lightning zapped those unsuspecting linebackers back more than thirty feet, knocking each of them out cold. Those thugs never knew what hit them.

"Seriously?" I asked, shaking my head incredulously at Jackson as I abruptly reappeared.

"Sorry. No time to waste," Jackson replied with a casual shrug. "Besides, they'll recover."

"Never tire of seeing you do that, dude," Oliver remarked with an approving wink as he strode in past Jackson and checked out the sleeping giants.

Taking charge, I stepped over the unconscious guards and forged ahead into the main area of the building, while Jackson and Oliver followed. I could see the place was completely empty except for one large thermal-testing chamber that was positioned at the other end of the facility. After a few more steps I saw that there was actually something inside—and it wasn't one of those satellites I had seen in Building 2.

"Yech. Smell that?" Oliver asked, cringing and putting his hand over his nose from the overpowering chemical aroma.

"*Oh my God*," I muttered, alarmed, pointing at the chamber.

There she was, imprisoned inside the sterile box like an exotic creature from the wild. Except the creature in this instance was my friend Maya. She was passed out cold across a blue air mattress.

Outside the chamber was an array of high-tech medical equipment, some of which I recognized, like EKG and EEG monitors. There was also a collection of serums, syringes, and pills, and enough supplies to outfit a small hospital.

"Maya!" I shouted out as I rushed over to the chamber.

Jackson and Oliver sprinted after me. I reached the chamber first and tried opening the door, but of course it was locked. I shook the door so hard that the entire structure rattled and shuddered. I was so enraged that I just wanted the whole thing to come crashing down.

"Easy, tiger," Jackson said, gently removing my hands from the door. "Allow me."

And Jackson stepped in front of me, preparing to zap the locking mechanism with some heavy-duty voltage.

Meanwhile Maya barely stirred inside the chamber. She seemed totally out of it. Except for a few empty plastic water bottles scattered around the floor, there was nothing else inside the chamber with her. I assumed that the powers that be obviously didn't want anything dangerous in there that Maya might use as a weapon if she got pissed off enough. The whole scene looked incredibly surreal to me—like one of those horrible cells inside a psychiatric hospital, except without the white walls and cushy padding.

Jackson unlocked the thermal chamber without breaking too much of a sweat. I pushed open the door, ran over, and knelt down beside Maya, taking her hand. She looked pale and had an IV in her arm. By the look of things I assumed they'd been sedating her to keep her quiet, so that she wouldn't be a threat.

"Maya, it's Nica. Can you hear me?" I gently swept the hair off of Maya's face, then patted both of her cheeks, trying to rouse her.

"We don't have much time," Jackson reminded me, keeping an eagle eye on the guards, who were still lying on the floor, passed out.

"*I know,*" I retorted. "I'm doing my best. Maya, c'mon, sweetie. Wake up. We need you to wake up."

After several much firmer slaps to her cheeks Maya

finally started to stir. She seemed a bit agitated, mumbling something I couldn't quite understand.

"Did she say something about Chase?" Oliver asked curiously, moving closer to hear a little better.

"You can ask her later," I replied. "In the meantime, give me a hand."

I was more focused on getting Maya up on her feet at that moment so that we could get the hell out of Bar Tech. I quickly removed the IV from her arm.

"Maya, do you think you can stand?" I asked.

Oliver and Jackson rushed over to assist me. They each took an arm and helped me get a wobbly Maya to stand up.

"Nica . . . ," Maya muttered, smiling but still incredibly groggy. "You're here."

"Yes, I'm here. So are Jackson and Oliver," I added, smiling and pointing them out to her.

"I knew you guys wouldn't forget about me," Maya said, overcome with emotion. "We're friends, right?" Her eyes welled up with tears.

"Of course we are," I responded a bit uncomfortably, with Oliver and Jackson there looking over my shoulder. "But we need you to focus on walking."

Maya nodded and tried taking a few baby steps before she stumbled. I caught her.

"Oops. I'm a little drunk," Maya said, giggling, obviously drugged.

"We should just carry her," Jackson suggested, anxious to get going.

"Hey, I may be able to leap tall buildings, but that's where the superpowers end," Oliver quipped, quite dubious about the prospect of transporting Maya out of the building and evading capture.

"No. I can do it," Maya insisted, shoving Oliver and Jackson out of her way. She proudly took a few more uneasy steps, her arms extended for balance.

"Look, Mom, no hands." A few more wobbly steps and Maya nearly tripped. But I swooped over to stop her from falling on her face.

"Easy," I said, steadying her.

"My head's throbbing," Maya said to me, grimacing in pain. "What happened to me? I had this awful dream that these men came to my house. They were sticking me with needles. I tried stopping them . . ." She was now becoming quite agitated.

"We'll talk about it later," I promised, trying to reassure her and keep her focused. "Drink some water," I ordered, handing her the last remaining bottle, which she eagerly gulped down as if she'd just spent an entire week in the Sahara desert.

"What about Chase? Is he okay?" Maya then asked with deep concern.

"He's in the hospital," Jackson replied bluntly. "In a coma."

"Oh my God." Maya choked back a sob, overcome with emotion. She was not taking the news well.

"I'm sure the jerk deserved it," Oliver quickly added.

I knew there was no love lost there between Oliver and his newly discovered half brother.

"You were just defending yourself, Maya," I interjected, shooting a disapproving look at Jackson and Oliver. No need to rile Maya up when she was still so fragile.

"He threatened me," Maya confessed with fear in her eyes. "Tried blackmailing me into telling him who else . . . was like me. I got upset." Maya's vulnerability was now spinning into rage. "I refused to tell him anything. I tried to get away from him. But he wouldn't let me leave his house. He got in my way and grabbed my arms. He was hurting me. I got so angry. Everything started whirling around the room. Next thing, this glass figurine gashed his head . . ."

I could see that Maya was overcome with enormous guilt over inadvertently hurting Chase.

"You did what you had to do," I said firmly, without an ounce of sympathy for Chase.

"I never meant to hurt him," Maya replied.

"Controlling this thing's a bitch," Oliver chimed in sympathetically, giving Maya a supportive smile. "But you'll get the hang of it."

Finishing off the final drop of water, Maya crushed the plastic bottle in her bare hand and tossed it to the floor. I could see she was trying to funnel all her anger and emotion into something productive. Taking several deep breaths, she blinked and allowed her eyes to focus. Then she nodded to me that she was ready to try walking again. I nodded back to her. Maya then took a few more steps. This time she seemed a bit steadier and more assured.

Then she turned to me and proclaimed, "Let's get the hell out of here."

Jackson opened the door to Building 4 and peered out into the darkness. Everything appeared quiet. Still. No one was waiting for us, not yet, at least. And the security guards that Jackson had zapped were still lying unconscious on the cement floor back inside the building. They'd most probably be down for the count a little while longer.

Jackson waved me out of the building first. Maya followed, clutching my hand tightly, and finally Oliver. Jackson picked up the rear and let the door glide shut ever so softly.

I led the way back in the direction of Building 2, stealthily retracing our steps on the same route we came in. I kept as close to the building walls as possible, staying in the shadowy recesses. Maya, still shaken by what had happened to her, never let go of my hand. A visibly nervous Oliver stayed close behind, followed by the ever-stolid Jackson, who kept glancing around to make sure no one was tailing us.

However, as soon as I rounded the corner of Building 3,

every single light in the Bar Tech compound flashed on all at once, illuminating the vast complex as brightly as New York City's Times Square on New Year's Eve. There was literally no corner or crevice for the four of us to hide in anymore. Our cover would be blown in no time. We were totally exposed—like a quartet of sitting ducks. I knew we had to make it down the hill and out of there pronto.

"Follow me," Jackson ordered as he brazenly darted out into the open, defiantly leading the way.

I hurried after Jackson, taking a few steps away from the building. Maya resisted, pulling back a little, still fearful. I turned and gave her an encouraging nod and then tugged her along. She hung on to my arm as we quietly darted between the buildings. I could hear Oliver's soft footsteps right behind me, not missing a beat.

The four of us had nearly made it around the perimeter of Building 3 when all of a sudden an alarm rang out. Loud, piercing. Shrill enough to nearly shatter my eardrums.

Maya immediately clamped her hands over her ears, face contorted into a painful grimace. I could see she was unraveling and on the verge of losing it right there.

"Run," Jackson shouted at us over the deafening blare.

"I can't," Maya insisted, shaking her head, eyes brimming with panic.

"*You can,*" I forcefully barked back.

I knew this was no time for a Maya meltdown, so I

grabbed her arm and yanked her as hard as I could across the compound road.

Meanwhile off in the distance I heard the screeching of tires on pavement and the loud rumbling of vehicles heading in our direction. The Bar Tech cavalry would be on us in no time.

The four of us charged down the hill, stumbling over jagged rocks and jutting tree roots. Jackson barreled ahead of Oliver, Maya, and me. He employed his expert snowboarding skills to slide down the hillside as if he were boarding down the powdery slopes at Aspen.

I clutched hold of Maya's arm as we slipped and tottered behind Jackson. Maya was still unsteady on her feet, her legs nearly buckling as we picked up speed during our rapid descent. I mustered every ounce of strength to hold Maya up and prevent her from going down and dragging me with her.

Hearing the hurried slamming of car doors from above, I instinctively glanced back over my shoulder. The blinding glare of headlights flashed down from the crest of the hill. A half dozen Bar Tech guards appeared in silhouette and just stood there menacingly. Looming . . .

"Don't look," Oliver shouted as he swooped over to my aid, supporting Maya's right arm with his left. The two of us were now practically carrying Maya aloft so that her feet hardly grazed the ground.

"Why aren't they coming after us?" I asked, perturbed by how the guards were just watching us scrambling down the hillside.

"Because we're so awesome," Oliver wisecracked, grinning.

Undeniable as our awesomeness was, I didn't quite buy that *that* was the reason they were just hanging back and not doing anything. My gut told me they were planning something else. And so, apparently, did Jackson's gut. He kept looking back at the guards with a suspicious eye.

"If we get separated," Jackson called out to us, "meet at my car in an hour."

"Just get me home," Maya pleaded, clinging tightly onto Oliver's arm and mine.

I knew that Maya returning home was not an option, but I kept my mouth shut, and so did Oliver. There was a time and a place for us to have that discussion. But it wasn't while we were fleeing for our lives down a steep hillside.

As the four of us continued down the final hundred yards toward our freedom, I noticed Jackson slowing down. I immediately saw the reason why.

A dozen Bar Tech guards, including Officer Korey and Officer Lorentz, appeared at the electrified perimeter fence, lying in wait for us. Like rats trapped in a maze, we were being driven right where they wanted us to go—directly into their hands.

"Let it rip!" Jackson shouted as he barreled straight toward the inevitable confrontation with the guards.

"Oliver," I shouted as I deliberately broke away from Maya and him. "Hang on to Maya."

Oliver nodded, intuitively sensing what I was about to do.

"Nica, no!" Maya cried, terrified, trying to pull me back.

But I was already willing my body to disappear and hide in plain sight. I couldn't risk Korey and Lorentz recognizing me.

Besides, the truth was Oliver couldn't do his whole leap-and-fly thing while carrying both Maya and me. And I knew that Maya was in no state to deal with any sort of conflict, whereas I could take care of myself.

"Hang tight, girl!" Oliver screamed to Maya.

As Oliver broke into a full-out run, he let loose his best Tarzan-inspired rebel yell. He then leaped through the air, higher and farther than I'd ever seen him jump before. Maya screamed in terror as they soared way over an astonished Officer Korey and Officer Lorentz. No way those two guards could ever catch Oliver or Maya, and they knew it.

Distracted by the Oliver-Maya flying spectacle, Lorentz and Korey as well as the other guards hadn't even realized that I had suddenly vanished into thin air, not to mention darted unseen through the opening in the fence. I literally breezed within inches of these unsuspecting guards without any of them even realizing I had passed so close to them. By the time they noticed that the fourth one of us had escaped, I'd be long gone.

Meanwhile Korey and Lorentz, now pissed as hell, whipped out their big-ass stun guns and aimed them directly at Jackson. They weren't going to risk letting this agitator who'd been stirring up trouble all these months slip through their fingers too.

Emboldened, Jackson continued heading straight for the line of guards, taunting them, his arms open wide as if saying *Come and get me.*

I watched with concern as Korey and Lorentz glanced at each other and then fired directly at Jackson's chest in unison, zapping him with thousands of volts of debilitating electricity. Instead of going down and squirming on the ground like a normal person would do after being tased, Jackson took the hit in stride. He remained standing, barely flinching. Then Jackson fired back at the guards with every volt of electrical energy he could harness from his body. It was the most awesome display of power I'd ever witnessed.

Dazzling white arcs of electrical energy surged back along the metal coils, literally blasting the stun guns out of the shocked officers' hands. Korey and Lorentz howled in pain, their bodies shuddering and vibrating, overwhelmed by the voltage. They collapsed on the ground, writhing, incapacitated. The other guards scattered in the confusion, which gave Jackson just enough time to rip the coils off his chest, then escape through the fence and dash off alone into the darkness–well before the rest of Bar Tech Security could come charging down the hill hoping to stop us from escaping.

# 18. THROUGH THE LOOKING GLASS

"You've got to leave here. *Tonight*," Jackson said, urgently pressing a set of car keys into Maya's right hand.

"Where am I supposed to go?" Maya muttered as she stared vacantly at the keys and shook her head, trying to comprehend the enormity of what Jackson was suggesting to her. "Barrington's my home."

In the aftermath of our narrow escape from Bar Tech headquarters, Oliver, Maya, Jackson, and I had rendezvoused an hour later in the school parking lot, where Jackson's Mustang was still parked along with at least two dozen other student cars. They had all been left behind in the morning's chaos, which already seemed like a distant memory to me. So much else had transpired in the span of only twelve hours.

"It's not forever, Maya," I said, trying to give her some comfort and hope. "Just until . . ."

I looked to Jackson, wishing he'd offer Maya some additional words of reassurance, since I had none left to give her. I was feeling pretty bleak at that moment too.

"We just want you to be safe," Jackson added, being straightforward and honest.

"Doesn't your sister live in Chicago?" Oliver piped up, attempting to put a positive spin on the situation, as if Maya were going on vacation or embarking on a fun adventure.

"Yeah. She's a senior at University of Chicago," Maya replied.

"That's great. Stay with her," I urged, giving Maya an encouraging smile. At least she wouldn't be alone. She'd be with family.

"For how long?" Maya asked, almost begging me for answers, which I sadly didn't have.

"We don't know," Jackson admitted somberly. "But we do know that Bar Tech has their sights set on you. You're in their system. They've run tests . . . they've got your blood. They know what you're capable of doing. And they want you. You're a high-value target."

"Can't we all just leave together? Run away?" Maya proposed, suddenly brightening and sparking with an idea. "We'll make it a big adventure," Maya continued, desperate to convince us to follow her plan. "Like one of those lame buddy movies where everybody bonds and learns the meaning of life . . ."

She let out a little laugh, all the while fighting back a flood of emotion, knowing she was just grasping at straws.

I felt awful for Maya. I knew how sad and agonizing it was to be the one who had to leave all her friends behind. Maya's perfect life had been totally upended in just a few weeks. And she had no idea when it would return to normal. As if that were even a remote possibility anymore for any one of us.

The truth was, our futures were just a giant black hole of uncertainty. This was our new normal. But right now Maya was the most vulnerable of all of us.

Maya ran her hand over Jackson's Mustang and shrugged. "Sweet ride. I always did want to drive her."

"Be good to her. She'll be good to you," Jackson responded, then handed Maya a cell phone. "It's prepaid. Untraceable. I even programmed in all our numbers."

"Our numbers?" I asked, wondering what he was talking about. "How can she call us when our phones don't work any longer."

"A minor inconvenience that I've rectified," Jackson then handed another new phone to me and another one to Oliver.

"Genius," Oliver remarked, admiring his fancy new smartphone from every angle.

"I'm not going to even ask where you got these from," I remarked, half-joking.

"Made a little detour by the family store after Bar Tech,"

he brazenly confessed, before turning his attention back to Maya. "Whatever you do, Maya, don't use any credit cards, ATM cards . . . ," Jackson advised. "Anything that can be traced back to you. They'll be looking for a paper trail."

"I don't have any cash," Maya reluctantly admitted, embarrassed.

"We took care of that." He tried to hand her a wad of money that Oliver, Jackson, and I had pooled together. "It's more than three hundred dollars. It'll get you all the way to Chicago."

"No. I can't." Maya shook her head, hands raised, refusing to accept the cash.

"You'd do the same for any of us," I declared, insisting she take all of it.

Maya looked at me and sighed. She knew this was one argument she wasn't going to win. I could be pretty stubborn. Finally she relented, taking the bills and stuffing them into her jeans' right front pocket.

"Oh, and take this," Oliver said, handing Maya a little USB flash drive.

"What's on it?" she asked, looking at the flash drive, quite curious.

"A video I made a few days ago explaining exactly what happened," Jackson replied, underscoring how valuable that flash drive was. "Think of it as an insurance policy."

I was surprised but impressed by his forethought.

Maya nodded, letting Jackson know she understood its importance. Then she slipped it deep into her jacket pocket and zipped it up.

"You better get going," I said with some urgency, keeping an eye on the street, watching for any security vehicles that might be driving by with their headlights off. "You want to hit the road before curfew officially kicks in."

"You're sure you guys will be okay?" Maya asked, her forehead lined with obvious concern for our well-being.

"For now." Jackson said, though I could discern just the slightest hint of doubt in his voice. "They may have recognized me, but they don't seem to remember much after the *shock* wears off."

"And those bozos never even *saw me*." I shrugged, with a sly grin. "Invisibility has its advantages."

Out of the corner of my eye I caught Jackson shooting me an amused glance, which immediately made me look away, self-conscious. My face flushed red, as I couldn't help but recall my highly inappropriate (but highly enjoyable) secret visit to his bedroom yesterday afternoon. Fortunately, no one seemed to notice with the exception of Jackson.

"We'll be fine," proclaimed Oliver with a newfound assurance he hadn't possessed that day I first met him. "You should hit the road, Maya. You've got a long drive ahead of you."

"Thanks, guys. I don't know what I would've done if . . ."

Maya couldn't finish her thought she was so overwhelmed with emotion.

"Hey. No good-byes," I insisted, looking at Maya, surprised that I had actually grown pretty fond of her.

"Yeah. Everyone knows they suck," Oliver said dismissively.

"Drive safely," Jackson said, avoiding any emotion. "And make sure you shift into fourth when you hit thirty-five."

"Got it." Maya nodded.

She then inhaled deeply, opened the Mustang front door, and slid right into the driver's seat. I could tell by her smile she liked the soft leather bucket seat. She slipped the key into the ignition and started the engine. Jackson's baby purred to life.

"Chicago, here I come," Maya said, shifting the transmission into first gear.

She gave us a quick wave before pulling out of the parking lot and driving Jackson's Mustang off into the darkness . . . and hopefully to safety.

"Think she'll be okay?" Jackson asked as his Mustang's taillights got smaller and smaller, receding from view.

"I do," I asserted, knowing that Maya was a lot tougher than she let on. And so was I.

"What about us?" Oliver probed, looking at Jackson and me. "You think we should've left town with Maya?"

"Let's go home and find out," Jackson said, heading

toward the street, ready to take on whatever came his way.

I looked at Oliver and shrugged. There was no way for us to know what would happen next, but standing around all night in the school parking lot was definitely not an option. Oliver nodded back, uncertain but prepared to face the inevitable blowback, whatever that might be.

Jackson and I delivered Oliver safely to the end of his driveway less than ten minutes later without incident. In fact the streets of Barrington seemed eerily deserted, way more than usual. On foot the three of us never encountered a single Bar Tech vehicle, which I attributed to a bit of good luck, not to mention clever maneuvering through neighbors' backyards and side streets. Or perhaps it was because of something else that I wasn't even aware of? Whatever the reason, I wasn't concerned. The only thing on my mind at that moment was exactly what I would say to my father when I saw him again. I looked at Oliver and could tell by his fretful smile that maybe he was feeling the same thing.

The lights were on in every room of Oliver's house. I even saw his mother sitting in the living room watching a big flat-screen television. Waiting for her son to return. On the surface the scene probably looked no different from a million other homes across America where parents patiently waited for their kids to return home, eager to hear about how their day had gone in school.

The difference here was that Oliver's mom had been anxiously waiting for her beloved son to return home all day. Her apprehension was apparent even to me standing way out in the street. I could read her tense body language, the way she sat perched on the edge of the sofa, as if she were preparing to jump off a ledge. It told me that deep down in her soul she knew that Oliver had changed. He was no longer the same happy-go-lucky, unquestioning geek whom she had raised for sixteen years.

Oliver was changing—*had already changed*—in more ways than even she knew. He had challenged his mother and taken on the town's status quo. And he had even dared to challenge his own personal history, beginning with his father's identity, which now was no longer a mystery. Richard Cochran was Oliver's father. Chase Cochran was his half brother. What that meant for Oliver's future I didn't know. And neither did Oliver.

What I did know was that Oliver hadn't yet fully processed any of it, let alone the physical changes to his body. I certainly hadn't processed the changes I'd undergone either. Not fully. Which was one of the main reasons why I wasn't ready to leave town just yet. I had questions I wanted answered. So did Jackson and Oliver. More importantly, I had unfinished business with my father. Today's events had thrown even more uncertainty into an already volatile mix.

So I wasn't at all surprised that Oliver's mother seemed so unsettled at that particular moment. I imagined that my own father and Jackson's parents were feeling that way too. All I knew for certain was that I felt strong enough to find out.

"Well . . . here goes nothing," Oliver quipped after exhaling audibly. He padded up the driveway toward the front door.

"See you in the morning at my house, dude?" Jackson suggested hopefully. "Be prepared to leave . . . just in case."

Oliver turned and saluted before taking out his key and unlocking the front door of his house. As he entered the house, I heard Oliver say, "Mom, I'm home."

"Will we? See him?" I asked Jackson warily as I watched Oliver's mom embrace her son through the window. She was visibly relieved to see Oliver had returned unharmed.

Jackson just looked at me and shook his head, having no easy answers. In spite of all the newfound power my friends and I possessed, *our parents* still wielded tremendous power over our lives. Which meant I was vulnerable along with Oliver and Jackson. True, we might have gotten Maya out of harm's way for the time being, but there really were no guarantees that we'd be safe too. As far as my future—our future—it was a vast unknown. To be determined . . .

Suddenly a pair of blinding headlights appeared down

the road, catching Jackson and me unaware. It was Bar Tech Security, and they were heading straight toward us, flashing their high beams.

Just as the lights were about to expose us, Jackson grabbed my hand, yanking me away from Oliver's house and out of sight of the oncoming vehicle. It wasn't clear whether the guards in the car actually saw us, but Jackson and I weren't about to take any chances.

The two of us darted across the backyard of the neighboring house, moving as stealthily as possible. We hopped over several fences, skirted around trash bins, and crisscrossed at least a dozen other backyards until we were several blocks away from Oliver's house. It seemed as though we had ditched our tail and were finally in the clear. Until I spotted the rogue vehicle passing through the intersection, turning at the next corner, and heading up the block.

Jackson and I quickly backtracked a street or two and decided to lie low for a few minutes. I hoped the car would eventually move on to another neighborhood. It methodically cruised up and down each block, flashing its searchlight across front yards and through the trees.

The two of us hid silently among a grove of spruce trees. Side by side, our bodies wedged close together, barely touching. I felt the hair on Jackson's muscled arms lightly graze the top of my hands. It was soft and tickled my skin. I couldn't help but let out a tiny laugh.

"You okay?" Jackson whispered.

"Yeah." I nodded, suddenly having an inappropriate case of the giggles. "Sorry. It's just . . ."

Maybe I was just overtired, or maybe it was the culmination of the strangest day of my life, but I couldn't stop giggling. All my pent-up emotion was finally bubbling to the surface, and I couldn't contain it. I watched Jackson's strong jaw set and neck muscles tauten. He was really getting pissed.

"*Shhhh,*" he ordered, shaking his head, his anger brimming. Which only made me giggle some more. I couldn't stop myself.

Suddenly I heard the cruiser riding up the street. Its search beam scanned the trees where we were hiding. Before I could even react, Jackson pulled me into his arms, just seconds before the beam was about to expose me.

And then Jackson kissed me. Deep. Hard. Jackson's mouth tasted sweet and just a little bit salty. I got so lost in the moment that my giggling immediately ceased, replaced by an overwhelming heat and desire to rip his clothes off right then and there. And unlike our prior kiss, this one felt different. This time I felt an equal desire rising up from Jackson. Like he really wanted me too.

Even after the squad car had driven down the block and disappeared around the corner, Jackson didn't stop kissing me. And I didn't stop kissing him. I let his hands discover the curves of my body the same way mine were discovering the taut contours of his sculpted torso. I had fantasized about this moment for so long I couldn't believe it was actually happening to me. In the middle of a thicket of evergreens, of all places . . .

I didn't want to second-guess what was happening or why it was happening to me. I just shoved all rationality aside. I wasn't going to worry about any of the reasons why this might be a really bad idea (for instance, Jackson's lingering feelings for Dana Fox). At that moment I was giving myself over to Jackson and to all these powerful feelings I had stifled for so long. And he was doing the same.

The simple truth was that I was in love with Jackson. I had been since I'd arrived a month ago. And in the heat of that moment I actually started to believe that he was allowing himself to feel something very real about me, too. He didn't need to shock me with his *power* for me to feel the electricity the two of us were generating together.

My hands shook as I unbuttoned Jackson's shirt and he unbuttoned mine. But our arms got tangled up in the sleeves as we tried to pull our shirts off each other. Not my most graceful moment. I was trembling and felt so nervous. We both started laughing at the crazy circumstances of trying to undress when surrounded by evergreens with large branches and very sharp needles. It was definitely not the most conducive place to make love.

Just then a blaze of yard lights flared on, interrupting our moment. From one of the nearby houses I heard a door slam and someone yell, *"Who's out there?"* The man sounded angry.

"Shit," I whispered, cringing at the thought of being caught with half my clothes off.

"Hurry," Jackson replied, grabbing me and whisking me through the trees before the guy discovered us.

Jackson and I pulled our clothes on as we ran through the streets, laughing at the absurdity of our situation. It might be the end of the world for all we knew. But as we turned up my block, he took my hand, and we strolled back toward my house, just like boyfriend and girlfriend. I looked at him and smiled. The moment felt so ordinary . . . so normal . . . so wonderful.

And yet I couldn't help but think about my mother at that moment. I wondered if this was the sort of ordinary (but special) moment Lydia had hoped I'd experience by moving to Barrington. Was this secretly what she'd had in mind when she'd conspired to send me to live with my father? Whatever my mother's reasons had been, at that particular moment, walking hand in hand with Jackson, I felt blissfully happy. All my fears and the other crap I had to deal with seemed to fade away for those few moments.

Jackson walked me to the back door of my house like we

had been out on a date. I took out my house key. We stood there staring at each other.

"You gonna be okay?" he asked in a whisper.

"Yeah," I replied, nodding my head, looking up at the house. I didn't see any lights on, though my father's car was parked in the driveway. "How about you?"

"Yeah," Jackson said with a smile, uncharacteristically nervous.

Suddenly I felt my pessimism rear its ugly head as I was filled with all sorts of doubts and insecurities. I couldn't help but question whether he was regretting what had happened between us back among the trees. Then his hand touched my arm affectionately. He smiled at me. Regret seemed to be the last thing from his mind. At that moment he seemed just like any other high school boy saying good night to his girlfriend. I didn't want to risk him changing his mind, so I thought it was time to go inside and end the day on a high note.

"Well I guess I should . . . ," I whispered, gesturing at the door. I hoped I could quietly slip inside and avoid a major scene with my father.

"Yeah," Jackson responded. "Text me if you need anything."

"You too," I snapped back. "I'm a light sleeper. So what are we going to do tomorrow? Stay? Leave? Alert the media?"

"Beats me," Jackson joked with a shrug. "Wing it, I guess."

"Sounds like a plan." I grinned, feeling as though I could take on the world—or Barrington, at least—with Jackson at my side.

Jackson then leaned in for a final good-night kiss. I leaned in to meet him. Our lips softly touched. He held me in his arms. It was sweet and tender.

"Better go home. Curfew starts in fifteen minutes," I reminded him, even though I didn't want him to leave.

"Night, Nica" were Jackson's parting words to me as he touched my hand. "Call me if anything . . ."

"I will." I nodded, assuring him.

Jackson then turned around and trudged down the driveway.

"Night," I called back with a half wave of my hand. Jackson looked back one final time, waved, then continued walking to the street.

I waited until Jackson disappeared down the block before going inside, bracing myself for the eventual inquisition and third degree from my father. Beyond that I had no clue what was going to happen.


I stood in the kitchen in the dark. The house was eerily quiet. Was it possible my father had gone to bed already?

I crept up the stairs to the second floor, where I heard him speaking on the phone to someone in a hushed voice.

Instead of just disappearing into my room and hiding under the bedcovers, I listened outside my father's study, eavesdropping on his clandestine conversation.

"Things are at a very dangerous stage," Dad muttered to the unknown person on the other end of the line. "It's too early to predict the outcome. I need time to do more testing."

I held my breath and tiptoed closer to the door, which was slightly ajar, carefully avoiding the sliver of light from the study that illuminated the hallway. I clearly saw my father sifting through confidential files from his locked cabinets.

"It's not clear what he's up to," my dad continued, "or who's involved."

*Oh my God.* It sounded like my father was talking about Jackson to Richard Cochran. I took out my new disposable cell, ready to warn Jackson. Perhaps we needed to leave Barrington before morning after all.

My initial impulse was to retreat away from the study and run, but then something deep within me made me stop. Was it anger? Or blind rage? Or just massive stupidity on my part? I didn't have a clue—just an overwhelming compulsion to confront my father head-on and stare him in the eye. Next thing I knew I was pushing open the door of my father's study. My dad looked up in surprise to find me standing in the doorway. Defiant. Demanding answers. Ready to have it out with him.

"I need to go," my father abruptly informed Cochran or

whoever was on the other end of the phone. Then he hung up and stared at me with a mixture of anger and relief.

"Where the hell were you all day?" He loomed large and he wasn't smiling. His face appeared lined and tense. In fact I was stunned to see my dad looking like he had aged since I'd last seen him early that morning. Had it really only been twelve hours ago?

"With my friends," I answered truthfully.

He came over and pulled me into his arms with a big hug, his anger dissipating. "You had me worried." I felt his heart thumping as he held me tight.

"I'm fine," I lied, slipping free from his embrace, refusing to be treated like a little girl any longer. "Jackson brought me home."

I stood there, waiting for the proverbial ax to fall on my neck. Was Dad acting the part of the concerned father just to butter me up and weaken my defenses? Would he ask me about the break-in at Bar Tech? Or if I knew what had happened to Maya? Was he going to use some other tactic to get me to talk? I couldn't pretend nothing had happened any longer. Just as my dad was about to turn away, I spoke up.

"What *happened* today, Dad?" I questioned, turning the interrogation tables on him for a change.

"Let's talk about this in the morning," he replied, quickly closing all the files on his desk so I wouldn't see the contents.

"No," I declared with authority. "This can't wait until morning. We're going to discuss this right now."

He stared at me and swallowed, not responding, as I pressed on with my questioning.

"I mean, one second the whole school is gathered in the auditorium hearing about Chase's attack and being in a coma . . . the next there's like this massive earthquake or lightning flash. And suddenly everyone's losing it. I'm talking mass hysteria. I've never seen anything like it."

"I know it must've been terrifying," my father replied, carefully measuring his words to me. "But you've got nothing to worry about."

*"Nothing?"* I responded with a sarcastic laugh. "Kids were freaking out. It seemed like the world was about to end."

"I promise you it wasn't anything that dramatic," Dad said, underplaying the truth. "In fact, it was actually a confluence of environmental factors."

"You're saying what happened today was a perfectly *natural occurrence?*" I was willing to give him a little rope to see how far he'd go with his lies.

"Absolutely natural. Like a solar eclipse or meteor shower." My dad must've read my disbelief, because he dug in with his pseudoscientific mumbo jumbo. "Remember what happened to those birds last month?" He was lecturing me like I was his student.

"Of course I remember. How could I forget? They all died."

"This is a similar situation," he asserted.

"You're telling me that whatever made those birds die was the same thing that happened today?" I shot him a suspicious look. Did my father really believe I was that gullible?

"Not to get too scientific," he continued, "but the earth discharges electromagnetic waves and radiation twenty-four/ seven. Ninety-nine-point-nine percent occur without us ever being aware or adversely affected by them."

"So you're saying this discharge of electromagnetic power, which made the town bonkers today, is that rare exception that proves the rule," I retorted back to him.

"More or less," he answered with a confident smile. "Fortunately, the effects were only temporary. Other than maybe people experiencing intense drowsiness and confusion or suffering a headache, you and your friends have nothing to worry about."

*Nothing to worry about . . .*

That seemed to be a common refrain I'd been hearing from my dad and other adults ever since I'd arrived in Barrington. It had worked on me for a short while. Unfortunately, I wasn't a trusting babe in the woods. My eyes had been opened to the truth. I knew too much. The four of us knew too much.

And yet I couldn't quite reconcile the kind, considerate man my father seemed to have been all my life with the deceitful doctor who was conspiring with Richard Cochran and Bar Tech. Why was he doing this? I couldn't believe it was just for money or profit. My father didn't live a lavish lifestyle and never seemed motivated to do anything because of money. So what else could it be? Perhaps his involvement was scientific? Maybe he was hoping to make some awesome discovery and win the Nobel Prize? It was killing me not to be able to trust my dad anymore.

"What are you involved in, Dad?" I questioned pointedly.

"It's complicated," my dad said, clearly not wanting to explain anything.

"No. It's very simple," I retorted as my dad looked at me, a bit stunned by my forceful attitude. And then the truth just poured out of me. "I know about the blood tests and the pulse and the fact that you're secretly working for Bar Tech and Cochran. That you're deliberately altering kids' bodies—turning us into genetic mutants."

"*You too?*" he asked, staring at me in disbelief and denial.

"Yes. Me," I declared without hesitation.

He shook his head and his shoulders slumped. My confession had hit him full force. "I hoped you'd be spared," he lamented. "That you wouldn't . . ."

"Go ahead. Call Cochran back," I dared him. "Tell him

the good news. Your daughter's been affected by the pulse. She can make herself invisible."

"Who else knows, Nica?" He approached me with urgency, looking visibly stricken.

"No one." I lied to protect Jackson and Oliver and Maya. This was between my dad and me.

"You've got to tell me the truth," he pressed, grabbing my arm.

"Why?" I snapped back, becoming emotional. "So you can turn them over to Bar Tech too? Like you did with Maya?"

"Nica, you're *wrong* about me." He shook his head, loosening his grip on my arm.

"I wish I was," I replied softly, sadly. "I overheard you with Cochran. You colluded with him."

"No. Don't you see? I've been trying to protect you. Ever since you arrived." I shot my father an incredulous look as he launched ahead with his explanation. "I knew your mother was pregnant when she worked at the facility. That's why I never drew your blood. So there'd be no record of you in the system."

"If that's true . . . ," I said, shaking my head in confusion, trying to process what he was telling me, "then why have you been helping Cochran?"

"Because that's my job," he proclaimed. "For him to *think* I'm helping him."

"What are you saying?" I looked at my dad, not knowing what to believe anymore. I was struggling to make sense of what was the truth and what was a lie.

He read the doubt in my baffled expression. Then he turned around and moved his desk chair away from the desk. "What I'm about to share with you is top secret. No one can know. *No one.* You can't tell a soul. Not Jackson. Or Oliver. Or even your mother." My father stared at me with the gravest expression I'd ever seen. *"Understand?"*

"Yes." I nodded, tentative, unsure what he was about to confide in me and whether I would regret my promise or not.

"Please believe that I never wanted any of this for you." My dad bent down on one knee and rolled up the area rug. Using a letter opener he popped out a small section of the floorboards, which concealed a secret compartment beneath. "I've spent years trying to infiltrate Bar Tech," confessed my father. "To gain Richard Cochran's confidence. He's a brilliant but dangerous man. And he's got big plans."

"Yes. He's selling *us* as covert weapons to the government for one hundred billion," I shot back, watching in shock as my father pulled out a small locked box from underneath the floor.

"No. Not to *our* government," my father responded cryptically but ominously, as he unlocked the combination of the box. I was incredibly curious to know what valuables my father had secreted away under the floorboards.

"Then where to?" I hesitated to ask, almost not wanting to know the ugly truth.

"China, North Korea, Iran, and Pakistan. Any nation willing to pay his price." He then reached in and pulled out something metallic. My heart practically stopped beating as I saw what looked like a nine-millimeter semiautomatic pistol.

"Oh my God . . . ," I muttered, horrified by the revelation of Bar Tech's despicable plans and never having seen a real gun up close and personal.

What the hell was my dad the doctor doing with a semi-automatic weapon? Much less a Walther PPQ, which I knew from seeing enough action films was the kick-ass weapon of choice favored by law enforcement? My head was spinning. What the hell was going on?

"I never wanted to burden you with this knowledge if there was no reason, if I could spare you," he explained sadly. "I'm so sorry for dragging you into all this."

Before I could process this information fully, my dad pulled out a slender black leather ID wallet. He handed it to me. My hand was literally trembling as I slowly flipped open the flap.

I gasped audibly when I saw what was inside. It was an official ID with my father's photograph.

I read the ID, which was issued by the United States government. By the Department of Defense.

*"Holy shit,"* I said aloud, looking up at my father in a completely new light.

"Now you know," he replied tersely as he took back his ID from me. "Your father's a government agent."

My head was spinning from information overload. Everything I thought I knew about my dad had been upended in less than five minutes. He was a deep-cover spy.

Before I could ask my dad another question, his cell phone buzzed, interrupting us.

"Dr. Ashley," he said as he answered the call. He listened intently to the person on the other end, nodding and looking directly at me. "Uh-huh. I see . . ."

I tried not to react or show that I was the tiniest bit paranoid. I couldn't help but worry the call had something to do with Maya or me.

"I'm on my way," he declared. "Keep him comfortable and quiet. Don't do *anything* else until I get there." And then Dad ended the call, looking distracted, his mind obviously elsewhere.

"Everything okay, Dad?" I asked, trying not to be too inquisitive but picking up definite apprehension from his troubled expression.

"Chase Cochran's out of the coma," he announced thoughtfully.

"Oh. That's . . . good news. *Right?*" I was trying to get a fix on exactly what my dad was thinking. But at the same time

I was also incredibly apprehensive about what Chase might say about Maya and the attack when he started talking.

"Listen, I need to get over to the hospital right away," he muttered, not directly responding to my question. "You'll be okay? Alone?"

"Yeah." I nodded my head, barely able to get a word out. I was so ready for the day to be over.

"I promise we'll talk more tomorrow," he assured me as he closed up his secret compartment.

"Okay," I muttered, still reeling over the explosive secret my father had just shared with me.

My dad nodded vacantly, then just turned on his heels and hurried off down the stairs without another word. A moment later he was out the front door.

I remained standing in the doorway to the hall, frozen, until I heard my father's car pull out of the driveway, at which time I finally exhaled. That was the moment when all the stress and craziness of the day finally hit me full force. It was also the moment I realized I had the world's worst headache, thanks to the pulse Maybe my father wasn't totally lying about those electromagnetic waves after all.

I felt dizzy and light-headed and leaned back against the wall for support so I wouldn't faint. Then I slowly slumped to the floor and started to cry. The tears just flowed. I couldn't stop them, and I couldn't stop my body from shaking. I wasn't sure what I was really crying about, but it felt like a relief to let it all out. I took out my new cell phone and wanted to call my mother and tell her everything. But I realized I didn't have her number stored in the new phone. Nor did she have my new number, which meant she couldn't reach me. Through my tears I started to laugh at the ridiculousness of my predicament. I was such a complete mess.

# 19. THE DAY AFTER

I woke up at six the next morning and dressed quickly. I wanted to get out of the house early so I wouldn't have to face my father. I was still so flipped out by his confession that he was a government agent—a spy. I had no idea what it all meant for me, or for my future in Barrington.

I had tried calling Jackson after my father had left for the hospital the night before, but the cell network was already down, no doubt deliberately disabled by Bar Tech. Even though I was sworn to keep my father's identity secret, I had to see Jackson. I had to talk to him. But what could I even say? The one thing I knew for sure was that leaving town was no longer an option. It would compromise my father's cover, not to mention raise way too many questions about me.

As I was scribbling a note for my dad, I heard him rustling around in his bedroom at six thirty. He'd be coming down to the kitchen in a few moments. He and I had a lot more to discuss. I had many more questions that needed answering.

Still, I wasn't quite ready to face him again. So I left my hastily written apology on the kitchen counter, informing Dad that I was going out to clear my head and that I'd be back later to talk. Our discussion would have to wait.

I bolted out the front door and hurried down the walk. I was immediately struck by the sensation that something had changed. At first I couldn't figure out what was different. Was the sunlight brighter than usual? Or was the sky bluer?

It was the birds. I heard chirping and singing again. Loud. Not many birds, but a few, perched high up in the trees and on front lawns. A whole new generation of birds had migrated to Barrington. I had no idea how or why, but it was as if nothing had ever happened. They were happily oblivious. I wished I could be too.

I arrived at Jackson's house. I had texted him that I was en route, so he was waiting anxiously for me. Apparently he hadn't slept much either.

"The birds. Have you noticed?" Jackson asked, opening the door to his house as I hurried up his front walk. We hugged each other for what felt like a long time.

"How could I not?" I replied, desperate to confide everything I had discovered about my dad, but I knew I couldn't. "Do you think it's because of the pulse?"

"Who knows? But something definitely feels different this morning," he admitted warily as we pulled apart from our embrace. "What happened with your dad after I left?"

"Not much," I said, shrugging and hating myself for lying to Jackson. "He was incredibly weird, though."

"In what way?" Jackson questioned, studying my face, trying to get a read on what I meant.

"My dad insisted that what happened yesterday was all due to some natural event. Then he dashed off to the hospital because Chase woke up from his coma." Could Jackson tell I was deliberately leaving out all the important parts in between?

"We have to hope Maya's halfway to Chicago by now," said Jackson.

"Out of reach of Bar Tech and this town," I added, hopeful that she had made it free and clear.

"I'm feeling like maybe we should've gone with her," Jackson blurted out, which totally threw me for a loop.

"Why?"

"Because my gut says that this thing goes a lot deeper than we even know." He took my hand.

I shifted uncomfortably. Did Jackson suspect or know about my father's secret? I so wanted to confide in him and confess: *Hey, guess what? My dad's a secret government agent.* But instead I bit my tongue and didn't say a word about it.

"What do we do now?" I asked.

"We stick to our plan and keep our mouths shut," Jackson reminded me. "I've got cash and supplies in case we need to leave in a hurry."

By then Jackson's neighbors had started emerging from their houses, picking up the morning papers off their driveways. Everyday life went on as usual.

Jackson and I watched in amazement how cheerful and normal everyone seemed.

"It's as if no one remembers yesterday's near riot," I said, completely bewildered by the level of denial that people appeared able to live with.

"Maybe that's better," Jackson wondered, embracing a cynical perspective. "Keeping the illusion that everything's all right. That we're all happy campers."

I just had to laugh. And I couldn't stop.

"Are you all right? What's so funny?" Jackson was bewildered by my odd reaction.

"Nothing. Everything. Us," I replied, suddenly overemotional. "The absurdity of our existence in this stupid town. What the hell does any of this matter?"

"What's going on with you?" Jackson pressed, sensing that I was concealing something big from him. "Is there something you're not telling me? Did something happen with your dad?"

"Is it crazy to want a do-over?" I evaded answering his questions, indulging in fantasy instead. "To pretend none of this ever happened to us? That we haven't changed. That we're just normal kids."

"We can leave today, Nica. This minute if you want,"

exclaimed Jackson, staring deep into my eyes with utter seriousness.

My loyalties were torn between protecting my father and the boy I loved. I didn't know how to tell Jackson that as much as I wanted to run away with him, I couldn't go. Not then. Not anymore.

Just as Jackson was about to speak, he got stricken with this sick look, suddenly turning ashen. Like he'd seen a ghost.

"Jackson? You okay?" I asked, worried that maybe he was having a stroke or some horrible reaction to expending all that electrical energy last night.

Jackson didn't respond to me. All he muttered was "Dana."

I turned around and saw her walking up the driveway. *Alive.* And very much in the flesh. That's right.

*Dana Fox was back.*

Dana beamed at Jackson as though the past months had never happened, as though her being at Jackson's house was the most normal thing in the world.

She walked over and embraced Jackson with a big hug, which stunned the hell out of him and me for that matter.

"Miss me?" She flashed a coy smile, as if no time had passed since she had disappeared without a word to Jackson or anyone else.

At that moment I spotted Oliver running down the block

toward Jackson's house. He witnessed the whole soap-opera reunion. He rushed over, heaving and panting, and could see by my shocked expression that I was devastated. It felt like everything was suddenly crashing down around me.

Jackson looked at me and I looked at him. There was nothing he could say. There was nothing I could say. I could barely breathe. Oliver instinctively came to my side, knowing I must be flipping out. I managed to hold it together. I'd been getting a lot of experience doing that lately.

All I said was "Hi, I'm Nica. You must be Dana. I've heard *so much* about you."

Dana in turn greeted me with a bright, warm smile.

"Pleasure to meet you too, Nica. Any friend of Jackson's is a friend of mine." She couldn't have been more gracious and friendly.

I smiled back at her even as an involuntary chill ran up my spine. My head was flooded with suspicion and doubt. Dana had supposedly fled town to get away from clingy, possessive Jackson. And now here she was nestled back in his arms. As if nothing had ever happened. I felt sick to my stomach, and I was pretty certain it wasn't just the green-eyed jealousy monster rearing its ugly head. Something else was causing my queasiness. Something else was setting off my alarms.

Was Dana's miraculous reappearance in Barrington the morning after all hell had broken loose just a bizarre coincidence? Was her reappearance just one of those fairy-tale endings? All my senses warned me that her return most definitely was not a coincidence. Though I hadn't a clue exactly *what* or *who* had brought Dana back to town, or what it was she wanted by showing up at Jackson's house. I suspected that whatever was going on in Barrington was far from over for any of us. In fact, the war had only just begun. . . .